PENGUIN BOOKS

WAS

Geoff Ryman is the author of *The Warrior Who Carried Life*, *The Child Garden*, and *Unconquered Countries: Four Novellas*. He lives in London.

WAS

a novel

Geoff Ryman

PENGUIN BOOKS

PENGUIN BOOKS

Published by the Penguin Group

Penguin Group (USA) Inc., 375 Hudson Street, New York, New York 10014, U.S.A.

Penguin Books Ltd, 80 Strand, London WC2R 0RL, England

Penguin Books Australia Ltd, 250 Camberwell Road, Camberwell, Victoria 3124, Australia

Penguin Books Canada Ltd, 10 Alcorn Avenue, Toronto, Ontario, Canada M4V 3B2

Penguin Books India (P) Ltd, 11 Community Centre, Panchsheel Park, New Delhi – 110 017, India

Penguin Group (NZ), cnr Airborne and Rosedale Roads, Albany, Auckland 1310, New Zealand

Penguin Books (South Africa) (Pty) Ltd, 24 Sturdee Avenue,

Rosebank, Johannesburg 2196, South Africa

Penguin Books Ltd, Registered Offices: 80 Strand, London WC2R 0RL, England

First published in Great Britain by HarperCollins Publishers 1992

First published in the United States of America by Alfred A. Knopf, Inc., 1992

Reprinted by arrangement with Alfred A. Knopf, Inc.

Published in Penguin Books 1993

20 19 18 17 16 15 14 13 12 11

Copyright © Geoff Ryman, 1992

All rights reserved

PUBLISHER'S NOTE

This is a work of fiction. Names, characters, places, and incidents either are the
product of the author's imagination or are used fictitiously, and any resemblance
to actual persons, living or dead, events, or locales is entirely coincidental.

Acknowledgments for permission to reprint previously published material may be
found on pages 370 and 371.

ISBN 0 14 01.7872 4 (pbk.)

(cip data available)

Printed in the United States of America

Set in Goudy Old Style

Designed by Cassandra J. Pappas

Except in the United States of America, this book is sold subject to the condition that it shall not, by way of trade or otherwise, be lent, re-sold, hired out, or
otherwise circulated without the publisher's prior consent in any form of binding
or cover other than that in which it is published and without a similar condition
including this condition being imposed on the subsequent purchaser.

Dedicated to It

This is the use of memory:
For liberation—not less of love but expanding
Of love beyond desire, and so liberation
From the future as well as the past. Thus, love of a country
Begins as attachment to our own field of action
And comes to find that action of little importance
Though never indifferent. History may be servitude,
History may be freedom.

—T.S. ELIOT,
Four Quartets

Contents

Contents

Part One

The Winter Kitchen

Manhattan, Kansas

September 1989

During the spring and summer I sometimes visited the small Norwegian Cemetery on a high hill overlooking a long view of the lower Republican Valley. In late evening a cool breeze always stirs the two pine trees which shade a few plots. Just south of the Cemetery in a little ravine is a small pond surrounded with a few acres of unbroken prairie sod. On the rise beyond the ravine a few large trees grow around a field. They are the only markers of the original site of my Grandfather's homestead.

My Grandmother once told me that when she stood on the hill and looked southwest all she could see was prairie grass. An aunt told me of walking over the hills to a Post Office on the creek there. I can remember when a house stood just across the field to the west and now I can still see an old tree and a lonely lilac bush on the next hill where a few years ago a house and farm building stood. Of the ten houses I could see from this hill when I was a child, now only two exist—but instead of the waving prairie grass which Grandmother saw in the 1870s, there are rectangles and squares of growing crops and trees along the roads. A few miles distant the dark green of trees, with a water tower, tall elevator and an alfalfa mill rising above them define the area of a small town.

—*ELINOR ANDERSON ELLIOTT,*
The Metamorphosis of the Family Farm
in the Republican Valley of Kansas: 1860–1960,
MA thesis, Kansas State University

The municipal airport of Manhattan, Kansas, was low and brown and rectangular, and had a doorway that led direct from the runway. The last passenger from St. Louis staggered through it, his cheek bristly, his feet crossing in front of each other as he walked. He blinked at the rows of chairs and Pepsi machines and then made his way to the Hertz desk. He gave his name.

"Jonathan," he said, in a faraway voice. Jonathan forgot to give his last name. He was enchanted by the man at the Hertz desk, who was long, lean, solemn, wearing wire glasses. He reminded Jonathan of the farmer in the painting *American Gothic*. Jonathan grinned.

He passed the man an airport napkin with a confirmation number written on it. American Gothic spoke of insurance and had forms ready to sign. Jonathan put check marks in the little boxes and passed over a credit card. He waited, trying not to think about how ill he was. He looked at a map on the wall.

The map showed Manhattan the town and, to the west of it, Fort Riley, the Army base. Fort Riley covered many miles. It had taken over whole towns.

Jonathan did not know there had once been a town in Kansas called Magic. There had even been a Church of Magic, until the congregation had to move when the Army base took over. The ghost towns were marked. Fort Riley DZ. DZ Milford. The letters *D* were ambiguously rounded.

Quite plainly on the map, there was something that Jonathan read as "OZ Magic."

It had its own little box, hard by something called the Artillery and Mortar Impact Area, quite close to a village called Keats.

"There you go," said American Gothic. He held out car keys.

"What's this mean?" Jonathan asked, pointing at the words.

"DZ?" the man said. "It means 'Drop Zone.'"

There were little things on the map called silos. Jonathan thought the silos might be for storing sorghum.

"At the end of the world," said the man at the Hertz desk, "it will rain fire from the sky." He still held out the car keys. "Manhattan won't know jack shit about it. We'll just go up in a flash of light."

Not a single thing he had said made any sense to Jonathan. Jonathan just stared at the map.

"Anyway," said American Gothic, "you got the gray Chevrolet Celebrity outside."

Jonathan thought of Bob Hope. He swayed where he stood. Sweat trickled into his mouth.

"You all right?" the man asked.

"I'm dying," said Jonathan, smiling. "But aside from that I'm pretty good, I guess." It was an innocent statement of fact.

Too innocent. Ooops, thought Jonathan. Now he won't rent me a car.

But this was Kansas, not Los Angeles. The man went very still for a moment, then said quietly, "You need a hand with your luggage?"

"Don't have any," said Jonathan, smiling almost helplessly at the man, as if he regretted turning him down.

"You from around here? Your face looks kinda familiar."

"I'm an actor," Jonathan replied. "You may have seen me. I played a priest in 'Dynasty.' "

"Well, I'll be," said American Gothic. "What you doing here then?"

It was a long story. "Well," said Jonathan, already imitating the other man's manner. "I suppose you could say I'm here to find some-body."

"Oh. Some kind of detective work." There was a glint of curios-ity, and a glint of hostility.

"Something like detective work," agreed Jonathan, and smiled. "It's called history." He took the keys and walked.

Manhattan, Kansas

September 1875

After the Kansas were placed on the greatly reduced reservation near Council Grove, a substantial decline occurred. For example, in 1855— the year their agent described them as "a poor, degraded, superstitious, thievish, indigent" type of people—the Commissioner of Indian Affairs reported their number at 1,375. By 1859 it was down to 1,035 and in 1868 to 825. Finally, while this "improvident class of people" made plans for permanent removal to Indian Territory, an official Indian Bureau count placed their number at "about 600." Clearly the long-range trend appeared to be one of eventual obliteration.

—WILLIAM E. UNRAU,
The Kansa Indians: A History of the Wind People, 1673–1873

The brakeman danced along the roofs of the train cars, turning brake-wheels. The cars squealed and hissed and bumped their way to a slowly settling halt. The train chuffed once as if in relief.

There was a dog barking. The noise came from within the train, as regular as the beating of its steam-driven heart. The dog was hoarse.

The door of a car was flung open, pushed by a boot, and it crashed against the side of the train. A woman all in black with a hat at an awkward angle was dragging a large trunk case. A little girl all in white stood next to her. The white dress sparkled in sunlight, as if it had been sprinkled with mirrors. The dog still barked.

"Where's my doggy? We're going to leave my doggy!" said the child.

"Your doggy will be along presently. Now you just help yourself down those steps." The woman had a thin, intelligent face. Her patience was worn. She took the child's hand and leaned out of the car. The child dangled, twisting in her grasp. A huge sack was thrown out of the next car and onto the platform like a dead body.

"Aaah!" cried the child, grizzling.

"Little girl, please. Use your feet."

"I can't!" wailed the child.

The woman looked around the platform. "Johnson!" she called. "Johnson Langrishe, is that you? Could you come over here please and help this little girl down from the train?"

A plump and very pimply youth—his cheeks were almost solid purple—loped toward the train, hair hanging in his eyes under a Union Pacific cap. The woman passed the child down to him. Johnson took her with a grunt and dropped her just a little too soon onto the platform.

The train whistled. The dog kept barking.

"Dog's been making music since Topeka. It's a wonder he's got any voice left. Trunk next." The woman pushed the trunk out the door. Johnson was not strong enough to hold it, and it slipped from his grasp to the ground.

"My doggy," said the little girl.

"Dot rat your doggy," muttered the woman. "Johnson. Do you know Emma Gulch? Emma Branscomb as was?"

"No, Ma'am."

"Is there anybody waiting here to meet a little girl come all the way from St. Louis, Missouri?"

"No, Ma'am."

"Well that's just dandy," said the woman with an air of finality.

"There's no one here? There's no one here?" The little girl began to panic.

"No, little girl, I'm afraid not. I'm going to Junction, otherwise I'd stop off with you. Why? Why let a little girl come all this way and not meet her, I just do not know!" The woman turned and shouted at the next car.

"Hank," she cried. "Hank, for goodness' sake! Fetch the little girl her dog, can't you?"

"He bit me!" shouted the porter.

The woman finally chuckled. "Oh, Lord!" She turned and disappeared into the next car.

The train sneezed twice and a white cloud rolled up doughnut-shaped from the funnel. Great metal arms began to stroke the wheels almost lovingly. And the wheels began to turn. A creak and a slam and a rolling noise and the train began to sidle away. It whistled again, and the shriek of the whistle smothered the cry the little girl made for her dog.

Then out of the mailcar door, the woman appeared, holding out a furious gray bundle. It wrenched itself from her grasp and rolled out onto the platform. It somersaulted into the child and then spun and righted itself, yelping in outrage. It roared hatred at the train and the people on it. The dog consigned the train to Hell. Johnson, the boy, backed away from him.

Sunset orange blazed on the side of the car. The woman still hung out of the doorway.

"Emma Gulch is her aunt! Lives east out in Zeandale!" she shouted. "Try to get word to her. God bless, child!" the woman waved with one hand and held on to her hat with the other. The air above the train shivered with heat. There was a wuffling sound of fire, and a clapping and clanking, and the brakeman did his dance. All of it moved like a show, farther down the track, fading like the light. The light was low and golden.

This was the time of the afternoon the little girl most hated. This was the time she felt most alone.

"What's your name?" Johnson asked her.

"Dorothy," said the little girl. She held up her white dress to make it sparkle.

"What's that stuff on your dress?"

"It's a theater dress," said the little girl. Her eyes stared and her mouth was puffy. "The theater people in Kansas City give it to me." She had stayed with them last night, and she liked them. "Are you going to stay with me?" she asked Johnson.

"For a little while, maybe."

"I'm hungry," she said.

"Well I ate up all my pie, or I surely would have let you have some."

The place was silent. The station had a porch and a platform and a wooden waiting room. The tracks ran beside a river. Dorothy could see no town. She recognized nothing. She pushed the hair out of her eyes. Nothing was right.

"Where is everybody?" she asked. She was scared, as if there were ghosts in the low orange light.

"Oh, next train won't be here till past six. Come on, I'll show you where you can set."

He walked on ahead of her. He didn't hold her hand. Mama would have held her hand, or Papa. She followed him.

Her ticket was pinned to her dress, along with a set of instructions. "Will this ticket get me back to St. Lou?" she asked. If there was nobody coming to meet her?

"I don't know," said Johnson, and held open the door of the waiting room. It had bare floors of fine walnut, wainscoting, a stove, benches. There were golden squares of light on the floor.

"You must be tired. You just rest here a bit, and I'll see if I can't find somebody to go fetch your aunty."

Don't go! Dorothy thought. She was afraid and she couldn't speak. Stay!

"You'll be okay. We'll get you sorted out." He smiled and closed the door. Dorothy was alone.

This was the time when Mama would lay the table. Mama would sing to herself, lightly, quietly. Sometimes Dorothy would help her, putting out the knives and forks. Sometimes Dorothy would have a bath, with basins of warm water poured over both her and her little brother, Bobo. Papa would come home and shout, "How're my little angels?" Dorothy would come running and giggling toward him. Don't tickle me, she would demand, so he would. And they would all eat together, sunlight swirling in the dust as shadows lengthened.

No dinner now.

And later people would come around, and they'd all talk and sometimes ask Dorothy to stand up on a chair and sing. The chairs would scrape on the floor as they were pulled back in a hurry, for cards or for a dance. Papa would play the fiddle. They would let Dorothy sit up and drink a little wine. People would hold Bobo up by his arms so that he could dance too, grinning.

So what happened to little girls with nobody to take care of them? How did they eat? Would it all be like that trip on the train? The train trip had seemed to go on forever, but this was even worse.

She was afraid now, deep down scared, and she knew she would stay horribly, crawlingly scared until dark, into the dark when it would get even worse, until she tossed and turned herself asleep.

Toto sighed and shivered, waiting out the terror with her.

The dust moved in the sunlight, and the sunlight moved across the wall, and no one came, and no one came. Time and loneliness and fear crept forward at the same slow pace.

Then the front door swung open with a sound of sleighbells on a leather strap, like Christmas. Dorothy looked up. A woman in black stood in the doorway, carrying a basket.

"Are you the little girl who's waiting for her aunty?" the woman asked. Dorothy nodded. The woman smiled and came toward her. There was something terribly wrong.

The woman's arms were too long. The bottom of her rib cage seemed to stick out in the wrong place, and she walked by throwing her hips from side to side and letting her tiny legs follow. As she moved, everything was wrenched and jolted. Dorothy backed away from her, along the bench.

"I brought some chicken with me," said the woman, smiling, eyes bright. Her face was young and pretty. "My name's Etta, what's yours?" Toto sat up from the floor, ears forward, but he did not growl.

Dorothy told her in such a low voice that Etta had to ask her again. "And the dog's name?"

"Same," said Dorothy. Etta sat down on the bench some distance away and began to unfold a red-checked cloth from the basket. Some of the fear seemed to go. "He's got the same name as mine."

Etta plucked out apples and cold dumplings and some chicken and passed them on a plate.

"The same name. How's that?"

"My mama got the two of us on the same day. So I'm called Dorothy and he's called Toto. That's short for Dorothy." Dorothy had the drumstick.

"Would Toto like some chicken?" Etta asked.

Dorothy nodded yes, with her mouth full. She stared at the woman's pretty face as she held out a strand of chicken for Toto. Dorothy was confused by the woman's height and manner. Dorothy was not entirely sure if she was a child or an adult.

"Are you middle-aged?" Dorothy asked. She did not understand the term. She thought it meant people who were between childhood and adulthood.

"Me?" Etta chuckled. "Why no, I'm twenty years old!"

II

"Why aren't you bigger?"

"I'm deformed," Etta answered.

Dorothy mulled the word over. "So am I," she decided.

"Oh no, you're not, you're tall and straight and real pretty."

"Am I?"

Etta nodded.

"So are you," Dorothy decided. The long arms and the twisted trunk had resolved themselves into something neutral.

Etta went pink. "Don't talk nonsense," she said.

"You're real pretty. Are you married?"

Etta smiled a secret kind of smile. "I might be someday."

"Everybody should be married," said Dorothy. It appealed to her sense of order.

"Why's that?" Etta asked.

Dorothy shrugged. She didn't know. She just had a picture of people in houses. "Where do you live if you're not married?"

"With my Uncle William."

"Could you marry him?"

Etta chuckled. "I wouldn't want to. There is someone I could marry, though, if you promise not to tell anyone."

Dorothy nodded yes.

"Mr. Reynolds," whispered Etta, and her face went pink again, and she grinned and grinned.

Dorothy grinned as well, and good spirits suddenly overcame her. "Mr. Reynolds," Dorothy said, and kicked both feet.

"People tell me I shouldn't marry him. But do you know, I think I might just do it anyway."

Dorothy was pleased and looked at her white shoes and white stockings. "Now," said Etta. "What we're going to do is wait here till your aunty comes. And if she can't come here today, then we'll go and spend the night at my house and then go to your aunty's in the morning. Would you like that?"

Dorothy nodded yes. "Is it nice here?" she asked.

"Nice enough," said Etta. She told Dorothy about the trees of Manhattan. When the town was planned, every street had a row of trees planted down each side. The avenues had two rows of trees planted on each side, in case the road was ever widened. So, Manhattan was called the City of Trees. Dorothy liked that. It was as if it were a place where everyone lived in trees instead of houses. Nimbly, Etta packed up the remains of their dinner.

Then they went to the window. Dorothy saw Manhattan.

There was a white two-story house on the corner of the road, with a porch and a door that had been left open. Dorothy could hear a child calling inside. There was a smell of baking. It looked like home.

And there were the trees, as tall as the upper floor. Beyond the trees, there was a honey-colored building. The Blood Hotel, Etta called it. There were hills: Blue Mont with smoke coming out of its top like a chimney; College Hill, where Etta lived.

"Are there any Indians?" Dorothy asked.

Not anymore, Etta told her. But near Manhattan, there had been an Indian city.

"It was called Blue Earth," said Etta. "They had over a hundred houses. Each house was sixty feet long. They grew pumpkins and squash and potatoes and fished in the river, and once a year they left to hunt buffalo. They were the Kansa Indians, which is why one river is called the Kansas, and the other is called Big Blue. Because they met right here where the Kansas lived."

Dorothy saw it, a river as blue as the sea in her picture books at home. The Kansas River was called yellow, and Dorothy saw the two currents, yellow and blue mixing like colors in her paint box.

"Is it green there?" she asked. She meant where the blue and yellow mixed.

"It's green everywhere here," Etta answered. They went back to sit on the bench. Etta told Dorothy about Indian names, Wichita and Topeka. Topeka meant "A Good Place to Find Potatoes." That made Dorothy laugh.

"But any place is what you make it," said Etta. "You've got to make it home. You've got to do that for yourself. Do you understand what I'm saying?"

Dorothy began to play with the bows on Etta's dress. Etta put her arms around her and rested her head against Dorothy's. They were nearly the same height.

"It's difficult, because everybody wants to be loved. And you think you can't have a home unless you are loved by somebody, anybody. But it's not true. Sometimes you can learn to live without being loved. It's terrible hard, but you can do it."

Then she kissed Dorothy on the forehead.

"The trick is," said Etta, pulling Dorothy's long black hair from her face, "to remember what it's like to be loved."

Dorothy fell asleep. She dreamed of knitting and the black piano and her paint box and picture books and all the things that had been left behind.

"Dorothy. Dorothy, darling, wake up." Someone was speaking. Dorothy opened her eyes to see a woman's face. Her skin was brown; the lips looked bruised; the flesh around the eyes was dark. "Hello, Dorothy. I'm your Aunty Em."

Toto gave one fierce bark of alarm and wriggled his way back onto Dorothy's lap. Dorothy was confused and rubbed her eyes.

"She's tired," said another woman. Dorothy remembered who Etta was.

"Of course, it must have been a terrible odyssey for her. I was so sure she would be on the number five! Dorothy, are you all right?"

Dorothy nodded yes and slipped down from the bench. Aunty Em moved away from her. "Etta give me some chicken," explained Dorothy.

"And a great kindness that was! Why, Etta, you must have been here for hours!" Aunty Em had a face like a horse, strong and full of bone. She had huge gray teeth. She stood still, her attention fastened on Etta. Bloated with sleep, Dorothy was confused. Were they supposed to be going?

"It was no trouble," said Etta. "Johnson Langrishe told me she was here, and I remembered how I felt once upon a time." Etta glanced at Dorothy.

"All the way from College Hill," said Aunty Em, grabbing Etta's hand, her face crossed with concern. "In your condition."

Etta's smile went a bit stale. "My condition isn't so very delicate. I'd gone to market, it was easy for me to bring some food."

"The whole county knows how hard you work. Oh, Etta, I'd just love to set and talk, but we've got to get going before dark. Dorothy? Are you ready to go home?"

Dorothy solemnly nodded yes, she was.

"Well, then, come along. Etta, I'll give you a hand."

"I don't really need one," chuckled Etta.

"Of course not," said Aunty Em, but didn't let go. They walked toward the door.

My trunk, thought Dorothy, looking behind her. What was going to happen to her trunk? She saw her dresses folded inside it.

"Dorothy dear, come along."

"My trunk," said Dorothy and found that she was near tears.

"Oh!" said Aunty Em and put a hand across her forehead. "Yes, of course." She pushed open the door and called, "Henry? Henry, please to come and give our little girl a hand with her trunk?"

Aunty Em kept talking, standing in the doorway. "I was just saying to Henry the other day that we don't see enough of you good people out on the west side of the city." Aunty Em's smile blazed, her eyes were hooded. "How is your Uncle Isaac? We never see him these days, running the entire state of Kansas by himself it seems!"

There was a clumping of boots. Aunty Em stood aside for a terrible, looming man who walked past her without speaking.

"Miss Etta Parkerson, Henry," said Aunty Em, in a gentle, chiding voice.

The man had a long beard of varying lengths and his hair was plastered to his scalp, curling at the tips. He wore a somewhat striped shirt and an open vest with patches of food on it.

"Morn'," the man said. There was a distinct whiff of manure. Toto hopped up onto Dorothy's trunk to defend it. He began barking, bouncing in place.

"Here, dog," said Dorothy, so softly only Toto could hear. He came to her whining, and she picked him up and hugged him and buried her face in his fur. Uncle Henry grunted as he lowered her trunk to the floor.

"Out of the way, dear." As Dorothy turned, Aunty Em ushered her through the door. The very tip of her finger touched Dorothy's shoulder and then jumped back as if from a hot skillet.

Dorothy knew that Aunty Em had just remembered the Dip. She thought Dorothy carried disease. She didn't want to touch her.

And Dorothy, who wanted everything to be pretty, soft, full of lace, stood outside on the veranda and looked at the street and a rough, gray, unpainted wagon. Toto wriggled free and dropped to the floor of the porch. Etta pulled Dorothy to her and hugged her.

"Isn't she a little heroine, though?" said Aunty Em. "All the way from St. Louis by herself."

"I'd say it was an epic journey," said Etta, giving Dorothy a little shake, and spoke to her alone. "And it's not over yet. You've still got to get to Zeandale."

"Oh, you know Henry and I regard ourselves as Manhattanites!" Aunty Em corrected her with a chuckle.

Uncle Henry came backward through the door, pulling the trunk. Toto began to bark again and harassed Henry's heels.

"Gone'n brought her dog," muttered Henry.

"I can see that, Henry," said Aunty Em, voice low, her eyes avoiding Etta. Her hair was raked back tightly into a bun, and her hands pulled at it. There was a row of curls across her forehead.

"Zeandale's nice too," murmured Etta. Toto whimpered, circling Dorothy's heels. Everything was confusion.

"Can . . . can we give you a lift up the hill, Etta?"

"Very kind of you, Mrs. Gulch, but I have my uncle's pony and trap."

"You mustn't overtax your strength, dear."

"I won't," promised Etta.

"Well, then," sighed Aunty Em, as if everything had been delightful. Her smile returned as gray as a cloudy day. "We must be on our way. Do remind me to your dear Aunt Ellen. And may I drop into Goodnow House next time I'm in town? I would so love to see you all."

"Of course," said Etta.

"And thank you so much. Say thank you, Dorothy."

"Thank you, Etta."

"Thank you Miss Parkerson," Aunty Em corrected her.

"Thank you, Dorothy," said Etta quickly. Then she kissed Dorothy on the forehead again. Dorothy could feel it, as if it glowed. For a moment she felt as though nothing could hurt her.

Dorothy sat on the trunk in the back. She looked backward as the station, the town, disappeared in trees.

"Well I must say, Dorothy," said Aunty Em. "You do make your acquaintances from the top social drawer!"

The wagon wheels thrilled over the surface of a stone bridge across the river and into shade. Overhead there was a high bank of clouds.

"Believe it's going to rain at last," said Uncle Henry.

"Hallelujah," said Aunty Em, her eyes fixed on the clouds. Then she turned and tapped Dorothy on the knee. "Out of the wagon while we go up the hill, Dorothy. Spare poor old Calliope."

Dorothy didn't understand.

"Calliope is our mule, Dorothy, and it's not fair to make her haul us up hills. So we'll have a nice walk."

The road had been baked into ruts. Aunty Em took her hand, and they walked in twilight into trees. "You should have been here in spring," said Aunty Em, "and seen the sweet William." Her face went faraway.

"I can remember going up this road for the first time myself," she said. "I was sixteen and your mama was nine, and we walked through here. It was just a track then. We walked all the way to Papa's plot of land. Through these beautiful trees. And then we saw the valley, like you will soon, all grass and river, and we camped there. And we slept under the stars by a fire, looking up at the stars. Did your mama ever talk to you about that, Dorothy?"

"No," said Dorothy. "No, Ma'am." Her mother had never spoken about Manhattan.

"Did she talk about your Grandfather Matthew? How he came here and built a house?"

Dorothy thought she better answer yes.

"Your grandfather came out here just like Etta's uncles, for the same reason. To keep Kansas a free state. And he worked on Manhattan's first newspaper, and then for the *Independent* with Mr. Josiah Pillsbury. We are educated people, Dorothy. We are not just farmers."

None of it made sense. Everything was so strange. It was like a dream. Dorothy knew that she would never wake up from it.

"There," said Aunty Em, at the top of the hill.

More shadows, more trees, fields.

"Isn't it pretty? Prime river-bottom land. They talk about pioneer hardships. Well, we must have been lucky. What we had, Dorothy, was pioneer beauty."

What Dorothy saw on the other side of the hill was flat, open land. There would be no secret places in Zeandale like there had been in St. Louis, no nooks and crannies, no sheltering alleyways. Even the trees were small, in planted rows, except on some of the farther hills, and they looked dim and gray. White, spare houses stretched away at regular intervals between harvested fields. Dorothy could see a woman hanging up sheets. She could see children chasing each other around a barn. The soil that was gray on top was black where broken open.

"We'll get you back home and give you a nice, hot bath, first thing," said Aunty Em. She was still thinking about the Dip.

It took another hour to get to Zeandale. They turned right at a school-house and went down a hard, narrow lane. The wagon pitched from side to side. Its old gray timber threatened slivers. Dorothy pushed with her feet to stay seated on the trunk as it was bumped and jostled.

Ahead there was a hill, mostly bald, with a few patches of scrub. To the right of that, more wooded hills folded themselves down into the valley. The lane bore them around to the right toward the hills. The sky was slate gray now; everything was dim. As the wagon turned, Dorothy saw something move beside the lane. Had it stood up? Its sleeves flapped. As it walked toward them, Dorothy saw it was a boy. He was whipping his wrist with a long dry blade of grass. As he neared the wagon, he doffed a floppy, shapeless hat.

"Good evening, Mrs. Gulch, Mr. Gulch."

"Good evening, Wilbur," said Aunty Em.

"Mother saw you leaving this afternoon, so I thought I'd just set by the road till you came back along so I could hear the news."

"I brought the news with me," said Aunty Em. "Wilbur, this is my little niece, Dorothy, come all the way from St. Louis to live with us. Isn't she the prettiest little thing?"

"Sure is," said Wilbur. He had a long, slightly misshapen face, like someone had hit him, and he had a front tooth missing.

"This is Wilbur F. Jewell, Dorothy, one of our neighbor's boys."

"Hello," said Dorothy. Across the fields, there was a white house, with two windows, and an extension. "Is that your house?"

"Yes indeed."

"It's lopsided," said Dorothy.

"Dorothy, this is Kansas, and in Kansas we take account of manners. The Jewells came here like your Grandfather Matthew and built that house themselves."

"We should have built a new one by now," said Wilbur quietly.

There was more chat. Some long-term trouble was spoken of: banks and payments. The smoke from Wilbur's house was blue and hung in the air like fog.

"Tell your mother I'll be along as soon as I can," said Aunty Em, sounding worried. The neighbors parted. Wilbur walked backward, waving his hat.

"Let's hope the rain don't wash the crops away," called Uncle Henry from the wagon.

"Goodbye, Will!" called Dorothy. She liked the way he was put together, like a bundle of sticks.

Aunty Em sat straight and still for a while, and then seemed to blow out as though she had been holding her breath. "Well!" she exclaimed. "Boy his age with nothing better to do than sit all day by the road like a scarecrow on a Sunday! What is his father thinking of?"

"I reckon old Bob Jewell's giving up," said Uncle Henry. His voice went lower and quieter. "The land can break a man, Em."

"Depends on the man," sniffed Aunty Em. She was pulling her hair again.

Home came slowly toward them. Home was small and gray, a tiny box of even, unpainted planks of wood, with a large stone chimney and no porch, just steps. It nestled between two hills that reached from opposite directions into the valley. Dark twisted woodland reared up behind it. The barn sagged. Dorothy took account of manners and was silent. Toto began to bark over and over.

Aunty Em covered her ears. "Dorothy, try to still your dog, could you?"

"Ssh, Toto," said Dorothy. Deep in his throat, teeth slightly bared, Toto kept growling.

There were fields, but tall marsh grass grew up among them, even in the drought.

"Dorothy," said Aunty Em. "See that grass there? That marks a wallow. Now you must be careful of the wallows, whenever you see them. They're quicksand. Children disappear into them. There was a little girl who got swallowed up in the buffalo wallows and was never found again. So when you play, you go up those hills there."

Dorothy believed in death. "Yes, Ma'am," she said very solemnly. Toto still growled.

Hens ran away from the wagon as it pulled into the yard. Toto snarled as if worrying something in his mouth and then scrabbled over the running boards. "Wow wow wow wow!" he said, haring after the hens.

The hens seemed to explode, running off in all directions. Aunty Em jumped down from the wagon, gathering up her gray skirts. She ran after Toto into the barn, long flat feet and skinny black ankles pumping across the hard ground.

"That's going to get your aunt into a powerful rage," said Uncle Henry, taking the mule's lead.

Inside the barn there were cries like rusty hinges and the fluttering of wings. Hens scattered back out of it, dust rising behind them like smoke, pursued by Toto. Aunty Em followed with a broom made of twigs.

"Shoo! Shoo!" she said in a high voice.

"He won't hurt them, Aunty Em!" said Dorothy.

Aunty Em brought the broom down on Toto with a crackling of twigs. He yelped and rolled over. She whupped him again, and he kicked up dust and shot under the house.

"Henry, get a rope," said Aunty Em.

"Got to take care of the mule, Em."

The house rested about a foot off the ground on thick beams. Toto peered out from between them, quivering. Dorothy saw his eyes.

Aunty Em sighed and caught an escaping wisp of hair. "Dorothy," she said, sounding somewhat more kindly. "Your dog is going to have to learn to stay away from the hens. Now let's get you inside."

Aunty Em held up her arms and lifted Dorothy down. She walked back to the house, holding Dorothy's hand. "We're going to have to tie Toto up, Dorothy. Just for a while. He can't go inside, or we'll never keep things clean, and he'll just have to learn not to worry the livestock." Aunty Em lifted Dorothy up to the level of the front door, and then looked into her eyes. "Do you understand, Dorothy?"

"Yes, Ma'am," murmured Dorothy, scowling, confused.

"Well, in you go," said Aunty Em, giving Dorothy's hand a rousing shake. "Let's have some food and get you cleaned up. Henry, please to see to the dog."

Then Dorothy saw inside the house. "Oh no!" she grizzled. It wasn't nice. There was only one room, and it was dark, with only one window with no curtains.

"Guess it isn't St. Louis," said Aunty Em. She flung open the door of an iron stove, red with rust, and lit two tallow candles. Immediately there was a smell of burned fat.

In the flickering light, Dorothy saw that inside, the walls were made of thick raw logs. There was a worn throw rug over a wooden floor, and a bare table and bare chairs; there was a wardrobe and a table with a chipped china basin and long handles on which towels hung. The chimney and fireplace occupied one entire side of the room, but were empty and cold. There was a bed crammed into one corner, and a blanket hung across the room. On the other side of it was a pile of straw.

Dorothy thought of Toto, who was still under the house. She felt disloyal being here. She wanted to hide, too, under the house.

Aunty Em took a deep breath and then sighed, a long, high, showy kind of sigh that she meant Dorothy to hear. She had decided to be nice.

"Well," she said, animated. "What have we got here but some nice stew! I think there's probably a little child somewhere who has had a very long day. Maybe she'd like something to eat."

Dorothy was not hungry, but she said, "Yes please, Ma'am."

"What a nicely brought up little child she is," said Aunty Em, still piping.

"Can Toto have some too?"

Aunty Em managed to chuckle. "Heh," she said. "This is people stew, Dorothy. We got special food for dogs."

Aunty Em passed her the stew. It was brown, in a brown cracked bowl. Aunty Em leaned over to peer, grinning, into Dorothy's face as she took a spoonful.

"There!" Aunty Em said, soothing.

The meat was hard and dry in the middle and very, very salty, and there were bubbles of salty fat in the gravy, and there were no vegetables with the meat. Dorothy's mother had always eaten lots of crisp vegetables, lots of fresh fruit, like she could never get enough of it. Dorothy was going to ask for some, but looked around, and saw there was no fruit or vegetables. Dorothy chewed and swallowed. But she couldn't lie. She couldn't say it was nice.

"It's greasy," she whispered. If this was what they fed people in Kansas, what did they feed dogs?

Aunty Em tried to be nice. "Well," she said, with another drawn-out sigh. "How about some nice hot cornbread to soak it up? Fresh-made this morning." She didn't wait for an answer. She turned away smartly, and began to saw away at the bread. Dorothy could see she was still mad. Aunty Em dropped the bread on her plate from high up. The bread was bright yellow.

From under the house came a low, warning growl.

"Nice doggy. Nice doggy," Uncle Henry was saying outside the front door. Dorothy's back was toward it. She didn't dare look around.

"You just eat up, honey," said Aunty Em. "I'll go make sure Toto's happy."

Dorothy heard Em's boots on the floor. Dorothy sat still and tried to swallow the meat and she chewed the bread, and it went round and round in her mouth, rough and gritty. She began to weep silently and slowly, listening to what they were doing to Toto.

"He's gone right under!" grunted Henry.

"Well, hook him out with the broom," Aunty Em was whispering.

Dorothy did nothing. If she had been big and brave she would have done something. She would have hit Aunty Em with the broom and called Toto and walked away and never come back. But she knew what the world was like, now. It was like that train ride. Here, at least, she would be fed.

"Got him," said Henry.

Aunty Em came back in, smiling at Dorothy. "It's going to rain, soon," she said. "Oh, you can smell it in the wind. We need that rain. And you, young lady. You need a bath."

Dorothy nodded, solemnly. She did. She liked baths. The water was hot, and it smelled nice, and she always felt pretty afterward. Aunty Em kept smiling. She pulled a big metal tub out of the corner, and poured a kettle into it. The water was boiling. Dorothy heard the ringing sound of the water as it hit the metal. It was a sound she had always liked. It was a sound from home.

"You want to get ready, Dorothy?"

"Yes, Ma'am." Outside, Toto began to bark. He went on barking.

"Toto's always quiet when you let him inside," said Dorothy, unbuttoning her dress.

"He'll bring in the dust, Dorothy," explained Aunty Em. "Here now." She pulled off the dress. Dorothy heard boots.

"Henry, please! Can't you see the little lady is engaged in her toilet?" Aunty Em was still trying to sound nice. The joke was an adult joke, made for adults, the kind of joke a child wouldn't understand. Dorothy, her head covered by the white fairy dress, could only hear Henry grunt and stomp away.

Dorothy was going to test the water with her toe. Aunty Em snatched her up and lowered her into the bath.

It was hot, far too hot. "Ow!" yelped Dorothy. The heat seared into her. "Ow, ow, ow," she danced back and forth in the tub and tried to climb out. Aunty Em held her in.

"It's hot!" wailed Dorothy. Em stuck her hand in.

"It is not too hot, Dorothy."

It was. Very suddenly Dorothy and Em were wrestling. Dorothy jumping, leaping, trying to keep out of the water, held by Em's hands.

"All right!" said Aunty Em. She pulled Dorothy out. Dorothy stood naked, rubbing her shins.

"It was so too hot!" Didn't she know that adults and children felt heat differently? Her mama knew that.

Bath time here was not going to be nice. Aunty Em stopped smiling. She dumped a pail of cold water into the tub. "Now let's try again," said Aunty Em. She didn't let Dorothy climb in by herself, but yanked her up and dropped her, as she had dropped the cornbread. The water was now too cold, as Dorothy had known it would be. She said nothing and sat down. Aunty Em came at her with the soap.

Kansas soap smelled like the stew and burned. "Ow!" Dorothy yelped. Aunty Em kept scrubbing grimly. "Dorothy," she said. "You came from a house where there was sickness. That means we got to get you extra clean."

There was a pig-bristle brush, and Aunty Em began to scrub her with it. That was too much for Dorothy. Bath time or not, she was leaving. She began to crawl out of the tub. Aunty Em pushed her back down. She probably didn't mean to hurt her, Dorothy knew that, but she slipped anyway and landed, hard, on the bottom of the tub. Was everything in Kansas hateful? It was that thought, more than the pain, that set Dorothy wailing again.

"I have never known a creature to make such a fuss," said Aunty Em. She scrubbed anyway. She imagined she was stripping away a miasmatic coating of contamination. The bristles bit deep, scraping away skin.

Dorothy knew. She was being punished. Punished for being here, for being Dorothy, for coming from a household with the Dip. She bore as much as she could. "Ow oooh. Ow," she kept saying, knowing it would do no good, trying not to do it, but the brush hurt so badly. Aunty Em held her hand out flat and buffed away at it with the brush.

"And I do believe this hair of yours has never been cut."

Dorothy had black shiny hair, down the middle of her back. Her mother used to sing to her as she combed it. Dorothy knew she would lose that too.

"You can't have long hair like that trailing everywhere in the dirt," said Aunty Em.

"Are you going to cut it off?"

"Seems a good time," said Aunty Em. She imagined disease could linger in hair like perfume. "Now hold still."

"I don't want it cut off."

"Well, you're a big girl now. Big girls have their hair cut."

Dorothy was in simple terror now. It froze her. She saw the scissors, big and black. Aunty Em held Dorothy by the hair. The scissors came. Dorothy could feel them as they closed, cutting through part of her. She made a kind of screech and bounced forward. Her hair caught in the joint of the scissors and was torn out. That really hurt. She squealed.

"Hold still!" Aunty Em was beginning to lose patience. Dorothy began to fight again, not because she wanted to be bad, but simply because she couldn't help it. She began to beat her hands around her head and to jerk her head.

"Hold still!" The scissors bit again, Dorothy pulled again, more hair was torn, and Dorothy screamed as she had never screamed, a high-pitched squeak that was like nails on a blackboard.

"Stop that!" quailed Aunty Em. It was a sound she could not stand.

Uncle Henry stomped in. "Em. What are you doing to the child?"

That was all it took. Aunty Em threw a towel at him. "I am trying to get this child clean!" she shouted. "I guess we'll just have to leave it like that, half-cut, until tomorrow. But it is going to be clean, at least." She worked the soap up into a lather. "Keep your eyes closed," she told Dorothy.

The lather went into her hair and into her eyes and seemed to scald them, worse than the water.

"I told you to keep them closed," said Aunty Em, as the battle started. Dorothy was beyond thinking of anything at this point. She hit and kicked and tried to clamber out of the bath.

"Hold her, Henry," said Aunty Em. Uncle Henry's hands, as rough as the soap, grabbed Dorothy by the elbows. Aunty Em worked the hair. Dorothy's eyes seemed to sizzle like eggs. Then suddenly she was pushed underwater. She swallowed and coughed and came up coughing. They let her go.

"I never saw the like," said Aunty Em. "Never!"

"She's still got lye soap in her eyes," said Henry. He clunked away and came back.

"Put your face in this, Dorothy," he said.

"No," she whimpered.

"You got to wash the soap out."

"It hurts."

"Everything hurts," said Aunty Em.

"You got to."

Dorothy did as she was told. She put her face in the water and opened her eyes. They stung like before. But maybe, maybe, they were a bit better as well. Had she been good enough now? Would they leave her alone, now?

She opened her eyes, and everything was bleary, and they still stung around the edges.

Aunty Em was opening her suitcase. "Now, Dorothy," she said. "You come from a household with diphtheria. It killed your mama and your little brother, and it will kill us too, you especially, if we don't get rid of it. So we got to burn your clothes."

"My clothes," Dorothy whispered. There seemed to be no point crying.

"I am going to have to scrub the skin off my own hands after dealing with you. It just ain't clean."

"It's cleaner than this place," said Dorothy, numb.

"I expect my sister didn't have to cope with a valley full of dust or mud," said Aunty Em. She swung open the red rusty door of the stove. Dorothy saw the fire. She saw her white theater dress, sequins flickering in firelight. Dorothy grabbed it and ran, wet and naked. She jumped sprawling down from the front door and fell onto the ground. The dust was splattered with drops of rain.

Toto was gasping. There was a rope around his neck, and he had pulled and pulled against it. He tried to bark and could only cough. Dorothy tried to untie the rope. It hurt her hands. She saw Uncle Henry on the doorstep. She screamed as if she had seen a monster. He came down the steps toward her.

Dorothy turned and ran. She knew she had lost. Her clothes would be burned—except for the white dress that had been worn only once by a fairy in a play.

It was night now, black. Dorothy ran clothed in darkness, as the rain came, hard. "Dorothy!" called Uncle Henry. "Dorothy!" called Aunty Em.

Down in the fields, there was death. Dorothy ran uphill, feet pattering in mud. She slipped and the mud peeled away in a damp layer, like flour. She stood, coated in mud, still clutching the fairy dress, now besmirched.

Sssssh, said the rain, as if comforting her.

Suddenly branches clawed at her face, catching her half-chopped hair. She plunged through a thicket, her face scratched, and her hands were suddenly scrabbling at the rough bark of a tree trunk. She went deeper into the woods. She would stay in the woods; she would live there like an Indian; she would never go back.

"Do-ro-thee!" called a voice down the valley.

"Holy Jesus," said a voice closer at hand.

Dorothy stopped running and looked around her. Rain ran over her face. She imagined wolves or giants.

"Is that Dorothy?" It was Wilbur's voice. "Is that you crying?"

"She's burning my clothes," said Dorothy.

Rain like tiny people running on the leaves.

"It's raining. You better go back."

"I don't want her to burn my clothes."

"I guess it's because your papa and mama died."

"My papa didn't die. He left."

Wilbur said nothing for a moment, in the dark.

"Oh. I thought that's what your aunty said."

"I've got my fairy dress. I want to hide it."

"I know a place," whispered Wilbur. "There's a hollow tree just around here. Hold on to my hand." Dorothy reached out and their hands met. He seemed to be carrying a big stick. She could hear something thrashing the leaves.

"Ow!" cried Dorothy as she skidded barefoot over a gnarled branch. There was a hollow thump as Wilbur's stick hit something.

"Give me the dress," said Wilbur. He took it from her. Dorothy had an impression that it was lifted over her head.

"You can come back and get it later," he said.

"She'll never find it, ever," said Dorothy. She squished mud between her toes. Wilbur's hand reached back for her.

"What have you got on?" Wilbur asked, feeling her shoulders. He gave her his shirt. It was huge and wet, clammy and musty at once, but at least it covered her. They walked blindly, feeling their way down the hill.

They came to the lane and saw a lamp.

"We're over here, Mr. Gulch," called Wilbur.

Uncle Henry had a coat draped over his face, over the lamp. Dorothy saw his face solemn in its red light.

"Thankee, Wilbur," said Uncle Henry. He took Dorothy's hand.

"You be all right, Dorothy," said Wilbur. He and Dorothy had a secret.

Aunty Em was sitting at the table, reading by candlelight. She wore steel spectacles.

"Time for bed, Dorothy," she said.

"Yes, Ma'am."

Aunty Em stood up, pulling back her chair. She pulled back the old blanket that hung across the room. She pointed to the straw.

"This is where you sleep. We will be getting you a bed as soon as we can afford it, but for now you'll have to sleep on straw. Not what you're used to, but it is good clean Kansas straw." She took a rag, soaked in the bathwater, and used it to wipe the mud from Dorothy's feet. "At least the rain got you clean," she said. She gave Dorothy one of her own old, darned nightdresses. "This has already been cut down for you."

Aunty Em unfolded blankets over the straw. She stood up, wincing, hands pressed against the small of her back. "Good night, Dorothy," she said.

"Good night, Ma'am."

"That was quite an introduction we had."

"Yes, Ma'am."

Dorothy crawled onto the blanket, and felt the straw underneath it. She pretended to go to sleep. She listened. She wanted to hear what Aunty Em said. She heard pots banging on the stove. She smelled food burning. She heard the rain on the roof.

"I'd say that was as thorough a job as she could manage of showing me up, with the Jewells," Aunty Em said, a long time later.

Uncle Henry sighed. "I don't reckon Wilbur will say anything about it."

"She had a scarlet dress. Scarlet. For a child. God knows what sort of life she had in St. Louis with that man."

Dorothy heard creaking. Uncle Henry was crawling onto the bed.

"Work," he mumbled.

And Dorothy heard Aunty Em pace. She heard her boots clunking back and forth, back and forth on the hollow floor. She heard Aunty Em weep, brief, breathless sobs. She heard the garments slip off. She heard the lamp being blown out. Everything went dark. She waited until she heard Aunty Em snore. Aunty Em's snores were loud, enraged. Then Dorothy took off the sour old nightdress and she padded on light child's feet across the floor, and she stepped out into the rain again, and she slipped under the house. It was fairly dry under the house, except for where the water trickled in little streams like blood.

"Toto," she whispered. "Toto."

He crawled toward her whimpering. She hugged him and he licked her face. He shivered. They both shivered. Dorothy had to be loyal.

I will wait, Dorothy promised Aunty Em. I will wait until you are sick and old, and I'll put lye soap in your eyes, and I'll take some shears, and I'll cut all your hair off, and you won't be able to do a thing, and I'll say, It's for your own good, Aunty Em, because you're dirty. And I'll just let you cry.

Dorothy had learned how to hate.

Lancaster, California

Christmas 1987

1876—When the Southern Pacific Railroad Company laid its tracks through what was to be Lancaster in the summer of *1876*, many of the early settlers stated the railroad named the train stop at that time . . . The Southern Pacific also built the first house in Lancaster, for their employees.

1881—Nicholas Cochran passed through the Valley on the train and recognized its agricultural possibilities.

1883—The first artesian well in the Valley was sunk near the Southern Pacific track for locomotive use. Soon after this, several men from Sacramento, connected with a bank there and other businessmen of that city, purchased land from the railroad company and prepared to colonize the Valley.

1884—M. L. Wicks purchased 60 sections from the railroad company at two and one-half dollars an acre, laying out a townsite in streets and lots.

An English corporation called the Atlantic and Pacific Fibre Company, with Col. Gay and Mrs. Payne as managers and J. A. Graves of Los Angeles as attorney, contracted to furnish paper for the London Daily Telegraph. They bought up a good deal of yucca land around the Valley and sent a large number of Chinese laborers in to cut down the trees . . .

The early streets of Lancaster were easy to find. Starting at 8th St., now Avenue I, continuing South, the streets were 9th and 10th (now Lancaster Blvd.), 11th and 12th streets. Starting at Antelope Avenue, now Sierra Highway, and going west were: Beech, Cedar, Date, Elm and Fern . . .

—*Lancaster Celebrates a Century*

There was snow on the Joshua trees. It rested on and between the spines. It was as if giant cotton bolls had grown thorns. Jonathan made Ira stop the car for yet another photograph. Jonathan photographed the clouds in the sky, the points of the spines, the snow on the ground. Jonathan shivered in shorts and a baseball hat with a short ponytail sticking out the back. He hopped back into the car with an actor's brown-legged spring, and a flash of a perfect smile.

"I'm a photo-realist actor," he said.

"You're playing a Joshua tree," said Ira. "Good. I'm glad. It's got to be better than most of those parts you play." Ira was a lawyer. He worked in offices and was plump and pale.

"Private or otherwise. Listen, just content yourself. I could have another hobby, like practicing the drums. Drive on, MacDuff."

"Jonathan?" Ira asked. "Mind telling me what we're doing here?"

Jonathan just smiled, gave his eyebrows a Groucho Marx wiggle. They both adored Groucho Marx. Ira adored living with Jonathan. It made life more interesting. Ira was very proud of living with Jonathan. The guy was maybe seven years older than he was, but already some people thought Jonathan was younger. He did strange, slightly mysterious things like this, drag Ira out to Lancaster, with a secret smile. Ira was so proud that he wished he could tell the people at work about Jonathan. But it was easier if they thought he lived alone and pitied him. Ira carefully looked over his shoulder before signaling and pulling out.

Ahead the road stretched straight for miles. The distant hills were either blue and smooth or rocky and craggy. There was nothing on them, not even a pimple of shrub. A perfect desert complexion.

"Why would *anyone* come to live here?" Ira asked.

"House prices," said Jonathan. "And anyway, it didn't used to be like this. There used to be grasslands and so many rabbits there was a plague of them. People came and it just stopped raining. The climate changed. They don't know why."

They came to a town called Pearblossom and another called Littlerod. There were tiny, wooden-frame houses that were like a child's stereotyped drawing of a house.

"Woe-hoe!" said Jonathan, which meant photo stop. Just outside of Littlerod, there was a stone ranch-style house with a low wooden front porch. The car's turn signal went click click click and Ira pulled the car over to the side. They kept pulling over. Jonathan scanned the landscape, scanned maps, his eyes fierce, his hair in spikes.

In Palmdale, Jonathan nearly killed them both. Hunched over a map, he suddenly shouted, "Turn! Turn here, now!"

With an illegal but magisterial sweep, the car did a U-turn. There was a screech of brakes and Ira found himself hemmed in by other vehicles in the middle of the intersection. Ira's breath was taken away. "This better be worth it," he said. As if embarrassed, the car crept forward into a broken, ordinary street.

"What's wrong with Highway 14?" Ira asked.

"It's not from Back Then," said Jonathan. "This is the old Sierra Highway. See? The old railway tracks run beside it." His voice was hushed with something like lust. The car tires hummed a broken melody on the road surface.

"Woe-hoe!"

Jonathan stopped to photograph an old water tower, perched on wooden beams, with a faded, flaking advertisement painted in a circle on it. They passed a low, stricken arcade of brick shops—"Happy Hocker Pawn Shop." Jonathan photographed that, too.

"Why?" Ira asked.

"It shows no one uses this road anymore."

Jonathan stopped to photograph a railroad sign.

"Doesn't it take you back?" he asked. "I haven't seen a warning sign like that in maybe ten years." The warning sign had a round black plate with a long, sheltering hood over the light. In front of the crossing, there was a wooden X painted black and white. Jonathan photographed that too. When Jonathan started to photograph the telephone poles, Ira felt compelled to ask him why again.

" 'Cause of this little plate on it, see, embossed? Pure thirties." The picture was taken.

"What I mean is why do you do this at all? This whole thing?"

Jonathan smacked his lips as if tasting something. "I'm trying to piece it together."

"But why?" Their feet crunched in companionable unison back along the soft shoulder toward the car.

"Oh," said Jonathan, bundling himself into the car. He looked preoccupied. He put on a pair of mirror shades. Somehow, Ira knew, he gave Jonathan the confidence to dress as he did, despite his age, despite himself. Ira knew Jonathan was shy; Jonathan was quiet.

Ira eased the car back onto the road. Jonathan answered the question.

"I do it so that I can see it. Back Then, I mean. I want to see it, so I can catch some of the flavor. Of the people."

"So you can act them?"

"Maybe sometime. I just get this strange feeling of something gone. It makes me love it. I even fancy the guys in the old sports photographs. It's because they're gone, now, or old."

"I get it," said Ira. "It's necrophilia."

"It's just that, in some of those old photographs, only a few of them, they're so clear, like they were taken yesterday, you could almost just walk into the street, with the wooden houses and the funny windows and the cars with canopies, and the guys with straw boaters. And some of the faces, only some of the faces, you can see who they were, what kind of people. And some of them—some of the old flinty-eyed kind—they might as well be Martians."

"They didn't like being photographed either." Ira hated photographs of himself.

They went first to the public library. They nearly always did on Jonathan's expeditions. The library was on Avenue J.

"Imaginative street names."

"Oh hey, that's nothing, you want confusion, it used to be that all the streets running east to west were numbered. Then they turned them around sometime so the numbered streets run north to south. So you can never tell from a photograph if Tenth Street means Lancaster Boulevard or not."

"So who wants to know?" Ira asked. "Except you?"

AIDS? asked a cheery poster inside the library. YOU'RE NOT ALONE.

"Well, that must be encouraging for them," said Ira.

Jonathan asked at the reference desk for a copy of the 1927 local paper. It had been stolen. Jonathan took 1928 instead. Ira sat and read Jonathan's book.

It was full of photographs. There were Mexican railroad workers in the snow. A great cloud of rabbits, thousands of them, ran between picket fences, watched by women in high, folded formal hats. Someone called Mr. Hannah and his friends posed on the front porch of the Lancaster Hotel in 1901. The hotel had two floors and was three windows wide, and the upper floor of the porch leaned outward. Cowboys lined up on horseback in 1906. There were truckloads of alfalfa, and photographs of floods, horse carriages fording the main street. The Woman's Relief Corps smiled out at Ira from the turn of the century. Some of the women were named, but there was one woman with a particularly smiling, attractive face who was not named. No one, apparently, knew who she had been.

Ira began to be able to trace particular people. One face started as a watchful, rather handsome lad graduating from grammar school in the twenties. Then he was seen even more stern behind the counter of a grocery store. The sports teams began and there he was again, still stern until the 1930s when, disastrously, he smiled. His face looked plump, uncertain, unrecognizable. And there he was as a coach in 1948, looking suddenly lively, bright-eyed, gleaming. In one photograph, in the 1950s, he was portly, polished and beaming. It was the story of a man who had learned how to smile.

Ira looked up at the quiet, modern library, with its rows of books, its tan and varnished index-card files, and its very slightly battered computers. Redolent of its age. There will come a time, Ira thought, when Jo and I are gone. Or one of us is gone. It wouldn't be the same, with one of us gone.

An athletic-looking man in running shoes strode past and left behind him a disturbance in the air, a bit like body odor. Ira looked at Jonathan, his long, fan-shaped back, his nonexistent butt, his wiggly, knobbly legs, and the effect on Ira was bland, neutral as if the body were invisible. A perfect relationship, except for one thing.

Ira went over to see how Jonathan was doing.

As he approached, Jonathan seemed to flicker sideways somehow, and he flipped the microfilm forward.

"You really don't want me to see what this is all about, do you?" Ira chuckled.

"I wanted you to look at this," said Jonathan, oblivious with enthusiasm. A headline in quaint serif type said: STERLING RINEAR TALKS TO KIWANIS ABOUT EISTEDDFOD.

The Eisteddfod was the Welsh bardic festival—another one of Jonathan's enthusiasms.

"It just all connects," said Jonathan.

Like electricity. Even Ira felt the jolt, but only through Jonathan.

"Look at this. And look at this," said Jonathan, showing him ads for Safeways and banks.

"I mean the Bank of Italy. What was it doing here? Except that it became the Bank of America." He paused. "You bored?"

"A bit," admitted Ira.

Jonathan rubbed his forehead and looked helplessly at the unending trail of stories, advertisements. "Yeah. Okay. I just wish I could photograph the whole thing."

It was impossible to catch the past. "You know, someday they'll do a computer model of every town every ten years. The shops, the cars, the parks, the houses. The people in them, the clothes, everything. And you'll put on your electronic glasses, and your earplugs, and you'll walk through it. You'll say hello to women in cloche hats and brown silk stockings and they'll say hello back." He paused, and Ira saw that he was almost near tears. "In very slightly tinny voices."

It was Ira's private conviction that he had married a genius. Ira never said anything about this to anyone, especially to Jonathan. But Ira had seen Jonathan act Shakespeare and had heard him talk. No one else knew what Jonathan was. The TV shows, the horror movies in which Jonathan appeared, were rubbish. This only made it more poignant for Ira, so Ira joked.

"Wouldn't you bump into them if you had electronic specs?"

"This isn't some dumb joke, Ira." Jonathan's face had suddenly gone solemn, and slightly ill-looking.

"No," said Ira gently. "No, it isn't." Ira kept watch over Jonathan. There was a downside to the hyperactivity that glittered in Jonathan's eyes.

Suddenly the downside was dispelled or, rather, cast out. "Get out of here!" said Jonathan, bullish again, and he stood up with a kind of whiplash smartness to his spine. He tossed the microfilm up into the air and caught it effortlessly. He was strangely put together, too long in the back, but top-heavy, with small thin legs. He had wonderful coordination and he always beat Ira at everything. Ira had to try hard at everything. Jonathan tried hard at nothing. Ira was the success.

"On," said Jonathan, "to Cedar Street."

"What's there?" Ira asked.

"A house," said Jonathan, with another secret smile.

"If this is some dumb movie-star pilgrimage . . ." Ira threatened. He had been the kind of kid who preferred Mozart to Kiss. And Bach to Mozart.

"You'll do what?" Jonathan asked.

"I'll tell everyone you're a John Wayne fan."

"Well, he's from Lancaster."

"I know! Listen, it's not John Wayne, is it? Please. Tell me it's not John Wayne."

"It's not John Wayne," said Jonathan, still smiling with his secret.

The house was on Cedar Street, on a corner, by what had once been the grammar school. "That's it, it must be it, two-story!"

"You want to stop?" Ira asked.

"No, no, keep going," said Jonathan, ducking down.

"Are you or are you not the world's only photo-realist actor?"

"I'm embarrassed," said Jonathan, and the words were like lead. "That's someone's house. I can't just go up and start snapping pictures. Go on, go on!"

There was a hum as the car accelerated. "I'll tell you one thing," said Ira, "you'll never be a photo-realist journalist."

"Drive round the block," said Jonathan. He switched baseball hats.

"Hey, master of disguise. Do you really think they won't recognize you in a different baseball hat?"

"You're a lawyer," accused Jonathan.

"Whenever I think straight, you tell me that."

Jonathan looked afraid. Ira chuckled and slapped his leg. "You're nuts," he said.

"I know," said Jonathan very seriously.

The fake-Spanish bungalows, the tiny 1920s frame houses with porches and tile roofs, slipped past. Consistency was not Jonathan's strong point. It ruined his career. He would sometimes freeze like this on a part. Something about it wouldn't be right, and Jonathan would have to stop. No amount of ambition, or gratitude to the people who had worked so hard to get him the part, could force a performance out of him. "I'm sorry," Jonathan would say, helpless. "I'm not being funny. I want to do it, I wish I could, but if I tried now there would be nothing. I'm sorry. I'm sorry." And implacable, he would walk away from money, from opportunity, from reputation.

And it isn't even artistic integrity, thought Ira. I mean, he does those terrible monster movies. There's just something in those that he can grab hold of.

"Go by there again, and just park," said Jonathan quietly.

And then sometimes, when it all came right, Jonathan would step into the lights of the stage of a little theater, and his friends would not know him, and there would be a hush or even a gasp from the small and scattered audience. It would be like a dagger coming out of a sheath. Jonathan could take people's breath away.

"Too close, back up," whispered Jonathan.

So they parked a few doors down, across the street, and Jonathan peered in silence across Ira's lap, through the window.

It was a two-story house, painted the dull green that desert dwellers felt made their homes more Arcadian. It was a strange shape. A long, low bungalow running north to south and, perched on top of it, very narrow like the deckhouse of a ship, a second floor that ran east to west. There was a low front porch, with funny pillars that each split into two thin green columns. There were extensions added onto the sides and frames for climbing plants. There were trees and lawns and shade.

Jonathan was all angles, knees, elbows and wide hunched shoulders. He went more and more still. Ira looked at him.

"You're beginning to look like the house," Ira said. Talent was spooky.

"We better go," whispered Jonathan.

"Get out. Take a walk around it. Take pictures, ask if you have to. You'll regret it if you don't."

"Take it for me?" Jonathan asked, holding out the camera. Ira sighed, suddenly unwilling. Ira did everything else.

"You're right," said Jonathan, and took back the camera. He shrugged and stretched his way out of the house shape and twisted around to get out of the car. He stepped into sunlight.

The curtain seemed to go up. As he got out, Jonathan began to blaze with excitement. "It's all just like it was Back Then. Look, there's a child's tricycle on the porch!" This seemed to be very meaningful to him.

Surreptitiously, grinning like an elf, he started to snap and snap and snap.

"Is it in focus?" Ira asked.

"Yeah. I reckon that extension there is the kitchen, but it looks more recent, maybe thirties, so my guess is the kitchen was out back, probably on the right not the left, and the central staircase would go up just a bit behind the front door there, and maybe two bedrooms upstairs, or possibly the bathroom, 'cause they might have pumped the water up to roof tanks, to heat it, to store it. Come on."

He skittered nervously around the back, into the alley. "See, they still reckoned on some people having a horse and buggy even in the twenties. That's what this is for, bring the horses around to the back. Like mews in London."

There were bicycles and baskets and large colored plastic objects. "Toys," whispered Jonathan. There were large old leafless trees and a crisscrossing of heavy wiring in midair. The rear extension had windows that seemed too large. "That was a door," said Jonathan. The camera kept making a noise like it was chewing gum. Jonathan was not even looking through the viewfinder.

"Okay, okay," said Jonathan, breathless. "Come on."

They went down Oldfield and turned left onto the Sierra Highway again. "Go slow," begged Jonathan, but he was disappointed. There was hardly anything left from Back Then. Everything was huge and flat and spread out, a car lot, a Swedish smorgasbord, an empty stretch of bare brown earth alongside the train tracks. MICHAELS COACHWORKS, boasted a sign, SINCE 1974. "Slow," said Jonathan. They passed a brick building with mildly Art Deco decoration along the roof.

"What are we looking for?" Ira asked.

"An old movie theater. It was made out of brick. It burned down." They both looked, but saw nothing like it. They came to Lancaster Boulevard—Tenth Street as it had once been. "Might as well turn," sighed Jonathan. As they did, a movie house with huge, decrepit, late fifties, early sixties lettering slipped past. "No, that's not it, and it wouldn't be here anyway," said Jonathan. He looked disgruntled.

Lancaster Boulevard looked left behind by the postmodern world. The flat-roofed, flat-fronted storefronts tasted of the early sixties. There were cars parked, but no people walking, and a hush. The shadows were long. Ira was about to say, as if it were his fault, that he was sorry.

And then Jonathan sat up. "Oh wow!" he said, like the old hippie he secretly was. "Pull over."

They did. There was plenty of parking space. "Will you look at that!" said Jonathan.

An old wooden building, scarred in a line where a porch had been torn away from its frontage, stood perched absurdly on stilts. It looked like a woman afraid of a mouse, holding up her skirts.

"I reckon I know what that is," said Jonathan, his grin fierce. He grabbed the Lancaster book and flipped through the pages and turned a page of photographs around. "Yup," he said. "Look, see these photographs? They were taken in '36 from the water tower, so you see about half the town. Now the water tower was on Cedar. And look!"

Jonathan pointed. Ira waited for an explanation.

Jonathan read from the caption, " 'Far left is the Western Hotel.' See the two palm trees?"

By the sidewalk, on the other side of the chain-link fence from the old building, there were two tall palm trees. In the photograph, taken from high up, the palm trees were smaller, below roof height. They shaded the doorway.

"What they've done is hoist the whole building up and move it back," said Jonathan, and grinned. "They're saving it!" He was pleased.

He sat still for a moment. Then suddenly he said, in a gathering voice, "Oh boy!" He jumped out of the car. Ira turned to look.

On the corner of Cedar Street, there was a theater. Behind the large white plastic sign, there was another, smaller one. The letters were slotted into bars of metal, Art Deco, three-dimensional:

LOS ANGELES COUNTY
OFFICES AND ASSEMBLY HALL

On either side of the entrance were two Art Deco lamps and beside them a long, narrow, frosted window with a kind of trelliswork of metal holding in the glass. On the wall, clumsily hand-painted in black, was another sign, with an arrow:

MENTAL
HEALTH
UPSTAIRS

Ira sat in the car and looked at Lancaster Boulevard. There was a shop called Windsor, and a J. C. Penney Co. It couldn't have been more ordinary. But it interested him now.

Ira began to look at the book again, the photographs from the water tower first. It was a shock to see just how much of the old town had gone, with its dust, its trees and its wide, wide spaces. He flipped back a few pages and saw a photograph of three sisters on the steps of an airplane. Ira read the caption. Ira covered his face.

Of course! That's why they were here. It was because of Jonathan's play! He was playing the Scarecrow in *The Wizard of Oz*.

"Jonathan," Ira said aloud in a joke schoolmistress voice. "This is unbelievably tacky."

Ira had only seen the film once, when he was seventeen, and had not thought much of it. The songs were mediocre, the dialogue silly, and the sentiment—*There's no place like home*—was nauseating. It was all right for kids, but why adults?

Jonathan was loping back to the car. He was carrying a handbill, smiling with anticipation. Jonathan looked sweet and goofy and he could dance. Perfect casting for a scarecrow, Ira thought. Ira looked at the man he loved but did not desire.

"A theater on Cedar Street!" called Jonathan, as if something had been vindicated. "They're still doing it. They're still putting shows on for each other just as if L.A. were a thousand miles away."

"Jonathan," Ira said. *"Judy Garland?"*

Lancaster, California

1927

Where is Vaudeville?

—Confused child to Jack Haley

In 1894, Horace Henderson Wilcox, a Kansas prohibitionist, bought 120 acres near Los Angeles for his country home. His wife called the place Hollywood . . .

The fine weather was certainly a major incentive for many companies to move their entire organisations to the West Coast, but Hollywood offered another advantage. An industrial dispute, known as the Patents War and fought with weapons and violence enough to justify the term, had forced several producers to flee . . . These producers had infringed the Edison patents by making equipment built from pirated designs . . . Hollywood offered an ideal sanctuary for refugees of the Patents War, for should trouble appear, the Mexican border was a mere hundred-mile drive away.

—KEVIN BROWNLOW,
The Parade's Gone By . . .

It was cool inside the movie house. Daddy kept it cool. There was a beautiful woman in the movie and Frances knew why it was so dark around her eyes. It was the black that you put on your eyelashes when you sing. Only people couldn't sing in movies because there was no sound. That was why people needed Frances and Jinny and Mary Jane. You could only sing on stage.

It was Daddy's movie house and everybody in town knew him and everybody in town knew Frances. They had come here from Grand Rapids, where Granny lived, but that was a long time ago, almost before Frances could remember, though it must have been nice, because everybody, Mom and Jinny and Daddy, they all said so, because Grand Rapids was cool and green. Lancaster was flat and hot. Hot enough to fry an egg.

In the movie a man had been running along the tops of the skyscrapers and had fallen off and now he was hanging on to the hands of a big clock. Frances laughed, ha ha, very forcefully and kicked her legs and looked to make sure her sisters were laughing. If her sisters were laughing, it would mean the movie was meant to be funny, and Frances wouldn't have to be afraid for the man. Virginia and Mary Jane were laughing and looking at her, to make sure she was okay, so she grinned, very hard, to make sure they could see she was happy.

Daddy's movie house. Frances said it to herself. They were all together in Daddy's movie house. They were all part of the show together. Mom played the piano and Daddy sang, and Jinny and Mary Jane sang. Baby Frances sang. And everybody came to see them.

The man in the movie was swinging from a rope now. It was caught around his ankle. He swung between skyscrapers, up and onto a roof and suddenly he was safe, and his girlfriend was there and hugged him and everybody clapped. Frances clapped too, though she always found the endings of movies a mystery. Why end there, when it could have ended anywhere? Why end there when he could have gone on running for as long as he liked? But Frances cheered. "Yayyyyyy!" She cheered because it was Daddy's movie, because they always cheered each other.

"You like that, Baby?" Mary Jane asked, as the lights went up.

"I surely did," said Frances, with a sideways wobble of her head that she had learned from her father. Frances liked Mary Jane just a bit better than Jinny, her middle sister. Mary Jane was older and kinder. And she had a huge, wide smile. Frances wanted to have a smile like hers when she grew up. Everybody always said that Jinny was pretty and they never said that about Mary Jane, but Frances thought different.

"We're going home now," Frances announced, and slid down from her seat, her pretty white dress riding up. "It's time," she explained. Her sisters smiled and shook their heads and followed as Frances stomped up the aisle in round-toed buckle shoes. One strap flapped.

Frances generally did whatever she liked, expecting people to like what she did. She went up to Harriet, who wore a red kind of suit and a red hat. "Have you seen my daddy?" she demanded.

"He'll be out front, Baby," the usherette said. "Good movie, wasn't it?"

"Oh yes, it surely was," said Baby. "But movies can't sing." She didn't really like movies. "Can you buckle my shoe for me?" She stuck out her foot, toes curled down like at ballet class. "It came unbuckled."

"That's okay, Harriet, one of us will do it," said Jinny, echoed by her older, shyer sister. It was her older, shyer sister who crouched down to do up the buckle, quickly, almost furtively.

"You don't have to buckle my shoe now," Frances reassured Harriet. She didn't want Harriet to feel she had missed out. "You coming along to the show tonight?"

"Um," said Harriet.

Jinny laughed. "She's probably already seen it a hundred times, Baby." Jinny did not always make Frances look good.

Frances knew how to deal with that. "That's why we do it different each time. We do different songs, don't we, Harriet?"

To Frances's great pleasure, Harriet agreed. The shoe was buckled. "Goodbye, Harriet!" called Frances as they were leaving. Then Frances ran up the aisle to find her daddy.

She found him in what her mother and no one else called the foyer. Daddy was there talking to some men, and Frances ran up to him, shouting, "Daddy, Daddy, it was good!"

Her father laughed and scooped her up and swung her around. "You bet it was!" he said and gave her a shake. "I was thinking of you when I booked it!" He turned toward the two men. "Hey, boys, this is my little girl. This is Frances."

Frances saw then that the two weren't men at all, but teenagers. Frances didn't like them. They didn't know how to smile. Their smiles were all twisted, and their feet shuffled, and their hands were in their pockets. They looked like they could be rough. "Hiya, Kid," one of them managed to say, with a voice with a catch in it, as if a string had been plucked.

"These are my other daughters, Mary Jane and Virginia." They had just come up. Mary Jane hid slightly behind Jinny, but both of them looked scared, or something like it. Frances was going to say something to make them all happy. She was going to, and then decided not to. There was something nasty about those two men. Why did Daddy know people like them? Frances could see her daddy wanted to get away too. His voice went breathless, and he began to talk too fast and move his head a lot. "Got to be getting on."

"Sure," said one of the boys, his smile even more twisted, and Frances felt something she had no words for. She felt the contempt the boys had for her father. Her father turned and quickly walked away.

"Who wants a swing?" he asked as he turned. Why did he let them talk to him like that? Frances hugged his thick neck that smelled of aftershave and was prickly with stubble.

"Me," said Frances, coyly, forgetting the boys in her affection for her father.

"Jinny?" her father asked, eyebrow arched.

Jinny said nothing but got into place beside him. Her father lowered Frances, and they each took a hand, and Frances felt a delicious tingle in her stomach.

"One . . . two . . . three!" they all said in a chorus and swung her over the movie-house carpet.

"Again," she said and giggled.

"One . . . two . . . threeeee!" Frances was swung up high over their heads, and Mary Jane had run ahead to push open the big glass door, and as if flying, Frances soared up out of shadow, and down into a blanket of hot Lancaster air.

"Now it's Jinny's turn," Frances said.

"You can't swing me, I'm too big," said Jinny. "And besides, it's too hot out here."

"I can swing you," said Frances and chuckled at the idea.

"No you can't," said Jinny, beginning to giggle too.

They all played a game. Daddy and Frances pretended to swing Jinny. One, two, threeeee! and Jinny would whoop. "Golly, that sure was some good swing," Jinny said, joking. Mary Jane followed quietly. Frances didn't want Mary Jane to feel left out so she turned and winked at her. Mary Jane smiled back, gently, her arms folded in front of her.

"Who were those boys?" Mary Jane asked quietly. Daddy walked on a couple of steps. "Those boys in the movie house?"

"Just some kids, honey," said Daddy, walking on ahead. "They come in for the show on Saturdays. Nice boys."

"They didn't look nice," said Janie.

"No, they did not," said Frances, holding on to her father's soft, fat finger.

"You don't like anybody, Janie," said Jinny, and there was enough truth in it for none of them to say anything else.

"Race you to the car," said Daddy.

Only he and Frances ran.

"It's too hot," said Jinny, behind them.

The car was a special treat. Mom had driven to and from Los Angeles again, and she had left the car outside the theater, so the girls, particularly the Baby, wouldn't have to walk home in the heat.

It was a Buick. Frances liked the word and said it over to herself. Big, beautiful Buick. Her daddy concentrated on opening the door, and she clambered in, hoisting herself up onto the large front seat. Janie came up, scowling in the sunshine, hand sheltering her eyes. Janie didn't like Lancaster. She was always uncomfortable in it. Frances bounced up and down on the big seat.

"It'll be cooler when we get going," said her father. He pushed open the windshield in front, so that the air could blow in. The Buick had a little metal awning that hung out over the windshield like the brim of a hat. The hood was dusty again.

"We'll wash the car tomorrow," announced Frances.

"And I'll turn the hose on you."

"No," said Frances. She loved washing the car and being hosed down in the heat. Janie reached forward and scratched the top of Frances's head. It was a familiar game.

"Don't," said Frances and pretended to slap her hand away. Janie did it again. Frances squealed. "Don't!"

Her father turned the key in the car and it started the first time, with a low rumble and a delicious smell of gas fumes. The Buick pulled away, with Frances giggling as both sisters tickled her from behind.

Daddy always drove quickly, to get the air moving. Suddenly the car roared and shot forward. It sped along Antelope Avenue, a current of air pouring in through the open window. Frances stood up on the seat to feel the wind on her face. The wind seemed to make her eyes shake. She saw the low flat buildings shivering past them, out to where Lancaster straggled to an end. It was late afternoon, and the shadows were long. The hills seemed to have more shape in the low slanting light, their clefts and gullies full of blue shadow, their crags kissed pink. The high desert looked more gentle, less bleak and blasted.

"Daddy, be careful!" said Mary Jane.

Frances realized something was wrong.

The car was going faster and faster, and Frances's father had a strange, set expression on his face, and his eyes looked gray and blank. He looked angry. Frances giggled to make him turn to her with his eyes that could be so gentle. He didn't. Frances began to sing—that almost always worked. But her father kept staring ahead and his face stayed grim, and the car kept roaring forward.

A jackrabbit suddenly darted across the road. Her father blinked and tried to swerve, and the car skidded around on the sand and gravel that had blown onto the road. Mary Jane screamed. The car turned right around in the middle of the road. Thrown sideways, Frances was lifted up and hurled onto her father's lap. The car stopped.

Silence and sudden settling heat. Frances could feel her father. He was shaking. He put his hands on her head, as if trying to cushion it. "Sorry, girls," he murmured. He helped Frances sit up and started up the car again. It coughed and shuddered. Very slowly, carefully, he turned the car around in a wide arc, back into its lane, back toward the town.

Frances stood up on the seat again. "Faster, Daddy, faster!" she said. Wordlessly, looking ahead, her father reached out and gently made her sit. The car moved slowly home.

One side of Antelope Avenue was lined with telephone poles, the other with tamarisk trees that made long, cool shadows. A woman walked under them. The car slowed and stopped, and Frank Gumm wound the window down, prepared, as he must be, to talk a spell. He always said if you were in business, you had to set and talk a spell with folks. Frances thought it meant he talked magic.

They didn't know the woman. She looked quizzical as the car crept up to her. Frances's father stuck his head out of the window and said loudly, too soon, to reassure her, "Hello, Mrs. Story, I don't believe we've met." He leaned out of the window, resting his arms on the sill of the car door. "I'm Frank Gumm."

"Oh," she said, surprised. "Hello, Mr. Gumm. Pleased to meet you." Her eyes flickered over him. Mr. Gumm was wearing a sporty checked cap and sporty checked jacket that didn't quite match, and without doubt was also wearing golf trousers with long checked socks up to the knees. "How did you know it was me?" she asked.

Frank Gumm grinned widely. "Just a process of elimination, Mrs. Story. Mrs. Abbot tells me you haven't been to see the show and you're one of the few folks around here I haven't spoken to yet. Can I offer you some free tickets?"

Definitely sporty, Mrs. Story seemed to think. A plump little man done up to look like he plays golf. "Well, I hardly . . ."

"These are my little girls, Mary Jane, my oldest, and Virginia— we all call her Jinny—and Baby Frances. They're the ones who do all the work."

Mrs. Story still looked uncertain. Frances thought she would pep her up.

"Howdy, Mrs. Story. I like your hat!" In fact she did. It was a nice felt cloche like Mom wore.

"Frances," murmured Janie, embarrassed.

"Well, thank you, honey," said Mrs. Story.

"It's a good, clean family show, Mrs. Story," smiled Frank. "And it's the coolest spot in the valley. When it's one hundred degrees out here, it's seventy inside my movie house."

"Well, it is hot, Mr. Gumm, I won't deny."

"Now you just do me a favor and take two of these, Mrs. Story. Good for any night of the week, just come and visit and take in the show when there's something on you want to see."

The tickets were held out.

"Well . . ." Mrs. Story took them. "Thank you very much, Mr. Gumm."

"Terrible name, isn't it? Frank Gumm. Just remember. Honest and sticky."

"Daddy, don't say that," said Janie, wincing.

"I'm sure I will remember, Mr. Gumm," said Mrs. Story, looking at the tickets.

"And say hello to Mrs. Abbot for me."

"Will do. Thank you for the tickets."

"Goodbye Mrs. Story!" Frances shouted as the car pulled away, and was flung back onto the seat.

Frank Gumm kept smiling, looking in his rearview mirror, until Mrs. Story was well behind them. The smile fell then. "She'll be pleased enough when she sees you girls sing," he murmured. He chewed the tip of his thumbnail.

He stuck out his arm to signal and turned onto Cedar Avenue. They passed the grammar school. Whenever he stopped grinning, Frank Gumm looked worried. "The summer's almost over," he told his girls. "Janie, Jinny, you'll be starting school again here soon."

"I won't," said Baby Gumm.

"Ho-ho, no," said Frank Gumm, darkly. "No, your mother has other plans for you, Baby."

"Where did Mama go today?" asked Janie.

Frank Gumm didn't answer. He didn't say anything else until the car slid to a stop outside their new house.

It was painted white, two-story, on the corner across from the school. Grandmother Milne was on the steps waiting for them.

"Now come along, Frances, your mother wants you straight upstairs to wash. Mary Jane and Virginia, help me please to set the table." She said nothing to Frank. He helped Frances down from the car, and walked with her. She held on to his finger.

"I'll be downstairs, Baby," he murmured to Frances. "You run upstairs and have your bath and get all pretty for the show. Saturday night tonight."

Grandmother Milne held the door open with one hand, and took charge of Frances with another. But Frances stood her ground, in the hallway, turning to her father.

"Afterward can I show you my ballet steps?" she asked.

Her father smiled his huge, too-wide grin.

"Sure, Baby. I'll be here," he whispered.

"Come on then, Granny, let's get this over with," said Frances with a theatrical sigh.

"Cute as a button," grunted Grandmother Milne. "Knows it too."

Her daddy was left behind in the hall.

Upstairs, her mother was waiting. She knelt down in front of Frances to kiss her, as if coming back from Los Angeles were like returning from an even longer journey. "Hiya, Baby," she said, smelling of makeup and lipstick and perfume. She was slightly damp with the heat. Honest and sticky. "Good picture?" Mama asked.

"Oh yes, it was about a man running around the skyscrapers."

"Many people there?" Her mother's face was crossed with concern.

"No," said Frances in a small voice.

"Well, early days yet," said her mother, her voice wavering.

"There were two boys talking to Daddy, but they didn't look very nice."

Mrs. Gumm went very still. "Were there? What wasn't nice about them?"

"They looked funny," said Frances, watching her mother. She had meant to cheer her up by telling her about people who had come to the show. "He says they come every Saturday."

"I bet they do," said her mother. She started playing with her daughter's hair, rubbing it between her fingers. "You're as dusty as a welcome mat," she said, with a sudden wrench of emotion. "Honestly, this place! You need a brush just to walk down the street."

Then she kissed her daughter, hard, on the cheek, and stayed there, on her knees for a full moment. Then she pulled back. She was trying to be cheerful, but Frances could see that she wasn't. "How about a bath?"

"Will it be cold?" Frances asked.

"Yes, Baby, nice and cold," said her mother, and stood up.

Frances skipped toward the bathroom. The bathtub was already full, and Frances held her arms over her head, dancing to have the dusty little dress pulled off. There were two kinds of clothes: ordinary clothes, which usually had once been her sisters', and show clothes. Show clothes were nicer, but scratched more and were specially made.

The gray little dress was hoisted off. "Janie and Jinny start school soon," said Frances, under its momentary shelter.

"Yes, Baby. Seventh and fifth grade, if you can credit it." Mrs. Gumm shook her head as she folded the dress. Frances shook her head too, at the unattainable heights of the seventh grade.

"How long before I'm in the seventh grade?" she asked. It was the summit of her ambition.

"Oh, years and years yet," said Mrs. Gumm, leaning over and testing the bathwater with her plump hands.

"How old will I be then?"

"Oh, about thirteen."

"And will I go to school just like Janie?"

"Maybe," said Mrs. Gumm.

"Daddy says you've got some other plans for me."

"Did he?" said Mrs. Gumm briskly and looked at her daughter.

"Yes," said Frances, pleased, because the plans meant that she was someone special. She tried to hug her mother again, but her mother swept her up and put her in the cool water.

"Oooooooo!" said Frances, squirming with the shock and with delight.

"Don't splash, Baby."

"It's nice and cool." Frances slid down under the water. She liked to hold her breath underwater. She felt the edge of the water close in over her bobbed and dusty hair. Her mother lifted her back up.

"Are you going to wash my hair?"

"Yes, honey."

"With 'poo?" asked Frances and giggled because it sounded rude.

"Yes," said her mother. "See?" Her mother held up a bottle of baby shampoo. She poured shampoo onto her hands. "Now turn around. Close your eyes."

Frances loved having her head rubbed and she loved the smell of the shampoo and the feel of her mother's hands working it up into a lather.

"Did your father say what the plans were?" her mother asked.

"No. Are you gonna tell me?" Frances asked.

"Well. You won't be starting school for a while yet. So I thought we could drive you into Los Angeles from time to time for special lessons."

"Singing and dancing?" asked Frances, her eyes screwed shut. She kicked her legs to show that she was pleased.

She had done the right thing. Her mother laughed. "Singing, dancing, anything you like, Baby." Rubbing the lather and the hair together.

"Is that why you were in Los Angeles today?" Frances asked.

The hands stopped.

"Yes," said her mother, not sounding pleased any longer.

"Oh, boy. That's going to be fun," said Frances, to make her happy again. But her mother said nothing else. They had lived in Los Angeles for a while. Frances remembered it, as if in a dream, a little low brown house with red tiles on top. "It's Spanish," her father had said, trying to make them happy. But Mama hadn't liked it. Maybe her mama didn't like Los Angeles.

The hands began to work again. Afterward there would be the big woolly towel and running cool and naked into the bedroom to dress.

Downstairs the piano began to play, and her sisters to sing. Eyes shut, lather slipping down her face, Frances began to breathe out the words with them.

You didn't eat in show clothes, of course. You got to wear a soft white shirt and shorts. Frances hopped down the stairs. She went gerump, like a frog.

"Daddy," she said at the bottom of the stairs. "I'm a frog, Daddy."

"Good Lord, Ethel. Do you see? There's a frog in the living room." Ethel Gumm was following her daughter down the steps.

"Well, it must be feeling good because it's just had a nice cool swim," said Frances's mother. She smiled at her child and then walked on, toward the kitchen.

"A wet little frog," said Jinny, and began to thump a bit harder on the piano.

Nobody can be louder than me, thought Frances.

"Gerump!" she shouted, hopping. "Gerump! Gerump!"

"Frances," said Jinny, a warning rising in her voice, "I'm trying to practice."

"Let's see how high the frog can jump," her daddy said. He bent over and picked her up.

"Bounce," he said and let her feet touch the ground and swooped her up again. "Bouncy . . . bouncy . . . bouncy!"

Each bounce was higher. Frances was bounced across the hallway, out of the living room and into the dining room. Her father picked her up, as high as he could, all the way up to the ceiling.

"It's a flying frog!" he exclaimed.

"Don't!" giggled Frances. "No."

Janie came in, carrying plates. She looked tired, circles under her eyes, tired and unhappy, and she took no notice of either of them.

"I'm flying, Janie!" called Frances. Janie turned and gave her a flicker of a worn, dim smile and then went back into the kitchen. Grandmother Milne came out, carrying a vegetable dish. "Don't make the child giddy before dinner," Grandma said.

Frances was lowered to the floor. Sssssh, Daddy went with his finger on his lips to show they should both be quiet.

Sssssssh, went Frances back.

"Are you going to show me your ballet steps?" he whispered.

Frances nodded yes. She pushed her daddy back toward the wall, to get him out of the way. Then she held her arms out straight and ran, not quite on tiptoe but very quickly, scuttling across the dining room floor.

"Very good," said her father.

Ssssssssh, said Frances, finger on lips.

He pretended to go "Ooops!" and covered his mouth with his hand.

Sssssh, Frances reminded him again.

Ssssss, he said back. She did her ballet steps, running back across the room again.

The kitchen door swung open. "Supper's on the table," said Grandmother Milne. Frances could only see her long brown skirt, under the table.

"Daddy, be quiet," said Frances, now that it was all right to talk again. She marched to her chair and climbed up onto it, hoisting a leg across it, and then rolling over. She did not sit on the chair but, rather, knelt. The table was at her chest height, and the knife and fork were huge, but Frances was proud of her ability to eat with them by herself. She made a point of being very adult at the table. Jinny came in carrying a pitcher of water, then Janie, Grandma, and Mama next to her. Daddy sat at the end of the table away from Mama, away from everybody, it seemed.

"All right, Frances," said her mother.

"For what we are about to receive," said Frances, eyes closed with devotion, "may the good Lord make us truly thankful. Amen."

The food was served mostly in silence. Grandma Milne spoke twice. "Frank. This is yours," she said, holding out a plate of chicken and mashed potatoes, stretching toward him. She looked only at his hand as he took it, to make sure none of the food was spilled. "Virginia," she asked, "are you hungry?"

"No, Grandma," said Virginia.

"It's the heat," said her mother. "Jinny, you must try to eat something." She nodded to Grandmother, and a heaping plateful was served. Frances was next. She ate well. She always ate well. Chicken and gravy and mashed potatoes.

"Don't stir it so, Frances," said her mother.

Frances had forgotten how to eat mashed potatoes. She knew you were supposed to pile them on your fork, somehow, but they kept slipping off.

"Frances, you're making a mess," said her mother, and reached forward to help her eat.

"Uuuuhhhh!" said Frances in protest. She tried again. The fork was too big to get into her mouth.

"Take less, Baby, just with the tip of the fork."

Frances scowled and thought about what that could mean. It's like dancing, she told herself. You step with your hands. Tap is done with the toes. So I eat tippy-toe.

Delicately she picked up a fluffy piece of potato on the end of the prongs and twisted the fork around, so that just the tip could go into her mouth.

"That's better. Good girl. See?" Her mother was pleased.

Frances knew they all depended on her. She knew that without her, none of them would talk to each other. They only talked when there was company, or a show, or when Baby Frances did something to make them all laugh. It all came down to her.

Supper was cleared up in a hurry. Mother went up first to bathe and change. Jinny went to help Grandma wash up. Janie and Daddy played with Frances.

They played a game of catch with Loopy. Loopy was a hand puppet, and there was a certain thrill of cruelty in throwing him about the room. Whenever Janie caught him, she put him on and pretended to make him hide behind Daddy's back.

"I've got something to hide," she would say in a funny voice and make Loopy peek out from behind Daddy's back. Frances would laugh, and try to catch Loopy in a lunge and always miss. Loopy would duck away.

"I'm doing something you can't see!" said Loopy.

Her father stepped away, his grin too wide. Frances ran forward, hands outstretched to try to get Loopy, and Janie threw him, high over her head, to Daddy.

"Daddy's got the secret now," Janie said.

"No, I don't," he said, his queasy smile suddenly unsteady. He flung Loopy away too quickly, as if the puppet could burn him, too quickly and too high. Loopy careered into the mantelpiece. A tiny dish was knocked off it.

"Uh-oh," said Janie, in alarm, and looked at Daddy.

"Oops," said Daddy, and they both laughed. Frances decided to laugh too, even louder than they did.

"Quiet," said Janie, her mouth stretched downward from tension. Both she and Daddy knelt down and began to pick things off the carpet.

Loopy was forgotten. "What are you doing?" Frances asked, walking toward them.

"We've knocked over your mother's seeds," said Daddy. "She's going to plant them in the spring."

"They're from home," said Janie. Home was still Grand Rapids.

Frances knelt down too, and all of them pecked at the seeds with their fingers, like birds' beaks.

"Looks like these are going to grow a healthy crop of throw rugs," said Daddy, holding one up, covered in fluff.

"Fran-ces!" called her mother from upstairs. "Come on up, honey, and I'll do your makeup."

"Show time," murmured Frances, and rolled her eyes. Sometimes she found the whole thing bored her.

There were always two movies shown at the Valley Theater. The songs came between the movies. Tonight the first feature was a Western. As she watched, Frances played the parts along with the actors. Her face mirrored the shapes the actresses made with their mouths, the wide O's, and their wide eyes and their fanned-out fingers held up in surprise. Frances thought they weren't putting enough into it. She would make a great deal more fuss. She would run around and help the hero more.

She wondered if silent actors bothered to talk when they were being filmed. She wondered if they stayed as silent as the movies.

Suppose everything was silent. Suppose you wanted to scream, but couldn't make any sound. You couldn't make anybody notice you. You could wave your hands, but people might not see. It would be like you were drowning.

Suppose no one knew they were in a silent movie? They would all think they were talking. They would move their mouths and nod their heads, but no one would say anything.

Frances watched her mother play piano to make some sound for the movie. Her mother was reading a book at the same time. Her mother was always doing two things at once. Like living in Lancaster and driving to Los Angeles all the time.

Frances was scowling in the dark. Whenever there were guests, Frances could feel the whole family launch itself forward together, forward like it was a show. Mama took Papa's arm, which she never did otherwise. Papa smoked cigars and swaggered, talking to the men, and Mama would laugh with the ladies. Then they played cards. Their voices would be smooth, modulated, flowing.

"Oh, Frank always thinks that shows should be for free, and I agree. If folks can't pay for it now, they will someday. And a full house is always better, for everyone. So you'll always see Frank, giving tickets to people who might not otherwise go. Young boys, you know?"

A full house always seems better, thought Frances, because movies are silent. Only people can talk.

The movie ended. Applause. Not much. The first feature wasn't that good. Mama stood up from her piano, looking pretty, proud and plump in her delicate blue dress. Frank Gumm sprang up onto the stage and took her hand. They gazed lovingly into each other's eyes, for a perfectly timed beat, and broke apart.

Jinny tapped Frances on the arm, and the girls crowded around to the side of the stage.

"Hello, friends," said Frank Gumm. "Welcome to the Valley Theater, the only stage in the Antelope Valley providing the finest in kinematograph and vaudeville entertainment. Though I reckon some of you are here because it's cool."

A light scattering of chuckles. Janie adjusted Frances's collar.

"And so, on with the next part of the show. Ethel?"

Her mother smiled with love at Daddy.

"Girls?"

Frances crowded up behind Jinny, as they lined up in order of height on the narrow steps.

"Ladies and gentlemen, together, the Trio Unusual . . . the Gumm Sisters!"

They came dancing onto the stage as their mother played, into the lights as the theater darkened, and there were the faces in rows, there never seemed to be enough faces in enough rows, but the faces transformed into those of friends, watching with anticipation. And Janie was with her, and Jinny was with her, and Mama, and Daddy, standing by.

"When the red, red robin comes bob-bob-bobbing along, along . . ." in something like harmony, and Frances knew she was the loudest, waving her arms, and she could hear people chuckle, and she knew that they liked her, that everybody liked her, there in the lights, where everything worked, and where there was love.

Frances woke up in the night. She didn't remember being loaded into the car, or being carried up to the house in her father's arms. She thought she was back in the theater, and that she would have to talk to people.

It was dark and it was silent. Then there was a shout, and a forced whisper, a whisper of hatred that made something in Frances's chest prickle with horror. She heard the voices of her parents.

"It's starting again, isn't it? It's starting all over again!" her mother's voice was a whisper, but the whisper rose up with a keening wrench, like a bird taking wing from its nest.

Baby listened. The whispering was like a scratching on her eardrum or a record at the end when it goes round and round in the same groove.

"I'm the girls' father, Ethel, you can't do that."

In this dark world, without the lights, without music, Baby Frances began to sing, softly, to herself. It was like having to sit through a movie. All you could do was sit and watch and hope for a happy ending. Frances hated movies.

Somewhere there was a movie that sang. Daddy had told her about it. It already existed. Al Jolson began to sing, right at the end.

If movies sang, would people want to hear them, the Gumms? What would hold the Gumms together? Maybe the movies were talking now, and not her mother and father. Maybe movies flickered on walls at night, whispering, a new kind of ghost. Maybe it was not her mother and father who were talking at all. If sound could come from nowhere, spoken by no one.

"Don't touch me! Don't touch me!" Her mother's voice was high and breathy, panicked. "Keep away from me!"

Nothing is hidden. Frances knew she existed to hold her parents together. She was the still point around which all the others turned. She and the music. She and the music were the same thing. Both of them had to stay in the center of attention. The center bore the weight, and if it slipped there would be disaster.

Her sisters were going to go to school, Daddy was hiring other acts, and she was going to go to Los Angeles. Frances began to hear the unaccustomed sound of her father weeping. She sang louder, to cover the dissonance. The words of the songs were not important. The meaning behind them was, a meaning that could not be put into words. The meaning needed music. The meaning needed her, to sing it.

Manhattan, Kansas

Christmas 1875

Chapman's favourite film was The Wizard of Oz, in which Judy Garland travels continuously looking for the lost farm, the loved faces . . .

And here is Judy, Chapman's first love, who had the same name as Garland . . .

Vince Smith, the director of the YMCA camp where Chapman worked for seven years: "He was particularly good with children, like a pied piper. I didn't see a fault in Mark. His camp name was Nemo." He gave that name up when someone told him it meant Nothing. And Cindy, who was a sobbing child in pigtails when Chapman comforted her in his camp: "He truly cared for me and that is very odd for an adult." The last time she saw him she backed off. "His face looked different. He had shark eyes and no feeling in his face."

In Hawaii he tried to kill himself . . . "You could always read Mark's mind like a book," said a fellow worker. We know the book. Holden Caulfield found adults phoney and Chapman fixed on Lennon, now living as a rich recluse, as the ultimate phoney . . .

Nemo does not, of course, mean Nothing. It means a Nobody.

> —NANCY BANKS-SMITH,
> reviewing a television documentary
> about Mark Chapman,
> The Guardian, February 3, 1988

Wilbur F. Jewell killed himself just before Christmas. No one seemed to know why. Some people blamed the weather.

It had been a strange December that year. Thermometers showed eighty-eight degrees if they were on a south wall out of the wind. It made the children restless, people said, to have summer in the middle of winter.

Then, as hard and sudden as a fist, winter slammed into them. The snow piled up in drifts, and schools were closed. Everything closed, even the sky which hung dark and low and heavy overhead. A few days before Christmas, Wilbur Jewell went missing. Uncle Henry and Will's father spent a day out in the snow looking for him. Dorothy was rather excited. Will had always talked of getting out of here. She thought he had done it. She thought he had run away and got on a train and become a steamboat pilot on the river or even gone out to the Territory, to join the Indians. She wished he had taken her with him.

Wilbur had walked clear to the other side of Manhattan to the telegraph poles.

Dorothy was in bed, listening, when she heard Uncle Henry's boots clunking up the stairs.

"The boy went and hanged himself," was all he said.

"What! God have mercy. Has his mother been told?"

There was silence for an answer.

"Well we just got to go there," said Aunty Em.

"She don't want nobody now, Em. She just sits in the corner rocking, and there's no comforting her. She don't want comfort. She just knocks it away."

"Oh! It just tears the heart! What does she say?"

Dorothy heard Uncle Henry slump down onto the chair. "She says he was a happy boy. She just says that over and over. He was a happy boy. And she says how she doesn't have anything to remember him by. Bob told me outside, he was going to get a photographer in. Photograph the remains."

"Horrible habit. I suppose they'll have a wreath with it that says, 'Sleeping in the arms of the Lord.'"

"It'll be all the woman has."

Dorothy could stand it no longer. She could very finely gauge what would annoy Aunty Em, what was safe and what was not. She could sense from the fine fierceness in Aunty Em's voice that almost anything would be all right.

"What's happened to Wilbur?" she said, walking out from behind the blanket.

"Oh, darling, did you hear?" Aunty Em sounded worried for her, instead of angry. Dorothy had been right.

"Wilbur's dead, Dorothy," said Uncle Henry.

Aunty Em tried to hug Dorothy. She somehow always missed, all angles and elbows. "We just have to hope that he's happy in the arms of the Lord," she told Dorothy.

Dorothy did not need to be told what dead meant.

"Was it the Dip?" she asked very quietly.

"Oh honey, now, it wasn't. Wasn't your fault at all." Aunty Em tried to kiss her. "No."

They weren't going to tell her why her friend had died.

"What does hanged mean?"

"Dorothy. That's something you must never mention. If you talk about it, it will only make it worse for everybody. I'll tell you, but you must promise not to talk about it. Say yes."

"Yes, Ma'am."

"It means he killed himself, Dorothy. I'm not going to tell you how because it'll just give you nightmares. But he killed himself."

Dorothy didn't ask why. She knew. It was a way of leaving. She nodded and went back to bed.

"Dorothy?" asked Aunty Em, her voice trailing after the child. It was Aunty Em who needed to talk. Dorothy didn't. Dorothy threw herself on the tick mattress and pretended to be asleep. She heard Aunty Em pull back the blanket to look in.

"She's asleep."

"That's a blessing. Leave her be."

Dorothy listened again.

"I knew there was something wrong with that boy."

"He was all right, Em."

"There's something wrong, Henry, with a boy that age who prefers to play with little children."

A few days before, Dorothy and Wilbur had made angels in the snow on the top of the hill. They had lain down on their backs and waved their arms up and down. That made a shape like wings. The trick was to stand up from the snow and then jump away, so that there were no footprints leading from the image. Then you could say that it was a place where an angel had gone to sleep. Will would lean out and lift Dorothy out of hers. So hers were the best.

Then Dorothy and Wilbur and his little brother, Max, had made three snowmen. Dorothy loved the way the snowballs got bigger and bigger, in layers like a cake, and the crunching noises they made on the snow underneath. Will helped them roll the biggest snowball and lift the smaller snowballs up on top. He would make snow castles.

Wilbur made an ice road. He carried buckets of water up to the top of the hill and poured them out on the ground to freeze. You didn't have to walk on an ice road. You would run at it and stop walking. And then you'd slide. It was like flying. They made an ice road all the way down the hill. They could ride down that inside hessian sacks, spinning and giggling and landing in a heap at the bottom. It almost never hurt. When it did, Wilbur would get worried and rub Dorothy's ankles until they were better. He never hit her, like Max did. He would stop Max from hitting her. "You don't hit girls," Wilbur said.

"Why not?" said Max.

"Because they're smaller than you. If you hit her, then I'll hit you, just so you know what it's like."

"And I'll tell Mama."

"And I'll tell Mama that you were hitting on Dorothy, which is why I hit you."

Max thrust out his jaw with hatred of his bigger, stronger, wiser brother and walked away, back down the hill, leaving his snowman behind.

Max was all right most of the time. You needed Max for most of the games. But it was nicer when it was just Dorothy and Will. After Max had gone, Will and Dorothy talked together about how much they hated Kansas.

"Just a big pile of dirt," said Wilbur.

"Just a big pile of dirt and nothing to do," said Dorothy.

"Nothing to do but work."

"You just got to wait and wait."

"And do your chores or go to school." The way Will said it made it sound like something disgusting.

"Sk-ew-ew-l," said Dorothy, imitating him. She admired Will because he had been to school and then quit and never went back.

"Stuff your head until it hurts and then tell you you're stupid."
Will glowered and kicked at the snow. Dorothy kicked at the snow too.

"One day, I'll get out of here," he said. "One day, I'll just get on
the train, and go West." West was the approved direction. Nobody
ever went Back East, that was giving up. Everybody talked about going
West.

"I want to see an Indian," Dorothy said.

"I seen loads of 'em," said Wilbur. "Till about three years ago,
there used to be a whole reservation of the Kansa, out at Council
Grove. Most of 'em dressed like poor white people and were drunk a
lot. I saw one once kept waving a letter and my papa read it and it was
from a judge and the judge said that this was a good Indian."

"He didn't wear feathers?" Dorothy was disappointed.

"Well, that was before all the Kansa left and went down the
Nation. I expect they dress like Indians now."

"Aunty Em talks about the Indians a lot."

"She don't know nothing about it," said Wilbur.

Dorothy wanted to believe that, except that Aunty Em really did
have a lot to say about the Indians: how they spoke, what they wore.

"Down the Nation, the Indians wear feathers," Dorothy said, reassuring herself, "and they're bright red, and they ride horses without
a saddle and don't have to do anything they don't want to do."

"They live in tents, not houses," said Will. "And when they want
to move, they just get up and go."

"And they hide in the grass, and nobody can see them," whispered Dorothy. "They're invisible."

Will was smiling, crookedly. "Well, we can't see 'em. Maybe
they're all around us all the time, only we don't see them."

"Maybe they live underground," said Dorothy. It was a game of
pretend. Will still smiled. "Maybe you can hear 'em sing at night,
under the ground."

"I wish I was an Indian," said Dorothy.

"There's some kinds of Indian I'd want to be," said Will, leaning
back and looking terribly adult. "And some I wouldn't. I wouldn't want
to be one of them tame Indians that try to be farmers. I'd want to be
out in the Territory."

"Let's pretend we're going to run away and join the Indians,"
said Dorothy.

Will smiled again and shook his head. "Nope. I don't want to pretend that. No point doing that unless you're going to do it for real."

He was right, of course. It would have been fun to pretend, but pretend was for things that could never happen. But there *were* Indians, and they *did* have a land of their own, the Territory, and you really could go there. You don't pretend something like that. You plan it. Dorothy was suddenly sure that she knew Wilbur's secret. Will was planning to go there. It was a secret she would lock in her heart and keep safe away.

Will was almost a man. He was calm and kindly like an adult, but he talked to kids. Dorothy knew that that was somehow wrong, talking to her as if she were anyone else, but she liked it.

She could tell him about how mean Aunty Em was, how she made her do things, and Will understood and didn't say anything to his parents, who would only go to Aunty Em and tell her what Dorothy had said. And he would tell Dorothy in turn about his parents. He made her understand that they weren't mean. In fact they could be nice. But his daddy was drunk all the time and didn't do anything, and the farm was falling apart and his mama was unhappy and kept complaining.

"Craziest place for gloom," he told her. "They just can't wait to hunker down and be unhappy. And I can't run that place by myself and I'm not going to. I don't want to be a smelly old farmer."

"Uncle Henry smells," said Dorothy. "I can't stand it."

"That's 'cause he's got bad teeth," said Will.

"He tries to kiss me with his beard. And his beard smells too," said Dorothy.

They sat on the hessian bags listening to the gentle hiss of snow landing on fresh snow. It was nice, doing what they weren't supposed to do, letting snow fall on them. The snow fell in big, light clumps that sat on their stockings.

"Eskimos are Indians that live right far north, all the way up in British America," said Will. "They make their houses out of snow."

Dorothy could see the Eskimo houses, sparkling in one of those bright, blue-sky days in winter. She saw an Eskimo town, their snow castles all lined up.

"Doesn't it get cold?"

"Nope. You see, you get enough snow, it shuts the cold out, just like anything else."

Another wonderful thing. Snow was warm if you got enough of it. There was a logic that made the world beneficent. It was a nice world, if you were an Indian.

"Indians are a lot nicer," said Dorothy.

"Except when they get mean and kill people," Will reminded her.

Dorothy scowled. That was the trouble with Indians. That was the thing that never made sense. Everybody liked Indians, even the adults. They bought Indian blankets. The Jewells had one up on the wall, and it was bright red and yellow in bumpy shapes. And they had an Indian buffalo hide on the floor, with the horns still on. Everybody liked Indians, but everybody was afraid of them too, and Indians tried to kill them.

"Why do they do that?" Dorothy asked in a small voice.

" 'Cause this used to be their country and we took it."

"But they got the Territory."

Will was silent. It didn't make sense to him either, even to him. They listened to the snow falling.

"I used to think the snow came straight from God," said Will, looking up. "Used to think it fell straight off Him in pieces. Asked my papa if His dandruff was snow."

"I used to think rain was God crying," said Dorothy.

"Then it freezes over Kansas, 'cause Kansas is so cold."

"Let's just sit here," said Dorothy. "Let's just sit here so the snow covers us up and see if it keeps us warm."

They let the snow settle over them. They sat shoulder to shoulder and watched themselves turn white. Then they heard Mr. Jewell shouting. He was far away in the fields, standing in the snow, a small dark smear, like charcoal. He was angry. Shouting for them to come back inside. What the blazes did they think they were doing?

"Your daddy swears," whispered Dorothy.

"Does a lot of other things as well," said Will, with a grunt, and stood up.

It was like the two of them were putting on masks. "We're terrible sorry, Mr. Jewell," said Dorothy. "We weren't cold. The snow would keep us warm."

"You get on into the house," said Mr. Jewell to his son. You couldn't move around adults without doing something wrong.

It was the last time Dorothy saw Will.

The funeral was held in Zeandale village. Uncle Henry, Aunty Em and Dorothy all squeezed up together on the front bench of the wagon. Now that Dorothy had been scrubbed and boiled and shorn for months, she was clean enough to sit next to Aunty Em. They huddled under lap robes and put their feet on stones that had come red-hot out of the stove. Their toes were warm, but everything else stayed cold.

Across the iron-gray fields, there were scarecrows. Aunty Em had planted them over the buffalo wallows to warn Dorothy. They were as well dressed as the rest of the family. In the icy wind, their sleeves moved, as if beckoning.

The first stop was the Jewells' farm. Bob Jewell was holding the family's mule while they got into their cart. Bob Jewell looked raw, like stripped meat, all gray and red and splotchy, with the undefended look of someone who was not used to washing. Mrs. Jewell was fat and helpless, wallowing in flesh and grief. Aunty Em took her arm as she walked toward the Jewells' wagon, and silently kissed her.

"Now you just let us all do everything, Mary," said Aunty Em. "Don't take it on yourself again. This day is for you, above anyone else." Aunty Em did not look at or talk to Bob Jewell. Aunty Em and Will's older brother, Harry, helped Mary Jewell up into the wagon. Max glared at Dorothy.

It was the cold of the Devil, hard as a sword. Their fingers, their toes, their eyes, were gnawed by the cold. Dorothy's eyes ran with water, stinging with cold. Aunty Em got back into the wagon and thought Dorothy was weeping for her friend. She patted her hand.

"We must learn to love what God takes away," murmured Aunty Em. She was recognized by everyone to be a good woman. No one would ever believe that she wasn't. Dorothy let her think what she liked, and scowled.

Dorothy was trying to feel what she was supposed to feel. She knew she was supposed to cry and carry on and need comforting. The thought of Will made her go hard and cold like stone, and that worried her. She knew she was supposed to feel more than that. The thought of mourning made her feel weary and stale. The ride there and back would be boring, and she would have to be good. She began to rock back and forth to occupy herself.

Aunty Em held her still. "Try to bear up, Dodo," she said. "We're nearly there." They were not nearly there at all.

Dorothy hated the whole business. Ahead of them for miles she could see other wagons, lined up along the road, going to the funeral, as black as beetles.

There was a picture frame behind Dorothy's knees. Each time the wagon slipped on the icy road, it knocked against her legs. It was a flower under glass, a flower made out of Dorothy's own hair. It made her feel sick.

"That will be your present to Mrs. Jewell," Aunty Em had told her. She had written a note on it. "From a young friend," it said.

Dorothy had made another present of her own. She kept it folded up inside her mitten. She would give the present to Mrs. Jewell herself, try to tell her, if she could, why Will had died. Nobody had given Dorothy a chance to tell her, even though Mrs. Jewell had said she didn't understand why. Dorothy thought she wanted to understand.

Dorothy had seen Zeandale ahead of them as soon as they had left the Jewells' farm and got onto the road. Zeandale seemed to creep toward them forever and never get any closer. The gray road, the gray sky, the gray earth, did not seem to change. It took on close to an hour.

All there was to Zeandale, the village, were a few houses and a post office store. EVERYTHING FOR SALE, said a fancy sign outside the shop. Tin tubs and pans and horse clothes were hung around the porch. The schoolhouse looked like any other building and had no steeple. Wagons were gathered all around it.

Dorothy knew Aunty Em didn't like having to come to Zeandale. She knew Aunty Em would be looked down on by the people here. She knew it from the stiff-backed way Aunty Em climbed down from the rickety wagon and from the way she folded up the hides, with a series of smart snaps, as if they were something rare and precious, to be protected. She stowed them under the seat quickly, so no one could see them.

"Now, Dorothy, the people here don't know us, so we got to show them that we're worthy of respect." The truth was that people in Zeandale did know them and only too well. The people here knew how small the house was and how poor the farm. In Manhattan, Aunty Em was still a Branscomb, the educated daughter of a local dignitary. At least, that was what Aunty Em thought. No one from Manhattan was ever invited back to see the unimproved homestead or the unimproved Henry Gulch.

Aunty Em swiped at the shoulders of Dorothy's black dress and pulled down hard on the bottom of the jacket. The dress was slightly lopsided. It had been one of Aunty Em's own.

"It was a sacrifice, cutting down this dress, but it was for your friend, Dorothy, and I was pleased to do it." Aunty Em's eyes flickered toward the Jewells, who were helping their mama toward the church. Aunty Em knelt down and smoothed the collar and shoulders and looked into Dorothy's face and breathed out wreaths of icy vapor.

"And you mustn't talk, child, not a word. We look at the good, Dorothy, and we turn our eyes from the bad. What Wilbur did was the greatest sin anybody can do. We are burying that sin today. The good men do lives on after them."

"Yes, Aunty," said Dorothy. The rule was: When you don't understand, agree.

Aunty Em pursed her lips and narrowed her eyes into an expression of cramped sweetness. She stroked Dorothy's face. "You are my own sweet sister's child," she said, with misgiving.

"Yes, Aunty." Dorothy's toes and fingers ached with the cold and she wanted to get inside.

Aunty Em was still scanning her face for imperfections. "Can't see a shadow of that man at all," she said. That man meant Dorothy's father.

"Yes, Aunty," said Dorothy.

The funeral was being held in the schoolhouse. Zeandale had gone to the effort of building a church, but the roof had blown off in a cyclone almost as soon as it was finished. Aunty Em kept an eye on the front door. When the Jewells finished maneuvering themselves through it, she stood up, and finally, finally, she and Dorothy could go inside. They walked together hand in hand; Uncle Henry followed with the framed hair flower. The Kansas earth underfoot was frozen as hard as rock. Dorothy tripped and stumbled; Aunty Em hauled her up by the hand. No one was to fall.

Dorothy knew that there had been some kind of trouble. There was a graveyard in the hills outside of the town. Some people had not wanted Wilbur buried there because he had killed himself. Dorothy wondered if they had done something to the ground to close it against him. Would God freeze the ground to stop someone from being buried?

They went into the schoolhouse, and it was colder inside than outside. The little stove had been stoked that morning, but all the heat rose up into the ceiling. As thick as a muddy river, currents of cold air flowed about their feet. The walls were white; the windows were white. The mourners had to sit on school benches. The place was full of adults all in black like some giant species of insect. There were children, too, some of them from Sunflower School, where Wilbur had gone. They were all real quiet and hung their heads and scowled. Dorothy knew that scowl. It was the Indian scowl. You made it when something didn't make sense.

There was a wall of memorials. In midwinter, there were no flowers. There were woven pine branches and pillows stuffed with potpourri and scrolls with writing on them. Aunty and Uncle filed past them. They looked a long time at each one. Dorothy wondered why. Uncle Henry pushed the frame at her.

"Put yours here, Dorothy," whispered Aunty Em. Dorothy leaned it against the wall without ceremony. She was glad to be rid of it. Aunty Em pushed her shoulders. Down. Like at prayers, Dorothy had to kneel. So she did. Then Aunty Em tapped her on the shoulders and she stood up. You just did what you were told. Then they went and sat on the cold, cold bench, next to people they didn't know, and Dorothy knew she would hate it. It would be long and full of words and nobody would be allowed to move. Dorothy started to rock. Aunty Em stopped her. The Jewells went to the front bench and sat down together.

Dorothy watched Mrs. Jewell. She rocked too. She rocked from side to side, and she was shaking, like some old cart on a bumpy road.

"Is she rocking 'cause of the cold?" Dorothy asked.

"Sssh," said Aunty Em. Of course you weren't supposed to talk, but Dorothy had thought one question would be allowed, about a nice woman who was cold.

The Preacher came in. He was a young man, slightly plump. He had come in from Deep Creek to preach. People coughed. He looked up at them.

"Thank you all for coming in this terrible weather. I think it is a measure of Kansas sympathy that everyone here managed to show."

They were told to sing. Dorothy tried to look behind her at the people singing and was turned around. Then they said a prayer. Dorothy had to make sure that Aunty Em heard her say the words. It was one of the worst things Aunty Em had found out when she came, that Dorothy did not know her prayers.

> The power and the glory
> Forever an never
> Hay men.

Dorothy didn't know what they meant.

Then the Preacher spoke.

"This is the saddest of occasions," he said. "The death of a young man in a way that in a less generous community would have precluded Christian interment. It is something that is hard for all of us to face, most especially his parents, who must be wondering how and why they failed him. All of us share that sense of having failed. I knew Wilbur Frederick Jewell as a boy and as a young fellow approaching manhood and knew him to be a well-mannered youth, who gave no outward sign of the worm within. We must all of us, in the privacy of our thoughts, come to our own conclusions about Wilbur. But in this memorial service, we must remember his virtues and pray that they weigh heaviest in the scales of justice when his soul is judged in Heaven. Perhaps the prayers of those who love him and the true love of the Lord Jesus can atone and win forgiveness."

It went on like that. Mrs. Jewell shook so much the pew rattled. Aunty Em clicked with her tongue. Dorothy could feel her aunt go harder and fiercer. There were more songs and another prayer. They all bowed their heads and prayed for the young man's soul. Dorothy didn't know that one, so mumbled, looking sideways to see if Aunty Em was angry. She looked angry, but Dorothy thought perhaps not at her.

Finally it was over. Why did everything have to last so long? Mrs. Jewell was making her way toward the church door, with the speed of clouds on a rainy day. They all had to sit for her. Dorothy's legs wanted to move, and started to twitch, and once again, of course, Aunty Em stilled her.

They waited while other people went out one by one. People shook hands with the Preacher and then spoke to the Jewells, offering a few words as if from a high platform looking down. Or they looked embarrassed, nodding, shaking hands, and then left, ducking for some reason, though the doorway was not low.

Dorothy felt her own secret gift, folded and crisp, inside her mitten.

Aunty Em patted her and then pushed her: now it was time to move. Dorothy swung her legs around and jumped down to the floor. The school students were ahead of them. They were the very last. Dorothy couldn't wait to be gone. The students had little to say. They ducked the most and gathered outside. From somewhere far enough away came the sound of laughter. The Preacher stood next to Bob Jewell, hands clasped.

"A cold day, young man," said Aunty Em to the Preacher. "And an even colder sermon. Perhaps when you are a bit older, you will also learn to be wiser."

The Preacher was not used to being criticized. He looked dumbfounded.

"I simply mean," said Aunty Em, "that it is not your job to increase the grief of the bereaved."

"I'm sorry if I left that impression," he said.

"It is not to me, but to the young man's mother that you should perhaps address a few more kindly words," said Aunty Em. "I may say that it would not have happened in our congregation or with another preacher."

The Preacher chuckled. It was a very nasty chuckle. Dorothy thought: Why is he laughing? He chuckled and shrugged.

Aunty Em took Mary Jewell's hand. She took it and then suddenly seized it hard, a different gesture altogether. Then she moved on.

It was Dorothy's turn.

"I've got a present for you, Mrs. Jewell," said Dorothy.

Aunty Em turned. What present?

Mrs. Jewell leaned over, with her great breathy wrinkled weight. Dorothy unfolded the piece of paper from inside her mitten. The present was a drawing. Dorothy passed it up to Mrs. Jewell.

"Thank you, Dorothy," said Mrs. Jewell. "What is it?"

"It's an Indian," said Dorothy. "I only had a pencil so it had to be a Kansas Indian. That's gray. A real Indian would be red."

"That's very nice, Dorothy, now come along," said Aunty Em, advancing.

"That's why he hanged himself," said Dorothy. "He wanted to be an Indian, a real Indian. But he wasn't brave enough."

"Oh-ho!" cried Mrs. Jewell, unsteadily.

"He didn't like it here. He didn't like school or anything. He wanted to get away."

But he was too frightened to leave, and so he felt ashamed. It was shame that made him kill himself. Dorothy could taste the shame and feel the shape it had, but she didn't have the words for it.

"Dorothy!" raged Aunty Em, stepping forward. Dorothy was seized, pulled, hauled away. Mrs. Jewell seemed to sag, waving Dorothy away. The drawing fell to the floor.

"But Uncle Henry said you didn't understand!" said Dorothy. Aunty Em gave her arm a savage tug. Dorothy knew she had done wrong, but she didn't care. It was the truth.

Aunty Em got her to the wagon and bundled her up onto the front seat. "Hurry up, Henry, let's get away." Uncle Henry speeded up somewhat. The mule was untied.

"Dorothy. What am I going to do with you?" Aunty Em's hand covered her face. Her face moved from side to side. "That poor woman."

Dorothy didn't want to hear what she had done wrong. Everything she did was wrong. "It was a present," she murmured.

"It was a present that opened a wound. I told you, Dorothy, not to mention what he did!"

"But I'm the only one who knows."

Knows that there is a nothingness in the wilderness, a great emptiness in the plains and sky, a nothingness that needs to be filled, not only with houses and horses and plows, but with imagination, an inhuman nothingness that could suck you in and kill you.

There was no point talking. How could Dorothy make anyone understand that? She could not explain it; she had no words. She could only endure the incomprehension and the harsh words and the silence.

It was dark by the time they got home. Scarecrows waved in moonlight. Instead of going inside, Dorothy hopped down from the wagon and ran.

She ran up the slopes of the bald hill to where the snowmen were.

There were still three of them, in a row, as glossy and hard as marble. They were white-blue in moonlight. They were here and Wilbur was not. When the sun came, they would melt, and nothing Dorothy could do would stop it. They would melt away like memories trickling out of her head. There was very little Dorothy could do about anything at all.

And there were the angels in the snow, a tall one next to a little one. The trick was to leave no footprints, as if you had lain there for a time and flown away to Heaven.

And suddenly, Dorothy was crying. She found she could cry. "Will-hill-bur!" Maybe there were Indians in Heaven. Maybe Wilbur had found them there. Maybe he had finally joined them.

Maybe not. The tears were soon over. Dorothy had faced death before. She was weary of it, bone-weary. People were here and then they were gone and you had to live as if they had never been here. What once had been, what might have been, could give her nothing. Powdery snow whispered in the wind as it blew. The scarecrows lined up over the wallows, though there was no need for them in winter. Even the wallows were as hard as stone.

The clouds in the sky were as white as ice, and they raced in thin crystals over the surface of the moon. The stars were cold. The valley lay under a sheet of white, and smoke from chimneys hung like freezing fog.

Only where there were houses was there light, was there warmth. It shone out of the windows, orange, fire red, faintly glowing. Those houses were the only place to go, the only life available.

Dorothy finally saw what adults wanted her to see. She saw pioneer beauty, from the top of a hill. It was a trade. In exchange, she had to become resigned. Dorothy knuckled under. She heard Aunty Em call, and she walked back down to punishment and food and a new clean bed.

A few days later, across the naked fields, Dorothy saw Bob Jewell armed with a shovel. For no reason, he was beating one of the scarecrows flat, in a rage.

Zeandale and
Manhattan, Kansas

Winter 1875—1876

*"That would make me very unhappy," answered the china princess.
"You see, here in our own country, we live contentedly, and can talk
and move around as we please. But whenever any of us are taken away,
our joints at once stiffen and we can only stand straight and look
pretty . . ."*

—L. FRANK BAUM,
The Wonderful Wizard of Oz

Dorothy knuckled down to learning to read. She would sit by the window, and Aunty Em would open up some huge volume smelling of mushrooms and dust. Toto would tug at her dress to go outside. Toto was kept inside now to keep him from freezing, but he was tied up most of the time.

"What's the first letter, Dorothy? Look at the book, child. Toto, set. Toto, get to your corner. Dorothy, what is the first letter?"

Dorothy was ashamed. "E?"

Another bad thing that Aunty Em had found out when Dorothy came was that she did not know her letters.

"No, Dorothy, that's a W. Now what does W sound like? A W with an H after it. Whuh. Whuh sound, Dorothy. Now I'll just read this first sentence for you. 'Whether I shall turn out to be the hero of my own life or whether that station will be held by anybody else, these pages must show.' "

Beyond the walls, the woods on the ridge sighed in the wind. Both the sky and the ground were the same white color. Aunty Em asked her to recite the alphabet. Dorothy forgot *F*.

"Don't start all over again," said Aunty Em. "That's just learning by rote, parrot fashion, and I want you to really know this. I don't want people to think we're ignorant, Dorothy Gael, and they will if you go to school without your alphabet and the rudiments of ciphering!"

And then she said, "What was your mama thinking of?"

Dorothy began to hate her mother, for all the things she had left out: prayers and table manners and numbers. Dorothy helped at candle making. She swept up the floor. She watched Aunty Em repairing shoes, repairing trousers, jabbing the needle so hard that she sometimes stabbed herself with it. She watched Aunty Em cook in a rage.

In the evenings, Henry would come in moving slowly with his long, stick-thin limbs. He would slump in his chair as Aunty Em threw pots about the stove, spilling, burning, humming hymns to herself. She made terrible mistakes. She baked cakes with salt instead of sugar. Meat came out of the oven burned black outside but red raw inside.

"You could plant an extra crop," said Aunty Em, one night.

Uncle Henry was baffled by exhaustion. "What crop?"

"Spring wheat, corn, I don't know."

"Most of this land is hillside turf, Em, or it's covered in woods. What you reckon on clearing it?"

"We could keep hogs in the woods."

"We got any spare cash to buy hogs with?"

"We would have with what fifty acres of river-bottom prime would earn anyone else."

"It's not prime land, Em. Your father didn't do too much with it either."

The pot slammed down as if on a head. "My father was writing the newspaper at the same time, instead of sitting around here with his boots off."

"So we're back to wheat. Every year since I come, people say it's going to be eight-row wheat, and then 'long comes the drouth or the hail or the wind or the bust. This year, last year it was locusts."

"Such a good excuse for you, weren't they?" said Aunty Em, talking over him.

"Or the herd laws means somebody's cows trample it. Worst thing of all is when you have a good year and the price just dries up till you get nothing for nothing."

"Well, I don't see the Aikens or the McCormacks or the Allens in poverty."

"They got sons, they got brothers."

"Well, hire yourself a hand."

"We don't have any money," said Henry, his voice muffled by the hand that rubbed his eyes.

"Well, we got to do something!" shouted Aunty Em, and the stove hissed and steamed with spilled water. "We got that child to feed now and send to school soon as she's old enough. Poor little creature."

Uncle Henry hung his head. Aunty Em's back was toward him. He said, very slowly, "We could sell some of the land."

"That's the only thing you can think of to do with it! My father settled this land."

"Don't I know it."

"And you aren't going to be the one to sell any of it!"

"Won't have to," said Henry Gulch. "Mr. Purcell at the bank is going to get it all anyway."

Mr. Purcell was the enemy. He ran the bank and he wanted to take away their land and give it to people Back East. How would that be possible, if Aunty Em didn't want him to have it?

"Him too," said Aunty Em, throwing food onto a plate.

Reading, ciphering, and hogs and banks. Dorothy admired Uncle Henry and Aunty Em. They knew so much, all kinds of things, but everything rode on them; if anything went wrong they would be alone. And they never rested, never let up on themselves. Dorothy was grateful, but she didn't ever want to be an adult.

Aunty Em sat down to eat and began to rail against the people of Manhattan. Aunty Em never went to Zeandale village. It was always to Manhattan that they went for church, for stores, for company. It was Manhattan Aunty Em talked about, but not with love.

She talked about Mr. Purcell, and also Mrs. Purcell, who was always organizing things and neglecting to invite Emma Gulch. There was L. R. Elliott. He had bought the *Manhattan Independent* from Reverend Pillsbury and then fired Grandfather Matthew.

"Killed him, killed him just as surely as if he shot him!" Aunty Em said. "Him and his talk of real news. He bought the paper and then killed both it and my father and waltzed off to be a land agent, if you please. And railroad agent. And anything else he could lay his hands on." Stew roiled forgotten in her mouth.

"The Higinbothams, and Stingley and Huntress. They're all in it together, all those people. They come here and take the town over from the people who built it up. And the good Dr. Lyman with his friendly little reminders—'You owe the good Doctor money.' " Aunty Em let her fork drop, and covered her eyes.

Later, she piled the tin plates one on top of the other. Aunty Em could produce a fine clatter of rage, and she plunged her raw hands into the water, which was near to boiling. She passed down the steaming plates for Dorothy to dry.

Then she said, "Dorothy, it's your bedtime. Say your prayers." Aunty Em would stand by the blanket that hung across the room. She would listen to what Dorothy had to say to God. Dorothy prayed for God to bless everyone and then crawled into bed to be kissed on the forehead. Then Dorothy would listen. She listened to the whispering.

"You ask me it wasn't the Dip my sister died of, but shame. That man used her and then left. An actor, if you please, with I am told another wife and children Back East. And he was about as Irish as I am. Anthony Gael indeed. More like Angelo or Chico if you want to know the truth!"

"You're fretting, Em."

"Well, don't I have enough to fret about?" A pan rang like a gong as it was hung on a hook. "Every time I look at Dorothy I can see that man's face. It's bad blood, Henry, and it will come out."

Uncle Henry would begin to snore, too exhausted to find the bed. Aunty Em would begin to recite. Aunty Em wrote verse. She would declaim it as she paced, the thumping of her boots punctuating the rhythm of the words. Throughout that winter, it had been the same poem, over and over:

> By day across those billows brown
> Across the summits sere
> The fierce wind blows; the sunlight streams
> From blue skies cold and clear.

It was a poem about the beauties of Manhattan when it was first settled. The Congregationalist Church was about to have its twentieth anniversary after the New Year. With her whole being, Aunty Em wanted to recite her poem at the banquet. The pastor's wife had also written a poem. It too was about the beauties of early Manhattan, and it was certain to be read at the banquet.

> By night along those meadows broad,
> In gleaming tower and spire
> O'er rolling hill, o'er rocky crest
> Creep crooked lines of fire!

Her voice would be fierce and whispering. Sometimes Aunty Em would change the words; sometimes she changed the way she said them. Sometimes the words came shuddering out of her, full of meanings for her that they would have for no one else. Sometimes she wept, reciting to the stove, the empty room, her husband's crushed and empty boots. Dorothy would pull the pillow down over her head and hide.

Aunty Em was always in Manhattan, working for the Church. She set up socials or church suppers; she chaperoned dances or sat on ladies' committees or organized drives. She decorated the church for Easter (Christmas was not much celebrated). She took baskets to the poor, though Dorothy heard people say that Emma Gulch was poor enough herself.

"We are people of note in this community," she told Dorothy once. "And we continue to be, despite straitened circumstances, which should be no bar in any civilized society."

And she and Dorothy would take the long road to Manhattan. Aunty Em inserted them both into the homes of women she considered to be her social if not economic equals. All through the autumn, into the first hot weeks of that strange December, Dorothy would find herself in the corner of Manhattan parlors, mollified by muffins or drinking chocolate.

Aunty Em visited Mrs. Parker, the Reverend's wife. She visited Harriet Smythe, who also threatened to give readings. She visited Miss Eusebia Mudge, daughter of the famous Professor Mudge. Miss Mudge was to provide the musical program by playing the organ.

"And how is your dear father?" Aunty Em asked. "Is he still occupied with his pterodactyls?"

"Oh, yes indeed," said Miss Mudge. "He will be returning to

Wallace this spring. He hopes to send a complete pterodactyl to the university in Topeka."

Aunty Em turned to Dorothy. "Dorothy. A pterodactyl is a giant flying lizard. The Professor discovered them in Wallace."

"They are extinct now, Dorothy," explained Miss Mudge.

"They have been, for millions of years. Just think of it!"

After so many conversations about buffalo, Dorothy certainly knew the meaning of the word "extinct." But she didn't know how you could discover something that had been dead for millions of years, or how you could send one to Topeka. She thought it best not to ask. Aunty Em might think it was insolent.

"The Professor also discovered a missing link in the evolutionary chain, am I right, Miss Mudge?" said Aunty Em. "A bird with teeth."

Dorothy wasn't too sure that all birds didn't have teeth. She tried to remember if their hens had teeth and decided that they did. By the time Dorothy resurfaced, the conversation had moved on.

"Well, we simply have to get Brother Pillsbury and Reverend Jones to speak, though at opposite ends of the program for reasons we can both imagine," said Aunty Em. Brother Pillsbury was a spiritualist, as well as a Christian.

"Certainly both should be acknowledged," said Miss Mudge with caution.

"Not to mention Mrs. Blood," said Aunty Em, smiling, in one of her flights of efficiency. "She's still alive, I hear, and there is time still to get a message to her in Illinois, so she can send something to us. I'm sure she would be most pleased."

Eusebia agreed. Aunty Em kept flying. She reminisced about the first Congregationalist services held in a tent or in Dr. Hunting's house. She rehearsed the story of how a tornado tore the roof off the church just after it was built—it seemed to be the fate of most churches in the county. She talked about Dr. Cordley, who had ridden all the way from Lawrence to give the dedicatory sermon. Did Miss Mudge know that his famous horse Jesse was lost during Quantrill's raid? Dorothy began to swing her legs. Eusebia Mudge bided her time.

"Evergreen branches, I think," said Aunty Em, talking of the decorations. "So in keeping with the season." She talked about food. "I can certainly make a lemon jelly, if you, Miss Mudge, would oblige with your famous angel cake."

"Speaking of cake," said Miss Mudge, whose time had come. "What are we to do with Mr. Sue?"

There was a Chinaman in Manhattan. He had come with the building of the railroad. To everyone's consternation, he was a member of the Congregationalist Church. He donated unsuitable cakes. They had unsuitable writing in icing.

"God made the world," the icing said. "Tzu made this cake."

Everyone called him Mr. Sue. Using a woman's name made people smile, while preserving their old abolitionist consciences. When they smiled, Mr. Tzu thought they were smiling with pleasure at seeing him. Or at least, he smiled back. He had suddenly imported a wife, whom no one had seen. She was said to live in the rooms behind his store.

"And you've heard of his invitation, perhaps?" inquired Miss Mudge.

"Why, no," said Emma Gulch.

"He has sent a card to every church saying that his wife will be at home to receive visitors on New Year's Day."

If anyone was so lost in good works as to go, it would be Emma Gulch.

"How splendid of him," said Aunty Em. "I'm sure we will all be happy to visit."

"I'm glad to hear you say that," Miss Mudge replied and permitted herself a smile.

On New Year's Day, Calliope the mule was hauled out, snorting with cold, and was hitched to the wagon. Inside the house, Toto was barking over and over to be let out, to go with them.

"Couldn't we bring Toto with us?" Dorothy asked.

"What, bring a dog into Mrs. Purcell's parlor?" said Aunty Em. "She can just about bring herself to let us in, let alone Toto."

All the way down the lane, the sound of Toto's barking followed them.

"That's how much he misses us. But just think how snug he is next to the stove."

Even from the lane, Dorothy could see Blue Mont, on the other side of the river, four and a half miles away. It took two hours, and the mountain never seemed to get any closer. The sound of Toto followed them across the valley. They rode beside the woods, the trees as bare as burned black skeletons. Branches passed by overhead. Dorothy broke off a piece of ice and looked at the perfect imprint of the twig. "Don't suck it, Dorothy," said Aunty Em, "or you'll perforate your stomach." Dorothy began to hum to herself. Aunty Em sang hymns. With each turn of the road, Dorothy hoped for the rise and fall of the road that would signal their sudden decline toward the river.

Finally, finally they got to Manhattan, frozen stiff as always. The church ladies were gathering at Mrs. Purcell's house on South Juliette. There was an alleyway with stables behind. A boy took hold of Calliope, and Aunty Em rather grandly pressed a penny into his hand. She inspected Dorothy's dress, tugged and thumped it, and then took her hand to walk around to the front of the house, to be admitted as guests.

The door was opened by a maid. There were gas lamps everywhere, frosted glass globes, and the tops of the chairs were dark and polished and carved into the shapes of leaves. From somewhere behind all the front rooms, there came a chorus of baby cries. The ladies, buttoned in black, sat in a circle amid a forest of tea tables.

Mrs. Elliott was there for the Methodists, the wife of the man who had brought Grandfather Matthew's career to an end. Mrs. Parker was there from Aunty Em's own church, as if Aunty Em were not sufficient in herself to represent the Congregationalists.

The Purcells were Presbyterian and owned the bank that had sold the mortgage to Emma Gulch's farm.

Dorothy knew of these people. She was interested to see them. She wondered how it was that Aunty Em could bear to smile at them. Dorothy looked at the frosted lamps, at the line of fuel within them like water under ice. She pretended to herself that the lamps had grown naturally frozen out of the Zeandale marshes.

Mrs. Purcell, no longer young, but very brisk and pleasant, came in with baby John. He had just been born a few months before. He was passed around the ladies, who complimented him and talked to him. Baby John beamed like an ancient old man. "Happy New Year! Happy New Year!" the ladies piped.

"His little hand!" cooed Aunty Em.

Dorothy peered into his soft, unformed face. Intelligence in his eyes met hers.

"Bah bah," he said. "Mo ta woe?"

It was how babies talked.

"Oh yes? Oh yes?" said Mrs. Parker too brightly, as if she understood. Maybe she did. The baby was passed to a maid to be taken upstairs. Tea and cakes were served, and the adults talked about Chinese people.

"Apparently they fry all their food in very hot oils," said Mrs. Elliott. "My cousin visited such a home once, and her fur collar smelled peculiar for weeks. They couldn't think what the odor was; it was so unpleasant, but not at all identifiable. Finally someone said it was burned sesame seed oil."

Mrs. Parker produced a nosegay from her purse and silently held it out. "I shall endeavor not to resort to this, since I'm sure Mrs. Sue will do her utmost to be polite."

"It's not the oil, it's the incense that will choke me," said Mrs. Lyman. She was the doctor's wife and she was beautiful and young, with red hair. Aunty Em made a point of chuckling. Mrs. Lyman was from St. George, just across the river from the Gulch farm. Aunty Em always made a point of saying how enchanting she found her. "Just a good, plain-speaking Kansas beauty," Aunty Em would say, again and again.

"Well," said a woman whose name Dorothy did not know. "My tablecloth came back cleaner than the gravel by the river."

Dorothy did not know much about the Chinaman herself, but she could see that the adults were frightened of him.

The seven ladies, Baptist, Methodist, Congregationalist, Lutheran, wrapped themselves in scarves and pinned on hats and were helped into coats that nearly reached the ground. They walked unsteadily on the boardwalk of South Juliette, north toward Poyntz, the main avenue. They walked past one Methodist church and Mrs. Elliott's house. They walked across Houston, past the Bowers' and the Buells'. On the corner of Poyntz and Juliette was Aunty Em's own church, white limestone, small. They turned right and swept down the broad main avenue.

Poyntz was lined with wooden-frame buildings, with wooden awnings that stretched out over the wooden sidewalks. The ladies passed another Methodist church, with a tall, graceful spire, and an Episcopalian and a Presbyterian. They passed the Manhattan Institute, which was a hospital built of brick. There was Huntress's Dry Goods, a two-story building of stone. On Poyntz Avenue alone, there were four banks, three land offices, three drugstores, a lumberyard, several general stores, clothing stores, hotels and two county offices. There were many businesses, with many owners, but amid those many names, a favored few kept reappearing: Higinbotham, Stingley, Elliott, Purcell.

The street was shuttered and closed, peaceful and safe. An old black man everyone called Uncle was sweeping the ice that covered the boardwalk. Someone Mrs. Elliott knew passed them, tipping his hat, breathing out vapor into the sunlight, nodding "Good morning, ladies," as he passed.

Mr. Sue's shop stood near the corner of Humboldt and Second, opposite the Wagon Shop.

There was a wide space around it, a market garden that was the town's only source of sorrel and green peppers. The laundry hissed out back, white steam rising up even on New Year's Day. Dorothy took hold of Aunty Em's hand, afraid.

The store was dark. Mrs. Purcell took it on herself to try the door. It opened with a clinking of bits of metal hung across the doorway. They peered inside, into scented shadow.

"Mr. Sue?" called Mrs. Purcell. Dorothy began to wish she hadn't come.

Mr. Sue emerged from some inner recess, smiling, smiling.

"Good morning, ladies. So kind to come. I hope you are not cold. Thank you, thank you."

He looked funny. Dorothy wasn't sure how. He was small and quick, wearing perfectly normal clothes and a bowler hat. Dorothy was miffed. Didn't he know it was impolite to wear a hat indoors? Then she saw him take it off, over and over, once for each of the ladies.

Inside the store, the air smelled a bit like soap, nice soap, and there were things in pretty boxes, nice colors, very pale and gentle. There were bolts of shiny cloth and little cups and teapots. There were china people, white with pink cheeks, frozen forever, looking shy and a bit afraid.

Dorothy began to be afraid for Mr. Sue. China was made of clay and so, said the Preacher, were people. China could fall and break. Maybe that's why the adults were frightened. They were frightened that they could shatter him. They walked so carefully around him as he smiled and smiled. He pulled back a curtain and held out his hat to show them the way they should go.

They went into a room, and Dorothy wondered if China people lived in tents like Indians. The wall seemed to be made of blue cloth. Dorothy pushed the cloth. There was a solid wall behind it. Perhaps wood or stone was too rough for China people.

There were cushions everywhere, with cloth flowers sewn on them, and the little room was hot as a stove, and full of the soap smell.

"Oh!" said Mrs. Purcell, looking around the tiny place in surprise. She looked large and clumsy, as if she would knock something over. But Dorothy felt at home. Everything was the right size for her.

Then Mrs. Sue came in and Dorothy knew she was right. China people could be broken.

Mrs. Sue walked in with breathless child steps, small and very quick, and her eyes and her face were lowered from shyness and she smiled shyly. She wore blue trousers and a blue top, very shiny, and she was painted like the frozen people outside. Pink on her cheeks, black around the eyes, red on her lips.

"Da doh, da doh," she seemed to be saying, unable to look at the ladies, bowing to them. She held out her hands.

The ladies looked at each other.

"She doesn't speak English, and she wants to take our coats," said Aunty Em, crisply. "Dorothy, please to help Mrs. Sue with all these coats. Mind you take them where she shows you."

Aunty Em passed her own thick, black, worn coat to her. "Thank you, thank you, Mrs. Sue," she said loudly, very plainly, smiling with her leaky gray teeth.

Mrs. Sue averted her face and bowed, again, and said something with the gentleness of the wind.

"May I help you?" Dorothy asked, looking up at her.

Mrs. Sue could bear to look at Dorothy but not at the adults. She looked at Dorothy and smiled. Dorothy strode boldly among the ladies, taking coats. She knew she would not knock anything over.

"We are to sit on the cushions," announced Aunty Em.

The ladies raised their eyebrows. This would be indelicate. Dorothy wanted to see how plump Mrs. Purcell and bony old Mrs. Elliott would manage it. Mrs. Sue, in a soft and singsong voice, was trying to tell her something, so Dorothy turned and saw she was to follow through another curtain, into an alcove. There was a white statue in the alcove, of a fat and naked smiling man. There were pipe cleaners all around it, burning. Did Mrs. Sue think you were supposed to smoke the cleaners and not the pipe? Mrs. Sue reached and hung up the coats. She folded and smoothed down the ladies' scarves. They looked beautiful, the scarves, folded so tidily. Mrs. Sue smiled her gentle, withdrawn smile, and Dorothy knew she was to go back to the adults.

Back in the hot room, the ladies were sitting, backs straight. Mrs. Purcell and Aunty Em had adopted the side saddle position they had learned as young ladies. Mrs. Elliott was thrashing, trying to fight her way upright. She kept slipping off the cushion.

"Knees under you, Emeline," said Mrs. Purcell.

Mrs. Sue came toddling in, carrying something that was neither a tray nor a table. It was made of beautiful brown wood and carved in funny shapes, and there was a teapot with red and blue crisscrosses on it. The tray was placed on the floor. There was tea and little pink cakes. Mrs. Sue lowered her head and held out her arms with a sweep over the tea and cakes.

"Isn't it exquisite," announced Aunty Em, determined they would all feel the right thing. "And so charmingly presented." She inclined forward, with her broken and horsey smile. Mrs. Sue tried to look pleased, but she could not bear the huge, coarse visage and had to look away, lest the distaste show.

Dorothy felt she was having some kind of revenge. The adults all looked wrong, like pigs or straggly plants. The only beautiful person in the room was Mrs. Sue.

She began to pour the tea, and to pass the cakes, looking up hopefully to make sure that everything was all right, that she had done nothing wrong. And Dorothy knew, just from looking, that Mrs. Sue was alone in Kansas, and that she was trying as hard as she could, but that she and these women would never be friends, no matter how correct they all were, no matter how polite. It was all done in hopefulness and was doomed to failure.

"The cakes," said Mrs. Purcell, in horror. "I think they're made out of fish."

Dorothy tasted one of them. It was bland and chewy.

The pink bland cakes were followed by sweet spicy ones that were also to no one's taste. And Mrs. Sue, trying hard, adopting all the right postures, sent signals of sociability that were only partially received. They were swamped by the heavy-handed and insincere gestures that came in reply.

"These are very unusual. Very unusual. Nice," said Aunty Em, loudly, holding up the spice cake.

Mrs. Sue kept smiling, looking nowhere. She leaned forward like a river reed to fill more cups with tea.

"Shouldn't she let it steep more?" wondered one of the ladies without looking at the others.

"Chinese tea is famous for its delicacy," Aunty Em informed them.

"I wish the incense was," said Mrs. Parker.

It couldn't go on much longer. Tea and cakes can only do so much without conversation. More smiles and nodding, and Mrs. Sue knew she had failed. Her eyes were veiled as she tried to look pleased and honored when the ladies left. Dorothy went to help her with the coats.

Dorothy wanted to say something. But how could you say something to someone who had not learned to talk?

She had an idea. She talked like a baby would talk. She made sounds without the words that she found she lacked. Dorothy whispered, sadly, "Da toh nah sang ga la ta no rah tea so la tee ree." Without having to find words, Dorothy said that she was sorry, sorry that Mrs. Sue was alone in a foreign country, and that her cakes had not been liked, and that no one else was coming, and that her husband would probably be cross.

Mrs. Sue knew that the little girl was really trying to say something, something kind. And she could see what she was not supposed to notice, that the child was poorly dressed. Mrs. Sue had a happy idea. It was a season of gift giving. She turned and gave the child a folded-paper doll, dressed in crepe paper, with a folded face and a painted smile.

"Thank you," said Dorothy.

They filed back out through the hot, cushioned room, through the curtain, down the cooler, wooden corridor, back into the store. Mr. Sue was smiling, thanking them for the call. Do tell your wife how charmed we were, said the ladies, what a lovely room, what a lovely blue . . . um . . . ensemble she wore, a delightful tea, such a departure from the usual. Why, Dorothy wondered, do adults always lie?

Back out into the cold.

"Oh," said one of the ladies, a safe distance away. "Back out into God's own air!"

"Poor little thing. Fancy not speaking a word of English!"

"She was the soul of courtesy," insisted Aunty Em. "I cannot imagine how her behavior could be in any way improved."

"Perhaps by using less incense so a human body could breathe!" exclaimed the Reverend Parker's wife.

"That was like your nosegay," said Dorothy. "She was frightened that you'd smell."

"Dorothy!" exclaimed Aunty Em. "Apologize to Mrs. Parker." But she sounded less angry than usual.

When they were back in the wagon, Aunty Em laughed. "Dorothy, your mouth!" she said, shaking her head. "The things you come out with! Mind, your mother was the same."

Dorothy could see that she had done something right, but did not understand what it was. Aunty Em was a mystery, to be watched, to be solved.

A few days later, Aunty Em learned that her poem was not to be read at the Church anniversary. Her own suggestion had been taken up. Mrs. Blood in Illinois had been written to, and the old woman had responded with a detailed reminiscence of life in Manhattan's early days. It would be read in full to the congregation, as would Mrs. Parker's poem. Aunty Em had a letter from Miss Mudge, thanking her for all her efforts.

That night Dorothy heard her pacing around and around the little room in silence.

The next morning, Toto slipped his rope and disappeared, into the snow.

Manhattan, Kansas

Spring 1876

Go east, and you hear them laugh at Kansas; go west and they sneer at
her; go south and they "cuss" her; go north and they have forgotten
her . . .

— *WILLIAM ALLEN WHITE,* in an editorial called
"What's the Matter with Kansas?"

Suddenly it was spring in Kansas. There were wildflowers all along the
roads and in the thorny hedges. Dorothy was relieved. It was as if some
part of life had smiled on her at last.

Today was Sunday, no school, and it was sunny, a strange sort of
sunlight that glowed in haze near to the ground. It was comfortable
riding in the wagon. Dorothy still had to wear her coat, but the lap
robes weren't necessary, and her feet and toes were no longer an agony.
It was as if the whole of Kansas had sighed in relief.

Aunty Em was in a strange mood too. In the morning, as she had
hitched the mule to the cart, there was a kind of secret smile on her
face, and she moved with more of a bounce in her step.

"C'mon, Dorothy, it's just you and me today. Your Uncle Henry
don't come, because he don't have the Spirit," said Aunty Em, feeling
chummy. "So it's just us two, Dorothy. We're going to go and have
our souls raised up like summer flowers. I tell you, when the Spirit
moves, you don't mind anything, because God is with you, and nobody
can take that away."

They weren't going to church. That was very strange. Meeting
was obviously going to be slightly like church, there could be no escape

from something holy on a Sunday, but it was obviously something more delicious and exciting, a kind of spring church. Aunty Em clucked her tongue, and the cart jerked forward, and they moved out into the fields.

Dorothy caught her aunty's mood. "We're going to Meeting! We're going to Meeting!" she exclaimed excitedly.

Aunty Em chuckled. "Yes, we are, honey, and we're going to meet all kinds of *nice* people." There was a kind of snarl in Aunty Em's voice, on the word "nice," that made Dorothy breathless with anticipation. Nice people. It had been so long since she'd met any.

"Nice people," Dorothy repeated. Saying it made her feel small and warm and comforted.

"It'll be like going to church in Lawrence," said Aunty Em. "We just had the one old cottonwood meeting hall, and the sun made the boards curl up, so the wind blew between them, and we'd all sing just to keep warm. Sometimes your grandfather would read the lesson. He had a fine voice for reading, he'd make the words come alive. He would read the Sermon on the Mount and make people weep from the truth of it. That was his most favorite passage in the Bible. And we'd stand up from those wooden benches and sing those grand old hymns just like in New England. And your mama, she was the littlest and she would sing such a sweet little song."

Suddenly Aunty Em was no longer smiling. "I don't suppose your mama ever told you about Lawrence."

Dorothy could feel the sun going behind a cloud. "No, Ma'am."

"She never told you?"

"No, Ma'am."

"Well. That was where we lived first. Kansas was just being settled, and we wanted it settled by Northerners. So the Company was formed to help us move across. We came from New England, Dorothy, from Massachusetts. Your grandfather was one of the first to say he'd go. He was a very brave man. He came all the way across the United States to Kansas, and he was one of the first. He left July 17th, 1854, one of the first thirty men. And it was a triumphant progress. They were cheered at the train stations."

Dorothy half imagined it, the flags and excitement, and people cheering a good man. It was all part of the Meeting feeling.

"Your grandfather wrote letters about it back home to the newspapers, Back East. He was such a lettered man, your grandfather. We followed the next year. I came across when I was thirteen years old. Oh! This was a beautiful country then! Nothing between horizon and horizon. I can still remember my first sight of Lawrence, across the river, in the trees. We came across in the ferry and stayed with such nice people, a minister. He had an Indian servant girl, and she gave me a buffalo rug to sleep on. Then we went out to look at our new house that your grandfather had built."

Aunty Em paused, looked at the fields, the flowers. "I can remember the first time I heard a Western voice. A woman from Iowa. She told us a store had 'a right smart chance of calicoes.' Your mother and I laughed and laughed, and no one could understand why two little Yankee girls would find it funny."

Aunty Em went silent again, listening to the mule. "Anyway," she whispered, "it's the children of the Company we'll be meeting today."

Aunty Em drew a deep and shaky breath.

Lawrence sounded beautiful and happy and full of laughter.

"Lawrence had trees?"

"Lots of them, honey, all over the place."

"And Indians and buffalo?"

"Not so much even then. People were planning to make their living farming. The hunters had already moved on, to places like Wichita."

"Why are we living out here?" Dorothy asked.

Aunty Em's face went darker. "We had to move out here, Dorothy. Didn't your mama ever tell you why?"

Dorothy shook her head.

"Border ruffians attacked the town. Called themselves Federal Marshals and carried the flag of South Carolina."

Aunty Em flicked the reins. "I remember getting up in the morning and seeing them on top of Mount Oread. The birds kept singing, the sun shone, and there were five hundred armed men on the hill. They fired cannon at the Free State Hotel until it fell. They destroyed the office of the *Herald of Freedom* where your grandfather wrote his paper. They came to arrest him, but he had already given them the slip. They came into our house, all leering, and asking for the man of the house. And I told them they knew where he was, driven from his own home. So they ransacked it. They were as drunk as skunks and singing 'Katy Darling' and 'Lily Dale.' And they read our letters and stole our clothes. They even destroyed the only daguerreotype I had of my mother! Then they set the house on fire. My little sister and I had to push a burning bed through the window. After that, my father thought we would be safer out here."

Aunty Em's rage seemed to subside, then flared up again. "And they did it twice! Once in '56 and again in '63. Only the second time they killed every man they could find. And not only men! They killed boys, children. They even killed babies if they were little boys."

"Why?" whispered Dorothy in horror.

"Oh! Because the South wanted to own slaves. They wanted to own people like dogs. And because of them the whole country had to go to war!"

"Why did they kill children?" Dorothy asked.

"Because their minds were twisted. They were so deep in evil, they couldn't find a pathway out. The glorious South. And your mother went to live there! In Missouri, St. Louis, the city that tried to stop us from even getting to Kansas. She has to go and move there, not four years after the ashes of Lawrence were finally cold."

Dorothy could not remember a war. She could not remember anyone in Missouri killing people. But it would seem that her mother had lied to her, not to tell her this.

"How could she do it to us?" said Aunty Em, helpless with anger and unhappiness. "Go off to St. Louis with that man."

Dorothy's mother was a bad woman. Dorothy had no idea her mother had been that bad. She began to be afraid that she was bad, too.

"Those Southerners owe every Union family five hundred dollars at least. Clemency indeed! You let them go and look what you have. Outlaws, that's all they are. You hear of the James gang, Dorothy?"

Dorothy shook her head.

"Murderous, thieving scoundrels. They were Southerners. They were there in Lawrence that very night. They were there, killing children. They ought to have been hunted down like dogs."

Aunty Em drew in a long, shuddering breath, and Dorothy hung her head and picked at her nails. "God forgive me. But that's what I feel."

It had been a beautiful day, and Dorothy had been happy. She had thought she was going to be happy. She began to cry now, for the horrible thing she didn't understand, and for the promise of happiness that seemed to have been broken.

"Oh, honey, I'm sorry," said Aunty Em. The sight of the child crying, crying for the right reason, crying for the reason Aunty Em wanted her to weep, moved her beyond measure. "We won't talk about that. We won't talk about that anymore. It's just too nice a day to spoil."

Aunty Em stopped the wagon and enfolded Dorothy in her sweaty hug. It seemed to the child that the very earth was bleeding. What other terrible secrets were there? She could imagine the terror, being in your own house, and having to run from bad men who wanted to kill you.

"I'm not a Southerner," said Dorothy.

"No, honey, of course you're not."

"But I lived in Missouri!"

"Well, that wasn't your fault. Your mother went to live there, and you were born there."

"But they still kill people!"

"Yes, but that's only a few of them. Now hush, there's no need to be scared now, the war's over."

Dorothy wasn't weeping because she was frightened; she was weeping because it had happened at all. Didn't Aunty Em understand that?

Aunty Em kept her bony arms around her. "We're going to Meeting," she said. "Meeting's in a big white tent."

How could a big white tent make up for murder?

"And there's going to be lots of singing, and we'll meet some nice new friends who'll be so happy to see you."

"Did my papa kill anybody?" Dorothy asked.

"No, honey. He was an Easterner."

"Is that the same as North?"

Aunty Em's face was crossed. "Yes," she decided.

"But St. Louis is East and people call that the South."

Aunty Em sighed. "Honey. Kansas is right in the middle, where North and South and East all meet." She went into a long explanation, of halves of the country, but it still wasn't clear. Then Dorothy understood. In Kansas, North and South and East and West were ways of calling the same thing good or bad, depending on how you felt about it. Dorothy's father had been from the North, but he was bad, so he was East, that's all.

"Am I from the North or the East or the South?" she asked.

"Well now, I'd say you were from the West," said Aunty Em.

They rode on, to the base of the hills. Roadrunners darted across their path. Birds with bright yellow breasts and black bibs sat on fence posts and sang. Their song was loud and very slightly harsh. Aunty Em sighed and said something very strange. "Guess neither of the Branscomb girls married very well," she said and shook herself, as if out of a dream.

They moved out of the fields and into the woods of Prospect. The eastern slope was covered with trees, but on top, the hill was smooth and windswept and crowned with a few low evergreens.

Down below, to the right, there were the orderly, patterned fields of corn and the straight surgical scar made by the MA&BRR. Beyond the train tracks was a line of tall willows, oaks and sycamores, marking the Kansas River. Only half hinted at amid the clouds of green was another rise, another hill on the St. George side.

To the people of Manhattan, this was still Zeandale, but to Dorothy, it was another country. Oak Grove, she called it, after its schoolhouse. There was always a breeze through that valley as if the river itself were breathing. On the wind, buzzards or hawks with huge wings were carried, their feathers spread like grasping hands. "Look!" Aunty Em exclaimed and pointed. A heron flew overhead.

Dorothy turned in the cart and looked behind her. Where the river curved inward, a line of trees seemed to reach out and meet the wooded slopes of Mount Prospect to form a nearly solid wall of green, except for one narrow passage. You would never guess there was an even broader, flatter valley beyond it, with Sunflower School and her aunty's house. Aunty Em called the passage the Gate, even though you never noticed when you were riding through it. Beyond the Gate, there were blue-gray hills, rolling off into the eastern distance, bald on the western side that looked toward the prairies.

They began to see other wagons. Aunty Em forgot herself and called out, "Harriet! Harriet Wells! This is Emma!"

And the woman turned around in her seat and nudged her man. "Why! Emma Branscomb. How be you? How was your winter?"

"Well as could be expected! Going to be a good year!"

"Most certainly. Lovely spring!"

Aunty Em smiled and murmured confidingly to Dorothy. "Old settlers," said Aunty Em. It was the highest mark of approval.

The road suddenly plunged steeply down the hill. Looking straight ahead, Dorothy could see the uppermost branches of the trees, as if she were flying, as if the cart were going to come to roost there. The curtain of leaves seemed to part and down below was the City of Trees and one of its two great rivers.

Trees lined the Kaw on either side, and Dorothy saw the river from above, big and slow and shallow and brown, winding off in either direction, nosing its way into deeper and deeper countryside, lands Dorothy had never seen.

The wagon moved on, down another dip through more trees. Then the road spread out, as if relaxing in sunshine, on the river's bank. There were tall, wispy grasses and pink flowers with leaves like rounded ferns. The soil was gray and baked like the crust of a pie, but the ruts the wheels made were full of glistening mud, crisscrossed with long grains of grass and the bodies of flies.

In the middle of the river, sandbanks rose, like the backs of giant turtles. On the other bank, there were huge, shadowed trees. The wagon bounced up onto stones; the shoreline was macadamized by them. The road began to climb again up the bank toward the bridge. The bridge was made of stone, and its stone supports rose up like towers from the midst of the river. Trees that had been carried by the spring currents were piled up around the towers. The trunks and branches were black, as if they had been charred.

Dorothy and Aunty Em got out and walked the wagon up and over the bridge. Farther downstream, there was the crisscross ironwork of the railroad bridge. The local line was joined there by the Kansas Pacific. Ahead of them was Blue Mont, and the lumberyards and train depots that formed the outer edge of Manhattan.

Instead of going into the town, the wagons turned left. Still walking, Aunty Em guided the mule over the train tracks. With a heave and a hollow thumping, the wagon went up and over the rails.

Beyond the tracks, between them and the Kansas River, there was a meadow of grass, ringed around with oaks and huge cottonwoods. In the middle of the field was a white tent with wagons drawn up all around it. People stood in groups, men permanently holding their hats off their heads. Dorothy wondered if Meeting might be like a circus. Boys in loose shirts ran up and offered to corral the livestock.

"The mule's name is Calliope, son, and she kicks so be careful," called Aunty Em, striding forward. Her eyes were beginning to gleam.

People knew who she was. They turned, stopped talking, and walked up to greet her. They hugged her, called her Little Em, kissed her breathlessly, called to other friends to hurry, Emma Branscomb was here.

"And I'd like you all to meet my niece, little Dorothy Gael."

"Why, you must be Millie's little girl," said a fresh-faced, fat woman bending over, smiling. "Dorothy, we're so pleased to see you here in Kansas."

It was the truth. The woman really was pleased. It was the first time anybody had said that they were happy to have Dorothy in Kansas.

Gratitude poured over Dorothy. "And I'm so pleased to be here!" she piped, hopping up. There was laughter.

"Pretty country, isn't it, Dorothy?"

"Oh yes, Ma'am. We saw lots of flowers."

More laughter. Dorothy had said something else that was right.

"I tell you, ladies, there are times I have to ask myself if this is a human child or a little angel who's dropped to earth. I can't stop her from doing her chores. She just works and works, sweeping, washing the dishes, taking care of the hens. I've never seen a child like her for helping out." Aunty Em's hand was firmly on Dorothy's shoulder.

"She must be just such a comfort." The fat woman looked back up. "After all that terrible business."

"Well, we are sent trials in order to test us, Harriet, and there's no bed of thorns that doesn't also bear a rose." Aunty Em patted Dorothy again.

They began to talk of adult things. Aunty Em pretended that the farm was going well. "We're thinking of bringing in some hogs."

"Oh yes, that's good if you can stop them from rooting out the crops."

"Well, Henry's planted a hedge, keep them in."

Before the winter there had been a murder. A colored man called George Hunter had killed someone in anger. Everyone said the dead white man had been trouble. But still, it was the first violence around those parts since Monroe Scranton had been lynched for stealing Ed Pillsbury's horses, and that had been back in the sixties. They talked of Negroes crossing the border and wanted to know Aunty Em's opinion.

"The South created the problem and wants us to solve it. And it's our Christian duty to welcome them."

"Hard enough for anybody making any kind of business work," said one of the women.

"There's some of them that are as honest and hardworking as you could wish. Edom Thomas for one."

"Oh, certainly. Some of them Exodusters have settled in right smartly."

They went from group to group, and people exclaimed, "Emma! Emma Branscomb!" More greetings, more hugs and kissings and kindly questions. Aunty Em's face became fixed; her smile and bright eyes glazed with happiness. The eyes were famished. Feed me, they seemed to say, I have hungered for this. Dorothy clung on to her hand, feeling forgotten.

"I tell you, I await the Spirit," said Aunty Em. "I tell you, after last winter, I need the Spirit."

"Amen, amen" came the replies, in clusters like flowers.

"There's this world, and there's the next, and sometimes the next just reaches out for you, and you yearn for it, yearn for its refreshment."

"Hallelujah."

Hally hoo hah, Dorothy thought they said.

Em looked hungrier. "Is it this new boy?" she asked.

"Reverend Salkirk? Oh, yes."

"How is he?"

"They say he called powerful good up in Junction City last week. First of the season."

"He was good by the end, but a bit roundabout," said another woman, rail thin like Aunty Em. They might have been sisters. "He doesn't know how to go for it direct."

"Nobody called like your father, Emma," said the man who was with her. He was much older, with a long white beard. "God rest his soul."

"For me nobody could and nobody ever will," said Aunty Em. "But let's see what Reverend Salkirk can do."

"I'm ready for the call," said the fat pink lady. "I feel just like a calf let out in the spring field for the first time."

The people were farmers like them, and they dressed like them, not like the folk of Manhattan. Their children ran about in groups, slightly older than Dorothy. Dorothy watched them, shyly, slightly hiding behind Aunty Em. She knew the children wouldn't say they were happy to have her in Kansas. She felt safer with the adults.

Then, as if rising out of the mist and the flowers, a figure in black came limping and twisting its way toward them. For just a moment, Dorothy thought it was a ghost, as if her bad mama were coming out of the South.

The face was familiar, as if in a dream, and that held a certain terror for Dorothy too. And then dimly, as if someone had called the woman's name from across a far field, Dorothy remembered who it was.

It was Etta Parkerson. She was wearing another black and beautifully made dress, all scallops and ruches, and she walked with a tall, sad-eyed man, old enough to be her father.

"Etta! Etta Parkerson!" said Aunty Em, her smile somewhat sour, caught as she was between two social worlds.

"Etta Reynolds, now, Emma."

"Oh! Of course!" said Aunty Em, hand on forehead as it shook from side to side. "Everyone. This is Etta Reynolds. She is niece to the Goodnow family, and only this February was married to Mr. Reynolds."

Hands were shaken politely. Mr. Reynolds's hands seemed to be made of stone and looked large enough to have torn his wife in half.

"I'm glad you could join us, Mrs. Reynolds," the old settlers said, meaning, cordially, what are you doing here?

"My husband is a follower," replied Etta. "How are you, Dorothy?"

Dorothy murmured that she was fine. She had first met Etta in another lifetime. She dimly remembered that Etta had been kind to her; she also seemed to remember that Etta had said something that even now disturbed her, though she could not remember what it was. This time, Dorothy did not warm to Etta.

Aunty Em launched into another performance of Dorothy as domestic angel, how she cleaned and tidied and helped around the house. Etta listened for a while.

"Emma," she said. "Do you think you could look after my husband for a while? I'd like to show Dorothy some of the field flowers."

"Why, that would be a great kindness, Etta. Alvin, do you feel safe with us?" Alvin Reynolds grinned and rocked in place and plainly did not feel safe at all. Etta held out her hand toward Dorothy. There was nothing for Dorothy to do but take it. They walked together down the slope of the field, toward the river. Etta's boots swept the top of the grass, sideways, as if kicking it. What does she want? Dorothy wondered.

There were flowers, like ground-hugging buttercups, the size of

Dorothy's hand. There were vivid little stars of blue on the tops of long stems, and plain white flowers clustered together. There were echoing cries of children, running to the river, and the shade of the giant trees, showing the silver underside of their leaves in the wind.

"Drudge, drudge, drudge, eh, Dorothy?" asked Etta.

Dorothy said nothing. She had a wildflower in her hand and was picking it apart.

"You can work until you disappear, Dorothy. It won't be enough. People don't love a drudge. But sometimes they love selfish people, for doing what they always wanted to do themselves." There were the sounds of wind in long grass and other children playing together.

"You look tired," Etta said. "Tired and scared. I find Emma Gulch scary, sometimes." Etta crouched down and tried to peer up into Dorothy's face. "They're never grateful, Dorothy. You can never do enough in someone else's house. They always think it's their due. You're always the poor relation."

What is the point, Dorothy thought, of talking to me like this? This is talk for adults. What am I to do? Leave? Where could I go? Fight? How can I fight Aunty Em?

"I want to go back," said Dorothy.

Etta sighed and said, "All right. But promise me, Dorothy. Promise me if things get too bad, you won't pray to God to change you. You'll pray to God to change them?"

What did that mean? Dorothy began to walk on ahead, back up the gentle slope. It was some kind of truth and Dorothy didn't understand it or need it. There was nothing the truth could do for her except give her pain. The truth was harsh and for adults. It frightened her. Dorothy needed lies.

"Did you have a nice talk?" Aunty Em asked as they approached.

"Yes, Ma'am," said Dorothy, head down.

Etta said goodbye. Dorothy did not look up. She heard her boots through the grass. Swish, swish, swish, with a cripple's gait.

"What can she be thinking of?" asked the pink lady in a low voice. "Don't she know about women's troubles? Poor little thing is only the size of a child herself."

"I reckon the Goodnows were surprised," chuckled one of the men. "I reckon they thought the Parkerson girls would be marrying some nice young men from the college."

"They're moving to Wild Cat. Out of harm's way, I guess."

Dorothy realized that she might not see Etta ever again. Her eyes seemed to swell from something like sorrow, something like anger.

"She thinks," said Dorothy, pink-cheeked, looking down, with a child's voice, "that she's going to be happy." That ended the conversation.

"Which seems a good enough reason to marry," said Aunty Em. "Shall we go to Meeting, brethren?" She took Dorothy's hand, and gathered up her skirts to march. The others followed.

It was hot inside the tent. Sunlight glowed on the white canvas. There were benches set on grass. It was as if there could be buildings with grass floors, grass floors with flowers growing in them, as if people could sit down to breakfast amid flowers.

They were sitting down to prayer. They passed the prayer books among them. Their voices seemed louder in the tent, men reaching across to shake hands, women calling out across the tent and waving. Aunty Em walked down the center aisle holding up her best black skirt, and she looked leaner, taller, back straighter than ever. When she turned to sit down, her dress whisked smartly around, and she nodded to the people near her and gathered up the dress and sat down slowly. It was as if she were someone else.

There was a banner across one side of the tent. Dorothy couldn't read it. "What's that say? Aunty Em? What's that say?"

" 'Gather ye unto the Lord,' " said Aunty Em. "And that little part underneath says 'Revival and reform.' That means to drive out sin and evil." Aunty Em's eyes still gleamed. She was still hungry.

A young man in black walked quickly across the front of the tent and hopped up onto a wagon. The Meeting quietened at once. Children's attention was drawn with a pat or a slap; a baby was howling, there was a hissing into silence.

The young man had wavy blond hair and a blond beard. "Good morning," he said simply.

"Mornnn'," came back a mumbling reply.

Aunty Em drew back and cast a critical eye. Dorothy turned and watched her. So far it was like an ordinary Sunday. There would be prayers and song, and Dorothy would get bored and have to sit still. Maybe the best part had been outside when they were all talking and being nice.

"Seems to me we got a lot of fine folk moving into Kansas."

No response. People weren't sure they agreed with him.

"They come from all over, North, South. Fine people with some money to spend, or no money to spend, and not all of them see much of a future in working the land. Some of them move out to Abilene, or out to Wichita. I hear Dodge is going to be next, following the quarantine line wherever the money is cheapest and nastiest."

The silence was the silence of approval. The people understood now.

"And in these fine new cities of the new Kansas, where the business is brightest and fastest, these thriving cowtowns that seem so proud, with their money and their banks, there are sights the like of which could strike a righteous man blind, and from which all righteous women would shrink like flowers from a flame."

Murmur of agreement. They would shrink away, the poor women of the land.

"And I have to ask myself: Do these fine people know what Kansas means, and what Kansas stands for? Do they know that this is the free state, the place to which the righteous flocked, to say 'No more!'?"

Hally hoo hah, said the Meeting.

"No more to sin and greed. No more to exploitation. No more to the cross of slavery. Or the cross of the Eastern banks and Eastern factories!"

Hally hoo hah.

"But lo, brethren, sisters, behold what comes slinking silently in. After the war, after the locusts, after the storms, and the broken hearts, what comes following in, after the people of Kansas have broken open the land, but people whose only god is the almighty dollar, whose only joy is in alcohol or bad women. Pray for them, brethren. But pray for yourselves too."

No cries as yet. Too indirect. He wasn't working them.

He changed tack. These people were not the farmers near Wichita. Politics did not move them.

"It could be that I don't know much. I have seen no blinding light from Heaven, I have seen no angels in the sky. I call the gospel because I love it. I can bear witness, and I will bear witness long as I can, loud as I can, that there is more to God's children than flesh alone or blood alone . . . or land alone or money alone, either."

That was more like it. Meeting made more noise. It wanted to touch the Lord, to feel Him brush past them, as if His robe swept their souls.

"I don't see no light of Heaven, it's not given to me to see it. That is given to prophets to see, and I ain't no prophet. But I'll tell you. I see the light of Heaven, just a glint of it, in the eyes of each and every one of you here today. That glimmer there? That's God shining out through you. And you can damn the bankers! You can damn all the fine folk."

There was some sound here of disapproval. He overrode it.

"They damn themselves!" A roar of agreement. "This is where the word of God shines!"

There were cries now, shouts. A man stood up, lean, lean under thick clothing, and shouted. Dorothy thought he was angry. She flinched and drew closer to Aunty Em. Were people mad? Why were they shouting? Dorothy thought perhaps she liked church better.

Aunty Em kept staring ahead, a thin smile on her face. But her eyes were full of yearning. A hand crept up to her breast.

"So let it shine, brothers, sisters. Let the Word shine in you! Let the Lord Jesus come to you in the Spirit. Open up the gates! Don't shut Him out. He sings in the wind. He whispers in the breath of every innocent young babe. He is all around us, to heal, to salve, to bring comfort, to warm the heart and bring peace to the mind."

Hally hoo hah. Hay men. Oh, he was good, this Preacher, who started out so slow.

Aunty Em seemed to melt. She listed sideways like a candle, hand still over her heart. The young Preacher prowled about his wagon. He'd started out so slow, and now he was waving his hands, commanding.

"Why are you so silent? Are you afraid of the Lord? Are you afraid of your speaking sins? Don't you know the Lord Jesus knows your sins, knows your pain, don't you know He loves you, and forgives you, leaves you as innocent as the child, the little children, whom He suffered to come unto Him? Go to Him as a child, be a child again in His presence!"

Aunty Em rose up, arms outstretched, her head shaking from side to side.

"The Spirit, the Spirit's on her!" called Harriet.

The old man with the beard grabbed her arms. Harriet stroked her brow.

"Brrrrrrrrrrrrrrrrr!" said Aunty Em, her tongue rattling loose in her mouth. Her hands shook; her lined cheeks flapped loosely.

Dorothy wailed in terror. "Oh!" she cried, the shadow of the terror of Lawrence still on her.

"Bulor ep ep ahhh no up shelopa no no no shelopa apa apa no ma!" cried Aunty Em.

"Oh, the Spirit's strong, the Spirit's good!" said Harriet, wrestling.

"I've never seen it like this," said the old man, looking worried.

Then the train came, with a whiplash whine along the metal rails nearby and a piercing shriek of steam through a whistle. A bell began to clang over and over. The horses in the corral whinnied and snorted.

And Dorothy remembered. The train had come once before and taken her away and shown her a world full of reasonable people who did not love her. The train came closer with a sound of steam and smoke, and Dorothy saw her aunty tossing her head back and forth, held down by other people, back and forth as if saying no, no, no. Aunty Em wanted to be hauled away from this world, from the farm, from the past. Dorothy was suddenly afraid.

"Don't die, Aunty Em! Don't die!" Dorothy shouted. The shadow of the train was cast on the white canvas.

The skinny woman leaned down, all pine-tree smells, breathing into Dorothy's face. "Your aunty's not going to die, darling," she said. Dorothy clung to her aunty's dress.

The Preacher had stopped preaching. He fought his way through the other people. Dismayed, he knelt down to look at Aunty Em.

"If you gentlemen could help me carry her outside," he said.

"You shouldn't have stopped, Preacher," chuckled Harriet. "It's what she came for."

The men carried Aunty Em out to her wagon. The train was far down the track, leaving a slight haze over the field.

Broke it up as soon as it got going, said voices, complaining. Dorothy followed, a fist rubbing her eyes to make the point that she was unhappy too.

"It's all right, darling, this means your aunty is with Jesus."

"Will she want to come back?" Dorothy asked.

The old man lifted Dorothy up into the wagon. Aunty Em was looking at her dimly. "Hello, Dorothy," she said gently, warm and soft and kind and far away.

"Oh, Aunty Em," said Dorothy, and lay down on the rough boards. "Oh, Aunty Em. I love you, love you, love you, love you."

"Why, child!" chuckled Aunty Em, pleased. She hugged Dorothy and kissed the top of her head.

"I thought you were going to die!" the child said.

"Oh, no," said Aunty Em, recalling the impact of Christ's love. "Not die."

A dog tied to a wagon began to bark. Dorothy looked up. "Toto?" she asked.

Aunty Em's hand, stroking her hair, froze.

Toto had lived throughout the winter in the buffalo wallows. The wallows had frozen hard, and the marsh reeds heavy with ice had fallen against each other to make ice shelters.

All through that winter, Toto would appear as if from nowhere, barking as he ran out of freezing mist that blazed with sunlight. He would bring Dorothy sticks to throw for him. They sparkled with frost. He bounded across crisp frosty ground to bring them back and drop them again at Dorothy's feet.

When blizzards fell, making a low grinding sound as if the sky were being milled, Toto would bark as Dorothy passed the barn. She would find him in the hay, and he would whimper and lick her hands. Dorothy left him food in a broken bowl and would return each morning to find it clean.

Aunty Em's hens began to disappear. "It's that dog. He's gone wild!" Aunty Em exclaimed. Toto unnerved her.

She would find him in her own yard, crouched and snarling at her, baring his fangs. When Aunty Em tried to grab him, he would scamper just out of reach and growl at her again.

"Dorothy! Dorothy! Come and call your dog!" Aunty Em would demand.

In the spring, the thaws began. Dorothy started school. She would walk every morning along the lane, between the ruts filled with muddy water and crusted with patches of ice. Toto would come out of the wallows from under the open arms of the scarecrows to meet Dorothy. He would be filthy, blinking and covered in mud. Dorothy would chuckle, and kneel down. "You got that old lady real mad at you."

He started to bring her presents. He brought her the Jewells' chickens, murdered and whole.

"Dorothy, you must control that dog. The Jewells are good neighbors to us and they can't afford to lose their livestock any more than we can. Now the next time you see him, you have a rope with you and you catch him and bring him back."

"Yes, Ma'am," said Dorothy. She somehow always forgot the rope.

Dorothy wanted to be good. That was why she worked so hard at her chores and her school exercises. She could sense goodness within her, like a pouch in her breast, to be opened. She wanted to love her aunty; it would be good to love her aunty. She loved Toto.

Toto was not good. He dug up the green shoots in Uncle Henry's fields. He tore down the washing from the clothesline into the mud. Once in the lane, he bit through the sleeve of Dorothy's only coat and tried to drag her with him, away.

"We can't go back, Toto," she said, stroking the rough gray hair of his terrier head.

She began to see him less and less. Sometimes he disappeared for days at a time.

Then one day, in late afternoon, Dorothy walked back from school hugging her books, head down. Aunty Em was at the stove, slamming pots, loud as she could.

"Good day, Dorothy?"

"Yes, Ma'am."

"What did you study, child?"

"Sub . . . subtraction."

"Hmmm."

They heard a bark.

"That dog. Back again."

Aunty Em wiped her hands on her apron and opened the door.

The earth was soft, muddy, thawed. It was about four-thirty in the afternoon in late March, what had been a nice day, a sunset blur of orange and blue across a flat and featureless sky. Toto the dog sat waiting.

"We'll have to try to catch him," said Aunty Em. She swept her coat on in one motion and put on gloves and took a rope. Dorothy followed, not wanting Toto hurt.

They opened the door again, and Toto had not run away. He was still there, at the end of the yard, waiting beside one of Aunty Em's dead flowerbeds. He barked as if to say: Here.

"What's he brought with him this time?" said Aunty Em, striding.

He had dug something up. He waited over it, eyes fixed on Aunty Em.

Aunty Em suddenly gave a kind of coughing, stricken cry. Her hand went to her throat, and she dropped the rope. Dorothy knew then that Toto had done something terrible.

Aunty Em broke into a run. "Horrible, horrible animal! Horrible, horrible dog!" she said, sounding as if she were coughing. She ran toward him, trying to pick up a handful of mud, to throw at him. She slipped onto her knees and kept sliding toward the thing from out of the ground.

"Rob Roy," cried Aunty Em, sobbing. "Oh, Robbie! Rob Roy!"

Toto barked at her, just out of reach. He ran around her, bouncing furiously.

Toto had dug up the corpse of another dog. Dorothy walked up next to her aunt and stood watching.

"Toto, stop," she said weakly.

There was bone with some wet and bedraggled fur still clinging to it, and hollow eyes, and a doggy smile full of teeth, a large skeleton with some skin still attached, a long, big corpse of a huge long-haired animal.

Aunty Em knelt in the mud, sobbing, covering her face.

Raf raf, raf raf, said Toto. He came hopping toward Emma. He was small and fierce and full of hate. You see, you see? Toto seemed to say. You had one too.

"Toto. Leave her alone," whispered Dorothy.

Aunty Em spun around and grabbed Dorothy and shook her, thick spittle clogging her lips, gray eyes wild. "Look at it! Look at it!" she demanded. "See it? See it? That's death. That's what your mother looks like now, in the ground."

Dorothy looked and saw the hollow eyes, the somewhat surprised and empty face that seemed to ask what had happened to itself. Where had it gone? Dorothy knew it was the truth. Her mother had no flesh now, or eyes, in the ground. Aunty Em wept, and Toto trotted back away, revenge taken. Dorothy saw him go, his tiny legs strutting across the gray mud, between the rounded gray humps.

Uncle Henry kept a shotgun leaning in the corner.

Toto did not show up for a day or two. Dorothy knew enough not to mention him. She thought he was hiding, keeping low for a while. He was such a clever dog.

But how low can you keep without disappearing, until you fade into less than a memory? When almost a week had passed, Dorothy asked if Aunty Em had seen Toto while she was away at school.

Aunty Em was scrubbing. "No, I haven't," she said, lightly.

"He's been gone a long time."

"I expect he's gone away," said Aunty Em, not looking at her.

"He wouldn't do that," said Dorothy.

"Well, he kept staying away for longer and longer," said Aunty Em.

But he wouldn't leave her, he wouldn't leave Dorothy, she knew that.

"Why would he run away?"

"Guess he didn't like it here."

Dorothy slumped down onto her mattress. Aunty Em couldn't stand it when anyone else cried. If anyone had a right to cry, it was Aunty Em. She looked around the edge of the blanket.

"There's no point going against the will of God, if that's what He's decided," said Aunty Em. Aunty Em looked at the good little girl who was so unhappy and relented a bit.

"Toto wasn't happy here, Dorothy. That's why he kept barking all the time and running off and did all those terrible things. So, I reckon he's gone off to find somewhere happier. Maybe he's gone off to find your old house in St. Louis. Maybe he thinks your mama's there. He's a dog and doesn't know any better."

"He wouldn't leave me!" said Dorothy.

"Well he has, and there's no way around it but to get used to it," said Aunty Em. Dorothy heard her boots on the floor as she walked away.

Dorothy waited for Toto to come back. Maybe he had gone away because he knew he was bad and would come back when he thought he had been forgiven. Maybe you could find out you were bad, and go away from shame and come back when you were good again.

Every day after school, when she came to the track that led to the farm, she would expect to see him again. Maybe this time, maybe this time, she thought every day all through the rest of that

March, into April, into the fullness of the Kansas spring. From time to time, she would call his name, expecting to find him lying close to the ground, ready to spring up and run yipping to her.

She knew just how she would feel when that happened. She knew there would be a leaping up of joy inside her, and she would say "Good Toto, good boy, good Toto," and he would roll over and over and over, like he always did when he was especially glad to see her. That would happen, and everything would be all right.

Whenever she heard a dog barking at night, the sound coming across the Kansas hills, she thought it was Toto. She would get up.

"Dorothy. Where are you going?" demanded the voice in the darkness.

"I think it's Toto," she would reply. "I think he's come back."

"It's not Toto. Get back to bed," the voice would order.

And Dorothy would slink guiltily back onto her bed, in an agony in case Toto came back and found no one there to greet him. She learned how to slip out of the window, into the cool spring night in just her nightgown.

"Toto?" she would whisper, teeth chattering, icy mud between her toes. "Toto?"

She started hiding her boots under the mattress. She would go out and hunt for Toto at night, stumbling across the Kansas plain, following the sound of the dogs. She would be sure that he was just a field or two away, lost, not quite able to find the tiny single-room house in the wide flat valley.

One day after school, Uncle Henry met her at the crossroads and they walked together.

"You're still worried about Toto, ain't you?" he said. His kindness was inseparable from his smell. He still reeked, and there was food in his beard.

"When he can't find my mama, will he come back here?" she asked.

"Well," he said. "It's possible that Toto is dead, Dorothy."

Dorothy saw the bedraggled fur, the empty eyes.

"If he is, then he's with all the other good little dogs in Heaven, and we should be happy for him."

Dorothy said nothing.

"So maybe he has found your mama," said Uncle Henry.

"And your little brother. Maybe they're all together, just like they used to be."

"Maybe Wilbur's there too," she said. She still thought of Wilbur sometimes.

"I should think that's right," said Uncle Henry. "So you say your prayers, and be a good little girl, you'll join them one day. They'll be waiting for you at the gate."

"By that time I'll be too old, and I won't care," said Dorothy.

But she didn't stop hoping. She just knew she had to hide it. Whenever she heard a dog bark, she would look up in hope.

But in another sense, Toto was always with her, silent and invisible, bouncing and spinning around her as she walked to and from school, or sleeping by the rusty stove while Dorothy did her homework. She could almost feel him, tiny and coarse-haired, growing warmer next to her at night.

She told stories to herself to account for why he was still there. She could see the stories happening very clearly. There were thieves and they came and tied Aunty Em up and were going to steal money from the tin box behind the flue, but Toto came back and saw them and fetched Uncle Henry, and the thieves were foiled, so Toto was a hero. Aunty Em let him lick her face.

Dorothy daydreamed many things, walking back and forth from the crossroads. She daydreamed that an angel came down, right in the middle of school, where all the other children could see her. And the angel said that because Dorothy was so good, she could have three wishes. And Dorothy would wish that her mother was back, and that her father came back, and that they all lived together in St. Louis. And the angel would smile and say, "Your wishes are granted," and there would be a great wind that would pick Dorothy up and blow her through the sky, back home.

She daydreamed the size of gravestone she would have. She thought that gravestones were earned by goodness, rather than paid for by money, and she imagined her gravestone, as big as a house, with angels carved all over it. Then she felt guilty because she knew her mother didn't have one like that.

She felt guilty remembering her mother. To dream that her mother was back, rocking Dorothy in her lap, singing to her, divided Dorothy in two. Because the mother who Dorothy remembered, soft-faced with pursed lips, was nothing like the mother Aunty Em talked about. She wasn't wild, she was hardworking. She had to practice the piano and she had to rehearse. She wasn't a poor, silly little thing. She was sensible and kept a cleaner house than Aunty Em did. She was often away and tried to make it up to Dorothy. Dorothy remembered her mother kneeling down on the floor with her to make cakes in the shape of men with sugar faces. She was sure she could remember her mother and her father having a snowball fight in the park. She could also remember her mother on the settee, sobbing, clasping her hands and saying, "Dear God, please don't let me ask him back. Don't let me call him back." Outside on the street her father was walking away.

To imagine she was back with her mother would remind Dorothy that something was wrong. Aunty Em was wrong. And Dorothy loved her Aunty Em. She had to love her. Everything depended on Aunty Em now. Her mother may have been beautiful and kind and sometimes terrible, but she couldn't help Dorothy. She wasn't there.

Dorothy would have to divide and find different places to keep things within herself. Memories here, love here, hate there, dreams here, school there. And hope?

She talked to Toto as she swept the floor, as she told Aunty Em she loved her, as she greased Uncle Henry's boots.

"Toto, you bad, bad dog," she would tell him, in imitation of Aunty Em. She would whup him, and he would cower in the corner, shaking. She would beat him mercilessly with the broom, kick him in the ribs and out of the door.

"Sit up and beg," she would tell him, and he did, feet pumping helplessly in midair, waiting for an answer that never came.

On the wall, there was an old sampler, slightly charred in one corner. It was signed in needlework: Millie Branscomb, aged 8, 1856.

"There is no place like home," it said.

And there wasn't, not anywhere.

Culver City, California

February 1939

*We have also seen, that, among democratic nations, the sources of po-
etry are grand, but not abundant. They are soon exhausted: and poets,
not finding the elements of the ideal in what is real and true, abandon
them entirely and create monsters. I do not fear that the poetry of
democratic nations will prove insipid, or that it will fly too near the
ground; I rather apprehend that it will be forever losing itself in the
clouds, and that it will range at last to purely imaginary regions. I fear
that the productions of democratic poets may often be surcharged with
immense and incoherent imagery, with exaggerated descriptions and
strange creations; and that the fantastic beings of their brain may sometimes make us regret reality.*

—ALEXIS DE TOCQUEVILLE,
Democracy in America

*If I only had a heart, lamented the Tin Man, close on half a century
ago. In our contemporary fantasies, the androids are made of sterner
stuff . . .*

—SHEILA JOHNSTON, in a review of the movie *Robocop*,
from *The Independent*, February 4, 1988

It was five-thirty when Millie got to work. Five-thirty in the morning,
that is. Took the bus. Knew most everybody on it. They all worked for
the studio too. She said Hello to them; they murmured back. She got
a couple of minutes' shut-eye, forehead on hand. She could feel the
cough and throb of the bus through her elbow as it rested on the edge
of the window.

A few minutes before they arrived, Millie put a fresh piece of Wrigley's Spearmint in her mouth, gathered up her bag and thermos flasks, and got up. She stood by the middle door, early, to avoid the exodus. Practically the whole dang bus got off at MGM.

The morning smelled of unburned gas and it was dark. There were pools of light around the studio. Millie said hi to Joe at the gate. She always brought him a thermos of coffee.

"Hi, Joe. Boys here yet?" she asked him.

"Yup. They'll be in the chair. Most of the kids are here too." He thanked Millie for his coffee and passed her yesterday's empty thermos.

"Welp. Off to work," said Millie. "Say hello to Joyce for me."

Millie had been over to their place. Lived in Santa Monica, right near her. Nice, ordinary people. Most of the people working at Culver were nice, except for the bigwigs and some of the actors. Even most of them were okay. So how many folks are wonderful at five-thirty in the morning?

Sometimes actors were. There were some of them who were just never offstage. They'd talk to you and keep you entertained while you worked. It was one of the many good things about this job.

Millie's shoes clicked on the concrete as she walked to the trailers. Cold this hour of the morning. Her gum clicked too. Millie liked the sound of punctuation and of process. She liked things to move, for herself and other people. Why she was so good at her job. Lots of people around who could do makeup. But there was more to the job than that.

Millie managed the team when Jack Dawn wasn't around. She would check out her boys and girls, get them all lined up, schedules ready. They were good kids, hardworking. This danged picture is made of makeup, Millie thought, hours of it every morning. Latex and fur and all of that stuff.

But nothing ever again, Millie thought, could be as bad as those darned Munchkins. One hundred and twenty-four of them all lined up in Rehearsal Hall 8, moving from chair to chair like it was an assembly line. Hard work, but the Little People were fine to work with. Millie had no time for the stories. Millie told her crew to treat them as adults, call them Mr., Miss, or Mrs. and to watch out for knives. Only one or two of them had knives, the real deadbeats, the drunks. Most of them were sweet and looked kinda lost. Like they woke up in the wrong world. But all this sexual business that people were saying. That was just their own dirty minds. The Little People were sweet as could be and as innocent as lambs. Heck, a lot of them had to be. There was something wrong with their glands. A lot of them had foreign accents and got totally lost in the studio. Had to be led around like a class of schoolchildren.

Humiliating for them really. Dressed up in those horrible clothes that pansy had designed for them. Get you, sweetie. Put them in big collars, loose sleeves, to make them look even smaller. Costumes were so bad, they had to have people help them out of them when they had to pee. People were just so mean. One minder used to carry them to the john, one under each arm. "What am I, a nursemaid?" Insulting. They didn't like it either, Big Man. That poor little fellow who fell into the john and couldn't get out? We put big ugly red spots on their cheeks. Supposed to look like they were made of porcelain. Big deal. I just told the kids to treat them with respect.

Lights on inside and warmer.

"Hi, Millie."

"Hiya, Tony."

"Storm last night."

"Yeah, big wind. Any damage to your place?" Millie asked.

"No. But we got a lot of sweeping up to do. Lots of eucalyptus, and you know how they shed bark."

"Not a problem we ever had in Missouri. Got all your gear?" Tony had been new, brought in to help handle the Munchkins. Jack had him stay on to train. "Got your pencils, spirit gum?" Millie asked. Her fingers rattled through the box.

"Mmmm hmmm," said Tony, sharpening an eyebrow pencil.

"You mix this today?" The spirit gum.

"Uh, no, that's yesterday's."

"Well it looks like it. That stuff's murder at the best of times. You better mix it new."

"Okey-dokey."

Nice ordinary people.

Millie looked at the schedule. "How come you're doing Frank?"

"Jack had Harry and me switch."

"Oh, sorry, he did tell me. Slipped my mind this hour of the morning." Millie thought of Frank Morgan. "Don't light a match," she warned the kid.

Tony smiled. "I know."

Frank Morgan liked his tipple.

"See you later."

"See you."

Just a quick hiya to the old hands. They knew enough to mix their gum fresh. Hi Tommy, Hi Mort, Hi Bill. Bad storm last night. Drains on our street's all blocked. This city is not designed for rain.

Millie got to her own locker and hauled out her kit. Looked like a toolbox. My little pirate's chest of goodies, thought Millie. All kinds of colors, hard to get. If I lose this, I might as well close up shop for good. Now let's see. Bit of mascara, eyebrows. Today is black-and-white, isn't it, so the lips are going to have to be even lighter than usual or she'll end up looking like Theda Bara. There now. Take all this over, have it ready, and pull back the Technicolor stuff so I don't make a mistake.

Millie loaded it all into a bag and walked down the hall away from the dressing rooms. She walked down the corridor, stepped outside. Everything was a beautiful blue color now, cool, with quite a wind blowing. It whipped the back of her coat up. She walked onto Stage 27. Monkeys were all over the rafters, fixing lights. Paint was still drying on the Kansas backdrop outside the window. Twelve-foot-wide moat between the wall and the set, filled with a bank of lights. Thank God those lights were off for once. Millie was cold, but not that cold. She went to the stars' dressing room, a trailer they had wheeled on to the stage, and opened it up. Millie had a key. She opened it up and laid the makeup out on the table.

Millie never talked about the people she worked with. If people asked her, she'd just say, oh, so-and-so's really nice. Millie would have a thing or two to say about the Kid, if she had a mind to. Oh, she was charming and all that. Went out of her way to be charming. But the stories she told. Like the story she told everyone about the dressing room. Stood outside it crying, saying that they hadn't given her the key. Just had to be the center of attention. Make a little drama out of anything. And as for that graduation business. Told Margaret Hamilton that she would have to miss her high-school graduation because the studio was making her tour. Said it was Hollywood High. Well, she goes to University High, which is clean across town from Hollywood, and she doesn't graduate until next year. So I know better than to believe anything Miss Judy Garland says. There now.

III

Millie, chewing her gum, locked the door behind her. Better go see about the boys.

Millie went down along the stage, into the next room. Six o'clock, there was Ray Bolger, getting a shave.

"Howdy, Ray."

"Oh, hello, Millie," he smiled, his mouth ringed with shaving soap. She liked Ray Bolger. Quiet and nice.

"Everything okay?" she asked Bud, who did Ray.

"Yup," Bud answered, looking up, smiling. "For once Ray's out of that mask. Just a standard paint job now."

"I feel like a used car," said Bolger, hugging himself. "The only thing I'm going to remember about this picture, Millie, is sitting in this chair. Even a dentist's appointment doesn't take as long."

"Well, at least today you're out of that mask."

"And it's black-and-white." He pretended to sob with relief. Black-and-white meant cooler lights.

"Jack'll be able to sit down," said Bud.

Jack Haley's Tin Man suit dented. He couldn't sit, for eight, ten hours, so he had to lean on a board.

"Bert'll have to find something else to worry about."

"Yeah." Ray chuckled. The boys were a pretty swell team, actually.

"When's the Kid due?" asked Bud, wiping the last of the suds off Ray's face.

"Not till six-thirty," said Millie. "I'm going to the canteen, get some breakfast. You boys want anything?"

"Had mine, Millie, thanks. I'll just—"

"Sit around and wait, and sit around and wait some more." She, Bolger and Bud said it in unison.

"See you," she said.

Millie loved working in movies. Never wanted any other job. Because of the people. It wasn't glamorous. There was nothing glamorous in it at all, really. She hated the whole concept of glamour. It was more than glamour. It was people working together to make something good, and when you worked for a class act like MGM, you knew you were doing something worthwhile. There were times when Millie could feel the whole giant enterprise ticking away. The sets, the lights, the makeup, the costumes. Like this morning. One set finished with yesterday, it gets struck overnight, painted again, and a new one put up. People working around the clock on something that reached out and got to people. That was what Millie liked. The sheer sociability of a lot of it. She looked at the rafters and the Monkeys, whipping wire. Been there all night probably. Wouldn't even know the story of the picture. But they could go and see it and say, I put that set up. You wouldn't have believed how phony it looked, either, but it looks good on film.

With a small, contented smile, Millie went to have her breakfast.

Mind you, she thought, listening to her shoes, feeling the delicious California chill again, this one's shaping up pretty poorly. I mean, doing a fairy tale as vaudeville is pretty risky. You got two different elements. Lahr and the other boys are great, but there is no getting away from it, what they do is pure vaudeville. The Kid, too, she's pure vaudeville. But the sets, the whole works is Viennese operetta stuff with a little bit of Hollywood Hotel thrown in. And there is just no script. Everybody keeps adding lines. The songwriters add lines. Lahr and Haley throw in old stage routines. They had God knows how many writers on it. And God knows how many directors. Thorpe. He went. Tried to make the Kid into Shirley Temple, and with the best will in the world, she's not curly-haired and cute. Brought in Cukor, who got her out of the wig, and then Fleming, who at least gets things done, then King Vidor. Picture will be a mess if they aren't careful. Black-and-white here, color there. And some of the filming really is sloppy. Like that Monkey, flipping a wire out of the way, right in shot, and they went and used it anyway. I just can't believe that.

Millie sighed, shook her head. Well. Ours not to reason why.

More coffee. Doughnut. Bacon and eggs. Long day today and it's cold. Millie remembered farm breakfasts in Missouri.

"Hi, Hank," she said to the man in the white cap.

Our own little world.

Millie sat by herself. Not many people in for breakfast just on six. She carefully unloaded things from her tray, like she was setting the table at home. She sat down and sighed. Bushed already.

Still, things sometimes come together for a picture. Like that coat.

Frank Morgan says he found it, him and Hank Rosson. They went looking for a coat for the black-and-white stuff. Found it in a second-hand store and showed it to Vic. They wanted something that would look shabby but genteel. The Wizard wears it when he's Professor Marvel. Vic turns out the pockets, and the label says "L. Frank Baum." Man who wrote the book. He used to read it out loud to kids on his porch, lived in L.A. and that was his coat. Got an affidavit from his tailor, they say. Mind you, they'll say anything. Too good to be true, like most things around here.

Millie thought about the Kid. She was nice really. But funny-looking. She wasn't pretty at all. Our little hunchback, Mayer called her. And her expressions were peculiar. Her smile would sort of twist around and look a bit sour sometimes. Then she'd pull herself together for the camera, stand up straight, look like a different person.

A lot of them could do that. That weaselly little private-school boy who played all the tough guys. Tiny, ropy-looking little thing until he had to act. One star Millie could name looked like an effeminate toad, until the lights came on. Then suddenly his toad neck looked burly, his hands developed wrists, and his voice went deep. Women all over the country swooned. Thought he was the epitome of beefcake.

Funny about the Kid. She liked guys like that. There she was, the world at her feet, going to premieres, the whole bit. And you'd see her hanging around with all the little fairies from the offices or from Wardrobe. Being real nice to them, nice to everybody, why not? Still it's funny. It's like she wants something from them. That little light in her eyes. Odd.

Millie lit a cigarette.

God, this hour of the morning, who wants to think about anything?

Numb.

Oh. Is that the time? Better move on.

Millie put everything back on the tray, carried it over to the rack, took out a fresh piece of gum.

Mind you, Millie Haugaard, who are you calling ugly? Tall, big hips, thin shoulders. Nice tan and nice hair, but thirty-seven is no spring chicken. They say they keep the Kid on some kind of diet. Seems to work. Wish they'd tell me. Millie could feel weight around her midriff move as she walked. Well, there's no way I could get any more exercise. There just isn't any time. She decided to check out her own makeup before doing the Kid's and swept into the powder room. Better get it all over with. It's a long day till lunchtime.

*   *   *

Millie got back to the trailer and waited outside it. Kid was late again. She'd be in, all breathless and apologetic. Millie watched as the lights were adjusted. One patch lighting up, then going dark, gels and over-lays being tried. It's like being in a stage show, she thought. Only you constantly set up, hang around, and no one ever gets to act.

Only sometimes they do act up.

Millie looked at her watch. Six forty-five. It's cutting it fine, Kid, starting this late anyway. Too late, you hold people up.

Then she saw her, the Kid, in a plain cloth coat, hugging herself, looking at the floor as she walked. She walked head bowed as if her shoes were the most interesting things in the place. That, thought Millie, is one unhappy girl. Millie stood up, put out her cigarette and said, "Hiya, Kid."

"Hiya, Ma."

Kid called her Ma.

"Anything wrong, honey?"

The Kid was wrestling with the key to her trailer. "Naw," said the Kid in a downward-turning drawl. She sighed and stepped inside and turned on the lights and slumped into her makeup chair.

"You sound like it," said Millie, fetching the foundation among the lined-up tubes and tins. Panchro No. 23.

"I don't sleep, Ma," said the Kid, her voice and her face somehow puffy.

"Should go to bed earlier then." Briskly, Millie applied the grease-paint in short dabs over the face and neck.

"I do," the Kid whispered.

Kid looked forty. The Hollywood life. At least you're not drink-ing. Yet. I'd smell it on your breath. Actors smell like skunks in the morning. Millie looked at the Kid's face in the mirror. Always was a funny face. Looked pinched and plump at the same time. Gonna have to put some white stick over those bags. Good thing I brought some along case I had to tone the colors down. Usually only have to use it on someone older.

Millie poured some water over her fingers and began to spread the paint thinly, perfectly. It had to be perfect.

"I went back to Lancaster yesterday," said the Kid, like it was some kind of confession.

"Oh yeah?" Millie filled in the pores. The slightest little thing, and it would show up.

Lancaster?

"That's way out in the desert somewhere," said Millie.

"Yup."

"Why'd you go there?" Millie leaned over to get the bit over the ear right.

"It's where I'm from. Went to see an old friend of mine. I always called her Muggsie." The Kid smiled finally, just a wisp of a smile, kind of twisted. "Got there, suddenly found I couldn't remember her real name. Just Muggsie."

"So how was she?" Millie asked.

"Oh. Just normal. She's a couple of years older than me. So she's about eighteen now. Going to get married. It was strange."

"Thought you were supposed to be from Grand Rapids."

Another studio lie?

"Well, I am in a way. We lived there until I was two. Then we upped stakes and moved to a dump like Lancaster because my mother wanted to be near Los Angeles so's we could all become *stars*." The Kid sounded sarcastic. "Daddy just wanted to run a movie house and keep us all together. Lancaster was the only place he could find."

That face is going to have to have some tone put into it. Millie placed a little jab of darker paint on each cheek. Fresh-faced country kid, so get a nice glow in the cheeks, without it looking like rouge.

"Thought you spent your whole life touring with your sisters," said Millie, selecting the right jar from the counter.

The Kid laughed. "No. You can't do that, Millie. You've got to go to school."

"Guess so," said Millie, chuckling too. Wide streak of something down-to-earth in the Kid.

"I mean everybody thinks we were some big vaudeville family or something. I'll tell you what we did. We sang in my daddy's movie house between shows. All of us. Mom played piano; Janie, Jinny, me, we just sang. The only place we were stars was in Lancaster. My daddy was the biggest star of all. He used to sing all the time." The Kid was staring through to the other side of the mirror, remembering.

"What's your daddy do now?" asked Millie. Eyes next. The eyes were the most important thing in the makeup.

"He died," the Kid said.

"Oh, honey, I'm sorry, I didn't know," said Millie.

"Nobody knows," said the Kid. "He died three years ago."

The Kid looked like she was going to cry. So, thought Millie, she went back home on the weekend and it stirred things up. Poor kid.

Millie took time out from the makeup. "Sounds like your daddy was a nice man."

"The nicest. He had a temper on him though. He was Irish, through and through. He'd just turn on people, say they weren't treating his girls right. Then he'd go and let half the town into the show for free. If they were poor or anything. So we always had a full house. People would come over and we'd sing. All of us."

"Sounds like fun."

"Thing is that I remember hating Lancaster. I remember thinking it was a really nasty, small-minded place. But when I was there, I started remembering all kinds of good things about it."

"Like what?" Millie asked, over her shoulder. Getting out the old Panchro—and her little white stick.

"Oh, like going swimming with Muggsie. We used to run around the old sheds a lot, just playing like kids do. Me and Muggsie and the Gilmores. We had a lot of friends there. People were really very nice to us. We'd go to parties and I'd just hop up onto pianos and sing. There was this place opened up called the Jazz Café, and they asked us in to sing there. And people kept coming to the shows at the theater. They never got tired of the shows, and they must have seen us every week." The Kid managed to laugh again. "To tell you the truth we probably weren't all that good. For years and years, the only thing I knew about singing was that you had to be loud."

"Oh, every place is a mixture of good and bad," said Millie. "I got pretty mixed memories of Missouri. Everybody gets into everybody else's business all the time."

"They sure do," agreed the Kid. She went silent, perplexed, hugging herself. Millie took advantage of the stillness to get the white stick and draw two quick lines over the bags under the eyes. You had to be quick. All these stars got such frail vanity.

"Okay, now. Hold still, Judy. I'm going to do your eyes." Millie smoothed even darker brown, No. 30, across the whole of the eyelid and then up to the natural eyebrow. It was a good design, this makeup. It made her eyes look bigger in her face, like a real little girl's, by darkening everything to the eyebrow and putting on these absolutely enormous eyelashes. Millie had thought it would look phony. Instead, the eyelashes seemed to match the Kid's own huge dark eyes. And then you didn't put a thing on the lower lid at all, except for the slightest bit of mascara.

The huge dark eyes were looking at her, and the Kid was saying something.

"That's what I can't figure," said the Kid. "I just don't understand. They were so nice, and then they drove my daddy out."

"Drove him out. What you mean?"

Millie leaned over and painted in eyebrows lightly with a brush. You had to be careful with eyebrows. Too much, too little, both showed up bad.

"After we started to get big. They drove my daddy out of town, took away the lease from his movie theater, shoved him out, and a year later he was dead."

Millie was silent. She was not sure this was the truth.

"Why would people do that to him?" the Kid asked, her voice rising.

"I don't know. If you were starting to get successful, maybe they were jealous."

"He was such a nice man. They killed him, Ma. One year later he was dead!"

Okay. Millie stopped, put down the brush. She knelt down so that she and the Kid were face-to-face. "What did he die of, Judy?"

"Spinal meningitis," the Kid admitted.

"That's not Lancaster's fault."

"They still drove him out," she said, picking at the arm of the chair. "The town drove him out, and my mother had left him for all those men."

Millie stood up. Don't want to hear about that.

"I've talked to your mother," Millie said carefully. "She seems to be a nice lady." Millie used the tip of the brush to sketch individual eyebrow hairs.

"Seems," said the Kid.

"I met a lot of kids' mothers," said Millie. She meant the mothers of child actors. "Most of them were real pushy. Yours wasn't."

"She's just better at it." The Kid's mouth went firm, drawn tightly inward. "You better hurry up with the makeup."

Okay, Kid, end of conversation.

"She just sat in the limousine," said the Kid.

Okay, not the end of conversation. "Who?"

"My mother. We got driven out to Lancaster in a studio limousine." The Kid said it in an imitation English accent, to make it sound snotty. "We drove up in a limousine to Muggsie's house, and my mother sat in it outside so I wouldn't stay too long. I mean, she could have gone to see the Gilmores or somebody, but she didn't. She said she didn't want to get dusty."

Does sound pretty snotty to me, thought Millie.

"She thinks limousines are the best thing in the world. She thinks it's real great driving all day. Every weekend, I'd have to leave Daddy and go with her all the way to Los Angeles. To take lessons or go to auditions. If it was schooltime, Janie and Jinny would stay behind. And I'd have to sit in the car alone with her. For hours and hours and hours. All along the Mint Canyon Highway. She used to make me wear the same dresses as my sisters. Only mine were real short so I would still look like a baby. And she put my hair in ringlets. Twelve years old and I looked like somebody's doll."

The Kid shifted in the chair, fuming.

"The day we finally left Lancaster, I leaned out of the car, and I gave Muggsie a photograph. Just some photograph of me, and I wrote something on it for Muggsie. And you know what? My mother got mad at me. She said I shouldn't give away a professional photograph like it was a snapshot. To my best friend. And there was Daddy, waiting left behind, trying to smile, trying to look like we were still a family. And we drove away and left him behind."

Okay, okay, so your mother was human. Millie thought of her own teenage boys. They all go through this phase. It isn't pretty. They all go through this phase of hating their poor old parents. Who are only doing the best they can.

"She was the real Wicked Witch of the West," said the Kid.

"She probably just wanted the best for you," suggested Millie.

"She thought that whatever she wanted was the best for us."

Well, that was probably true. Millie was keeping an open mind. Some of what the Kid was telling her was probably true, some of it probably not. Millie couldn't judge which was which and wasn't going to try. Not judging between truth and falsehood is called keeping an open mind.

"After that, Daddy followed us around like a puppy dog. We'd go to Chicago, or up North, and he'd drive all that way, just to see us. And my mother would take us farther away. She left him and took us, and he was all alone." The voice went thin with pity. "He was left all alone when everything went wrong, and he lost his movie house, and the town turned on him. He must have thought even we didn't love him."

"It would have come right again," said Millie. She knew. Boy, did she know.

"Listen, honey," said Millie. "I moved out here with my husband, oh, about 1927. We moved out here, and I didn't know a soul, and then our marriage broke up, and I was left with two boys. I thought it was the end of the world, but I got a job here at Metro, just as it was starting up. So everything came out right. It would have gone right for your daddy, too."

The Kid shook her head. "The only way it could have come out right was if he got us back. And he never would have. My mother would have stopped him. He got another movie house in Lomita. We were already calling ourselves the Garland Sisters. And so he called his movie house Garland's Theater, after us. He started calling himself Garland. Just so people would think of us as a family still."

Either that, thought Millie, or he was cashing in. She kept it to herself.

"The night he died," said the Kid, and her voice started to shake, "I had to go on the radio. I had to hug old Wallace Beery and giggle and say how pleased I was to be back on his show." The Kid spoke in a nasty, piping voice.

"I had to pretend I was oh so happy. Because they were going to announce that I had a contract with MGM, and I was supposed to pretend that it was because I had gone on his radio show, and of course it was the other way around, the whole thing was a lie. So I did my little routine and then I had to sing, and I knew Daddy was dying in the hospital, but they had a radio by his bed."

The Kid had started to cry, and Millie didn't believe a word.

"And I had to sing this stupid stupid song. 'Zing Went the Strings of My Heart.'" The Kid rolled her eyes at its stupidity. "The words didn't mean anything, but I sang it for him just the same."

The Kid's voice clogged. Millie passed her a Kleenex. Well, there go the eyes. At least I haven't done the mascara yet. If she's lying, at least she believes it herself, thought Millie.

"I don't know if he ever heard it," the Kid said, in a voice like a rusty hinge. "He never knew. Any of this." The Kid made the Kleenex take in the whole of Metro-Goldwyn-Mayer.

"When people die," said Millie and coughed, "the people who get left behind have lots of feelings. When my father died, I tried to put the blame for it on all sorts of things. I thought there had to be a reason for it. Sometimes there isn't. And that seems the worst thing of all, that you can lose something for no reason. And so you start to blame other people."

"We all left him alone."

Ah, thought Millie. Now I got it.

"Or even worse," whispered Millie, "we start blaming ourselves."

The face in front of her was puffy, closed against her.

"Well, you don't need a lecture from me, I guess," said Millie and stood up.

"I hate it here," said the Kid. "I don't want to be here."

"You don't like being a movie star?" Millie didn't sound surprised. Most of them didn't, one way or another. But they hated it when it was taken away as well.

"It's okay, I guess," said the Kid. "I don't know." She'd stopped crying, and merely sounded dispirited.

The way they worked this kid over. Pulled all her teeth together, put her on diets to beef her up, put her on diets to slim her down, sent her to physios for her shoulders. No wonder she feels all spun around by everybody. Even me, painting on a different face.

"A lot of people would like to be Judy Garland," Millie reminded her.

"So would I," said the Kid.

Millie caught a whiff of self-dramatization. Poor little movie-star stuff. Well, you are a movie star and, until you decide to quit, we both have a job to do. In about fifteen minutes. Millie examined the makeup. Still got the lips to do, and the fall. And her eyes will be all bloodshot. I don't have any eyedrops.

"Listen, honey, I've got to go and get something. You going to be all right on your own till I come back?"

"Sure," said the Kid. She leaned forward, arm across the counter, and rested her head on it.

"I'll be back in a minute," said Millie, but the Kid didn't answer.

Outside the trailer, the studio was in full boom. Millie always thought of the phrase as "full boom." That was how she had heard it when she was a kid. It made her think of noise, people shouting, getting things done. The sound stage was crawling with people. "You got half an hour, Millie," Continuity shouted to her across the bare concrete.

"Don't worry, I know," she shouted back.

Outside there were actors everywhere in all kinds of costumes, coming out of the canteen, finding their sound stage. Props were being rolled in or out. Somebody was carrying a stuffed elephant's foot. And the secretaries and the clerical help walking to their office the long way round, just to feel part of the excitement.

What did Millie think? That is one unhappy kid, is what she thought. It's true what they say, success don't mean happiness. Funny thing about working with actors was that all the clichés turned out to be true. The blond bombshell really does get ahead by using men, and she really is pretty smart and pretty dumb at the same time. The great actress really is as temperamental as hell and impossible to be around. The clichés were true and that was surprising, more surprising in a way than to find out they weren't.

So the Kid doesn't like the whole schmear, and who can blame her. It is pretty phony. But she asked for it. She doesn't quit it. She's the one the whole thing benefits most. She is the center of attention, it all focuses on her. Maybe it's the responsibility. Like my husband Bill, when he got promoted, he didn't really like it because it meant more work. But he had to pretend to like it, because you have to pretend you like success.

Like he pretended he loved me.

Now, now, Millie. He liked you well enough till he met that little girl from Encino.

Back in her bungalow, Millie found the eyedrops. Collected up other bits and pieces too. Time I got a bigger case, with all these stars. Maybe a degree in psychology too. So's I can handle them when they start to act up. I wonder. You know, it wouldn't surprise me one little bit to find out that Frank Garland is still alive and running a movie house in Lomita.

She put a fresh stick of gum in her mouth. Kinda kept the breath minty when you had to talk into people's faces doing makeup. She said hi to the Monkeys as they filed out of the stage. Bill, Mark, Tomlin, she passed them all, said something to each of them. One big family. Those guys must have been working from well past midnight on top of everything else. Well, the other studios are good; we're just better, the best. Makes people feel worth something, like they're doing something in life.

Back into the dark and the blaze of lights ahead. A wave to Continuity, who's getting all antsy. Millie saw she hadn't closed the door to the trailer properly. It hung open, resting against the latch. She walked in without making much sound. She heard the Kid say:

"You going to be all right on your own until I get back?"

Millie heard her own Missouri twang. The little minx, she thought. She's imitating me.

"Ah-yale be bay-yak in a min-uht," said the Kid. Her voice rose and fell in swoops. She was sitting up in the chair. Lily had been in and pinned the fall onto her hair already. And I see she's polished up the eyes for me and put on the lashes. The Kid was in costume, too, dressed like a little girl. The Kid was staring ahead, and it was spooky. She was staring ahead and smiling.

"Bay-ack in a minute," she repeated, turning the words into music. That's how she does it, thought Millie. She turns the sounds into notes, even when she talks. That's why it sounds so good. She modulates it. That was the word. She modulates her whole self.

Kid didn't seem to realize she was there.

"Frank," the Kid whispered. "Frank Gumm."

That child has indeed suffered a loss, thought Millie.

"Honest and sticky," the Kid said. She was smiling and looking kind of weepy at the same time. "And my name's Frances."

"You ready?" Millie said, trying to sound like she had just climbed in and hadn't heard.

"Yes, I'm ready now," said the Kid. That's a line from the picture, thought Millie. That's just how she says it to Billie Burke before she goes home.

Millie didn't say anything but worked quickly. She put a towel around the shoulders, over the mutton sleeves of the child's dress. No time for eyewash now—it would make the eyes run.

"Judy, I just got to finish your lips," explained Millie.

She used a pencil to outline them, no time for a brush, and then used brown for lipstick, just a few shades darker than the skin tone.

Finally a bit of powder over the whole thing to kill the shine. The Kid sat still.

My, but I've had to do this in a hurry. Too much talking.

"Okay, sit up. Now remember, don't scratch your hair, even when it's hot. Suppose Lily told you that, too. Should be cooler today anyway with black-and-white." Kid said nothing.

They walked out of the trailer, and Judy Garland was on.

The Kid modulated. Her shoulders went back; the curl to her lip relaxed. She went up to people.

Kid saw Continuity heading their way and went straight up to her. "Hiya, Jenny, howya doin?""

Continuity looked a bit surprised that someone was friendly, then remembered to smile. "Uh. Fine, thank you. How are you today?"

"Oh, you know. Was your place okay after the storm?" The Kid sounded real concerned.

"Why yes, thank you." Continuity's clipboard strained forward, like it was on a leash.

"Now, the braids are the right length for Kansas, Jen," said the Kid. "I know, because in Kansas, they're not long enough to help hide my tits."

Continuity's face froze. The Kid winked at her. Continuity actually laughed.

"And my makeup *is* keyed for black-and-white, 'cause I checked the color numbers as Millie put it on. So everything's okay."

"I guess so," said Continuity, shaking her head.

Kid did that to everyone. Went up to them and said hi. It was like she was vacuuming them up or something.

She went up to Bolger. "Say," she said, looking serious, "don't I know you?"

He wasn't entirely sure she was joking. Poor old Ray.

"Oh, I know, you're playing the Tin Man!"

Then she giggled and kissed him on the cheek.

She waved to the Monkeys overhead amid their lights and wires. She swaggered up to the technicians on the ground and she was as confident as they were. She played poker with them sometimes—and won. She crept up behind King Vidor and hugged his back. He yelped and spun around.

"What the—oh, Judy!" the little guy said with relief. He would have taken it only from her. Kid jumped back giggling and covered her mouth. You just had to laugh with her.

Well, thought Millie. Got to hand it to the Kid. You'd never know there was anything wrong in her life at all. You'd really think she was just some sweet, ordinary kid. Except that she's a demon poker player and knows all my Panchro numbers. And her lines, from seeing the rewrite just once. And the names of all the technicians. She's smart. She's real smart, like some kind of genius or something. Millie found it just the slightest bit creepy.

They ran through the last scene of the picture. Doesn't usually work out like that, filming the last scene just about last. The set was tiny, so small they had the Kid's bed jammed right up against the corner of the window frame. There was only just room for a little table squeezed in between the bed and the other wall. It was the little girl's bedroom. The wallpaper was covered in poppies.

It was a simple setup. The camera pulls away from the Kid in bed, and she wakes up and sees the family; Frank sticks his head in through the window and the boys crowd in.

Only there wasn't room for them all.

Vidor intervened. "Uh, Clara. Look, when you take the cloth off Dorothy's head, put it on the table. Listen to her for a while until the boys need to get on—leave on the dream line. Pick the cloth up and take it to the kitchen."

"Why would I do that if my little girl's just woken up from a coma?"

Vidor had an answer. "It's wet and you're worried about the varnish on the table."

Blandwick didn't look convinced. "Look," said Vidor. "You're a farmer's wife. You're practical. So you make sure the Kid's all right, then it's up, brisk, quick out and then back in."

Blandwick held up a hand to stop. "Okay, I've got it."

Went for a take. No problem. Kid was bright, smooth. There was a bit when Blandwick lifted up the cloth and it pulled up some of the Kid's hair, right where it was wound into the fall. Kid looked up at Frank Morgan, and brushed the hair back at the same time. It looked real like the little girl had done it without thinking, but the Kid was managing her wig. She knew she had to keep the hair the same from shot to shot.

Millie watched Vidor. He was smiling, telling them it was fine. He's not happy with it, thought Millie.

"Let's just have a few reaction shots," he said, the lights reflecting on his funny round glasses.

"Judy," he said to the Kid, waving at her to stay on the bed. He sat down and began to talk to her in a low voice.

Millie wanted to hear. She crept up a bit closer.

"Like this," he was saying. "Just breathe out at the top of your register, a whisper right in the front of your mouth." He said the line for her. Reason he was so good. A bit eccentric. Studios were full of stories about how he would tell producers off. Maybe why he sometimes ended up finishing other people's pictures.

The Kid lay back as Continuity fussed with the quilt.

And something happened again. The Kid's eyes went faraway.

King was bustling around with the camera, looking through it on tiptoe. A small man physically, lots of energy. Kid closed her eyes and went still as a corpse.

"Okay, going for a take."

It was just the Kid on the pillow, her eyes closed, and she began to murmur over and over the last line: "There's no place like home. There's no place like home."

Millie felt a prickle down her neck. Kid really sounded like a little girl, for all that the brace had to hold down her chest.

"Right," said King, sounding surprised. "That was just what I wanted."

They set up another shot. More huddling between Vidor and the Kid. Millie went to freshen her makeup, but didn't hear what Vidor said. As Millie touched up the eyebrows, the Kid started to sing to herself. "Zing Went the Strings of My Heart."

She kept on singing it, softly, as the lights and the cameras were moved.

There was a rustle of paper on a clipboard.

"Dog," said Continuity. "The dog jumps up on the bed halfway through the scene. And Dorothy is already sitting up and holding it."

"Terry? Terry?" called the dog's trainer. "Dog's shy," he explained to Vidor.

"Where's the dog?" called Vidor, annoyed.

"Here, dog," whispered the Kid. Only Millie seemed to hear her. "Up'n the bed."

It sounded like Missouri. Or Kansas. Darned if the dog didn't come too, right up on the bed out of nowhere. You are a country girl, aren't you, honey, thought Millie. They couldn't have found somebody better for this part in a million years. A country girl who got picked up, spun around and dropped into Hollywood and Technicolor.

Vidor sat Blandwick down and pulled her shoulders into the frame. Cameraman kept shaking his head.

Ten minutes, maybe twenty. Hours of waiting. It was amazing how these actors could sit and wait and wait and then just launch themselves into it. Mind you, that's why they were paid. To be able to say lines like they believed them. The Kid started singing again.

Finally Vidor said, "Okay, let's go. Dorothy, your last lines from 'Anyway, Toto, we're home.' "

The camera whirred, Vidor pointed, the Kid said her line, and it was wrong.

On the word "home," her face crumpled up and she started to cry. Not modulated. Ugly, wet, snotty.

"No, no, no, no, no," said Vidor, waving at the cameraman to stop.

Vidor stepped forward and spoke loud enough for most of them to hear. "Uh, Dorothy. That's probably a bit too sad. Remember, she's home, she's happy, everybody she loves is back with her in one place. She's probably never been as happy, and probably never will be as happy again. So what we want to see is joy. Joy like we've never seen it. This has got to be the happiest part of the whole picture."

The Kid smiled and smiled and nodded yes and darned if she wasn't still crying. Anything to please, thought Millie, rolling the gum in her mouth.

They tried again, and this time, the Kid sputtered and burst into tears with a kind of spurting sound. Vidor cut the air with his hand.

She went too far, sometimes, the Kid. When she first saw Lahr in his makeup, she went hysterical. They couldn't stop her laughing. She had to hide behind the set and say over and over "I must not laugh, I must not laugh," and then she came out and started laughing all over again. Finally Fleming slapped her right across the chops. That stopped her laughing all right.

Vidor scratched his brow with his thumb, thinking. Then he walked up to the bed and leaned over it and spoke low and soft, like a daddy to his little girl.

"Frances," he said.

The Kid turned to him, startled. "Frances, just pretend you've gone to sleep, and you wake up back in your own house, just like it used to be when you were little with your mommy and your daddy and your sisters. All there, all home. Just close your eyes."

He stepped back quietly. The Kid stroked the dog. It licked her arm.

"Now open them," said Vidor.

She did.

"And you're home," said Vidor.

The lights came up fierce, and so did the Kid. Suddenly she smiled, and the smile cut through the one wall of the set that faced her and the camera and the lights.

There was silence. They all waited in silence, and King motioned for the whirring of the camera to keep going. The Kid kept staring. Was she going to say anything?

She told Toto they were home. Home, like she couldn't believe it, it was so wonderful to be back.

And this was her own room, and they were all there together, everyone she loved, and she wasn't going to go away, ever again. Oh yes you are, thought Millie. Life takes you away. Don't believe that down-on-the-farm shit, kid. "And, oh Aunty Em? There's no place like home!"

It was strange. Everyone stayed silent for a while. Somebody coughed, like they were saying: Can we move now? People went back to work.

There was one thing that Millie could tell people about her job that was true, and that was that the good actors, the ones who could actually act, were really nice, nice inside. Oh, sure they acted up; they were childish; they were like little kids. There was something childish about each one of them.

"Ray, Bert, Jack," said King Vidor, and they came in a parade, dressed as farmhands. Lahr who couldn't sleep from fear. Bolger who wanted to go to college. Jack who showed them how to say their lines like children—rumor was he wanted to start a charitable foundation. He was the one who wanted a heart. Yup, thought Millie.

All these people working together on something, sometimes it all comes together. Looks like maybe this picture is. That business with the coat. The Professor is wearing L. Frank Baum's coat. If Judy Garland really is a nice country kid, then maybe the coat is real too.

And the Kid was beaming, still smiling, in the lights, where home would continue to be. The only place it would be, in the center of attention.

Santa Monica, California

January 1953

The only thing she was good for was spreading chaos and fear.

—JUDY GARLAND, of her mother

The parking lot looked empty. Ethel swung her car around, looking at the space she was aiming at, and nearly hit an old Ford. She slammed on the brakes, reversed, wrenching the steering wheel around, slammed into forward, straightening the car, and roared back neatly into the space. Her heart was thumping. Late. Late again, darn it, she was never late, and suddenly twice in one week. Why am I always late for everything, she admonished herself. Then she looked at her watch.

It said six forty-five.

It was like a blow to the chest. What? She was an hour early. Of all the stupid . . . She'd misread the time. All that panic, missing her breakfast, dashing out to the car, makeup to be done later. Screaming up Sepulveda, only half noticing how empty the streets were, praising the Lord that the traffic was light for once, tearing into the lot and then thump, here she was, thump, parked in the McDonnell Douglas parking lot an hour early with nothing to do on the coldest day of the year. She looked over her shoulder. Even the chow shop on the corner hadn't opened yet.

She sat and went very still. She closed her eyes. Something heavy and sluggish settled over her like mud. What a panic! And for nothing.

The little Dodge smelled of gas and Ethel felt sick, a queasy, floating nausea that was not altogether unpleasant. After the iron pressure of the race across town, it was nice to find she could sit for a spell and relax.

When was the last time I was able to do that? Ethel thought. She sat for a few moments with her eyes closed, just listening to herself breathe. Actually, she thought, this is rather nice. A whole hour just to myself. She took a deep, soothing breath and opened her eyes. I might even get used to this when I retire. I deserve it. But knowing me, I probably won't stop till I drop, just like Mother.

I can do my makeup, she remembered. Do it properly for a change, like in the old days. The visor was already down as a defense against the low California dawn. Her soft, sagging face stared back at her from the mirror. Her face was flushed. She looked, she thought, surprisingly healthy. Nothing like an early morning crisis to get the blood moving. The light showed the damage the years had done around the eyes, and neck and mouth. I have to smile all the time, she thought, smile just to stop looking like I'm frowning.

Still, can't show up for work looking like this.

I still have my old kit in the glove compartment, she remembered. It's like in the old days, before going on stage. You start with the base.

With a professional's jaundiced eye, Ethel began to pat on the foundation. All those years I did this for the stage, she thought. Who would guess I was ever on the stage now? All that time I spent, year in year out, up and down in that car, going into offices, negotiating contracts, doing all those things a man should have done. All of that.

Don't get bitter, she told herself. She managed the different parts of her personality as if they were a family or a team of performers. You can't repent what was done for love. And if your daughter doesn't feel she owes you anything for all your love and care, so be it. Your conscience is clear.

Your pocketbook, too, came another voice. You'll be in harness all your life.

The reply came: So who said life was going to be any different? Life was a harness. We knew you had to get on with it, do things; that was the way we were brought up. In those days. We'd rather die than take charity.

And I can see her point of view, Ethel told herself. She was the one who did all the work, after all. It was her singing, her voice that earned the money. Why should she support her old ma? Parents are there to support the kids, not the other way around. If she is prepared to see her old ma living in a Santa Monica bungalow on sixty dollars a week, what can I say? I can't prove to her that love and respect might indicate what the law cannot enforce. Maybe she has no love and respect.

Her hands stopped applying makeup. They sank to her lap. Face it, Ethel. Your daughter hates you. Everything's gone wrong for her, and she needs someone to blame. So old Ethel has to carry the can again. I have been carrying that can all my life. It might be nice if somebody else did, for a change.

And it was a mistake to go and sue my own daughter. It was undignified. It was a public squabble. I was the loser, in every way. People know about stage mothers, or think they do. What they don't know, they can make up for themselves. Suing my own daughter for support.

Ethel shook her head at herself. What would my mother have said? she thought. Well, Mother, Ethel thought, remembering her mother's face, I'm afraid we live in a colder world. Life was hard in your day, but other people made up for it. These days, it's just the reverse; we have our cars and our Frigidaires, but we don't have each other.

Ethel sighed and looked back into the mirror. Now. A bit of color on the cheeks. Her hands rattled through the assortment of compacts and lipsticks and old dried tubes of greasepaint. Her mind was not attending. The containers turned over and over in a jumble.

Suing was so messy. And vengeful too. All right, I was angry. I was appalled and angry and I really did need some help and I couldn't believe after all I'd done for her that she would treat me this way. Just cast me off, like I was a piece of stale meat. A dog or a cat would have had better treatment from her.

Another part of Ethel intervened, broke off the thought.

She isn't the same girl, Ethel told herself, she isn't my little girl anymore. My little girl is dead. Instead, there is some fat, shambling woman who can't control her hands. Someone who is, for want of a better word, a junkie.

People warned me. They told me Hollywood kills. They didn't say how, and I didn't see how it could reach right into someone and destroy her, how it could take everything and leave a desert.

She became a horrible person. My little baby, my sweet little Frances. She grew up so selfish, so mean. On another planet. My lawyer shows up to serve a writ and she bounces up to him and says, "Come and hear me sing." Takes him by the hand! Like he was a family friend. Like we were all still a family. She just did not understand what she had done. Those lies she told about me, those viperish lies. I read about myself in the paper, she tells reporters how awful I was. When all I ever did was try to help her, try to protect her, to get her away from what I knew was coming. It would be Grand Rapids all over again, only with my little girls old enough to understand.

Ethel Gilmore thought of Frank Gumm. She thought of the sweep of her life.

She no longer hated him. She thought of him infrequently now that she had remarried and divorced again. When she thought of him at all, it was with a kind of understanding. It must have been awful for him, too. I suppose he wanted to become normal, poor man, and couldn't. And I have to suppose that he loved me a little bit. I guess he loved playing piano with me. Like he loved playing a husband and father.

She dimly saw the little theater in which they had met. A memory of hands on keys. A memory of him leading the audience in song. "Follow the Bouncing Ball." Gosh, that was a long time ago. With me young and pretty with long hair wrapped around my head and thinking the world was foursquare and simple. I thought you fell in love like walking into some kind of mist, and something happened in the mist that you couldn't quite see or feel. I'd hardly even heard of what Frank Gumm was.

Pretty little lady with the pretty little hands, that's what Frank Gumm would call me when we were on stage together. I'd stand up and give a little smile; he'd take my hand; we'd bow. What a con artist. Both of us.

And everyone knew. Everyone in Grand Rapids, then everyone in Lancaster. I had to walk down the street and feel people's eyes on my face. What a world he pushed me into.

The pretty little lady cut her hair and became modern. The things I found myself doing because of Frank Gumm. I nearly didn't have Frances. I can remember driving to see Marcus, Marcus our friend, our doctor. It was like being in a dream, my husband driving the car beside me, looking

like such a man, being so gallant and soft-spoken. I couldn't put it together. It didn't make sense. A husband and wife driving off like dirty
strangers to kill their child, as if they were two kids who had been caught.

Sitting in Marcus's office. Trying to find a way to tell him, a way
to begin to ask him. We both sat grinning and coughing. We didn't
even know what to call it. An abortion.

Frank kept smiling. His whole life was a smiling lie. I was the one
who had to say it in the end, I was the one who always had to do
everything.

"What my husband means, Marcus, is that I am with child and
we don't want it and we were wondering if there was some way in
which we don't have to have it."

Marcus paused and looked back and forth between our faces.
Frank's fat, sweaty face all queasy and cheesy and I hated him then. It
was all starting to come out in his face. He was becoming a weaselly
little man.

Poor Marcus, what was he to say? "Um. There are some ways,
yes, but none of them anything I'd like to associate with you two. Do
you mind telling me the reason?"

I still can't remember what we said. Two children is enough. Can't
afford three. Can't afford the time. It must have sounded pretty feeble.
How could I say, My husband is a sodomite and I can't bear him, the
idea of where his hands have been or the thing that is growing inside
me, that he put inside me. I wanted it gone.

Baby sensed that, somehow. She must have. She must have felt
it inside me, no child couldn't. Maybe she half remembers that Mommy
wanted to kill her.

But only because I thought she would kill me, inside. Me, Ethel
Milne, wanting to do that to my own child. I'd been pushed into a
nightmare. What my husband was. The lies we told. And that was only
halfway through, halfway through our strange dance. Me and Frank.

We named her after both of us, Frances Ethel. She was supposed
to hold us together, and she did. There was something special about
Frances. But it all got too much for Grand Rapids. The women came
to tea and asked me about Frank's friends. One of them even called
them boyfriends, and my little girls could hear, and I wanted to die.

Running away somehow kept us together too. All the way across
America, going West and working on the stage.

That drive across the whole darn country. That little town with the cockroaches. They had a one-hundred-seater in a town of five hundred. We knew then that vaudeville was dead.

And Frances's Spanish trousers all in a tangle, not able to get them on. Poor little thing all naked in the wings and Janie, Jinny, singing the chorus over and over, waiting for her to make her entrance. Frank fighting to get her dressed so she could go on. And Baby Frances just smiled, grinning. She knew it was happening and thought it was funny. Everything was held up for Frances. That was all she cared about even then, being in the center. That little impish grin.

Well, imps grow up to be demons. Ethel saw the impish face, transmogrified into something medieval, a monkeylike, vengeful face. Gargoyle. Judy Gargoyle.

So where is the goodness in my life? Where is the joy? Where has it all gone?

Don't think about it, Ethel. There's more to you than that. Things go wrong, but they can't touch what you are inside. They can't touch what you once were. Or where you were from. They can't touch home.

Ethel Milne Gumm Gilmore remembered her first life.

I used to play tennis in a long skirt that went all the way down to the ground. Mutton sleeves, tiny waist. You had to play so that you didn't sweat too much. You couldn't play to win; you didn't give it everything you had. You were supposed to break everything off. We'd play tennis, the girls of Superior, Minnesota, and we'd laugh. We'd all get together Sunday afternoons after church, around the piano, the whole crowd, boys and girls in a group chaperoning each other. A date like they have nowadays would have caused a scandal.

Chasteness seemed so sensible in those days. Foursquare. No nonsense. Everything dirty seemed a continent away. Real people got married and were happy and if there were problems they'd solve them. We had a girl who did the scrubbing, and an old fat woman who did the laundry, and some tough skinny old bird who polished the house. All we had to learn was how to be beautiful. Taste and refinement. You learned how to speak properly and sit up straight. There were knives and forks and flowers on the table and laughter in the front hall. You cooked special dishes for church socials.

And the clubs. I would be the president of one and the secretary of another. Superior Chapter of the Order of the Rainbow. Young Ladies' Music Society. What were we going to do? We were going to make a good world by setting an example. By living well, we lived for everyone.

There was such a thing as progress. You learned about it. People talked about it; they believed in it. We talked about science and morality as if the two were the same thing. Light bulbs, motion pictures, flying machines, all the products of rationality. And rationality was always clean, calm, sensible. Enlightened. We thought mutton sleeves and laughter were a sign of rationality. Progress meant men who shaved and didn't drink in secret. We thought there was no need for secrets and that most people didn't have them. We thought passion was something sweet and orderly, smiling fresh-scrubbed behind glasses. Poetry was progress. Learning Tennyson by heart and singing simple songs. I was ever so daring, working in a theater. Lizzie, I can still see Lizzie, going all red. "Ethel!" she said. Brave, she thought, singing in public and risking approbation.

"I see nothing wrong in singing harmless songs and bringing harmless pleasure," I said. I felt ever so modern with white cotton up to my chin and my wrists and ankles hidden well away and a little watch hanging from my waist.

"You'll be smoking a pipe next," Lizzie said. Flushed face, bright spectacles.

How, Ethel wondered, how did I end up here? Half a century later? Airplanes in the sky and me driving a motorcar as if it were a bicycle. Me. I'm now some old divorced lady who works as a clerk. I'm some fat old lady called Ethel who nobody has to listen to or take care of. They all think that I've done nothing with my life. They take it for granted that there is nothing more to me than fat arms and cheap dresses and well-applied, scented powder. They think that I've done nothing but wash diapers and follow my husband around and grow fat. Fat and deserted when my children left me, with nothing to do but make ends meet. If only they knew.

Knew that I could once walk into a theater, any theater, and put people at their ease and get real work out of them. I knew how to do it. I treated it as a business proposition. And I knew my babies were good. And I knew darn well that when the second storm broke, when people found out what Frank Gumm was a second time, when we had to flee in shame again, I was darn well certain that I and my babies were going to be able to cope on our own, without him, without Frank Gumm to pull us down into the mud again.

I was ready for the next time they rode him out of town on a rail. I saw it coming. I saw those boys, hanging around the movie house. They blackmailed him into giving them free tickets. They sat in the front row, next to my babies, their faces, their smirks, joking about fat old Frank so that everyone could hear, everyone could know. His poor wife, everyone would say. His poor wife. Mind you, she puts up with it. What goes on behind that smiling mask of her face?

The men of the town would come sidling up to me, sideways.

Oh, they'd heard about Frank Gumm, and I suppose they'd heard about me too. They'd come up to me, talking without moving their lips, hardly bothering with pleasantries. "Come on, honey, you're a married woman. You know what it's about."

They knew I needed love. They needed something other than their wives. Adultery, to call it by its proper name. I took lovers. Me, Ethel Milne, took men who didn't always shave, who had secrets, who cheated each other in business deals. Who cheated me. Who treated me like a business deal.

There was Billy. Young, burly, blond. Oh, what a difference, to be really wanted. That look in his eyes. And the way I opened up to him. Opened up in that deserted shed, back of town. He was a barber. No. A barber's boy. Hah. Frank and I had the same taste in men.

What a world, after Superior, Minnesota. Where was the bright and coming world of flight and public railways then? When you were fending off a strong young man who you wanted just as badly as he wanted you. Fending him off in a shed in Lancaster, California. The two of us had dust in our hair, and the place smelled of chicken manure. Why was I fending him off? He was angry; I was angry.

Suddenly, that shriek of laughter, outside, the laughter of children exploring, and me leaping away, pulling my head back from Billy's chest.

And there was Frances, my Baby, looking at Mommy playing with strange men in a shed. Thank goodness our clothes were in place and we hadn't been doing anything. Her dark eyes scowling with a question. Where is Daddy? Why aren't you with him? Who is that man?

Brats, Billy muttered. He called my Baby a brat and I knew. It wasn't love he felt or he couldn't have called Frances that. He should have knelt down and reassured her and showed me that he could love her too. But she had interrupted, interrupted his sport, another man's brat who got in the way. His face was young and sullen, handsome, but soft too, and I suddenly saw how his face would go as he aged. He wouldn't look that different from Frank. He would be gone, chasing younger women. Women younger than me, younger than himself. I saw that we had no possible real life together, even as secret husband and wife. So I left him, left beautiful, blond, young Billy. After that I would drive into Los Angeles alone and find my men in Los Angeles.

Frances must have known. She knew what Billy was. She never asked. She never had to. She never said in front of Frank: Mommy, who was that man? She never said it because she knew, and she thought she had to protect Frank, and I suppose she still remembers Billy, and she remembers the things she saw in Los Angeles.

So she doesn't respect me. She saw her fat, ordinary mother chasing man after man in L.A. and always being dumped and disappointed. Treated like a towel on which men wiped themselves. Some fat old widow from Lancaster with a Buick, that's what people thought until it turned out her husband was still alive. She bounced her fat old hips like a mattress. And Frances, coming back early from Meglin's and her new dance steps, would sometimes see the men leave. She must have thought the lessons were just an excuse to get me to L.A. and to the men.

Can't you forgive that now, Frances? After all the men you've had? After the divorces? Can't you understand?

Nothing works out for either of us, Kid. Like me, marrying William Gilmore. The nice neighbor man with the dying wife. My life, Baby, is a parade of mistakes, and I still don't know what I did wrong.

I remember meeting the Gilmores for the first time. We were the nice new couple who bought the movie house. They were neighbors two streets down. We had them in for bridge. I'd serve iced tea and try to pretend that there was anything gracious about the gray bleached streets of Lancaster. Mary Gilmore would come into the kitchen after dinner to help me wash up, talking about the town. Mary didn't like Lancaster either. You couldn't like that heat. We'd talk about ways to keep cool, damp cloths and scent. We'd talk about the local school and how to keep the kids healthy.

If only we had seen the future, Mary and me. Me marrying her husband. Baby Frances becoming this thing on posters, this giant creature. Mary dying. I saw her die, of a stroke, like a rose in the Lancaster heat. I saw William Gilmore cry, and I thought, Who will cry for me? I saw a nice, decent man.

Two years later Frank was dead, Baby, and I was more sorry than you'll know. The strangeness of life. I had loved him once, Baby, when he was twenty-eight and still beautiful, and I had lain with him and we produced three children before the horror finally closed in on us.

Frank was dead, Baby, and the marriage had died years before, and I was alone, and Mary was dead too, and I confused sympathy in mourning for sympathy in life. So I married Bill Gilmore, and the nice decent man turned out to be dull, Baby. Dull, yes, after your father. I found I had married an old man who just wanted his slippers and his supper cooked. I had been permanently swindled, Baby, swindled out of a whole part of life, when you're married but still young enough to attract each other. I never really had love like that. Like peaches that fall before they're picked. You can't put them back on the tree. Nice dull Gilmore wanted two minutes out of me once a week, with his eyes closed, pretending I was something young and lovely. Or even pretending I was Mary. Too many ghosts.

I had nothing, Baby. My life had gone wrong again. And you danced when the marriage failed, Baby. I saw your smile. I saw you be so glad the marriage had died. Just because it wasn't your precious father, because I dared to have a life of my own, after you and he had gone. Why do you think you own me? And if you do own me, why don't you take care of me?

Well, listen, Baby, listen, Frances, I hate you too. I hate you for that smile when Ethel Milne passed through the name of Gilmore and out the other side. You wanted me to fail. As hard as I had wanted you to succeed, you wanted me unhappy. What was I supposed to do? Stay and hold your hand when you ditched friends and husbands? Be your mommy when all you ever did was tell me I was in the way? Where was I supposed to go, when I saw that evil light come into your eyes and I knew you were going to snap again or make me feel small? When I knew you were going to extract revenge like pulling teeth out of my head.

Your friends. They would look at me with that silent, smug little smirk, that Lancaster smirk that said we know the whole story, you don't fool us, we know what you are, Judy has told us about you. Those smart Hollywood young people, smirking as I tried to make myself useful, passing around the canapés as Baby barely bothered to be polite.

Oh, smart young people, blaming me for your precious Judy's red, red eyes and the fact that she lied, over and over, playing nervously with her hair. Going mad in front of your eyes, blaming me, and doing nothing.

Did they ever help you, Baby, all your smart young friends? What did they do for you except pour you another drink, or keep you supplied with the pills? What was I to do, Baby, but get out of your way for good? That was what you wanted, wasn't it?

So Ethel Milne moved again. Listen, Baby, I am of frontier stock. My people built houses out of sod, brought them out of the ground from nowhere. We don't need anything from anybody. My people made their own soap and made their own shoes if they had to. Here come the Redskins, move the wagons into a circle, duck the arrows, and take up a rifle and shoot. Then move on.

So I moved again, my little Gargoyle, when I knew you didn't want me. I moved to Texas. I went to live with Jinny, the plainest and plainest talking of all the Gumms. Who else did I have? Jinny didn't know me, but at least she didn't hate me. Didn't look gleeful when I did something wrong. Didn't relish every opportunity to curse me in my own house.

Texas was Lancaster all over again: another hot dusty town. It was a pattern by now. I still couldn't get away from the pattern. I opened a movie house, Baby. Only I didn't play piano anymore, and I had no one to sing with, and I had to be careful not to visit Jinny too much in case I overstayed my welcome. It wasn't home, Baby. If I had a home left anywhere, I would have gone to it. Back to Superior? Back to those bright gals, with their sensible husbands? Those bright sagging gals in their fifties whose faces had so changed I wouldn't recognize them, whose world was so far away from the one we were part of together? Mother dead, father dead. We all go down into darkness, Baby. It opens up under our feet. If we're here together for such a short time, why do we make life so hard on each other?

We were right, us girls in Superior. Right to be cool and sensible, tough but clean, right to believe in the rational. It was the rational that left us. What a world, what a world. Opening up inside us, opening up in the dark and fertile places. Good and evil mingle there, blood and darkness, where children are born and blood comes pouring out. A wound. All women are wounded, Judy Gargoyle. You more than any of them. What did I do to you?

You tried to cut your throat. I read about it in the papers. So I came back from Texas and you wouldn't see me, and your smart young friends told me I was the reason. And I had to see it then, see that you had an arrow in your heart, and you thought it was me.

It was your father, Frances. And the one good thing I've done in my life is never tell you. I know he is the only thing you still hold dear. So I don't tell you, and I will never tell you. You will go to your grave not knowing. So if there is a God, maybe He'll forgive me for that. Maybe there are Gates, and maybe they will open for me.

I left Frank Gumm because he would destroy us, Baby. I worked us so hard because we needed to be able to make a living without him. He was driven from Lancaster because of the things he did there, with everyone knowing. They tried to forgive him, poor Frank, poor poor beautiful Frank. They tried to forgive him, and tried to ignore it, but I guess without me there, he just went to pot. Went too far. Danny Boy.

Oh God, I'm crying. Why am I crying for him? Poor Frank. Poor fat balding little boy, always hoping every time he shook a man's hand that he had found it, love, a friend, something true out of a life of lies and horror. Poor Frank, trying hard to love me. And he succeeded. He succeeded in loving me, not for my breasts or my body, but loving me for the pattern we made, the pattern I can't escape, the pattern in the lights, the pattern in the song, the pattern in our three little girls, all of us singing in the magic circle of the lights. That was Heaven. If those Gates open, if I am forgiven, that is what I expect Heaven to be. The stage of the Valley Theater, with all of us together again, but in spirit, in the pattern. How could we lose so much? How could we fumble so badly? Maybe beyond the Gates, Baby, we'll all be healed.

Ghosts, Baby. We're ghosts, haunting each other now. We went back to Lancaster once, remember, back when you and I were still friends. I sat in the limousine, terrified, while you went to see that awful girl. I was terrified that if I got out, I'd stay. I'd find Frank still there, and the life of lies. I was frightened I'd see him walking down Cedar Street, and that he'd wave, poor ghost, not knowing he was dead, and that I was ten years older. That he'd go back to our house, and find someone else living there. Where are our babies? he'd ask. Did we fail, then? Did it happen in the end? And I would have to say, in a sour and weary voice, Yes, Frank, it happened again. What did you expect? It happened again, and it killed you.

So I sat huddled in that car, telling myself it was the heat that I was hiding from. But it was hotter inside the car than out. So I braved it. I got out and waited and wondered how long you would be. And then I went for a little walk.

And I felt it, a brush against my hand. And it was as if I had my Baby back, the little baby hidden away in that huge, bitter shell. And my Baby and I walked through those barren, flat, blistered streets as if the future had not come to destroy us. And I felt another hand, plump and soft and large and damp, and it was Frank. And Jinnie ran on ahead, Janie looked uncomfortable, and I knew we were still in Lancaster somewhere. Somewhere, maybe, in the wind. The wind makes a noise in the tamarisk. In the dust.

You haven't seen Muggsie since, and I'm not sure who you are married to now, except that I haven't met him and never will. But somewhere I still love my Baby, and I have to hope that somewhere in the wilderness she still loves me. But I can't touch the love, and I can't find the truth. So I still have to go on.

Go on calling the truth the Devil that only comes in idleness.

Ethel Milne Gumm Gilmore looked at her watch.

Thump.

Thump.

Eight-fifteen. Now I'm late. Late for real. Oh, Ethel, sitting here like a lump when you should be moving.

Her body didn't respond. It didn't want to move. Come on, Ethel. There's a time clock. You have to punch it to eat. You have to punch it and write on cards and file them and put papers away.

I don't want to, her body replied. I want to go play piano. I want to sit here and look at the sky.

Like moving through mud, Ethel turned. She turned and fumbled with the door. Makeup, she remembered. I haven't done my makeup. With terrible weariness, she looked at her face in the mirror. It was gray and covered with sweat and streaked with foundation that hadn't been worked and smoothed. The foundation slipped, skidding across her face she rubbed it. She smeared on some lipstick. Her lips were sweaty, as if she were melting. Getting up early doesn't suit the old, she told herself.

Shortcut. Cut between the cars. The car door felt like slippery rubber in her hands. Her feet felt like the shoes were too big, with heels that were loose. I should have eaten something. I feel so hollow inside. Empty. Empty. A nothingness, waiting to suck me in.

She began to hurry. She needed to get inside the plant. There would be shade there, and chairs, and she could sit, and fan herself, get herself together, tell her boss she was sick. There was a first-aid room, a couch to rest on. She was hot though the air was cold. She stepped outside and vapor rose out of her, from her nostrils, from the back of her hands.

She steamed out into the California morning that was so bright, ablaze with light so that it burned her eyes; she felt dizzy; she couldn't see. A shortcut, she told herself. A shortcut between the cars, the strangers' cars, gray and blue and red, other people's cars, not hers. All her life, living among people's cars, driving along the Mint Canyon Highway.

Thump. As in a cyclone, breath was taken from her. She tried to breathe, pull in air, but it wouldn't come. A fist seemed to have clenched her chest. It held her vengefully. Kneel, it said. Kneel before your God.

I don't have one, she thought, her thoughts in a thin and pitiful voice. A blaze of light that meant nothing, I have no God, and I am forced to kneel to nothing. She was down on her knees between the strangers' cars. Her arms were stretched apart, each hand clasping a door handle to keep from falling. All the big, washed cars were lined up in judgment, at the gates of McDonnell Douglas, the strange and unimagined ending place of her life. She knelt in the light and asked forgiveness, as we all must, for failing without knowing why, and for living so long without seeing so much. But kneeling in the light, settling through it, crucified between two door handles, it seemed to her that she was. Forgiven. Or rather, that there was nothing to forgive. Ethel Milne was borne away.

She did not know that her daughter had had a change of heart and was making plans with her lawyer to arrange financial support for her mother. The Gumm sisters came to the funeral and did not speak to each other. There was too much to say. For Frances it was one more tightening of the knot, one more loop in the tangle. One month later, in February 1953, the Valley Theater, Lancaster, was hollowed out by a fire, as if a revenging spirit had raged through its aisles. It was not rebuilt. It is now difficult, even with old maps, to reconstruct where it once stood.

Part Two

The Summer
Kitchen

Manhattan, Kansas

1881

. . . *the men burning houses and barns and horses so that for ten years and more the countryside was an inferno of revenge, broken by a fifth season of arson. The tramps who packed guns and overran whole towns. The old men who went mad with jealousy. The old women who jumped down wells. All those mothers: the ones who carried their children into the rivers, the ones who fed them arsenic and strychnine so that, if they had to die, at least it wouldn't be of epidemic disease . . . All the men who cleansed the putrescence of their lives with carbolic acid. All the others who killed themselves with the same insecticide they used on the potato bugs . . .*

By the end of the nineteenth century, country towns had become charnel-houses and the counties that surrounded them had become places of dry bones. The land and its farms were filled with the guilty voices of women mourning for their children and the aimless mutterings of men asking about jobs. State, county, and local news consisted of stories of resignation, failure, suicide, madness and grotesque eccentricity. Between 1900 and 1920, 30 per cent of the people who lived on farms left the land . . .

The people who left the land came to the cities not to get jobs, but to be free from them, not to get work but to be entertained, not to be masters but to be charges. They followed yellow brick roads to emerald cities presided over by imaginary wizards who would permit them to live in happy adolescence for the rest of their lives . . . It is this adolescent city culture, created out of the desperate needs and fantasies of people fleeing from the traps and tragedies of late nineteenth century country life, that still inspires us seventy years later.

—MICHAEL LESY,
Wisconsin Death Trip

Kansas was a go-ahead place. It had been the first territory in the United States to propose votes for women—in 1859. It was to be the second state to grant them, nearly thirty years later.

Prohibition was a women's crusade. Women couldn't vote, but they organized and lobbied; and an amendment to the state constitution forbidding the sale and manufacture of intoxicants was passed by a narrow margin in 1880. The state became dry, as far as could be managed with towns full of hot and sweaty men. The local newspapers ruefully reported that the most popular local song was "Little Brown Jug" and that kegs were seen going to private parties. Women raided pharmacies that were too free with their medicinal alcohol.

Manhattan was a center of progress in the go-ahead state. The town had its first telephone in 1877, wired up by Professor Kedrie of the State Agricultural College. Professor Mudge had died, and there was talk of erecting a statue to his memory. Barbed wire arrived, Devil's grass. It finally put an end to the question of the herd laws by ripping the flesh of cattle that tried to wander into farmers' fields. No less a personage than G. W. Higinbotham was severely wounded by barbed wire, which tore out a chunk of his chest.

In 1878, Manhattan built a fine new schoolhouse of stone. It towered above Poyntz Avenue, two stone floors with a stone tower. It had four main classrooms on each floor to accommodate the growing numbers of little scholars.

Aunty Em's instinct was to send Dorothy to the new Manhattan school. But Aunty Em did not approve of the school's Principal, Mr. J. McBride. It was a matter of public record, jovially reported in the local press, that he was fond of drink. He was succeeded by Professor Hungerford, but this was no improvement. Professor Hungerford was considered to be the local actor and singer. Aunty Em did not approve of actors. He had quite taken over her own Congregationalist church. In May of 1880, the church had staged an opera, *The Cantata of Joseph*, with full orchestra and sixty costumes. Professor Hungerford took the leading role. The *Independent* reviewed the production and called him, particularly, "brilliant."

"Brilliant indeed, like his hair," said Aunty Em quite mysteriously. "In time the people of Riley County will tire of all this old crony–ism."

So Dorothy stayed for a while in Schoolhouse Number 43, called Sunflower School. She was quietly content there. This was not enough for either Aunty Em or the teacher of the school, Miss Ida Francis.

Ida Francis and Emma had become firm friends. Miss Francis was a regular caller to tea, which she drank sitting at the Gulches' one rickety table, little finger outstretched as if the place were grand. She could pour her heart out to Emma Gulch.

"They have finally, finally repaired the stove," Miss Francis said once, eating Aunty Em's biliously colored cornbread. "The poor little scholars are not being introduced to smoking via the school chimney any longer."

"We must be grateful for that," said Aunty Em with a chuckle. "The next thing is to do something about the books."

"I must say again, Mrs. Gulch, how grateful we are for your donation."

"I do what I can," said Aunty Em, smiling, with her eyes closed.

"Would that Squire Aiken took such an interest."

Squire Aiken lived on the slopes of the hill south of the river, on the wooded side. He had peach orchards. His family had settled there from Kentucky. His family had been slave-staters.

"Are you surprised, with that background?" murmured Aunty Em, eyebrow raised.

"Hmmm," said Miss Francis, without commitment. Aunty Em did not know that Miss Francis's parents had favored the South.

"And how is my dear little charge progressing?" said Aunty Em, gazing on Dorothy with fondness.

It was the moment Dorothy dreaded. The bilious cornbread went round and round in her mouth. It was supposed to be a treat, to have tea with Miss Francis.

"Well," said Miss Francis looking around, pressing down a smile. "Everything Dorothy does is as neat as wax."

"You should see her at her chores," said Aunty Em, nodding.

"All her work is quite brilliantly presented," said Miss Francis, "but it must be said that the content of her figure work and ciphering is not what it should be."

"Dorothy, are you paying mind to your teacher?"

"Yes, Mmm," whispered Dorothy.

"Speak up, Dorothy," said Aunty Em. "Sit up straight, and pay

Miss Francis the compliment of your regard." She turned back to her ally.

"Dorothy is always beautifully behaved, a very model in all respects," said Miss Francis, still smiling at Dorothy. "Except one. She is still stone silent. She does not put herself forward. Nor does she appear to fraternize with the other children."

"Even now," sighed Aunty Em, looking at the table in sadness and concern. "It is the tragedy, hanging over her."

Dorothy was so weary of being reminded of her tragedy. She did not remember it. It was a universe ago. She did not remember the old house, she sometimes forgot she had once had a little brother, and her mother was the flattest and dimmest of memories. She had long ago given up dreaming that her father might come for her one day and take her away. Her father didn't know or care. It came as something of a surprise to remember that he was still alive, Dorothy had grown so used to telling everyone that he was dead. The tragedy, as Aunty Em called it, seemed to have nothing to do with her.

"Perhaps also," said Aunty Em, "it is that the other children do not wish to mix with her."

Aunty Em was coming to blame the rough local children of Zeandale. They ran barefoot in the dust and stole fruit from orchards and raided wildlife by the river. All sorts of mischief, while her Dorothy sat at home and polished and sewed and scrubbed and grew beautifully less.

Then Professor Hungerford left teaching to take advantage of all his many connections. He opened a business, offering abstraction and insurance. Aunty Em's loyalty to Miss Francis persisted for two years. Dorothy sat in the kitchen silent and still, sinking even deeper into a scholastic quagmire. Aunty Em felt compelled to ask Miss Francis to dinner.

Aunty Em told Miss Francis that something had to be done about Dorothy before it was too late. It was no reflection whatsoever on Miss Francis's program, but it was time that the child was given a different and more varied setting. With Professor Lantz now in charge, and Mrs. DeEtta Warren as his assistant, Aunty Em now had renewed confidence in Manhattan education. Miss Francis could do nothing but concur and skillfully manage to disguise a measure of relief.

So, though Zeandale now had a stone schoolhouse as well, Emma Gulch sent her quiet little mouse of a ward all the way to Manhattan rather than have her educated in the country. This was considered by the other farmers to be of a piece with the rest of her behavior.

It fell to Henry Gulch to take her in. All through the autumn of 1881, he and Dorothy would be up with the dawn. Through the long gentle ride to Manhattan, they would see the sun rise on fields and in forest. They would see the birds, though Uncle Henry would not insist on Dorothy naming them. He would let the birds be themselves. He let Dorothy be as quiet as she wanted to be, finally resting from work, her books in a bundle in the back, out of her arms. Often she fell asleep, leaning against him, listening to the plod of the horse's hooves in the dust.

Aunty Em was running the farm now, and running it well. It was prospering, and they did have hogs and they did have horses. There were plans finally to build an extension. Nothing grand, just a summer kitchen for Aunty Em to cook in during hot weather so that the single room in which they slept and ate would stay cool.

Winter came and was a bad one. Dorothy and Uncle Henry shared the same lap robes and jostled their feet on the hot stones taken out of the oven. They huddled together, and he tickled her. Uncle Henry tickled Dorothy and started to laugh, with broken teeth.

One night, in the middle of that winter, Dorothy started to bleed. She woke all wet and sticky down there. Something dreadful had happened. There would be blood on her nightdress, blood on her sheets. Bad blood, it was as if her bad blood were leaking out of her. Had she done anything unwittingly down there to cut herself? How could she explain to Aunty Em that she was bleeding down there for no reason?

It would require desperate action. She would have to say she had cut her hand. That would explain the blood on the sheets, perhaps, but not the blood on her nightdress. It was wet around her middle, there was no saying that was from her hand. Dorothy, who was always neat and tidy, who hated to see anything flow, was appalled at the mess she felt all around her.

She would have to burn the nightdress.

Very slowly she slipped out from under the blankets. The mattress rustled. She stood up, already in an agony of chill, but she could not put on her shoes for they would clump on the floor. She had to slip the nightdress off, over her head like a whisper. She nipped around the blanket that hung from the walls to divide the room and padded across the kitchen floor.

Dorothy knelt and lifted up and opened the door of the stove and threw the nightdress in, over the black and orange embers. She could see the steam of her breath in the faint light. Her bare legs rose up in goosebumps and her teeth began to rattle against each other.

"What are you doing?" demanded Aunty Em. Dorothy spun away and pushed the hot iron door shut with her hand. Had Aunty Em seen her, crouching naked in the light? Had she seen what she had done? Dorothy's throat went tight with terror and cold. She could hardly breathe. She couldn't talk.

"She's just feeding the stove, Em," said Uncle Henry. "She just wants to keep us warm."

"Well, be careful with the fuel," said Em. There was the sound of settling down under the bedclothes. Dorothy leapt into her bed, shaking for warmth and other kinds of shelter. How would she get up in the morning without being seen? What if the nightdress did not burn? What if it was found in the morning, laying cold on top of the coals? And what, what if she hadn't stopped bleeding? What if she bled to death? Dorothy began to weep, curling her lips inward and pressing them shut so no sound would escape. Her hand. She would have to cut her hand. Dorothy cursed herself for forgetting to bring back a kitchen knife. But how would she explain the cut of a knife in the middle of the night? What was she to do?

Then Dorothy knew what she had to do. She placed the thick flesh below her thumb into her mouth. That would satisfy Aunty Em. That would propitiate her. As her teeth overcame the resistance of her flesh, Dorothy had a single thought that mingled comfort and distress.

The thought was this: at least Aunty Em had not seen her naked. But Uncle Henry had seen her. He had been lying awake in the night.

Dorothy never remembered when it began. One day, she got snow deep into her boots. Her toes were an agony. Beyond a certain point, cold burns as harshly as fire. Dorothy wept with cold all the way home, scurrying into the winter kitchen in a kind of flatfooted shuffle. She dropped down on the floor and tried to tear off the boots, but her hands were white and blue and as lifeless as sausages. She could not undo the laces. Uncle Henry knelt in front of her and pulled the boots off and rubbed her bare feet.

"Poor little toes," he said, smiling tenderly at them.

After school, when he met her at the bridge over the river, he would walk out to her, and back to the cart, holding her hand. Sometimes if the cold was too bad, if she couldn't talk, he swept her up in his arms and carried her, and how grateful Dorothy was. She didn't even mind when he suddenly kissed her, his mouth full of dead and rotting, reeking teeth.

The snows melted, and the road to the farm became a muddy track, mashed up by wheel tracks and the back-and-forth marching of their own boots. They would go into the barn sometimes before going into the house. Henry would grin naughtily and pull Dorothy in with him. They both understood. They were escaping from Em. They would play together in the straw. He would begin to tickle her, again. It was not so much fun, being tickled all the time.

When did it begin? Dorothy never remembered, it crept up on them so stealthily. One day he did not meet her at the bridge in the evening. The Allens were passing by, laden with stores. What was Henry Gulch thinking of, leaving the child to wait in a winter afternoon with cold descending? Up here with us, Dorothy, they said, though they had never been particularly kind to Dorothy before. Kindness foxed Dorothy. It made her go wary and suspicious. She did not even know that she was enraged at Uncle Henry.

When the Allens let her off, Dorothy went into the barn to find him. Uncle Henry's back was to the door. He wasn't doing any chores, he had no tools in his hand; he had simply been standing with his back to the door. And then he turned and looked at Dorothy as if he hated her.

What have I done now? thought Dorothy in dismay. She had come to think of Uncle Henry as her only friend, even if he did smell. Henry glowered at her, darkly, and he seemed to loom larger in the half-light. He seemed to fill the lopsided crib they graced with the name of barn. His eyes burned. Dorothy said nothing. She shook her head, trying to say: I've done nothing. I didn't know I'd done anything.

I didn't mean to do anything. Henry stood stock-still, full of what looked like rage.

Dorothy crept back toward the house. Every limb felt weighted down by cold. She wanted to lie down and die. Whatever was wrong with her, the bad blood, had done it again. Even Uncle Henry hated her. She thumped slowly up into the wooden house.

"Evening, Dorothy," said Aunty Em briskly, looking up from her account book. She wore little round spectacles, and her eyes blinking behind them looked huge, like a frog's. "Nice day at school?"

"Yes, Mmm."

"Nice drive back with your uncle?"

Aunty Em didn't know. Aunty Em didn't know Henry had not come for her. That must mean he really hated her, to do that and not tell Em. He must not have ever wanted her to come back.

"Yes, Mmm," replied Dorothy, devastated. The house seemed to be made of bone.

"Once you've got yourself warmed up, there's some cuts I fetched up from the cellar for frying. They've still got enough lard on them, so you won't need to use any more. Waste not, want not."

Aunty Em went back to her business. Dorothy cooked the evening meal, watching her hands move, as if they were someone else's. The months-old pork, sealed in its own lard, was gray and flabby and slightly damp from delayed putrescence. Dorothy watched it smoke and steam. There was a scar on the bottom of her thumb. She took rags to bed with her at night. She watched the smoke rise and wished her bad blood could be similarly consumed, burned clean. She wished she could be burned clean. Perhaps if she drank carbolic, that would burn her clean from the inside, and then she would die clean.

Uncle Henry clumped into the house, with eyes as desperate as butterflies flitting. He was smiling. It was a thin smile, keen and sharp, and his movements were changed. Gone was the dear, slow, sad Henry. This man flickered, hands and eyes darting. Dorothy passed him a plate of food and he did not look at her. When she sat down, he turned away, crossing his legs in the other direction. Dorothy ate the tired old pork as if it were her due. It tasted of old wooden floors and rancid fat. They would all smell each other, all through the night.

"That was a right smart supper, Dodo, thank you," said Aunty Em, with a smile. The only thing Dorothy knew about dodos was that they were extinct.

"Don't you worry about the washing-up," said Aunty Em. "You just get on with your home studies. Henry, please could we clear a space for Dodo's books?"

Henry said nothing, but stood up and went out into the night.

Aunty Em looked at Dorothy, smiling crookedly. "I surely hope he manages to produce something tonight."

They were all bound up tighter than drums with pork and no vegetables. Aunty Em's face was kind. It was taking Dorothy into her confidence, as if she were almost an adult. This confused Dorothy mightily. No! she thought. It's too soon for that. She didn't want to be treated like an adult. She wanted to be treated like a child. She wanted to be sat on someone's knee and be told a story; she wanted to sit on someone's knee and do nothing, leave the work behind.

"Dorothy," chuckled Aunty Em. "No need to be shocked, child, there are some things that are perfectly natural to talk about sometimes." She stroked Dorothy's hair with fondness.

"Now you get settled in," said Em with a sigh, and stood up and collected the dishes with a fine clattering of clay.

The next morning Henry got up and gave her a ride in to school, and neither of them mentioned that he had left her alone, waiting at the bridge. They sat coldly side by side but at a distance. He did not even ask her how she had found her way home.

Dorothy passed the day at school in even deeper silence than usual, hugging the books that she yearned to lose forever.

In the afternoon, she walked back down Poyntz and along the road toward the bridge. She had made plans. If Henry was not there, she would slip back into the school and sleep by one of the stoves. But Uncle Henry was there, blue in the dusk, waiting for her, holding the horse's lead.

And that night, as he led the horse and the cart toward the barn, he grabbed her wrist, and pulled her with him. Inside the barn, he held her to him and blurted out a kind of a sob. He rested his shaggy, smelly head on her shoulder and neck, and his cheeks were damp and he pressed her to him.

He did love her after all. Dorothy went weak from gratitude. She hugged him back, and his huge, rough hands pushed her even closer to him. The whole length of his body was against her, and he kissed her cheek. Was he saying he was sorry? He must be. Dorothy kissed him back. She meant to kiss him on the cheek, but he turned his head and their mouths met. That startled Dorothy and she jumped back. He worked her shoulder, and his smile crumpled and went grim. He turned away, and Dorothy wondered again if she had done wrong.

The next day, the ride was joyful. Uncle Henry sang old campfire songs. Dorothy had never seen him like that. She giggled and he turned his eyes toward her and they had a sparkle she had never seen before. It suddenly occurred to her that Uncle Henry had once been young. He would have been a young, broad-shouldered man with sparkling eyes. And bad teeth.

So when did it begin? Every evening in the barn, or sometimes in the woods, when it was dark, he would pull the wagon to a stop, and hidden under lap robes, he would tickle her. Dorothy was getting bored with being prodded and tickled. Henry kept looking back and forth up the road as if it were something naughty, something bad. She pitied him. Poor Henry, old Henry, she thought, and she hugged him. Was that bad? He was just hugging her, and he loved her, so was it bad?

His hands were blunt and large and rough. They kept rubbing her shoulders. When did they begin to rub her legs?

She remembered him cupping both her tiny breasts in his hands. "Pretty little things," he had said, forlornly. Even then, Dorothy was not sure that it was bad. He looked into her eyes. His eyes were blue and large, cold and soft at the same time, and his cheeks were always bright red on deep brown and covered with tiny purple veins all over the surface. He looked lost.

"Do you like it when I touch you there?" he asked.

She didn't like it, not really at all. It was private and it wasn't nice, but he was Henry and he loved her.

"You're so kind, Dorothy. You're so good to old Henry."

One evening in the barn, his trousers came down, and she saw his thing, and she knew then that this was bad.

"No, honey, no, Dorothy, don't look away, don't look away from old Henry. Here, look, I put it away, see?"

The only thing that Dorothy had thought was good about her life was bad. All her life was bad; it was something to do with her. She must be bad, if this was what happened. The thought of her badness made her go still. It must have made him go still too.

He didn't do it right away. He tried to hold off. But it was too much for him, alone with the flat wilderness, his drying fields, and Em.

Finally he did it, quickly, in the barn, while Em sat with her books. The thought of her own badness made Dorothy go small and still. Dorothy looked at the straw and the wooden beams and knew that everything would change. When he was done, he was scared. He pulled up his trousers and began to weep. "Oh God, oh salvation. There's no praying that can heal this."

She knew it was truly terrible then. Dorothy watched, as if pork were frying. He did not look at her. He will hate me now, she knew. She was ready. It was all she deserved. There was more blood. More bad blood. She was so full of that bad blood, it just oozed out of her.

"You better get into the house," he murmured, looking away from her.

That night at dinner there was a terrible silence. Even Em could sense it. She was full of rage. It was Aunty Em's turn to cook and she banged down the plates and the coffeepot. She had boiled up some jerky and some dried corn and that was all they had to eat. Dorothy thought she must have seen them, that she must know. The silence was terrible, but Em did not notice anything unusual. For Em, the silence was always there, and always terrible. Em was oblivious to her own rage, but Dorothy ate in suspense. Later, Dorothy went out into the darkness and threw up, quietly, so Em couldn't hear. There is no pit, Dorothy thought, no hole in the ground deep enough and black enough to cover me. There was a hook on which they hung the bodies of the hogs. It went right up through their guts. Dorothy thought of putting the hook through herself.

Once again, Henry did not come for her after school. Dorothy had known that he would not. He'll be scared, she thought, beginning to feel contempt for him. He'll keep well away. He might be so scared, he won't do it again. Either way, she knew she could no longer count on Henry for anything. He might send her away. He might want to keep her near and do it again. He might ignore her and pretend that nothing had happened. There was nothing good that either one of them could do. She hitched a ride home with Max Jewell. He had grown up nice and polite and was very interested in Dorothy. He asked her all sorts of questions about Manhattan and tried to catch her eye. Dorothy saw Uncle Henry in him and answered coldly, yes or no.

It took a week. Uncle Henry let other people take her back home for a whole week. Neither one of them said anything to Aunty Em.

Max had found repeated excuses to come out to town, in order to give her a lift back. That in itself was ominous. It might be good to discourage Max.

Finally Uncle Henry showed up, waiting at the bridge. Max was there too. Max called hello to Henry, somewhat unwillingly, and his quick crumpled smile in Dorothy's direction was one of apology. Max assumed quite rightly that she might not want to ride with some smelly old man.

Dorothy felt herself go into abeyance. She watched herself. What, she wondered, am I going to do? She saw herself climb down from Max's wagon.

"Thank you, Max," she murmured. It sounded like a farewell.

She got into the wagon. Henry waved Max away. Henry pulled hard on the reins to keep the wagon still. Henry waited until Max was out of sight, disappearing over the top of Prospect.

"We don't share no blood," Henry said solemnly. "We're not blood kin."

That meant nothing to Dorothy. Did he mean that he had no bad blood? Did he mean that only she did? She waited, as an animal waits when it is cornered by a predator.

"I'm just older than you, that's all." He tried to smile, but there was a shaking in him. "You aren't going to do nothing, are you, Dorothy? You aren't going to go away, are you? 'Cause old Henry, he needs you. You are the light of his life. You are the only beautiful thing. And a man needs that, Dorothy."

He paused and looked at the wall of trees, full of spring buds, climbing the side of the hill. The buds gathered together on the trees looked from a distance like a slightly purple mist. "We'll have to be careful of her. We'll just have to watch our step. In summer, the corn will be as high as you like."

He means we'll do it in the corn, thought Dorothy. He'll wait for me here, and we'll go into the corn. He wants to go on doing it.

"She can't live forever."

He wants Aunty Em to die.

Then he gave her a ride home, a chaste distance from her. It was already late, so they walked into the house, Dorothy first, Henry a few minutes later. Chores, he told Dorothy. Got a few things to do. You just go right on in. He was lying.

The next day, they went into the barn. "I got to do it," said

Henry, grinning. "I just can't keep away. You are a wicked, wicked little thing." He smiled and rubbed his nose against her, and she went still and cold and quiet as ice.

"You like that, you like that, don't you?" he said, and it made no difference that she didn't answer.

It went on and on and Henry got rougher and rougher with his raw hands. Yes, I'm bad, thought Dorothy. I'm bad, I'm bad, I'm bad. She could feel herself twist inside. She hated Henry's smell, she hated his body, she hated the barn. And she wanted Aunty Em to see them.

She wanted Aunty Em to see them, so bad she could taste it. Her so God-fearing, her so church-loving, to walk in and see her husband pig-backing a kid, pig-backing me, doing what you should be doing Em, you old dried piece of beef jerky. You should see this. I can just hear you yelping.

So she pulled up Henry's shirt, and she pushed his trousers down, so that there would be no mistaking. No one hugs a child with their milk-white bottom bare in early spring unless they're doing that.

And one day, muddy, bleak, not so cold, his trousers were down around his knees, and he kept pulling them up, chuckling, "Don't do that, honey," and Aunty Em yelled out, real close to the barn.

"Henry, where are you?"

Henry gasped and ducked away, scuttled around behind the bales of hay. Dorothy stayed where she was. Her dress fell back down by itself, but she would not have pulled it down. Her flannels were still down around her thighs. She leaned against the post and waited.

Aunty Em came in, carrying a pan. Mocking her, Dorothy made a coy little-girl motion with her hips and head. Little old me do anything wrong?

"You seen your uncle?" Em asked.

"Sure, he's just around there," said Dorothy and pointed.

Em looked between Dorothy and the hay. "What you doing there?" said Em to Henry. "Why didn't you answer?"

Henry stood up. Down on his knees, he had managed to hoist and fasten his trousers. "Thought I saw a rat," said Henry, looking straight at Dorothy. Dorothy's eyes went wide. Did I do something wrong, Uncle?

"Well, get up off the floor and tell me when we can get into Manhattan. I can't use this pan. It's finally gone through."

"Friday. We'll go Friday."

"High time too. Dorothy, if you're through in here, come in and sweep up."

"She'll be 'long momently, Em," said Uncle Henry. "She's doing some chores in here for me."

"All right, but send her along." Aunty Em left, sensing something too big to even acknowledge. She left scowling.

Pause. Dorothy looked at Henry, with that cold curiosity.

He took two steps toward her and whupped her right across the mouth and onto the floor. Dorothy tasted blood, in triumph. Yup, yup, that was right. That was what it was. Now she could hate him.

"What the hell are you trying to do?" he said, whispering, shaking in fear. "You want her to know or something?"

"Did I do something wrong, Uncle Henry?" she asked in a little-girl voice. "She asked where you were and I told her."

"You just keep quiet. You just keep quiet about everything. Oh Jesus!" He hid his face.

"What am I going to tell her about my mouth?" she said. Dorothy puffed out her lips as she spoke to make it sound as though she were hurt worse than she was, all swollen.

"Tell her you fell. You're pretty good at making up stories."

"Like you are, Uncle," said Dorothy very quietly.

She was silent and smiling, and she knew that the smile said: Why should I lie for you? Give me a reason. Then she spoke.

"You gonna bring me back something nice from Manhattan?" she said.

Uncle Henry looked scared again. He leaned over and helped her up. He started to brush her dress. "Yeah, yeah, I'll do that."

Dorothy smiled sweetly at him, so that he could see all her teeth were red.

"Dorothy, I'm sorry I hit you, but you almost got us . . ." He could not imagine what would have happened. "Honey, we got to keep quiet about this. We got to keep as still as mice. It's like it's our own little world. It can't touch the other world at all."

"Okay, Uncle Henry."

He looked at her with love and great misgiving. His eyes were saying: What have I got myself into?

"I better go in," said Dorothy.

I got them dancing, thought Dorothy. I got Aunty Em with a pin through her, squirming like a butterfly, and she don't even know it. And Uncle Henry, he's just got to be so careful. All I got to do is make sure nobody knows, and I can just keep pushing pins.

She stopped at the barn door and turned. "Tell Aunty Em that I need some new boots," she said.

I'm bad, she thought, rejoicing. I'm wicked, I'm evil. I'm the Devil's own.

"You can get them for me, when you go to Manhattan," she said, and went into the house. She burned the pork, deliberately, burned it black, and she was smiling all the time.

The next day, or the day after that, in Manhattan, at school, a pretty little girl fell in the schoolyard and started to cry.

Aw, thought Dorothy. You poor little thing you. Is that all you got to cry about? Is that the only reason you have to cry?

Dorothy grinned and pretended to help the little girl up. She was so little and so thin and Dorothy was so big. She could feel her size.

"Does it hurt?" she cooed, and sliced the edge of her nails down the girl's wrist. The little girl looked up in bewildered horror.

"Hurt?" asked Dorothy, and wrenched the flesh of the wrist in two directions at once, wrung it like a cloth.

The little girl wailed.

"Shut up," whispered Dorothy, and punched her as hard as she could in the stomach. The little girl doubled up and went quiet.

Dorothy looked at the pretty white dress and had an inspiration. "You got any money? Give me some money. I'll stop if you give me some money."

The little girl wept in silence.

Dorothy put her nails against her cheek. "You better give me some," she warned her, and chuckled suddenly. "It's going to be real bad if you don't."

The feeble little girl reached for a pretty little purse kept inside her glove. Dorothy took it from her. "Tell your mother you dropped it," she said. "And you better not snitch, or I'll follow you home and whup you so bad you can't walk."

The other kids said that Dorothy Gael was farm dirt. They said she was poor and had fleas. They said she smelled, which she did, and they refused to sit next to her in class. I can shut you all up, Dorothy realized. There's nothing I won't do to shut you all up.

She was swollen with discovery. She hung up her coat and scarf right next to the other kids'.

"Ew!" they cried with gestures of disgust.

She very quietly grabbed one of them by the throat. She had chosen a boy, one of the bigger ones. She throttled him. She cut off his supply of air, and then relinquished just enough to hear him gasp.

"You want to fight?" she whispered. She shoved him away from her, into the wall. She turned and spat on his coat. "You ought to be more careful with your clothes, Sam," she told him. She looked around at the others. "Any of you little chickens tells, I'll come for you."

Dorothy turned away with complete confidence. If anything happened to her slimy old coat, she wouldn't mind. She wouldn't mind, and she'd beat them all hollow on the way home.

Dorothy walked down between the rows of desks, feeling like a queen. And there was Larry Johnson, pug-faced Larry who always made the jokes. Well, well, well. His desktop was lifted open. She slammed it down as hard as she could on his fingers.

No matter how tough he was, he had to yelp. "Ow!" Everyone turned. They saw Larry Johnson, sitting, looking up at Dorothy Gael, who loomed over him. They saw Larry Johnson having to fight to stop the tears, and he was big, in the eighth grade. A ripple of fear passed through them, as if across the surface of a pond. The people from the cloakroom came in, whispering. Dorothy Gael sat down and raked them all with her eyes. There's going to be some changes hereabouts, her eyes told them.

There was another poor, fat, ugly girl. She had a smile like a rat's. The other little girl saw her chance. She saw how it was done. Curiously enough, her name was Em too, just like Dorothy's aunt. When the teacher, Mr. Clark, came in, she raised her hand and asked, "Sir, can I move my desk next to Dorothy's?"

A sigh came from the class, a sigh of loathing. The two misbegotten were teaming up together. It was an alliance against them all, and they knew it. The teacher considered. Dorothy was dangerously isolated, he thought. He wanted Em to stay in the front of the class where he could keep an eye on her, but anyone being friendly to Dorothy Gael was a change for the better.

So this second Emma moved, cradling up her textbooks and slate. "All these slimy little Two-shoes," she whispered to Dorothy.

"Yeah," said Dorothy, with authority.

So it went, into summer. The corn came through. Couple of times a week, Dorothy and Henry in the shed. Sometimes he would drive the cart into the woods on Prospect. Dorothy would lie under the trees and remember the days when she went to Sunflower School. School had only been a half-mile walk across the fields then. As she walked, the birds, the red-winged blackbirds, would leap up into the air ahead of her, and the Jewells' cat Rusty Hinge would slink out from the corn and mew and come up to have his head scratched. In summer, the corn would move its leaves, and quail would run across the path. Sometimes the pinch bugs bit, but you soon got over that.

The children each planted a tree around the schoolhouse and that tree was named after them. It was as if a piece of each child had been left behind to grow.

Dorothy would lie down on the ground with Uncle Henry covering her, and she would look past his face. The trees would lean over as if in sympathy, and Dorothy would let her spirit fly up to them, to hide amid their leaves, to reside in them. She would make herself part of them. She felt herself bend and sigh with them; she felt buds and soft green leaves at the tips of her extremities. She was out of reach of Uncle Henry then. He could not touch her then. She was a tree. There were trees called Dorothy all over the hillsides.

In summer the corn came up and they would lie down between the rows. Henry brought a sack along for her to lie on. So the dirt wouldn't show, and she would look away from his face and up at the underside of the corn and see the fluted ridges of its leaves, the dance of the low afternoon sun through them. The hiss and rattle of the wind in the corn seemed to call her name.

Sometimes he would call her back. He would try to make her speak. She couldn't even hear what he said. You stink, Henry, she thought. You got wrinkles all over. You farmer. You stink like a hog.

"Do you love me, Dorothy?" he asked her.

"Course I do," she told him.

Manhattan, Kansas

1882

In a show of rebellion, Adolf decided to run away from home. Somehow Alois learned of these plans and locked the boy upstairs. During the night, Adolf tried to squeeze through the barred window. He couldn't quite make it, so took off his clothes. As he was wriggling his way to freedom, he heard his father's footsteps on the stairs and hastily withdrew, draping his nakedness with a tablecloth. This time Alois did not punish him with a whipping. Instead, he burst into laughter and shouted to Klara to come up and look at the "toga boy." The ridicule hurt Adolf more than any switch, and it took him, he confided to Frau Hanfstaengl, "a long time to get over the episode."

Years later he told one of his secretaries that he had read in an adventure novel that it was proof of courage to show no pain. And so "I resolved not to make a sound the next time my father whipped me. And when the time came—I can still remember my frightened mother standing outside the door—I silently counted the blows. My mother thought I had gone crazy when I beamed proudly and said, 'Father hit me thirty-two times!'"

—JOHN TOLAND, *Adolf Hitler,* as quoted in
For Your Own Good: The Roots of Violence in Child-rearing
by Alice Miller

Dorothy and Emma, her little ally, came to be called the Furies, or the Kindly Ones. The schoolteachers called them that. The schoolteachers knew Greek.

The teachers made sure no other children sat near the Furies. If a child did, and she had nice long hair, it would be tied to the back of her chair in so many knots that the hair would have to be cut off. Pockets were found full of ink. Cowpats were placed on the seats of chairs. The Furies talked to each other, loudly, while the teacher, Mr. Clark, spoke. At least Mr. Clark was better-looking than Henry. Dorothy hated him, too. The Furies developed a horrible screeching laugh that they used together. The other children went still with fear.

The schoolteachers knew Greek and that gave them the right to beat children. The boys, that is, were regularly beaten. It was thought to be good for them. Toughen them up. Some boys, the timid ones, were very difficult to beat, because they didn't do anything wrong. Even the teachers thought they were sissies.

"Can't stand a kid without any gumption," they might say. "That Jenks needs a hiding, just to wake him up."

And the chance would finally come. Somebody would throw a spitball, and blame Jenks. Mr. Clark would pretend to believe him. Mr. Clark was kind. He believed that beating Jenks would be for his own good, to make him less different from the other boys.

"Why did you do it, Jenks?" Mr. Clark asked, silkily. The other children squawked with laughter. The Furies screeched. They all knew the game that was being played.

"I did not do it, Sir," said Jenks, appalled.

"Did he do it, class?" asked Mr. Clark.

"Yes!" the class shouted.

It was very gratifying. Jenks began to cry. "But I didn't, Sir. I didn't do it!"

"Why should you be treated any different than anyone else, Jenks?" Mr. Clark asked. "Jenks, I think we better go to the Principal's office."

There was a theatrical gasp from the children. Jenks was going to get the Strap. The children terrified themselves deliciously with tales of the Strap. They said it had spikes on the end. It was a dark and terrible thing. Jenks began to blubber with fear. "Mr. Clark," he begged, his voice a whine.

"Angela. Take charge of the class, please." Angela was Class Monitor, a two-edged sword, who led the mayhem when he was out of the room, and then organized the tidying up before he came in, so that he did not have to deal with it. He knew that. The class knew he knew that. The class knew he secretly approved of a bit of mayhem as long as it was kept absolutely hidden.

Angela sat on the teacher's desk. "Jenks, getting the Strap. I never. I never would."

"They won't give him the Strap," someone said, knowingly. Jenks's grades were too good.

"They have to now, Mr. Clark said he would, and it would look too bad if he didn't. Who else do we want to have the Strap?"

Dorothy barked out a laugh and stood up. She looked at them all with undisguised scorn. "All of you. All of you little smarty-pants. You all think it's so great. I'd like to take you all and whip your asses."

Silence.

Jenks came back into the room with a face the color of sandstone from weeping. He couldn't sit down. But the class didn't laugh at him or tease him. They didn't lean forward whispering out of the corner of their mouths, asking him about the exploit. Something was wrong. The class looked cowed and silent. "Thank you, Angela," Mr. Clark said. He thought perhaps that Angela had simply kept them firmly in line.

Or maybe, maybe they hadn't thought it was right. Well then, if Jenks didn't do it, they should have told me the truth.

That Dorothy Gael, the children thought. We got to do something about that Dorothy Gael.

But the terror of the Strap meant there was one unbreakable rule: You never told, you never snitched. They couldn't snitch, and if they did, what would Dorothy do, what revenge would she extract? What, what could they do about Dorothy?

One day in spring term, her ally, Emma, said something. That was what broke it. Nobody knew for certain what it was that Emma said. She whispered it, but it sure was something Dorothy Gael didn't like. Em had trusted Dorothy a bit too much and grown too familiar. She teased her about something, her size, maybe, or her shoes, her dress. Maybe it was something about her family. Evangeline Thomas claimed she heard Emma whisper the word "Henry."

There was the word "Henry" and Dorothy Gael's face twisted up like a painting of the Devil, and her lips pulled back in concentrated hatred, and she slapped Emma across the face. The noise was so loud that Mr. Clark dropped his chalk. Emma wailed in shock.

"Dorothy Gael. Did you hit her?" Mr. Clark knew that this was his chance.

Dorothy said nothing. Her face was puffed out like an adder, arrested in an expression of utter rage and turmoil that unmanned Mr. Clark for a moment. He had never seen an expression like it on a child's face.

"Did anyone see what happened?" Mr. Clark asked.

That's when it broke. "No," said Angela, the two-edged sword. Her arms were folded. She had decided. The time had come. "But Dorothy is always doing things like that."

"She picks on people."

"She makes Amy Hugson give her money, and if she doesn't she hurts her real bad."

"She put cowpat all over Tommy's face."

"She hits people all the time."

In chorus, like a Greek tragedy.

"Dorothy Gael, is all of this true?"

The terrible head turned toward him. Not a Fury, he thought. A Gorgon. A glance turns to stone.

"Why are you asking me, Clark?" the child said. No "Mister," just a hard, blunt last name like in a bar room.

The child was smiling at him. "Everything I say is a lie. I got to lie all the time."

Mr. Clark was thinking he had never seen the like of it for pure evil.

Dorothy was thinking: My uncle does that to me every day in the dirt. Is that the truth you want to hear?

"Dorothy. You're going to come with me to the Principal's office."

There was no gasp, just silence. The children were almost sorry then. Girls did not get the Strap. This was a real change. Girls keenly felt the distinction of Straplessness both as a privilege and a penance. In part, they wanted to be beaten because it was an approved achievement that was denied them. But now that it was happening, the change, the revolution, was shocking. They were too young to have seen many changes.

"Let's go then," said Dorothy Gael. She almost sounded bored. As she walked up the aisle, she bumped her hips from side to side to say, That's what I think of you all.

The children had another shock. Mr. Clark boxed her ear. "You stop acting up," he said. The child stared back at him stony-faced. What else you going to do? the expression seemed to ask, as if she were invulnerable.

Mr. Clark marched her to Professor Lantz's office. There had to be a Principal and he had to be a man, so that there could be a Strap.

"I think the time has come to give Dorothy Gael what she's been asking for," said Mr. Clark.

The Principal was older, fatter, with ridiculous gray whiskers that went from one end of his face to another. He wore checked trousers. He leaned forward in his chair and adopted a smooth and soothing voice that was supposed to sound wise.

"Dorothy. I think you know why this is being done. You know the sorts of things you've been doing. This is happening because the other children have finally decided that they have to turn to us to discipline you. Are you sorry for what you have done?"

"No," said Dorothy.

The Principal sighed and looked at Mr. Clark and his female assistant, Mrs. Warren.

"You've brought this on yourself, Dorothy."

"Can we just get it over with?"

There had to be a woman present. The Principal had already taken legal advice. And he could not beat a little girl across her bottom. The proprieties had to be observed. It had to be across the hand—or the wrist if the child tried to pull away. The wrist was far more painful. All the children knew it was up to them not to pull their hands away.

"Hold out your hand."

Dorothy presented it. Mrs. Warren grabbed the fingers and held them flat. The eyes behind Mrs. Warren's spectacles were like tiny pebbles. The Principal struck, using a one-inch-wide leather Strap. It sounded worse than it was. He didn't strike too hard at first. He looked into the child's eyes for some sign of contrition. All he saw was rebellion. He struck again, looking this time for pain. The face went red, but there was no surrender. He hit her ten times. The hand was released.

Her eyes were full of heart-stilling hatred.

"One day," the child whispered, "I'm going to be bigger than you are and I'm going to break your nose."

"The other hand," said the Principal. He got more satisfaction this time. The face went red on the first stroke, and involuntarily, Dorothy tried to pull away. She decided she could not absorb the pain after all. She began to struggle; her hand and wrist darted about. All right then, be it on you, thought the Principal. The Strap lashed her about the wrist. Welts and little purple dots showed on the skin. He had to stop after another ten. They had never given more than ten to any child.

Dorothy Gael's face was puffed out like a serpent's, but she held her tears. Her hands were claws. Professor Lantz looked at her, panting. They all looked at her. With immense effort, Dorothy Gael managed to smile.

"What do we do now?" asked Mr. Clark, who realized that the punishment had done no good.

The Principal shook his head. "Take her back."

The child walked ahead of Mr. Clark down the hall. He could see her hunched and tense, determined not to cry. He had to hand it to her. She was tough. They made them tough in Kansas. She stopped just outside the classroom door.

"Open the door, Dorothy," he said.

"I can't," she answered him, with mere impatience. How stupid are you? she seemed to say. My hands have been beaten raw.

Mr. Clark understood then that they had made a terrible mistake, a tactical error. They had not punished Dorothy Gael. He saw her gather herself in. He opened the door and watched her enter in triumph.

She was smiling, beaming, and she held up both hands in triumph, both arms raised so that all the class could see the welts and the blood.

"What are you going to do now?" she asked them in a silky voice she had learned from the teachers. "There's nothing they can do to me. There's nothing any of you can do to me."

The class and Mr. Clark understood then that they had created a monster. And monsters have to be appeased.

Little Emma, the ally, had been whipped into line. She had learned never to tease Dorothy again and she knew that she was nothing without Dorothy. The second Fury was more than content to be Dorothy's lieutenant. And the teacher and the class let the Furies talk, and they let the Furies laugh. Angela began to lose power. Mr. Clark was helpless. Teaching became impossible. He dreaded going into the classroom. He knew he had failed the children, failed to protect them, and they saw no reason now to take him seriously. They all began to call him Clark, last name only. He became ill.

That's how they got the Substitute Teacher. The children knew the Substitute was not a real teacher because he was so soft. He had a round and smiling, handsome face, and he was young, only about ten years older than them. He had a lovely voice, very warm and soft and beguiling, and his movements were small and neat and quick. He wore a straw boater. He was like nothing the children of Kansas had seen.

He was, it turned out, an actor from New York. He told them about a play he had written called *The Maid of Arran* and he was touring with it and playing the lead role.

"Of course," he chuckled, "the handbills can't say written and directed and starring all the same person, so the posters say that the actor is called George Brooks."

What is your name? What is your name? all the children asked in chorus.

He chuckled, pleased. "Frank," he said.

You couldn't call a teacher by his first name!

"No!" the class chorused, laughing. "What's your last name?"

He told them, and Dorothy misheard. She thought his last name was Balm. Frank Balm. It was a meaning name.

"Honest Ointment!" shouted Larry Johnson, as if it were a quack medicine, and the actor bent forward with laughter.

"The original and genuine article. Every bottle is signed," grinned the Substitute. He sounded just like a hawker.

He lit a cheroot. In class, he lit a cigar. He sat on the desk and crossed his legs at the ankles, and he leaned back to let a serpent of cigar smoke rise up from his lips. There was a frisson of real excitement from the class, and the children looked at each other, eyes goggling.

"My other occupation," he continued, satisfied with the progress of the smoke, "was inventing chickens. I would breed new kinds of hen. My hens won awards. I even wrote about them. My new kind of Hamburg hen." He made a certain motion that may have been like a hen, or like something else. The children weren't sure what, except that it looked a little racy and made them laugh.

The Substitute had dash. He smelled of New York, he smelled of money, and he didn't care that teachers weren't supposed to smoke. He was small, what the children called a squirrel, but he was a nice squirrel. An unspoken agreement passed in silence around the class. As long as he doesn't try to make us do anything stupid, we'll be nice to this one.

Dorothy fell in love with him. My parents were actors, she wanted to tell him. They were like you.

She whispered the name to herself, all the way home. Frank, she thought, Frank, Frank, as her uncle put his hands on her and then moved them away again in fear. In summer evenings, there was too much light; they could be seen from too far away. Sometimes Uncle Henry didn't do anything, except smile and pat her knee. Tonight was one of those nights. All the trees seemed to whisper in gratitude. Could she plant a tree and call it Frank?

Frank, she whispered as she fried sausages. She thought of his smooth hands, his one clean suit, his funny hat, his groomed moustache, his light and pleasing tenor voice. She thought of his kind and handsome face. His name seemed to sum up everything that was missing from her life.

Frank, she thought, as she lay down that night. She thought of him, and she thought of her own unworthiness, and tears stung the lower edge of her eyes. It was as if she were in a boat cast adrift, never to come ashore to some green and happy land, where people laughed and everything was beautiful. She herself had cast the boat adrift, and there was no going back. Now she would never get home. Now she would never be where Frank was. He was too good for her. She began to hate him just a little. And said his name again.

The next day, the Substitute brought in a thick red book.

"How many of you," he asked them, "can speak Ottoman Turk?"

The class looked back at him in silence.

"Well, this is a book called the *Redhouse Osmanli–English Dictionary*, and it tells me what words are in Turkish. How many of you know anything about Turkey?"

Stupid question.

"Uh—you eat them at Thanksgiving," said Larry Johnson. The class laughed, somewhat shyly, because they knew they were ignorant. The Substitute smiled, too, lightly, happily.

"Turkey is a wonderful country," said the Substitute, his blue eyes going pale with wonder. "The Turks worship in huge domed buildings called *jamis*, bigger than any cathedral. Vast domes, with pigeons flying around inside and carpets on the floor and fountains where the faithful wash before worshiping. They have wonderful tiles on the walls, all blue and green. And the sultans have many wives and many concubines, so many that they all live together in beautiful prisons which no man may enter—or he'll be killed. In the palaces there are special fountains where executioners wash their swords."

This was very racy stuff indeed. The class was fascinated.

"Ask me a word in Osmanli," he whispered.

There was a shuffling and a shrugging of shoulders and birdlike exchange of nervous giggles.

"What's the word for sunflower?" asked Angela, who was brave.

"Moonflower," said the Substitute promptly, smiling with anticipation. He didn't have to look it up.

The class laughed, partly in relief that this was going to be fun, and partly from the pleasant strangeness of another language. It was like a mirror that reflected things backward.

"They pronounce it 'aychijayee,'" he said and turned and wrote it on the blackboard:

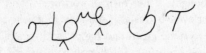

"It's the Arabic alphabet," he explained.

They asked him the word for hen and the word for school. Dorothy Gael put up her hand.

"What's the word," she asked, shyly, "for home?"

The Substitute blinked and then his face went soft. Just answer the question, thought Dorothy.

"*Ev*," said the Substitute. "*Ev* means 'home.'"

"What's your name in Turkish?" asked Larry Johnson, grinning.

The Substitute smiled, spun smartly on his heel and wrote, without hesitation:

Then he pronounced the word.

The class laughed in unison. "Ooze?" they asked.

He made a kind of embarrassed swallowing gesture. He pronounced it again. This time it sounded more like "Uz." "It means 'frank' in Turkish. And Frank's my name. It means a lot of other things as well. It means 'real and genuine.' It means 'pure and unadulterated.' It means 'kernel and cream,' and it means 'self.' It's the root word for 'yearning' and for 'homesickness' and for all the things that people want. It also happens to be the original name of the Turks. They were a tribe called the Uz, or the Uzbecks. Or the Oz, and they came out of the wilderness."

Dorothy was suddenly hauled out of herself by a gust of childish interest. "You mean like the Indians?" she blurted out, her voice loud and lacking in grace.

The class laughed until the Substitute, the full power of his smile trained on Dorothy, said, "Very like the Indians. They were desert nomads who lived in tents. They came out of the East and the North, they came out of the desert, and they conquered the Greeks and they conquered the Arabs. Turkey is a country where the Indians were the settlers. The Indians won."

He held up the book called *Redhouse*, like Red Indians, and he said, "And this is the Oz–English Dictionary."

The Substitute got bored just as quickly as the children did. The fire for Oz went out of his eyes, and he began to talk about other things. He told them the story of his play. He told them how it had run out of money, and how he was now "resting." They chuckled at his joke. "Mind you, actors are always resting. That is the attraction of the profession."

The class tested him. They mocked his New York accent. "I say, I am an actor from Noo Yawk."

He laughed. They waited. It wasn't a false laugh—that would have showed he was pretending to think it was funny so he wouldn't have to do anything about it. He didn't imitate them back, so he wasn't sarcastic or mean. And he didn't tell them it was wrong to make fun of people just because they were different, so he wasn't a pompous fool. Instead, he genuinely seemed to think it was funny.

He laughed and looked a bit mystified.

"Why," he asked, "is it that people laugh?" He asked it in wonder.

Was it a trick question? It seemed to be a pretty dumb one.

" 'Cause something's funny?" ventured one of the girls.

"Yes, but what do we mean by funny? I mean, what is funny?"

It was the sort of question a little kid about five would ask. Unanswerable. It was a real question, one the Substitute himself had no answer for.

Suddenly the Substitute was looking at Dorothy. He remembered her question about Indians, about home. It was as if he had recognized a kindred spirit. The look he gave her was questioning. He wanted a mystery solved, and he wanted to know more about her. The look, confiding and sincere, alarmed Dorothy. It was not unlike the look that Uncle Henry gave her.

"Dorothy," the Substitute asked. "Why do people laugh?"

"To show who's boss," said Dorothy Gael.

The smile of the Substitute slipped. "Yes, but for what other reason?"

Dorothy considered. "Sometimes it scares people."

"But your parents, why do they laugh?"

"My parents are dead," said Dorothy.

The nice squirrel looked stricken. "I'm so sorry."

"Why?" asked Dorothy. She was suddenly impatient with the Substitute. "I'm not sorry. Can't hardly even remember them. Nobody laughs around our place anyway."

"Nobody laughs?"

"Life's too hard," shrugged Dorothy. She wanted to shrug away her love of him. She hated his dazzle. The love hurt. "The hogs don't laugh, why should we?"

You stupid squirrel, Dorothy thought. You got a face like a pillow.

"That's a terrible thing," said the Substitute.

"Shut up," said Dorothy.

"Dorothy," said the Substitute, "that's very rude."

"Shut your squirrel's face up," said Dorothy. Is that rude enough for you to get my meaning?

The Substitute looked straight at her and looked sad and wise, and he smiled. "You're too old for this class, aren't you, Miss Gael?"

That made Dorothy afraid. The fear gathered strength and speed like a rockface slipping from a mountain. Dorothy was stricken with terror. No, she thought, I'm not old, I'm not too old.

The Substitute thought she was surprised at being treated with courtesy. He thought, quite rightly, that no one had ever been courteous to Dorothy before, but it was fear that made her go still. Dorothy was realizing that at nearly thirteen, she was almost an adult. At fifteen, two years from then, she would leave and go to work. As a child, she had power. She knew that as an adult, fat and ugly and slumped in dirty clothes, she would have none. Her childhood was almost over and she could not remember ever being happy.

"Could you do something for me, Miss Gael? Would you mind leaving the class?"

Dorothy began to grin a crooked grin. Oh, yes, you want to get rid of me that easily?

But he held up a hand. "I've got an idea for an assignment that I want you to work on. I want you to go into the bookroom and just sit quietly and write something. It doesn't have to be long. But it can be about anything you like. Anything at all."

Dorothy stood up, still grinning crookedly. She had been cast out before. She took pencil and paper. "I'd do anything to get out of here," she said.

"Thank you, Miss Gael. Take as long as you like."

Outside, Dorothy thought: So why on earth should I go to the bookroom? Stupid squirrel. Stupid groundhog.

Then she thought: Where else do I have to go? Only home. And I don't want to go home. I hate home. I'd rather stay here, but I hate it here, and everyone here hates me. I hate everybody and everything.

She went to the bookroom. Mrs. Warren glared at her. "Teacher sent me here," said Dorothy. There was one table and shelves of spare textbooks. Proud as they were of their schools, even the people of Kansas could not call this a library.

But it still smelled of books and varnish and sunlight. Sunlight came through the window, fierce and hot, Kansas sunlight, parching. It was warm and airless, and Dorothy felt sleepy. She wished she had come here before, to lay down all her cares. She bowed her head, to the table. She wanted to stay just here, in this one place, and never leave it.

Write something, he had said. Write about what? Write about all the kids who hate me? Write about how stupid little Emma is and how she follows me around because I scare people? Shall I write about how I am God's worst sinner, and how I know I am going to go to Hell and that that is the only reason I don't kill myself, because I see the Devil when I sleep at night, and that I smell Uncle Henry around my mouth all day long, and that nobody loves me. Not even God. Should I write that God doesn't love me? Or do I write about how beautiful you are and how I know how ugly I am and how you could never have anything to do with me?

But she found what she wanted to write about very close to the surface. She wrote about it, weeping. And then she dried her eyes and found she wanted someone to see it, just so that someone would know there was a bit more to Dorothy Gael than blows and bad blood.

She walked back into the classroom, hugging the paper to herself. She walked up to the Substitute's desk.

"That was quick, Miss Gael. Have you written something?"

Wordlessly, she passed it to him, a whole page both sides, and she stood over him and watched him as he read.

What he read was this:

TOTO

I have a little dog called Toto. He is a terrier which means that he has short wiry hair and is gray. He waits for me every day when I come home. When he sees me he comes running. He jumps up and down. He wiggles and nitters and wants me to pet him. I say to him "Good Toto, good boy." And he nitters again because he knows his name. We walk home together. He loves chasing sticks. I throw sticks for him, and he brings them back to me and drops them at my feet. When I throw them, he runs and runs, flat out. He even runs when I don't throw sticks. He runs all over the fields, yipping. It is like he is saying hello to everything. He chases the quail, but he never hurts them. He runs all over the hills. He runs and comes back to me and runs again. I can hear him barking.

I get home and Aunty calls hello and tells me what's for supper and I tell her all the things I did that day. So I fetch the water for Uncle Henry's bath, and Aunty Em says I can go and play with Toto. So we go out into the fields, for hours and hours and I sit down and eat an apple that Aunty Em give me, and Toto and I sit down, on top of a hill where I can see all the farm. Toto sits on my lap, and I scratch his ears and his neck under the collar. He licks my hand, and he goes to sleep on my lap. He has a cold wet nose. He goes to sleep with his nose against my arm. At night, I give him his supper in a red bowl. I fix him oatmeal and egg and a bit of jerky that Aunty lets me have for him.

I did not call him Toto. That is the name my mother gave him when she was alive. It is the same as mine.

That was where Dorothy had to stop writing.

The Substitute went very still and quiet. Dorothy knew he had finished reading, but he didn't say anything. Dorothy guessed that it wasn't very good. Nothing was very good, but that was as good as she could make it. So he had to say something.

He coughed and still didn't look up at her, and he said in a very rough voice, "Thank you, Dorothy."

Then he managed to look up and Dorothy saw that his face looked horrible and that he was trying not to cry. "I'm very glad," he murmured, "that you have something to love as much as that little animal."

You stupid, stuck-up, New York freeloader. You skinny little balloon-faced squirrel.

"I don't have a dog!" Dorothy shouted. Her voice went thin and screeching, and she kept on shouting, as loud as she had ever shouted, shouted to bring the walls down. "I don't have a dog because Aunty Em killed him! He was the only thing I got to take with me from home and just 'cause he barked and chased the hens, she killed him, and she didn't even tell me, so for years and years every time I heard a dog bark I thought it was Toto, and I run and I run after him, calling out his name, and she heard me do that and she never said nothing, she just let me call, because she hates me, she makes me work, and she never feeds me 'cause there's never any food and I'm always hungry and I don't have nothing and she never gives me nothing, and I can't say anything.''

The Substitute was on his feet and the class gaped in amazement. The child had gone hysterical, just as suddenly as a roll blind when it snaps up. He tried to take her in his arms.

He tried to take her in his arms and she screamed. It was a horrible sound, a sound like a spaniel caught in a bear trap, a horrible wrenching yelp that turned into a thin, piercing, seagull wail, and she pushed the Substitute away.

"And every day Uncle Henry does it to me, he pushes me up against a wall or down into the dirt, and takes up my dress and he does it to me, with his thing, he does it to me!"

The other children heard. The Substitute gathered her up and tried to bundle her out of the room, but she fought. She pummeled him about the face. His glasses broke. "You stupid, stupid squirrel. Why did you have to come here? You stupid, stupid man!"

And then the great galumphing gal curled up onto the floor and wept like a baby.

She tried to dig a hole in the floor. Her hands were gouging at the varnished wood. She curled up smaller and tighter and tried to dig, her eyes closed, her mouth closed, like a mole, and when he tried to stop her, when he grabbed her wrists she fought and was as strong as he was. Finally he let go, and she went still. She went still, making a small, squeezed, wheedling little sound.

"If she gets up, keep her here!" he told the class. He turned and ran. He heard his flat feet clatter in the corridor, and he felt his bad heart beat. At first the Principal didn't believe him.

"Collapse? Dorothy Gael? That girl has the constitution of an ox."

"Even an ox can die of heartbreak," said the Substitute. "There's been something terrible going on. She shouted it out, and all the children heard."

"Did they indeed? What's she been doing, stealing peaches? All right, Mr. Baum, I'll come and see."

She was still there on the floor, no longer wailing, but shivering, and she had stuck her thumb in her mouth. Professor Lantz walked in and one of the children giggled. They were all biting their nails.

"DeEtta," the Principal said to his assistant, "take the children out into the yard, please."

"Come on, children, there's nothing more to see here," said Mrs. Warren as the children gaped in wonder.

"What she said!" breathed out one of the girls.

The Principal looked up and waited until the children had left. He was taking Dorothy's pulse rate. It was a scientific thing to do.

"All right, Mr. Baum. What did she say?"

The Substitute found he couldn't say it. He had had a delicate upbringing. The Substitute could feel his cheeks roasting with embarrassment. He sighed and hissed with the difficulty of even finding words for it.

"Out with it, Mr. Baum, there are only us men here."

"She says that her uncle has relations with her."

For just a flicker, as if time had blinked, Professor Lantz went still.

"I mean, what she actually said was that he pushed his thing up her." Frank Baum felt his voice suddenly shudder and go weak. He was nearly in tears.

"Buck up, man," said Professor Lantz. "It doesn't surprise me. Dorothy Gael is quite capable of imagining anything. She said this in front of the other children?"

"Yes," said the Substitute, overwhelmed by the horror of it.

"Dorothy Gael," said the Principal, as if the child were not curled up under his hands, "is a very wicked creature. At times she almost convinces me of the truth of demonic possession. She has said before, herself, that she lies about everything. She is capable of uttering any untruth and, I'm afraid to say, of thinking up all manner of foulness by herself. You do not know the girl, Mr. Baum." The Principal was fat and had to grunt as he stood up. Without realizing it, he made a gesture of wiping his hands.

"We'll get your relative, Dr. Lyman, in to have a look at her. And then we will bundle her up and send her home and ask her never to come back to this school."

The Substitute followed him out of the room glancing back and forth between him and the girl. "Are you sure? Are you sure you should send her home?"

"Where else does she belong, Mr. Baum?"

"Whatever else may be true, she is desperately unhappy there, Professor Lantz. Please! Look at her! What would make a child try to dig her way into the floor?"

"I don't know," said Professor Lantz, looking back with a half smile. "Perhaps a handsome young actor from New York."

The Substitute found that dismay was turning to anger. You are going to blame me for that in there? "What," the Substitute asked, drawing himself up, "what if what she said is the truth?"

Professor Lantz stopped smiling and his gaze went steely.

"There must be a reason for it!" exclaimed the Substitute.

"The only reason," said the Principal, "is fantasy. Fantasy is pretty unhealthy as a general rule. I will remind you, Sir, that you are an itinerant actor invited here to teach class for a few days at the suggestion of Dr. Lyman. You do not know Dorothy Gael, nor her guardians, the Gulches. You could not hope to meet more God-fearing or civic-minded people. Her uncle takes her to and from Manhattan every day, the distance of four miles each way, simply to bring her here since her last school failed to effect any improvement. She gets the best care her people can afford. Particularly since she must be a very great trial to them. And I am afraid, Sir, that we will not be requiring your services tomorrow. After creating that incident in there I think you can see why. Cigar smoke and all."

The Professor waved his hand in the air as if to wipe away the stench of smoke, of actor, of fantasy.

Dr. Lyman arrived, with a weary glance at his worthless young cousin. "Sexual hysteria," he pronounced, having heard the story from Professor Lantz. "There's not much I can do for her, except take her home. Which under the circumstances I will do gratis. Not my normal policy." He glanced up again at the actor. "Frank, perhaps you would care to assist."

"I will ride back with her," said the Substitute.

"No," said the Doctor. "You will not."

They got the great lump of a girl to stand. She really was huge, the size of a grown woman and stronger than most boys her age. The Substitute took her hand, and she grasped his firmly, but he had the feeling she did not know who he was. The flesh on her face hung dead and limp and yellow. She was quite tame. She stepped up onto the

Doctor's coach as if somnambulating. The effect was curiously ladylike. She sat tall and straight. The face had a faraway expression, almost refined, and the Substitute had time to see that the face was beautiful. With the anger and the pain fallen from her, Dorothy Gael would have been a beautiful woman.

And then the child murmured, "Frank. Frank."

And the Substitute thought: Oh no. They were right.

"Frank," she said again, in a faraway, failing voice, and it was the voice of a little, little girl, calling for a story.

Dr. Lyman, his fearsome host, glared at the Substitute and raised an eyebrow and clucked with his tongue and shook the reins, and the coach swept around in a gracious circle. With the wheels spinning faster, making patterns across each other's faces, the coach sped away down Poyntz.

The Substitute turned and walked back toward the classroom. It was nearly dark now.

Was it his fault? It must have been his fault. He thought of his cigar and his stories and leaning on the desk, and he felt like a fool, a fool of a show-off actor. Damn, he murmured. Damn. And he needed the money, too.

He walked back into the classroom. It was silent and smelled of children and warm, dead wood. He gathered up his hat and his umbrella and sighed and opened the door to go. He looked back to check if he had left anything behind. On the desk there was a piece of paper.

He picked it up and read it again, and he was sure; he knew that he had been right, that the child had told the truth. He read it and felt the pit open up under his feet.

"Oh, mercy," he said aloud.

A place where no one ever laughed except to frighten or to crow victory, a place without love, a child who had no love, except when she dreamed that she still had a dog.

"How could they?" he said aloud, looking about him in anger. She was telling the truth and they were all determined not to believe her. The horror of it rose up and choked his gentle soul. "I wish I could do something, Dorothy," he whispered. "I wish there was something I could do."

He stared at the piece of paper and nearly let it drop. Then he folded it up and put it in his pocket with its names—Dorothy, Em, Henry, Toto. He picked up the red book of Osmanli, the language of Oz. Then he moved on. The door closed behind him and his footsteps echoed down the Kansas corridor.

Corndale, Ontario, Canada

November 1956–Spring 1957

The picture also opened well in the thirty-two key cities surveyed by
Variety, bringing in more money in the first week than such recently
successful MGM films as Goodbye Mr. Chips *and* Idiot's Delight.
But the picture didn't have enough legs to justify its cost . . . The Wiz-
ard of Oz cost $2,777,000 and grossed $3,017,000 for the studio.
When the cost of distribution, prints and advertising were added to the
cost of making The Wizard of Oz, *it meant a loss to the studio of*
nearly a million dollars. The movie edged into the black during its first
re-release in 1948–49, when it brought in another $1,500,000; but it
did not really make money until it was leased to television . . .

The film was shown for the first time on 3 November 1956 from
9 TO 11 p.m. Eastern Standard Time. With a 33.9 rating and 52.7 per
cent share of the audience, The Wizard of Oz *did extremely well—but*
not as well as it did in 1959, 1964, and 1965. As of July 1975, The
Wizard of Oz *was in 11th place on the list of the highest-rated movies*
ever shown on network television. (It was also in 12th place, 14th place,
16th place, 21st place, 23rd place and 25th place.)

—ALJEAN HARMETZ,
The Making of the Wizard of Oz

In his later years, Jonathan would look at old photographs of the house
in Corndale. There would be a kind of electric jolt from the photographs, a cattle-prodding of memory. The photographs were surprisingly
small, cracked, rather greasy-looking, with crinkle-cut edges like tiny pies.

In the photographs Jonathan would see his father's old drinking mug and Jonathan would remember its rich brown color and the black etchings of highwaymen printed onto its surface. It was silver around the rim and made everything taste slightly of beer. He would see the wicker basket in which logs were kept next to the fireplace. He would suddenly be able to feel in his fingertips the smoothness of the wicker-work, with its suddenly harsh edges. He would remember how dismayed he was as a child when the basket was displaced from its corner by a new desk.

He would see a brass elephant bell, and he would remember its sound and he would remember the shelving it had been kept on. It stood in a glass display case built into the wall next to the front door. The case went through the wall; its outside was frosted glass. Standing on the front steps, you could see all the treasures kept inside it: a brass ice bucket; a porcelain squirrel that was a souvenir of Algonquin Park. They would be seen as if through a mist.

In the photographs Jonathan would see his parents when they were young. He would see his mother, standing on a pile of dirt in high-heel shoes in the early 1950s. His mother was the picture of Canadian elegance, her yearning for style and urbanity revealed in immaculate hair and dress and the angle at which her cigarette was held. His father was standing beside her, with his shock of Einstein hair. He was young and slim and bare chested. A baby hung suspended from his arms. This was the ground-breaking for the new house in Corndale. Beside them, in swim trunks, with a shovel, there was a rather handsome Scottish-looking man whom Jonathan did not know. Neither, now, did his parents.

His first world. Through all the later changes in his life, Jonathan would remember his childhood as happening in that house. They had moved away from it when he was nine years old, but the interior of the Corndale house was the continent of his infancy.

The photographs would bring it back. He would remember the uncomfortable texture of the gray sofa. It had raised, rough surfaces in the shapes of flowers and vines. They made his skin itch.

He preferred instead to lie on the floor under the ultramodern chairs. He would trace with his finger the snakelike wiggle of the metal strands that supported the cushions. He liked the feeling of being enclosed, hidden, safe.

One of the ultramodern chairs was crimson, the other was bright green, and they stood by a lime-green throw rug that slipped underfoot on the polished pinewood floors which always smelled of wax. There were bookcases made of boards sandwiched between bricks, and on them stood small Indian vases, with bright blue and yellow flowers embedded in the red ceramic.

Jonathan could remember the colors, even though the photographs were black-and-white. This was very strange. Jonathan was color-blind. Except in the strongest light, green and red looked the same to him. Blue and purple were indistinguishable.

So how had the infant been able to see them? Jonathan could remember loving red, a color he could not now perceive.

Love is almost too feeble a word for the rich passion that red had inspired. Red moved the infant Jonathan like music. In his coloring books, everything was red. He wanted the whole world to be red. He tried to make it red.

He would steal his mother's ruby lipsticks and, to her misery, scrawl all over the walls, over the pale pinewood of his bookcase, over the prints of Canadian forest scenes. He alarmed her by painting his fingernails red with her polish. He would rub lipstick all over his face, surprising visitors.

Jonathan loved Indians. They were called Red Men. He had an Indian blanket that was red and a pink piggy bank that looked like Pow Wow the Indian boy. He loved his picture books that were full of pictures of Indians, hunting buffalo in the grass or dancing. He would coat them with layers of red—lipstick, jam and Crayola crayon.

It was difficult for Jonathan to imagine now, but he had been a very bad little boy. He was still surprised to hear his aged mother refer to him as a problem child. The person Jonathan remembered being was a horribly polite, cringingly well-behaved child who loved his parents and thought of them as his best friends.

But the photographs showed a burly, tough-looking boy. The Corndale house was growing around him in stages. He would stand chuckling amid its wooden skeleton holding a hammer, a wild destructive light in his eyes. He was a hefty little brute who looked as if he would grow up round and small and hearty. Jonathan had grown up to be tall and thin, distant and mild.

The little thug looked wonderfully happy. Jonathan the adult was tempted to say insanely happy. The eyes sometimes seemed to be stricken with a faraway vision, fogged with wonder. The smile sometimes blazed beyond delight. Something broken would be clutched in his stained and brutish, pudgy fist. The smiles of his parents would be sideways and nervous.

Jonathan needed reminding that Dr. Montemuro in Streetsville had diagnosed him as being autistic.

Jonathan had smiled and Jonathan had rocked. He would sit on the floor cross-legged and rock back and forth for hours. Jonathan the adult could not sit cross-legged at all.

The bad little boy had rocked himself to sleep each night. He threw himself back and forth, until the cot swayed dangerously, wood creaking. His parents said they had built the extension to give themselves a separate room in which to sleep. The rocking was very noisy, particularly as the little boy hummed and keened to himself. The songs would be wild, tuneless, like the crying of a bird, his mother said. He shook his head from side to side as if denying the world. He would fall asleep from sheer exhaustion.

He ripped his sheets. He tore holes in them big enough to crawl through. His mother thought it was his constant nightly exertions. In fact, he tore them quite deliberately with a guilty, almost sexual delight. He would work a small tear in the center and gradually prize it open.

He was trying to make a hole big enough to climb through. It was as though the sheet were a screen that separated him from somewhere else. When the hole was large enough, he would climb through it, hoping to emerge somewhere wonderful. It was a disappointment to him, to find himself still alone in his room. He kept on tearing sheets.

He was subject to fits of blinding rage.

He broke his Indian bow and arrow quite coldly out of hatred for something he did not understand. It was terrible because he had truly loved his Indian bow and arrow. He was stricken with remorse.

"Is that your bow? Your *new* bow?" his mother demanded, invisible from within the house. He wept as he held it up, like a broken bird.

"Well, this time your father is not going to fix it for you."

He hid under his Indian blanket in the driveway. He knew his father would coast into the driveway, up and over it, over him.

"You stupid child! Don't you ever do that again!" his mother said in alarm, shaking him, her eyes wide and fearful. Jonathan's face was covered in the red crushed juice of berries, as if he were bleeding.

What kind of kid was that? Jonathan asked himself, remembering. And why did he look so happy?

His earliest memory was of being small enough to be bathed in the bathroom sink. He kept striking the warm water, to make it splash over him. "Oooh, lovely warm water," his mother cooed. He understood her. He said something in reply, in the language of childhood, a series of sounds. His mother didn't understand him. Why not?

Jonathan could remember the moment of dismay when the infant realized that he would have to use the same word each time for the same thing. He could remember the horror: he realized the size of the task ahead of him. He became enraged with disappointment. The world should work so that everyone understood out of love, as he did.

Jonathan did not begin to speak until he was three years old. He was angry. He rejected the world out of rage.

The scrawls he made on the walls were writing without words, messages in Crayola and lipstick. "Walt Disney owns Cinderella and Mickey Mouse and Disneyland too," the scrawls would say in the swirling shapes of cyclones.

When Jonathan finally decided to speak, it was in a complete sentence. He had been able to speak all along. Every family has its legends, and this was one his mother was pleased to relate, entertaining visitors.

"I nearly died!" his mother might say, laughing and shaking her head. "Three years without saying a word, and suddenly he asks for a glass of water! After that his nose was never out of a book!" The implication for listeners was that Jonathan's extraordinary verbal skills were somehow brewing in that silence.

Throughout Jonathan's later career as a good little boy, his teachers expressed satisfaction with his ability to write, to speak, to act in schoolroom plays. In the tests they gave to measure potential, Jonathan scored, frankly, at near-genius level on verbal reasoning. On the strength of his verbal reasoning alone, Jonathan kept skipping grades until his skills matched the work load and he fell forever behind in mathematics.

The bad little boy's talents had not been verbal, but lay in the realm of color and shape. He layered strokes of Crayola crayon, fifty-two colors, as if each stroke was the plucking of musical strings. He had masses of plasticine, a nondrying clay, which he would mold and remold, making dinosaurs or Indian tepees that seemed to have been carved out of stone.

Jonathan could remember modeling a head in clay. He was playing at the back of the house, where his father was building a patio. His father was laying large slabs of stone, chipping the edges to make them fit in a patchwork-quilt pattern. For some reason, Jonathan had been given clay, real clay instead of plasticine. Jonathan's father had artistic ambitions as well, which the clay had been meant to fulfill.

And Jonathan was suddenly seized by the idea of clay. Out of it, from nowhere, he worked the head of a caveman. Jonathan loved cavemen, loved the idea of living in rock chambers, wearing hides and talking in grunts.

Jonathan the adult could still remember the caveman's face, his apelike brows, his monkey nose, his hedgehog ears and, above all, his expression. The flesh around his eyes was crinkled, ready to blink in dismay at the modern world into which he had strayed. The lips were half-open, as if the caveman were making up his mind to speak.

The tough little boy had even been sociable, in his own way. Hovering around the edges of the memory was another little boy called Robby Polk, who lived across the field. Jonathan's relationship with Robby was uneasy. Both of them liked to win, but Robby was better at it.

Robby looked at the caveman head and said, "That's lousy."

Jonathan was pleased. He felt he had caught Robby, trapped him into being petty. Jonathan's father had no kiln in which to bake the head. When the caveman finally dried, he split down the middle. Jonathan knew what Robby would say.

"Good," said Robby, and Jonathan knew he had made him look small. He smiled and looked away and pretended Robby was not there.

His mother looked at the caveman head and stroked Jonathan's disordered hair and said, "There are always compensations."

The bad little boy hated most books. He tore up the ones he didn't like. They were written by adults for children. Jonathan knew that not because anyone told him, but because he sensed it in the books themselves. They were not written for children at all. He tore up a library book called *Anatole*. It was about a French mouse and it told cheese jokes about Camembert and Roquefort. That was a joke for adults. What child would know anything about French cheese? Why write books for children if you knew nothing about them, if you were really writing for adults?

There were honorable exceptions. He loved a book about a monkey, called *Curious George*. George kept getting into trouble, breaking things. Jonathan also loved a book called *Space Cat*. It was rather long-winded, and Jonathan would torment himself by forcing his way through the languorous opening. It was about a cat and a space pilot who became friends. They went to the moon and Space Cat had his own spacesuit, with a sausage-shaped piece for his tail. On the moon, there were floating silver globes, full of light, that were alive.

And, Jonathan loved *The Wonderful Wizard of Oz*.

He did not have the real book. His parents did not know that he could read. They read aloud to him and thought he just looked at the pictures. They had bought him a slim, picture-book version. There was a pretty, blond Dorothy and a smiling Scarecrow. The Wizard was shown as several different things, a beautiful woman and a monster. There was only one page that showed a witch, but she soon melted away like all bad dreams.

Jonathan loved a few books and hated the rest. He hated mechanical toys and model cars. Most of all, he loathed television.

In the first place, it was full of murder. Dale Evans would be tied to a chair—horrible violation—and even though he knew Roy Rogers would arrive in time, riding Trigger, it was still terrible. Why, he thought, why watch anything that you hated, telling yourself that it would be all right in the end because it was a TV show? If the only comfort was knowing it was not real, why watch it at all?

He also hated the thing itself. His parents' television stood on four spindly legs. It was as if it could walk, with its one huge unblinking eye. Jonathan had dim memories of seeing a film on that one blind eye, a film in which an alien disguised himself as a television set. Jonathan could imagine, so clearly, the television suddenly lurching toward him, shooting electricity in lightning bolts from its blank screen.

If his parents turned it on and there was a Western or a cartoon, things he was supposed to like, he would scream and run away or howl until it was turned off. His parents, still grateful that he had recently ceased to smear lipstick over everything, would leap forward to turn it off.

But worst of all, everything on television was in black-and-white.

Jonathan loved color. He loved red. He wanted everything in the world to be full of color. So what, the adult Jonathan would often wonder, what had made him change?

In November 1956, Jonathan saw the first broadcast of the film version of *The Wizard of Oz*. The movie started at 9:00 p.m. and would go on until eleven. Jonathan had never before been allowed to stay up so late. He wore his red-striped pajamas and his red bathrobe. He was covered by his Indian blanket and he leaned against his mother on the gray and itchy sofa. His father passed him a cup of hot chocolate in the brown highwayman mug. Jonathan felt very adult.

His parents were obviously excited themselves. Television was still new. The idea of seeing such a great film for free seemed a wonderful advance. Jonathan understood that the film was something delightful that had happened to his parents when they were young. They talked about it at great length as the commercials unwound. They were a mine of misinformation about it.

They told him that the story was a very old fairy tale that someone had updated and made modern. They told him that the little girl who played Dorothy had only been twelve when she played the part (though that seemed very old to Jonathan).

Then the CBS eye, black and floating against clouds, came up, and a man said in a voice of portent, "CBS presents a Ford Star Jubilee." There were advertisements for cars. Then the talking continued. ". . . a masterpiece of literature," said the announcer, "which has fascinated children and adults for years, ranks with the great works of all times." An old man talked to a little girl about how her mother had starred in the movie. It went on and on. What *TV Guide* had not said was that the film itself was only 101 minutes long—but the slot was two hours. Even Jonathan's parents began to shift uneasily.

Jonathan was in a kind of panic. He knew that he would fall asleep soon. Why couldn't they have all the talking after the movie?

A picture of a record sleeve came up. It showed a girl, and—there they were!—the Scarecrow and the Tin Man and the Cowardly Lion! Jonathan squealed and kicked his legs under the blanket.

His parents beamed with pleasure. It was rare to get a reaction from Jonathan that was easily understood. The voice was asking people to write away for a special record album of songs from the film.

"I know a little boy who would like that," his mother said, smiling. And Jonathan went quiet with longing. He didn't dare say yes. Years later, he still regretted that they had never got the record.

Then suddenly it began. There were more clouds, like the CBS eye, and a chorus of voices rising up like a great wind.

Dorothy came running over a hill. She wasn't like Dorothy in his pretty little book. She was large and had dark hair, but as soon as she started to speak, there was something in her voice that soothed Jonathan as he worried. He was worried that it was so different from his book.

Her Aunty Em said a lot more things, and the farm was full of people. There was going to be more story. This was a delight to him, but he also felt betrayed. How could so many things have been left out of his book?

Jonathan remembered liking Dorothy swinging back and forth holding on to a huge barnyard wheel. It seemed like something fun to do. He was excited by her visit with Professor Marvel, who was brand-new and nothing to do with the story he knew at all. Then he grew suspicious. What if the movie was completely different and Dorothy didn't go to Oz at all?

He did not perceive Miss Gulch at all, nor was he badly affected by the threatened death of Toto. Jonathan had never had a pet to love. He had not learned to care for little animals. In fact, to him the eyes of animals seemed cold and alien. They chilled, rather than warmed him. Perhaps also he didn't understand the line about taking the dog to the Sheriff to have him destroyed.

The major disappointment was the cyclone. Jonathan was looking forward to seeing the cyclone almost as much as Oz itself. A few months before, there had been a cyclone warning, a great rarity for Ontario, and everyone had gone out and picked up loose branches and closed the shutters over windows. Jonathan had had to be dragged sullenly back inside the house. He had wanted to stay outside to see it.

But now the cyclone was lost for him amid the black-and-white blur of the television screen.

"There it is," his father said, pointing.

"Where?" demanded Jonathan, becoming angry. He had imagined cyclones as great, solid, spinning things that came from nowhere out of a blue sky. He peered narrow-eyed at the television, seeing only swirling clouds. "I can't see it!" he wailed. He saw Dorothy running, and behind her, beyond the porch of the house, he could just barely make out something moving in the sky. Was that the cyclone?

He forgot his anger when Dorothy woke up inside it. He loved the idea of being warm and safe, cradled in the wind. He loved the chickens flying about inside the storm and the people in a boat, rowing their way through clouds as if through water.

Then there was a lady on a bicycle. It had been a long time since Miss Gulch was on the screen; Jonathan had forgotten all about her. He didn't recognize her. He did recognize what she turned into.

Suddenly, clothes streaming behind her, there was a huge horrible witch riding a broomstick.

He screamed and hid under the Indian blanket.

"Jonathan!" laughed his mother, always taken aback by his sus-ceptibilities.

"Is it gone?" he demanded.

"Yes, yes," said his mother. Jonathan stayed under his blanket. He heard Dorothy screaming, and he screwed his eyes shut.

There was a line in Jonathan's shortened book: "The cyclone set the house down very gently for a cyclone." He had liked that. He knew what it meant. There would be quite a big bump, but not so big that Dorothy would be hurt. He wanted to see the house land so he forced himself to watch. He looked out from under his blanket in time to see the room and the house come to a stop with a tremendous bump. Oh, said Dorothy. Perfect! They had done it perfectly!

Dorothy was in Oz. Jonathan wanted to see the Munchkins and he wanted to see the Good Witch. Most of all he wanted to see her give Dorothy the magic kiss that meant no harm could come to her. Jonathan loved the idea that no harm could come.

Dorothy went toward the door. Jonathan was so excited, he almost had to pee.

"Look," said his father. "This is the part that turns into color. She steps out and everything is in color."

The commentary was an unwarranted distraction. Jonathan knew perfectly well that the television couldn't show color. He was gripped by both joy and edgy suspense. Dorothy peered out through the door. Then she stepped out onto the porch, but he still couldn't see Oz.

"There, that's when it turns into color!" exclaimed his father.

Oz was black-and-white. It didn't matter. Dorothy's eyes were wide and round, and she wandered through a strange gray place full of television mist and giant leaves. Jonathan went breathless and still. And then, there was a floating, silvery globe.

"That's like Space Cat!" cried Jonathan, overjoyed.

The bubble turned into Glinda, the Witch of the North. The magic kiss was to come.

Glinda asked, so very politely, if Dorothy were a good witch or a bad witch. Jonathan loved the idea of good witches. He loved the way Oz people spoke, very polite and slightly addled. When Glinda asked if Toto was the Witch, Jonathan shrieked with laughter and kicked his feet.

"Sssh, Jonathan," said his mother, worried about the way he could get overexcited.

Jonathan loved it that Dorothy had killed the Wicked Witch. It was good that she had not meant to do it, and it was so strange to see the Witch's striped-stocking feet sticking out from under the house, strange in the way that being tickled is strange, slightly fearful and gigglesome at the same time.

"She'll be all squashed and flat," said Jonathan gleefully.

The Good Witch was beautiful, and the Munchkins laughed in high-pitched voices, and Dorothy was a National Heroine because she had saved them. Out came the Munchkins to celebrate. In Jonathan's book they all wore what looked like witch hats, only cockeyed and crumpled and amusing, and they all wore blue and played fiddles. These Munchkins looked different from that—but oh! they were all happy and sang aloud and Jonathan could not tell if they were adults or children. They looked like both. It was a new world, in which adults stayed children and children could be adults.

And they sang. They sang that the Witch was dead, and that they were free of her. No more bad witches, only good and smiling ones, like Glinda.

Then, when everything seemed nicest and happiest, and everyone was singing, there was a boom and a bash and everything was ruined. The Witch was back. The Munchkins ran.

Jonathan emitted a piercing shriek and hid under the blanket again. He screwed his eyes shut and plugged his ears.

This had not been his pretty little book. Glinda explained: this was the sister of the witch who was dead. This was the Witch of the West. Were all witches, even Glinda, sisters?

"Who killed my sister?" the Witch demanded. Jonathan didn't

want to hear; he couldn't bear it. "Was it you?" the Witch roared at Dorothy, terrible with hatred, and Jonathan, under his blanket, wailed again. It was wrong to kill, even if it wasn't your fault. How would Dorothy explain?

"No, no, it was an accident, I didn't mean to kill anybody!" said Dorothy.

Why had they put the Witch there? He felt his mother's hand on his shoulder. He peeked out over the edge of the blanket again, and she was still there, swirling with hatred. He screamed again and hid again.

"Jonathan," said his mother, "if you keep this up, I'll have to turn it off."

Jonathan forced himself to come out. He watched, wincing.

The Witch promised death. She promised she would get Dorothy and her dog.

She screamed and cackled and then there was a great booming sound. The Witch exploded and went away, in front of horrified eyes. Jonathan did not learn until years later that in that flash of fire the actress who played the Witch was severely burned.

He stared numbly, bestilled by horror, taking comfort from Glinda's motherly voice. Quietly and gently, she was telling Dorothy about the great and wonderful Wizard of Oz. And then, and then, she kissed Dorothy on the forehead.

He waited for the kiss to stay there, glowing on her forehead. But nothing happened. Gradually Jonathan realized that in the movie, the kiss was not a spell. The kiss would not protect Dorothy. She could be hurt.

It was television, frightening him again.

"It's all right," said Jonathan's mother. "Look, she's off to see the Wizard." But her voice was solemn. Jonathan looked around and his mother's face was pinched and hurt.

Things began to get hazy. Jonathan wasn't rocking himself, but watching Oz was rather like being rocked. When he rocked himself to sleep, Jonathan saw things like Oz, wonderful things, colors and magic.

Half-asleep, he met the Scarecrow. Jonathan loved the Scarecrow the best, like he loved Indians. Nothing would shake his loyalty. He loved the floppiness, the weak ankles, the loud cries, the gentleness. In comparison, the Tin Man looked greasy to him and nasty, and besides he was a machine and machines had no magic for Jonathan. He almost disliked the Tin Man, even though he kept crying out of kindness.

The Witch came back, skulking in a corner, appearing on a roof. Terror jerked Jonathan awake.

She called to the Scarecrow like she wanted to play a game. Then, most dreadful of all, the Witch threw a ball of fire at the Scarecrow, fire to burn him alive. Jonathan's shriek was the most piercing yet. Someone, somewhere, had decided to terrify him. That was what frightened Jonathan most: that it was deliberate. They could have made a movie without a witch at all.

He glimpsed poppies. They were about sleep and he could feel his own limbs go still and heavy. The movie turned into color and he seemed to sink down into it. He sank down and settled very gently, his feet touching solid ground and seeming to spark with life. He ran, into Oz.

He could hear his own running feet, and he could feel cobbles underfoot through the soles of his shoes. The bricks were bright yellow, so bright that it hurt his eyes.

"Wait for me!" he called. And they all turned, Judy Garland and the Scarecrow and the Lion. He caught up with them.

"Can I come too? Can I come too?" he asked them, panting. The fields were bright red, and the sky was full of a white smiling face, and it was snowing too, flowers and snow together, and there was music, grand and happy at the same time.

"Why, of course you can," said Judy Garland.

Jonathan woke up in the morning in his own bed. The room was dim and gray, shadowed by a curtain. Except that at the foot of his bed, there was a flowering of color. He woke and imagined that the Lion and the Tin Man and the Scarecrow were with him. Jonathan could feel the weight of the Scarecrow, not too heavy, against his feet.

Wake up, Jonathan! Judy Garland seemed to say. We're off to see the Wizard!

"Hurray!" cried Jonathan. He threw off his blankets and hurled himself into the cold air. "We're off to see the Wizard!" He ran into the bathroom. His new friends crowded into the bathroom with him.

Dorothy brushed her teeth too, and the Lion used dental floss on his fangs, just like Jonathan's father.

It was November and cold, though it had not yet snowed, and Jonathan ran to sit in his morning place: in front of the ventilator duct by the kitchen door where hot air blasted out. He warmed his hands and feet. The Lion held the tip of his tail near it. The Scarecrow hung back in fear of the heat.

"Don't worry," Jonathan whispered to him. "It's not fire. There's no fire."

It was Sunday, and his father was home. Normally, Jonathan and his father ate Sunday breakfast together. Afterward they would check the boiler in the basement and make sure the water around the sump pump had not frozen and killed Jonathan's fish who lived there. This morning, however, Jonathan heard his father already hammering away in the attic. Jonathan was glad. He wanted to be with the people from Oz.

His mother walked in with a bowl of porridge. "You'll have to hurry this morning, Jonathan," she said. "It's late and you've got Sunday School."

He and his mother and the people from Oz all sat at the breakfast table by the front window. The people from Oz were going to have porridge as well. Jonathan's mother sat down opposite him, smiling with love.

"You fell asleep," she said, sympathetically.

"When?" Jonathan asked.

"Before the end of your movie."

"I did not!" Jonathan had felt very adult, being allowed to stay up late. It was a sign of great childishness to have fallen asleep.

"You did," said his mother, sweetly. She was utterly charmed. He had fought so hard to stay awake.

"I saw the whole movie," he protested.

"Did you?" said his mother. "What happened at the end?"

Jonathan thought back and found he couldn't remember. This was a truly terrible thing; he was sure he had seen the film, but he found he had no memory of the Witch's castle or of the inside of the Emerald City or of Dorothy's going home.

He went very silent. He wished his mother would stop smiling. He hadn't seen it, after all. He had slept through his movie. He would never see all of the story now.

"It will be on again," said his mother.

"I did so see it," he murmured.

He watched the brown sugar melt on his porridge. He liked that. He used it to help himself forget. Then he poured on the milk to cool it. Otherwise it was too hot. The aim was to get all the porridge floating whole on the milk, so that the sugar on top was not washed away. He blew on his porridge, and the friends from Oz blew with him.

He looked up at them, appraisingly. He must have fallen asleep and pulled them into his dream from out of the movie. So when he woke up they woke up with him and were still there, and that's how they joined him. So maybe it was lucky he had slept.

After the porridge, his mother bundled him into the bathroom again and washed behind his ears, which made him squirm, and then she put him into his own gray suit, with his own red bow tie. Then she put him into his mud-colored coat and his cap with flaps that could come down over his ears. She pushed his galoshes over his feet and then sent him off to Sunday School.

There was already a Christmas wreath on the front door, though there was no snow. The house stood on high Canadian foundations, out of the mud. There was a bank of concrete steps leading down from the front door to the earth. Just in front of the steps, waiting like a trap for the unwary, was Jonathan's wagon. His father had made it out of spare bits of wood. The rubber wheels had a suspension system his father had invented out of springs, too sophisticated for Jonathan to appreciate. He only knew that his wagon ran quietly and smoothly.

Jonathan loaded his new friends onto it and then he ran with his silent wagon, ran down the slope of the small artificial hill on which the house rested. The wagon rolled smoothly over the cover of the cesspit, which his mother was always telling him to avoid. He imagined it was a gate into the underworld or an entrance to an underground house, like Peter Pan's. He ran over the cesspit to the front drive and its broad opening through the white fence that enclosed the Corndale house as if it were a ranch. He left the wagon right in the middle of the entrance where he always did, ready to be flattened.

The people of Oz walked to Sunday School with him. He hoped that he would see no one else, just them. The Second Line West became the Yellow Brick Road. The circular tin culverts under the driveways seemed full of secrets.

Jonathan carried his secret into Sunday School. He told no one that the Oz people were with him. They were his friends alone. The Oz people sang "Yes, Jesus Loves Me" to the colored slide that showed Jesus and the words. They sang "Suffer Little Children." They listened to the story of the parting of the Red Sea, and on the way home, they and Jonathan imagined that they were walking between two high magic walls of seawater, pursued by Egyptians. Within the glassy green walls there were giant fish.

The Oz people were with him when his mother undid his bow tie and changed him into his ordinary clothes. They were with him when they ate Sunday lunch, roast goose with roast potatoes. "How did you like the movie?" his father asked Jonathan, having descended from the attic. Jonathan murmured something through a mouthful of food.

"I think he's forgotten it already," said his mother.

In the afternoon, he and his friends went out and played in the mud. Jonathan sank himself as deep as he could into it. It filled the tops of his galoshes. Together with the people from Oz, he made mud pies. They made patties of the wet cold soil. Jonathan had a bottle of poison from the bathroom. It was a bright red bottle of iodine with a skull and crossbones on it. It was a magic spell. Together, he and the Oz people put poison in the mud pies.

"We're going to feed them to the Wicked Witch," whispered Jonathan. He crept through the back door. He kicked off his boots, heavy with mud, and peeled off his smeared and sodden trousers and ran into the kitchen, trailing mud from his hands and socks. He put the mud pies on plates. He thought that mud was like melted chocolate and would go crisp and solid in the refrigerator.

His mother arrived to find her best china coated in mud and Jonathan in wet socks and underpants, shivering and leaning into the refrigerator.

"I'm poisoning the Witch," explained Jonathan. His round face was evil and eldritch. "Those are Poison Pies, so don't eat them!"

"I promise not to eat Poison Mud Pies," said his mother, endeavoring to find it amusing. "Where are your trousers?"

"Um," said Jonathan.

She went to find them. "Oh, Jonathan!" he heard her cry from the back door. She came into the kitchen holding out the trousers, a twist of cloth and mud. "How did you do this?" she demanded. There were wet footprints across her green rug, her polished floor.

Jonathan spent the rest of the afternoon indoors. He rubbed red poison iodine all over his face and lay on the green carpet, closing one eye. The fibers of the carpet looked huge, like trees, and he and the people from Oz walked through them, on their way to see the Wizard.

"Jonathan, wash your face, now," said his mother. He left red face-stains on the lime-green rug. "What are we going to do with you?" his mother asked.

He and the people from Oz hid in the shoebox. It was a great wooden box that filled one end of the corridor just outside the bathroom. He and the people from Oz lifted the lid and crawled inside it and nestled down amid the smells of rubber and leather and socks, the shoes and boots alternately hard and soft underneath them.

"We're going to disappear," Jonathan told the people from Oz. He burrowed down into the boots, piling shoes on top of himself. Later, when his parents began to try to find him, they even opened the lid and looked in and didn't see him.

Jonathan was as invisible as the people from Oz.

All that winter, Jonathan withdrew from the world to be with his friends. They wandered to the woods far down the Second Line West. They walked quickly and quietly, hoping no one would see them, past Billy Tait's house, past Jaqui Foster's house, all the way beyond the house of his parents' friends, the Harrisons. Jonathan looked down at his feet as he walked, as if ashamed, as if frightened of falling. When he thought there was no chance of anyone seeing him, he broke into a run.

Under a gray November sky Jonathan plunged into the forest through the tangle of shrubs and twigs. Inside, the woods were even darker and grayer. The ground was covered with brown leaves amid the smooth trunks of ash and sycamore. There were birch trees with their magical, white-paper bark that the Indians turned into canoes.

They were in Oz. They all sang and danced together, kicking up leaves. They danced along the banks of a tiny branch of the Credit River. Tree roots overhung the bank. Underneath them were secret houses, full of Munchkins. They would come out to join the Oz people, singing "Ding Dong the Witch Is Dead." The singing went on amid showers of fallen leaves.

Then, one morning, Jonathan got up and saw that the world had turned white and that the air was full of falling flakes. The last time it had snowed had been nearly a quarter of his lifetime ago. He greeted winter like a friend he had not seen in decades. He ran out in ordinary shoes and flung handfuls of snow into the air. The sky was white.

He loved winter. In the dark, as he lay in bed in the mornings, there would be the comforting sound of the snowplows, rumbling past. His father would have to dig snow out of the driveway before he could leave for work. There would be sliding on the ice and toboggan rides. The inside of the living room windows was coated in great leafy patterns of frost. Jonathan and the Oz people sat at the breakfast table, wandering among them, in a forest of frost. As soon as breakfast was over, he would run outside.

Jonathan loved sunlight on snow, and he loved the mystery of ice. One day he and the people from Oz walked on the frozen surface of the ditches, imagining water babies shivering underneath the ice. The surface cracked and Jonathan fell in, soaking himself in ice water to the knees. He kept on walking, enchanted by the world he and his Oz friends walked through.

There were high billowing clouds. Cold made them seem solid, like icebergs in the air. Television had once told Jonathan that there were things in the air called Mushroom Clouds. People saw them and died.

Jonathan pretended that Corndale was under threat from advancing Mushroom Clouds. Jonathan was the only person who had a coat made of Jet-Age Plastic. He was protected, no harm could come to him. He walked to the gate of each house, walking on the crisp surface of the snow on his numb and frozen feet, pretending to warn them about Mushroom Clouds. He forgot about the cold.

There were canyons of ice overhead. White light swung around him like a sword. The people from Oz said that each sparkle of light on the snow was a fairy. The snow plains of Canada glittered with them, were spangled with laughing souls. If all the snow had taken to the air at once, with cries of joy, Jonathan would not have been surprised. He stood and looked at the snow, his trousers drenched, his feet and the water in his eyes ringing with cold.

When he got home, his feet were frostbitten. He howled as his toes were lowered into a basin of lukewarm water. There were sad, sick patches of gray on his skin. His mother wept. "Jonathan. Why didn't you come inside?"

She had to go to the store for ointment. Jonathan listened to the car murmuring out of the front drive.

Then he went to the new extension and took out a stepladder.

"Sssh!" he told the people from Oz. "This is the best." He climbed up the ladder and pulled himself into the attic.

It was cold inside the attic, with a single bare light and the smell of raw wood. The underside of the roof was coated in thick sandwiches of paper stuffed like mattresses. Some of it was wound up in rolls. Jonathan sat on them. There were wooden joists, and between them the back side of the plasterboards, still with writing on them.

"Careful," Jonathan warned the Oz people. "You can only stand on the boards." Fearful, grateful for his presence, the Oz people tiptoed toward him, balancing delicately.

He reached out for them. He was shivering and his feet were bandaged. He was not aware of what happened next. He must have slipped. Very suddenly, he was somersaulting through space. There was a lovely crisp sensation of breakage, as if falling through potato chips.

Then he was lying facedown, amid dust, bouncing slightly as if dropped by a cyclone.

He had fallen through the ceiling. He screamed in terror at the idea. By sheer chance he had fallen onto a roll of wire netting that was used to hold plaster to walls. There was blood.

Then he looked up and saw a rough and broken silhouette of himself punched through the smooth white surface of the ceiling. It was like Bugs Bunny running through a door.

When his mother got back, she arrived to hear peals of laughter. She went in the extension's front door and found Jonathan, bruised and bloody, looking up at the hole he had made and roaring with laughter.

"You fell through the ceiling?" she shouted. She couldn't believe it. "You fell through the ceiling?" Each time she shouted it, Jonathan laughed even louder.

His parents left him alone after that, for a while. His mother discovered that if he was left to do as he chose, he grew quieter and quieter, and more safely housebound. He no longer rocked in place, but he did sing to himself all the time, drawing layer on layer of colors on paper or making castles out of plasticine or sugar cubes that sparkled like snow. Sometimes he spoke to people who were not there.

He had never been happier.

Winter became spring, filling Jonathan with misgiving. Where there had been snow, there was mud, and on the branches of the pussy willows were buds that hung like centipedes. There was a thaw, and Jonathan peered out of the window down the Second Line West toward the schoolyard.

There lay his future, crowded with other children, more outgoing and physically larger than he. He could see them sunbathing, leaning against the white wooden walls of the schoolhouse, or sitting on the steps. He retreated from the window and went back into his room for his afternoon nap.

He imagined that he and his friends went to a circus. There were no fast or terrifying rides in this circus. There was a Ferris wheel, slow and gentle, and the Cowardly Lion was the most fearsome beast among the donkeys and sheep and friendly pigs. Even so, in this gentle circus, someone got hurt. Perhaps it is not possible to tell a story without someone being hurt, without a witch appearing.

The Scarecrow was wounded. Jonathan knew you were supposed to tell an adult as soon as a friend was hurt. He didn't want to tell anyone. He had never told his mother about his friends. If the Scarecrow really was hurt, then he had to. Why didn't he? Jonathan challenged himself. What was he afraid of? Jonathan steeled himself. Feeling fateful, he left his room and went to his mother.

"The Scarecrow caught his penis in a door, but Judy Garland kissed it better," he told her.

His mother was alarmed on several counts. "No, she did not," she said, not appreciating how truthful and dutiful he had been. "It's a lie, and I don't want to hear you talking like that again."

"But he did," protested Jonathan, in a voice that was almost too weak for even him to hear.

"You are going to go outside," said his mother, "and find some other children to play with."

* * *

Jonathan found Helen and Matty Quicke. They were sisters who lived two doors down. Helen was the same age as Jonathan. She had a floppy page-boy haircut and there always seemed to be a dirty stain of orange juice around her mouth. Her nose was always running. It was always running, Jonathan's mother said, because her parents didn't feed her properly.

Helen's elder sister Matty took care of both her and Jonathan. She liked to boss people, which meant that if Helen and Jonathan started to argue, she would stop the fight and make a decision. The great thing about the girls was that they understood the point of playing pretend. The point was to believe, not to win. The girls made up rules and stuck to them.

They played House. Jonathan always played Father—they needed a boy for that. They went through elaborate rituals of cooking meals and washing up and taking care of babies and fixing cars. It was so much like real life, that each one knew what to do, except that Jonathan had two wives.

They played Vikings. They would stand together on the prow of a longship, and they would attack a castle, but they were always on the same side. "Okay, men!" Matty would say, and they would all run together, brandishing swords.

They went to Sunday School. The Oz people came as well, but Jonathan couldn't concentrate on them. He got confused and stumbled over the words of the songs and couldn't answer the questions asked by the Sunday School teacher. The teacher wore tartan trousers, and her nose ran, like Helen's.

Afterward, Matty would be elated by the idea of goodness and became insistent on righteousness. She would say that you should do whatever Jesus told you. You should never say "ain't," though Matty otherwise said it all the time. Enlivened by religious instruction, they would play Jesus. Jonathan stood on a fence post, his arms outstretched, being crucified while the sisters adored him on their knees. He liked that game. His mother made them stop.

His mother did not entirely approve of Helen and Matty. Their family offended against the world of style and grace she was trying to build. The Quicke home was ugly, with roof tiles over all of the walls. Helen and Matty's elder brother was only ten, but he wore his hair greased up. He smoked cigarettes and had a dog called Nigger. His eyes were hard, and he trained them on Jonathan.

Once, it was their father's birthday. Jonathan joined Helen and

Matty in singing "Happy Birthday" to him. Helen's father was a big man with big red hands and orange hair. Helen and Matty sat on his knees as they sang, and his rough face went kindly and soft. "I can't think of anything nicer," he said, "than to be sung to by two cute little girlies like you." Jonathan wondered why he felt so different from them.

The real world was pushing the Oz people to one side. They watched from the corner while Jonathan pondered the fact that rough Mr. Quicke could be kind. Outside again in the muddy backyard, the Oz people could only watch as Jonathan and Matty and Helen dug a hole to the Center of the Earth.

Why didn't he speak to the Oz people when Helen and Matty were around? He would try to, but fear would grip him. What was he afraid of? Jonathan decided that he would force himself, force himself to act as if the Oz people were there.

Jonathan knew how to behave. He had been drilled in politesse. He knew that you introduced people properly.

So one day, toward the end of that spring, he ushered Helen into his bedroom. He was going to do it. He really was going to do it.

"Helen," he said. "May I introduce the Oz people." He pointed to each one of them in turn. "The Lion. The Tin Man . . ."

He couldn't finish. Panic overcame him. Helen gasped and covered her mouth. He looked at her arms and the very fine, pale down on them. Helen stared at him, grinning, eyes wide. She knew what was happening. She knew that Jonathan thought the Oz people were really there. Jonathan tried to say something else, but the words stuck.

Helen squealed, hand over her mouth, and turned and ran. Disturbance seemed to follow her, swept in a spiral like a dust storm. It spun out of the doorway of Jonathan's bedroom, taking something with it.

Jonathan turned back to the corner of the room. There was no one there. He saw that there was no one there, that there never had been anyone there.

Shame covered him like darkness. Helen would know. Helen would tell. "Sissy," her brother called him. And he was a sissy, to make up people who were not there.

His room had been stripped bare of magic. It consisted now only of his parents' cast-off chest of drawers, the trampolined bed, some toys in which he had no interest. His room was devoid of interest. So were the grass and the trees beyond. It was this stark world from which he had been trying to hide.

He wanted to break every single toy, wrench off their heads, their butterflies on wires; he wanted to tear up all his books and rip to shreds all his drawings, everything he loved that was so thin and frail, and which could not defend him. The rage seemed to rise up into his eyes as an ache. He was blinded by anger, rising up in his gorge to choke him, overwhelming and complete. There was nothing that could satisfy it, but himself. He broke himself. He took the self he had been and broke it again and again. He called himself all the names he could think of: stupid idiot dope nincompoop sissy crybaby brat. Worm. He called himself a worm and seemed to see himself crushing himself underfoot. He stood absolutely still, with his elbow wrapped around his eyes. Then, very suddenly, he flung it away from his face and glared.

The world was diminished. It was smaller, duller, and he was unutterably bored by it. He didn't want to play with his crayons, his coloring book, his papers, his toys, his stupid plasticine. He prowled the field of his vision like a caged beast, restless, made aged and jaded and grim. He was five years old.

Helen's family moved away shortly afterward, to Brampton. In those days, there was a vast expanse of farmland between Corndale and Brampton. It seemed a long way away.

Jonathan was relieved. He and Helen had stopped playing together and her older brother was even more of a menace. Jonathan knew now that he would have to learn how to fight. He would have to learn how to throw a ball and to win at games. He was not a little boy any longer.

But one afternoon, just before they moved, Helen came running to Jonathan's house, calling his name over and over. It was an act of unexpected kindness. She wanted him to come out and look at the rainbow.

She rushed up the path, her pageboy bob flapping into her eyes and stains around her mouth. Jonathan sat disconsolately on his front steps.

"Jonny, Jonny, there's a rainbow!"

Jonathan had once yearned to see rainbows. He had seen them in storybooks, where they were short and thick and made of the brightest colors. Sitting there on the front steps, Jonathan was surprised by a tearful yearning for color, as bright as books.

He leapt up from the steps and ran down the artificial hill to meet her. "Where? Where?" he called.

They were suddenly friends, real friends, united in mutual excitement. "Up there! Up there!" Helen jumped up and down, over and over, pointing to the sky.

"I can't see it! I can't see it!" Jonathan cried.

As if infected by him, the rainbow disappeared for Helen as well. She walked backward, scowling. "Maybe you can't see it from here," she said. She led him running back to her house, back to the place where she had seen it. They ran up her drive and around the back and up the wobbly, unpainted wooden steps that led to the back door. The steps formed a kind of landing, high off the ground, above the deep foundations.

"There it is," said Helen, her arm pointing over Jonathan's shoulder. She jabbed her finger at it over and over. "There! There! There!"

Jonathan was being stupid again. How stupid could he get? He scanned the sky, trying to see something very short, an arch made of paint-set reds and greens and blues, all in sharply defined bands, as he remembered them.

"Cantcha see it, Jonny?" asked Helen's mother, Mrs. Quicke. She came out of her kitchen, wiping her hands on her apron. She leaned on the railings, a thin, worn woman with long hair pulled back in the fashion of ten years before. She wore glasses and had bad teeth.

"It's there, just keep lookin'," Mrs. Quicke said, with the rough, kind foreignness of someone else's mother.

"I can't see it," whispered Jonathan, as if in exile. Later, he would recall seeing dimly a wispy yellowish trail across the sky, like smoke.

Jonathan couldn't see the red or the orange; he couldn't see the green or the mauve. He could only see a brownish streak of mist and the blue beyond it.

Jonathan had become color-blind.

For him, green and red were muddled into a grayish brown. He no longer played with his box of fifty-two Crayola crayons. Color no longer sang to him. He could see no difference between blue and purple, between pink and gray. The world had become as dim for him as Oz on TV.

* * *

Jonathan became a good little boy. He did everything he was told. He called people "Sir" and said "please" and "thank you." Old ladies were enchanted. He went to school for the first time in autumn and was badly beaten up the first day by a gang of older boys. They had been waiting for him. It was the price of feeling superior.

In the photographs taken after that, Jonathan looked watchful and wary, suspicious and very adult. The good little boy only looked good in photographs in which he was scowling. His smiles were twisted, cheesy and false.

In life, he was timid and silent around others, embarrassed and awkward if made the center of attention. He was always ashamed of himself—of his clumsiness, of his many fears, of his fantasies, of all the things that made him inadequate. The things he enjoyed, he did in secret. He rocked surreptitiously at night. He dreamed surreptitiously, after memorizing his homework. He earned straight A's. His teachers wrote in his reports that he was socially backward.

Jonathan became a fan of horror movies. He watched them on TV every Saturday afternoon with another boy who eventually grew up to be a sadomasochist. The other boy would beat Jonathan, even at age eight, across the bottom, and Jonathan would bear it, for the same reason that he would bear the horror movies.

It was one more way of being a good little boy. He was proving he was no longer afraid of the Witch. He was proving he could take the pain, as the other boy butted him with his head or took a switch to his backside. Being beaten was no different from watching television. The role of entertainment is to toughen us up and whip us into line.

Jonathan wanted to be tough. Above all, he wished he could stop feeling things. He wanted to be a machine. He despised himself. When Jonathan was alone, hidden in his room or, even better, far away from the village, he would visit Oz in secret. He knew it wasn't real, he knew Oz couldn't help him, so he gave no outward sign and hated himself for it. But alone on his good-little-boy holidays, away from school, his mind would begin to wander. He would start to imagine things. Jonathan would walk through Canadian evergreen forests, up the sides of Canadian mountains, or across shelves of rock beside still Canadian lakes, and he would hum the songs of Oz. There were no Canadian songs to fill the silence. Jonathan would imagine the four companions ahead of him on their way through Oz. He saw their backs. The Emerald City would rise up over the brow of a Canadian hill in another part of the story that had been left out.

The story kept on growing. Jonathan imagined a new ending to the movie. Dorothy looks up at her bedroom walls in joy, as before. Then Aunty Em holds up a pair of slippers, slippers that should have been red but now look gray. Aunty Em says, "But Dorothy. Where did you find these shoes?"

And Jonathan would look down at his own gray feet.

Zeandale and Pillsbury's
Crossing, Kansas

1883

The Fields were Full of Life

*Title of a diorama in the Kansas State Historical Society Museum,
Topeka, Kansas. A rather small area is shown full of native grasses and
taxidermic wildlife, including one large, hunched, stuffed buffalo. On the
rail around the exhibit there is a block of wood covered with a worn
hide. A sign beside it says:*

BUFFALO HIDE—PLEASE TOUCH

Of course there was a scandal. All the children had heard, and told
their parents what Dorothy Gael had said. There was a queasy moment
in each Manhattan household as minds seesawed back and forth from
shock and indecision.

Nothing is hidden, but some things are blocked out. Everyone in
Manhattan knew, really, what was wrong with Dorothy Gael. It was
revealed in every twisted movement, each bitter and angry smile, each
horrifically knowledgeable look, in the hefty size of her body, in the
grimness of her aunty's face, in the child's rages and the way in which
she could brook all pain and insult. They all knew, really, what it
meant.

But nice people were not supposed to be able to recognize certain
things, because they were supposed to be so untainted that they couldn't
even think about them. People sincerely believed that they were
shocked and surprised and that they had had no idea such things hap-

pened. They sincerely thought they found it difficult to believe. There were veiled preachings from the pulpit. The Devil was here, in Kansas, but how to recognize his terrible face? The Devil, the Preacher said, could lurk within each of us. To recognize the Devil, we had only to look into ourselves. Let the other folks alone.

No one would tell Em what it was exactly that Dorothy had done to be expelled. "Some things are best left unsaid," the Principal had told her. "But she has told some wicked lies, and is something of a bully."

It was beyond Emma Gulch. It did not sound like her Dorothy at all. Her little Dodo, a bully? Quiet, shy little Dodo? At first she could not believe any of the stories. What could have been happening? Emma found that people would not speak to her unless she spoke to them. They murmured without looking at her and she began to realize that Dodo, little Dorothy, had been lying about Henry and about her.

"What has the child said?" she demanded to know, hands on hips. She stamped her foot. "I've been part of this town, woman and child, for going on thirty years. Will somebody tell me?"

People were unable to tell her. The words stuck. Their eyes skittered like ball bearings on grease. "Some things," they said, "are best left alone. You mustn't fret, Emma. No one believes her."

"Believes what?" Aunty Em yelped. No one would answer.

So she knew it was really terrible. And she also knew, really, what had happened. Emma knew her husband and herself and the life they led. For that very reason, she did not even begin to contemplate the truth. Instead, Emma made a point of coming into town with Uncle Henry, made a point of parading with him, normal as could be.

They looked normal. They were normal. Em was upstanding and bitter, made ugly by years of sun and drought and dissatisfaction. What could be more normal? Her husband was docile and sweet and unloved, confused and in terror and desperate for the next piece of sport, uncertain that there would ever be one. Underneath the dust and the poverty, the people of Manhattan saw themselves in Em and Henry, and they didn't want to look too deep.

"Mind you," some of the nastier males said, when drunk and alone with each other, "if I lived with a woman as fulsome as Emma Gulch, I'd be looking elsewhere, too."

The "elsewhere" and the "too" meant that they knew, really, what had happened.

But they decided, on balance, to blame Dorothy. Dorothy, they decided, had been lying. She was an unpleasant, ungrateful child with a diseased mind. She would contaminate the other children if left near them. The young, they said, must be protected. They spoke about Dorothy's mother, Em's sister, in dark tones.

"Now that sister of hers was . . ." theatrical pause, "an *actress.*" The word meant so many sinister things in Kansas. "She went off with one of them fast crowds, went East to St. Lou, and married some minstrel Irishman. Just look at the result. All these years, I wondered what was eating Emma Gulch, and now I know. She's been fighting this, that child, her sister. Mind you, it runs in families." The dark hint was that Emma Gulch had had to fight against it too, the lure of fast crowds. They all had to fight against quickness. They all resented their children, because children were fast and had to be taught to be slow. They all had to be what was called good, and it was a constant battle.

Dorothy Gael ceased to exist. She went into Manhattan only once more. She walked by herself the whole distance, for Aunty Em would not have allowed it. She walked into Manhattan and no one saw her, and no one spoke to her, and no one served her in a store. She was invisible, like the Indians. She walked past the schoolyard and only one child saw her, a little boy in the first grade. He ran to his older sister. She glanced at Dorothy just once. None of the others saw her at all. They jumped rope for a while and then turned and went in before the bell. Dorothy watched them go in, and waited. She thought maybe one of the teachers would come out and chase her away. Even that did not happen.

It was quite remarkable. The children would have taunted or physically wounded a less monstrous transgressor. The teachers would have surely come out and threatened her. But Dorothy had become a legendary figure of fear, as if the Devil would breathe fire on the children, on the teachers, if they got too close to her.

Dorothy was not upset. For so long her only hope in life had been to be left alone. She asked for no better for herself, because she believed what they believed, and believed that her punishment was just.

So. No one would talk to her, she was beyond hope, and that was that. She turned and left the school and felt herself go quiet and still inside. She stayed that way. Badness had not been enough. Badness had not protected her. It was a shield that had cracked. So she was deprived even of that proud sensation. She was not bad; she was nothing, a hole. She was an adult.

She was set to work by a baffled, wounded Aunty Em.

"I don't mind telling you, Dorothy Gael, that I am ashamed, deeply ashamed of you. You've got yourself kicked out of school, closed the door on your chances of success, so you better learn to work, and you might as well learn here. You'll have to get used to it."

Dorothy ceased to talk. She ceased to talk altogether. She washed the clothes; she fed the hogs; she shoveled muck; she looked after the hens; she swept the floor; she cooked; she sewed; she scrubbed, all without speaking. She ate without speaking. That suited Aunty Em, who could only bear to speak to Dorothy to tell her what to do next, or to tell her to do it more quickly. There was sometimes a quiet dreaminess to the child that annoyed Em. It made her work slowly. Ponderously, tamely, Dorothy did exactly what she was told. No more. She would sit until told to do something else. She would sit staring all day, if not told exactly what to do.

Em found she had no heart for business. She would open the books to begin her accounts and couldn't go on. She would sit, hand pressed over her mouth, her thoughts bitter with a sense of failure. Must everything in her life turn out so badly? Even little Dodo? It was too much, too much for Emma to bear. What else in life was there for her? Pushing Henry, pushing the dry land, pushing herself until she died? Aunty Em grew to hate the clumping of Dorothy's boots.

Uncle Henry avoided Dorothy out of terror. His escape had been too narrow. His escape had changed him inside. He loathed Dorothy now, hated the very sight of her as she had once hated him. And he hated himself as much as Dorothy had hated herself. He could not bear to be with her or with himself. Each of them was utterly and completely alone and stranded, in the newly whitewashed house with its extra room in the beautiful valley, with its trees and hills and its Kansas River.

Dorothy was fed corn and cornbread and sometimes a scrap of meat or a slice of lard. Dorothy grew fat and malnourished. Her plump legs jiggled when she walked. She ate her meals outside the house or in the barn.

She slept in the summer kitchen. It was honey-colored inside, the wood being raw. It was hot in summer, sleeping near the still warm stove. In winter, the wind rattled through the shakes. Aunty Em let her have dung and twigs to burn, but that meant the stove had to be lit each night, and Dorothy didn't bother. The blankets were as cold as the snow outside. She started to sleep on the hay in the barn where the animals were kept. It was warmer.

She liked it there. It smelled of the horses. She accepted banishment as her due. She knew she was not being punished for the act. People did not believe the act had taken place. But she thought the punishment was fit for what she had done. She was even grateful for escaping so lightly. If this is what people did when they said she was lying, what would they have done to her if they had known the truth? Dorothy learned not to pay much mind to anything at all.

She liked the pigs. They had round cheerful faces, and they knew her. They greeted her. Uncle Henry would slaughter them.

I am a pig, she thought, cheerfully. I smell like one, I shit like one, in the straw away from the house. She thought of wallowing in muck like a pig. Who would notice the difference? Maybe I'll just become a pig, maybe there's a magic spell that will make me one. I'd wake up one morning on all fours grunting. I'd marry a little pig of a husband and have lots of piggy babies and then one day they'd take me away and slit me open. The lining of white fat and pink-gray meat and blood on the walls.

She drifted off to sleep, dreaming of lines of butchered, gutted Dorothys hanging on the walls. That's what happens to us anyways, she thought.

She dreamed it was wartime. There was a war between children and adults. Adults were hunting children across the landscape, on wagons and horseback. The children had to hide under the leaves. If the adults caught you, they made you a slave like in ancient Egypt. But if it was your parents who caught you, then they killed you.

Dorothy would wake up under straw, counting snowflakes blowing into the crib. She would stumble across the icy desert of the yard to the house to feed the stove, to bring in wood or coal or dung to burn. She fumbled with frozen fingers to find eggs and she brought them in to cook for breakfast.

No one came to the house to call. It was as if the Gulch farm were haunted, full of tales now. No one saw how Dorothy was living, except maybe Max Jewell. He dropped by once, on a Sunday morning, to drive her to church. He saw Dorothy huge and shapeless in bundled torn cloth, a blanket tied around her with rope. The sight of her fat face, as heavy and numb as dead meat, appalled him. Max never came back. Dorothy went on into the house.

The winter drew on. Em said nothing. Henry said nothing. Dorothy felt like some great slug, a cocoon, about to hatch. She waited for the spring.

Spring was full of mud. Dorothy lost a boot trying to rescue chicks. The sun came and baked the mud into hard plates. Dorothy broke the ground with a hoe to plant the vegetables. She scrubbed the floors and everything else in the house, where it was warm, while Aunty Em sat in silence, darning. Still there were the dreams full of death and things far worse.

Spring to summer. Rising corn again. Dorothy dreamed that the ears of corn opened out and inside each one was a baby, Henry's children from mating with the earth. And that Aunty Em boiled them, five minutes only so that they were still crisp, and they were eaten buttered, with tiny forks stuck into them on each side. Dorothy dreamed of walking through the fields, to find the ground covered in white slime, smelling of Uncle Henry. Had anyone spoken in the house for months?

To escape the dreams, Dorothy tried to stop sleeping. As spring warmed toward summer, she began to wander all through the warm nights, lit by Kansas stars, Kansas moon. She would visit the trees that had her name, sitting under the boughs high on Prospect, as if in conversation with them.

Dorothy walked along the lanes of Zeandale. It was a different place at night. It was blue and balmy and all the flowers were moonflowers, turquoise or aquamarine or purple in the dim light. She slipped like a shadow past places where there were people. She would see golden light shining from windows or from porches. The light would have a hazy halo of bugs dancing around it. Across the wide flat fields, through the still Kansas night, there would come the sound of voices, the sound of laughter, the trailing of music.

Dorothy would creep closer to the tall white farmhouses; she would hide behind the barns or outhouses. She would watch the apple-bobbing, the taffy pulls, she would hear the calming sound of singing and piano keys, the rough and carefree scraping of a violin and the light applause after sedate dancing. Dorothy would watch and listen and try to understand.

The terrible, incomprehensible truth was this: that delight was commonplace in Kansas. Delight in summer, in being young, in being with friends; delight in the warm nights that came between storms, droughts, locusts and disease. Delight in simple games, in cards held out in concealing fans; delight in the river while floating in candlelit canoes. Delight in the broad shoulders and handsome faces of German immigrant farmers with ice-blue eyes; delight in the Kansas damsels with their tough, wry smiles.

Dorothy would hide in the corn and see the awkwardly growing children of Kansas walking out together in pairs, the beefy young men in bunched-up, ill-fitting suits walking chastely beside tall slim girls in long swirling dresses.

The sight of them devastated Dorothy. It was not jealousy. Dorothy did not believe she deserved someone to walk with and had given up even dreaming of it. What devastated Dorothy was that these young people should have each other and have the light and the games and the music, have the crowded parlors and the hot fudge and names to call out to each other. They had all these things and Dorothy's night as well. They also had the blue stillness, the stars and the moon, the only things that Dorothy had thought were her own.

The realization drove her deeper and later into the night, to even more secret places at even more secret times. She would walk across the fields to Sunflower School. She looked at the trees that children had planted and that had their names. She found her own tree. It had not withered or been cut down. It was growing tall and straight, and its leaves rustled as she drew near, as if to say hello.

Then Dorothy would stand on tiptoe and peer through the windows into the classroom that would be lit with moonlight. Sunflower School became Moonflower School. Shadows of window frames cast by moonlight fell over empty desks. There would be sweeps of erased chalk across the genuine slate of the true blackboard, and there would be the stove, and the glass jars in the inkwells, and the empty pegs on which would be hung the faded bonnets in summer and thick wool coats in winter.

The trees were getting bigger, like the children who had planted them. Most of her schoolmates were already gone, adults like her, and the rooms would be suddenly full of children she didn't know. Not even ghosts.

One night toward the end of that summer, Dorothy stepped out from Sunflower School back onto Rock Spring Lane and looked up its straight length toward her hill.

Dorothy remembered Miss Francis telling them about the Aztecs, the Indians of Mexico who had built such fine, high stone buildings. Dorothy's imagination had been caught, and Miss Francis told her about the pyramids they built, rising up in layers. And Dorothy had walked out and seen the hill. It rose in layers, too, as if someone had cut giant steps out of it. Dorothy had been convinced, had wanted to be convinced, that Indians had built her hill as well, and that they lived inside it, like Aztecs. She did not ask Miss Francis if that were so. She had decided that it was so, and that it was her secret.

Dorothy no longer believed in Indians. Rather, she believed in the hopeless, flat, beardless faces wearing dirty white men's clothes, like her own. Dorothy wore britches and boots like a man.

The hill stayed silent as she walked through the secret places of the night. Dorothy wandered through the orchards of Squire Aiken. She did steal a peach and ate it in starlight. She headed east and then south in a great curve around to Pleasant Valley Cemetery. All the dead were lined up as straight and foursquare as they had been in life. There were no terrors for Dorothy in Pleasant Valley Cemetery. She knew most of the people in it. There was Wilbur and Mrs. Jewell; there were some of the Pillsburys and some of the older McCormacks and Allens. She picked wildflowers in the moonlight and left them on the graves. And walked on. She walked miles. Cemeteries and dark woods were better than her dreams.

And suddenly the road plunged down into a hollow, and Dorothy was at Pillsbury's Crossing.

The first time that Dorothy had gone to the Crossing was with the school, her first year in Kansas. It was America's Centennial, 1876, and she was how old? Six? They had come here to have a picnic.

Dorothy remembered the road, plunging down straight across the river. The river was only inches deep, flowing over a single, huge rock. The children had waded in the water, delighting in the cool shade of the hollow. Dorothy had felt ripples under her feet, in the stone, like the ripples water makes in sand. Was rock sand? It was, in a way. Teacher said so.

Teacher said a glacier had probably left the rock there. She said that a glacier was a river of ice, but that didn't make sense. Dorothy thought that perhaps a glacier was some great animal, carrying stones on its back.

The river swept on, in a huge bend, and suddenly slipped over the edge of the rock in a great horseshoe waterfall. It was confusing, because the water started to flow diagonally across the stone. Suddenly it was pouring over it, right next to the road and in the same direction as the road. The other children had yelled and shouted to each other. Dorothy had not liked the noise or the slashes of sunlight through the leaves. Little Dorothy had hidden under a cleft in the great rock itself, behind the waterfall. She watched the flowing screen of water that concealed her. She had heard Miss Francis shouting her name over and over, but Dorothy was in hiding and it simply had not occurred to her to reply. Gasping in panic, Miss Francis found her. "Dorothy!" she exclaimed. "Why didn't you say something?"

Little Dorothy had not known why and could not explain. The next evening Miss Francis came to call for the first time, to have her first long talk with Emma Gulch about what to do with Dorothy.

Now it was night, and everywhere was a hiding place. Once again, Dorothy walked down the road toward the crossing of the waters.

It was very dark in the hollow, and she could only hear, rather than see, the river. She felt her way down a slope of stone toward the crossing.

And then, it seemed to her, she saw the glacier.

Something was stranded in the shallow, rippling water. It snorted a blast of air like a dragon and tried to raise its great head. It had huge hunched shoulders, and it thrashed in the water, pawing with its front legs, trying to stand, failing to stand.

Dazed with sleeplessness, Dorothy simply stood and watched. She waited until her eyes grew used to the dark, began to see things in the starlight that fell through the leaves.

There was a buffalo. A single buffalo alone. Here in Zeandale? There were no more buffalo in Zeandale. And buffalo moved in herds. They did not live alone.

The beast knew she was there. It held up its head, unmoving and watchful. There was a glint of moonlight on its living eyes and on its tiny horns. Dorothy seemed to feel the strain in its neck muscles. The buffalo snorted again and tried to thrash its way to its feet.

And then, the buffalo lay down its head in the waters of the Crossing.

And Dorothy understood. This was the last buffalo. It had come back home to die. Its home would have been the hills above Zeandale. Now those were pastures for cattle, ringed around with barbed wire.

The buffalo were becoming extinct. Like giant flying lizards, or dodos.

Dorothy could hear its breath, hoarse and panting. The beast was dangerous. Its head was huge and a single convulsion would knock her off her feet or tear her flesh. But Dorothy did not want to leave it. She did not want it to die alone, unnoticed. She did not feel that it wanted to be left alone.

She watched it from the shore, warily. It had stopped thrashing and its giant head lay still in the shallow water. She could feel its life draining away. Dorothy sat down on the stone and unlaced her boots and walked out onto the Crossing, toward the edge of the waterfall.

The water was cool, and she felt underfoot again the stone that was rippled like a sandbar. Dorothy walked as close to the beast as she dared.

Then she put her spirit into the buffalo. She felt the vast, exhausted bulk that had gone as immobile as stone; she felt the covering of wiry, curly hair caked with mud. She felt the tail wet and heavy, beyond flicking, floating in the shallow water. The buffalo was settling into the stone. Its huge pink tongue was lolling in the water.

Don't let me die alone, the buffalo seemed to say to her. Buffalo live together; we are taken by the wolves if we cannot keep up a march. If we lag behind, we are quickly torn away, but we do not understand loneliness. Don't leave me alone.

And Dorothy knelt close beside him and stroked his mighty head and the huge hump of his shoulders, and she felt how once he had been a king. No king should die unmourned. He went very still. Breath bubbled out of him in the water. His hide twitched.

Give me to the river, the buffalo said. Hide me away from men. I don't mind the coyote or the vulture; I don't mind the beetle or the muskrat. But I don't want men to get me. I don't want them to hang my brow and horns on their wall; I don't want my skin on their floor or on their backs. Let me go whole back into the earth.

Dorothy tended the king until he died. She stroked him until she was sure he was dead, until the chest no longer heaved with breath, until there was no bubbling in the water, until the flesh was still.

Then Dorothy tried to roll him over the edge. She was very strong and perhaps the current helped. She succeeded in half rolling the corpse of a bull buffalo up onto his haunches.

It was as though she had sparked something. The legs suddenly twitched. *Yes!* the muscles seemed to say, *Yes!* Dorothy heard the hooves scrabbling on the stone.

As though the buffalo had tried to leap into Heaven, the corpse launched itself into the air. It shivered its way over the edge of the rock, a moonlit sheen of water pouring over its shoulders. It fell over the horseshoe plunge, where Dorothy had once hidden herself.

The buffalo fell between the waterfall and a large boulder. He landed, with a rearing up of his small legs, which were now limp again. He reared up and settled back and it was as if he had sighed with relief, accepting the embrace of stone.

There was a large branch stranded on the edge of the fall, and Dorothy dragged that forward until it fell too. It slipped slowly sideways, hardly falling at all, it seemed, the heavier end of its trunk crashing down onto rocks and puddles. The upper boughs lashed the air at about the level they had been at before. Except that the buffalo was covered, hidden perhaps, safe perhaps from men.

Then Dorothy stumbled back home toward the summer kitchen. Her clothes were wet, but there was no one at home who would mind. Who needs dreams? she thought. This was better. As she walked, she felt her eyelids drooping. She picked up a stick to lean on.

It was blue-gray in the sky by the time she reached the woods over the farm. She planned to walk down out of the trees, unseen. She was idly slashing at the hickory with the stick. She thumped a large tree trunk and realized that it was hollow.

There's a hollow branch up there, she thought. And there was. Now how did I know that? She reached up into a broken branch and felt leaves and pulled.

Something came out, brown as Kansas. She shook it. It was a child's dress, very lacy. Would have been white once. And there were tiny, flaking platelets of metal sewn onto it. Dorothy held it up against herself. Definitely a child's dress.

Something stirred, as if there were something else alive within her. She felt it move. It was as if there were a dreamworld somewhere, which she could dimly see. Had she left the dress in the tree?

Dorothy remembered Wilbur. She remembered the first day and the train trip and something about staying with people on the way to Kansas. There had been another life, as if the world had divided in two. She had not always lived with Aunty Em. Dorothy rolled up the tiny brown thing and hid it in her coat.

Back down on the farm, there was nothing to greet her or welcome her. She dropped down onto her mattress and sank into the deepest kind of sleep, as deep as a well and dreamless. All unaware, she had dammed up a reservoir of dreams. They grew heavy, as if hairline cracks ran through the bones of her forehead.

As Dorothy worked that day, she stumbled. She stared ahead, terrible rings around her staring eyes. Aunty Em said, "I reckon you best rest a spell, Dorothy." Dorothy looked back at her, almost refusing. But I don't want to rest, she thought. I might have the dreams.

"Go on and lie down." Aunty Em's voice sounded sad and weary. Dorothy noted how it sounded even as she turned to obey automatically. It was easier to obey than to try to think. She plodded into the barn. Her feet were like heavy stones. She slumped down onto the bales of hay and curled up on one of them, boots drawn up under her knees. She stared ahead. She would not close her eyes. Aunty Em had told her to lie down, but she would not sleep.

Aunty Em came in.

"You're still awake," Emma said in sorrow.

Aunty Em came and sat next to her on the straw. "You don't sleep, do you, Dorothy?"

Aunty Em sighed when Dorothy did not answer. She moved closer and there was a rustling of hay. "Your clothes are soaking wet and your boots are covered in mud and grass and pine-tree needles. Where do you go, Dorothy? Where do you go at night?"

Dorothy didn't answer. She stared ahead. Aunty Em began to stroke her hair, as Dorothy had stroked the buffalo.

"What happened, Dodo? What happened to you? You were such

a beautiful little girl. You'd always help around the house and were so kind to your poor old aunty. And you used to make me laugh. Like when you told off all those old ladies about the way they treated the Chinawoman. Remember? Or when we caught caterpillars and put them in preserving jars with grass to see if they'd turn into butterflies. I thought that was the funniest thing."

A shabby black sleeve on bone-thin arms with a veined and muscular brown claw at the end, smoothing down Dorothy's hair, trying to untangle it.

"Did we do anything, Dodo? Was it something we did? Is it something we can undo?"

Dorothy couldn't think. Yes, probably, she thought, but she wasn't sure she had said it out loud.

"Dorothy," said Aunty Em. "Please come back. You were the light of my life. You were what kept me going all those years. Just to hear you laughing, or naming the birds, or working away at your books."

Dorothy thought just two words. The words were: too late. It was a very simple, very final thought, and she wondered how something so simple could be so complete. Too late. She could not think much beyond that and she did not need to.

"Come on, up. Let's get you into the house." Aunty Em coaxed her to her feet and led her up the wooden steps to the summer kitchen.

The next Sunday, Aunty Em went alone to Meeting. She went to howl in tongues, flushed with the love of Jesus, a stick jammed between her teeth to keep her from biting off her tongue. One of Dorothy's worst dreams had been about all of Aunty Em's talking tongues slithering out of her mouth, hydra-headed.

Uncle Henry was out communing with his fields, which meant masturbating into the dirt. It was a good summer, warm and gentle, though today was surprisingly cool.

Dorothy finished all her chores. She did them without questioning. She washed Aunty Em's clothes, her nightdress. She washed Uncle Henry's socks and his loose and baggy underwear. She went out to the clothesline with a basket and pegged all their clothes up on the line.

Then she stood up, as straight and sudden as if someone had called her name. That was it. She was finished here.

Dorothy knew she was big enough to go. Big enough and ugly as a pig's backside, but that made no difference. The weather was perfect, brilliantly sunny without being hot. Em and Henry were away, so she could steal what she needed.

She would go to St. Lou, or Abilene, or Wichita. She would go there and be one of those bad girls. It was better than scrubbing the yellow garments Emma Gulch slept in. Dorothy wasn't entirely sure what it was that bad girls did, but if it was lying with men like she had lain with Uncle Henry, she could stand it. She didn't feel anything when that happened. She knew she looked older than she was. And if they found she was younger, they probably wouldn't mind. They'd probably like it. But she needed some clothes.

She opened up Aunty Em's wardrobe and saw four dresses and stole two of them. She judged very carefully which ones she took. Em was wearing her second-best Sunday and had left her best Sunday for another occasion. If Dorothy took her good Sunday or the striped crinoline, Em would send the law after her. So she decided on the old bottle-green dress, stitched and darned back into shape. There was another old one, her coming-out dress Aunty Em called it, splotched and itchy blue. She took a dried-up old bonnet with wilted cloth flowers. It didn't matter if she looked poor. Poor meant bad and that would draw the men. It didn't matter what it looked like as long as it looked adult. Enough.

Right in the middle of the room, Dorothy changed. She had no shame left. If Uncle Henry walked in, she would not turn around. Let him see it, it would be nothing new to him. Nothing meant anything to her. She put on the bottle-green dress because it would not be so uncomfortable when she sweated and would not show the dust as the blue one would. She rolled the blue one up like a towel around the brown boots Uncle Henry had brought her back from Manhattan two years before. She could wear her old ones. She looked around the small dark room. It had never done her any harm. There was the bed and the new dresser with its rows of ill-assorted plates. The room had a face that seemed to smile. The old clock on top of the wardrobe. The Bible, and all of Aunty Em's old books in rows. The new table rocked when you tried to cut bread.

It might have been a home. Goodbye, she said to the room, but not the people in it.

She could imagine what would happen later that afternoon. Emma would come back from Meeting and call for her. "Dodo? Dodo?" she would say and then walk out to the barn. She would realize that Dorothy was not there. She would pace around the floor for a time, hoping that Dodo had only gone for a Sunday walk. Then she would think. She would check her cupboard and cry aloud, covering her mouth when she saw that the dresses were gone. Alone in the house, she would cover her face and weep.

When Henry finally came back in, she would blurt out to him, "Henry! Dorothy's gone!" Henry would try to look sad, and he would stand over Emma and pat her on the back and say, There, there, Em, and she would say: She stole my dresses! And they would decide that maybe it was worth the price of a few dresses to have Dorothy gone. And the house would return to silence.

Dorothy forgave them, almost forgave herself. They had all failed, failed in the most fundamental way—to make a way of life that was possible. Dorothy felt fear now, fear of the world beyond the familiar fields. She had no reason to suppose it would treat her any more kindly than her own kin. And she saw them in her mind and surprised herself with a mild stinging of tears in the bottom of her eyes. The Aunty Em she hated seemed to melt away. In her place was a woman who was nothing like as old as she looked, a woman who had not been loved since her father died, and who did not know how to say what she really felt and who hated her life, dressing in black, saving her good clothes for occasions that never came, stabbing at the rotten socks, trying to keep them together, stabbing them and her fingers with the needle. Too late. And Henry. Poor soft old Henry who could only have power over children. It was as if they had all stood back-to-back, shouting "love" at the tops of their lungs, but in the wrong direction, away from each other.

But goodbye, goodbye as fast as I can. If Dorothy had to eat one more meal from the hands of Aunty Em, it would choke her. If Uncle Henry so much as glanced at her covertly, something kindling again in his eyes, she might kill him.

Was there anything else she needed? Dorothy remembered that there was one thing only that was indisputably hers. She went to the summer kitchen, and from under her pillow she took the child's dress. She stood in the yard and took one final look, not to remember, but to forget, and then Dorothy walked.

There was no softening haze over the fields. It was a strange day, fiercely bright, but cool, very cool in a Kansas August. When a day was as fierce as that, it always meant it would be cloudy by noon. Dorothy was glad it was cool; she could walk farther. The corn would be tall; it would hide her as she walked. She could not be seen on the roads. The sunlight on the corn leaves engraved them with lines. The soil underneath was baked as firm as any roadway, in hard clumps that tickled Dorothy's hardened feet.

Dorothy began to skip. Witch, witch, Wichita. Which witch from Wichita, witch? Which Wichita? She was going to Wichita, to be a whore, but now, just for now, the sun was shining, and just for now, she could be a kid, one last time. She spun around and around and around. She knocked a stalk of corn. Goddamned corn, the whole country was corn. It used to be a prairie, full of sage and groundhogs. Her hands were like a scythe as she spun. She could feel herself chopping the corn down. She staggered spinning, giddy. Gol-danged corn, she thought and tore up a stalk of it by the roots. She began to march with it over her shoulder, like a soldier, and she began to sing a Civil War song and march to it:

> *When Johnny comes marchin' home again*
> *Hurrah! Hurrah!*

And it felt as if she were going home, or somewhere. She slashed at the corn with the stalk in her hand until it broke. She kicked at the corn, knocked it over, tore it up, broke it, giddy and grinning, and began to spin again, spin around, harder and harder, to spin the world away, spinning out of the plowed rows, through the corn itself, breaking the order of the lines, spinning until her stomach rebelled. It clenched and suddenly poured out the breakfast of grits in another circle, a great arc of gray and inferior food. The last breakfast from Aunty Em. Dorothy was free from that too.

Chuckling at the sudden outbreak of utter foolishness, Dorothy allowed herself to be spun onto the ground. The ground seemed to tilt up to receive her, and Dorothy was on her back, looking up through corn leaves to the sky, to the clouds gathering overhead, and the sky and the clouds seemed to spin above her. They seemed to spin and stay in one place at the same time, moving and not moving. The world's turning all the time. Only we can't see it.

Dorothy turned and looked at the ground. An old black beetle struggled up and over the clumps of gray dirt that looked the size of boulders. There were hills and forests under the leaves. The ground was splashed with pallid shadows and pallid fading sunlight, and the corn was taller than trees. It whispered, calling her name.

It was another world. Dorothy wished she were that small, to live hidden under the leaves. She would ride field mice and live in a burrow that had a little smoking chimney, and she and the other little people would dance and laugh and spin until they were giddy and hide when the big people came. Maybe when you grew up, part of you was left behind, to live unnoticed under the leaves.

The leaves began to rattle in a breeze. Was it cooler? Dorothy stood up. My green dress is dusty, she thought, but she didn't mind. I don't want to look like an adult just yet.

Maybe I'll just walk through these fields the rest of my life and no one will find me. I'll wear corn leaves or cobwebs, and I'd build a sod house so far underground that they'll plant the corn right over it. And I'll sit in my house and hear the plows go overhead and laugh. I'd rock back and forth and have the gophers in for dinner.

But it was time to move on. Dorothy began to walk again, reeling as if drunk. She stumbled on the baked clods of earth that were as hard as stone. The sun went behind a cloud and stayed there.

Did she really want to walk to Wichita? Was there anything else she could do? She could try to find her father and live with him. She didn't know his first name. Only Gael. And that may have been made-up. Gaelic to Gael. He was Irish and an actor, and she wouldn't know him if she saw him. And he would not know her. He was probably dead, or in New York.

Dorothy came to the end of Uncle Henry's fields. There was a screen of leaves between her and the end of her known world. The sky got darker. There looked like being a storm. She would have to walk through rain and mud.

And suddenly she hid her face and wept. What was she going to do in Wichita except starve and beg and get dirty and smelly and used? Who did she know in Wichita? Who did she know anywhere? No one in Manhattan, where people looked straight through her. No one in the only place she could remember living. All Dorothy needed was extreme cleverness, and fearlessness, and love and a home, and she had none of those things. Dorothy needed magic. She needed some magic spell that would change her, give her different clothes, a clean face. She needed magic to scoop her up and drop her down in Wichita as a famous actress. She dreamed of being rich, of taking the train, of being met by carriages, of wearing pretty clothes and having doormen greet her.

There was no way out. No way back. She kept walking. She began to have another fantasy, that she was walking backward. She was walking backward through the years, and she was going to walk back home, to St. Lou before the diphtheria, to find her mother and father waiting for her, in the home she did not remember, away from Is, into the land of Was.

She pushed aside the last of the corn leaves and found a pasture of sunflowers.

They were wild, multistemmed with tiny yellow blossoms. They bobbed in a gathering breeze. They looked like a field of lamps. Dorothy stepped down from the barbed-wire fence, her adult dress held up around her ankles.

She ate the sunflower seeds, like the Indians did when they had lived in a place they called Blue Earth. If only there were Indians, real Indians that she could go and live with.

Then she heard a giggle under the leaves.

High-pitched, as if the gophers had acquired human voices.

"Hello?" she asked. "Hello?" She crouched, looking under the leaves, thinking to see children. The Jewells had children. She remembered them. One was small and hard and jealous. What was his name? And the other one was tall and shambling. A scarecrow on a Sunday. Would they have yellow sunflower faces? They would have sunflower faces. She looked but couldn't find them.

"Hello?" she called again, chuckling kindly, so they could hear she meant no harm. Then she thought: Were the sunflowers laughing? And then she heard deep voices.

> *Wichita ta ta*
> *Wichita ta ta*

It was a chant.

Wichita ta ta

Wichita was an Indian name, it was the name of the tribe of Indians the white adults had pushed aside, marched into the desert so that they died. But some of them escaped. They had stayed in Kansas, to live secretly under the cornfields. They had finally, finally come out to dance.

Wichita ta ta

She saw them, under the sunflowers. They were tiny brown men no taller than her knees. They were naked except for the feathers of birds and they were slightly wizened, like children that never grew up, or adults who had decided to stay children. They danced in a circle, chanting. They were Indians who had won. They were the Indians of Oz.

Wichita ta ta
Topeka
Manhattan
Ha ha
Tan tan

The gophers were standing in a ring to watch. There was a slight change to the sound.

Wichito to
To to
Topeka
Wichito to
To to
Toto

And suddenly she heard a dog bark, far away.

All the sunflowers began to bob and bend in a gathering wind. There was a low animal whine from all around her. The wind plucked at her adult clothes and there seemed to be smoke. It trailed across the ground, between the flowers, over her shoes. Smoke from Indian fires? The air was full of dust and smelled suddenly of soil. The chant went on: Toto, Toto.

Suddenly, all the sunflowers broke free. They rose up, leapt into the air, and spun away as Dorothy had spun.

Wichito to
Topeka

The sunflowers spun smiling all around her, like the scythes of her hands. There was a blast of wind and dust. Dorothy's dress was whipped about her legs. It spun around her like a sheep caught in barbed wire. The dust was flowing now like a wide thick river. She was standing in the middle of it. Dust blew up into her eyes, stinging, she had to look away.

The dust was making her weep. The Indians kept chanting. She let her eyes water, to clear them, and when she opened them again, the whole of the field had risen up into the air, spiraling sunflowers, a plowed line of dirt drawn up into the air like soda through a straw. Still blinking, Dorothy looked up and saw it.

A twister. A twister.

And Dorothy froze. She went stock-still.

The twister loomed over her as huge as a man, spinning, turning, trawling its vast single foot lazily across the fields.

Dorothy thought she was calm. I made it, she thought. It came out of me. I spun and spun and I made it, as twisted as I am. And now it's coming for me. There is no place to hide. I ran away, and there was no escape. I ran into the fields, the one place you are not supposed to go in a cyclone, and I can't go home. You need to have a burrow in the earth. And that was what I wanted. Somewhere to live hidden. And now I'm going to die. I'm going to die.

It seemed to her suddenly to be the way out, to let the wind blow her away, like dust, to somewhere else.

She watched the twister as it came, passive as she had been before Uncle Henry. She waited as if for a lover. She was unable to move.

*   *   *

Then suddenly there was a bright, fierce little bark, a sound like shattering mirrors. Dorothy looked down, and there was Toto, bouncing with rage, turning around and around in the dust.

Toto, she tried to say, but the wind pulled the breath out of her lungs.

He was full of life and anger. You don't want to die! he seemed to say. Run!

Dorothy broke free. She screamed and covered her eyes. With a thrill of self-love, she began to run.

Toto ran with her, yipping, on tiny terrier legs, circling her ankles. She ran blindly, arm across her tender eyes.

In a twister, you set the horses free, free to run. Some know to run away from the twister. Some run into it, and no one knows why. Some want the twister, betrayed by something inside them.

Toto shepherded her. He drove her away from it, toward the hills, out of the valley. She ran with long hungry strides over the broken earth toward shelter, the Aikens' house. She ran listening for the howl of wind in a peach orchard. The twister turned and changed shape, the blast sucking one way and then exploding in another. *Our Father who art in Heaven.*

The cyclone was behind her, then in front of her, dodging like a clever, nasty boy weaving his way toward a touchdown. Toto barked. This way! This way!

Hallowed be thy Name.

The wind clutched at her adult dress and tore at it viciously.

Thy kingdom come.

Lost in a world of burning dust.

Thy will be done.

The ground beneath her suddenly gave way. She felt her boots flood with water.

On earth as it is in Heaven.

She had run into the wallows. She felt the mud suck at her feet and pull her down. Oh God, don't do this, oh God, I'll be good. I promise. Dorothy fought her way forward, thrashing with her hands. Hands were cut. Was it a thorn bush? Dorothy fell forward into rolls of barbed wire.

It had been nailed to stakes, to keep it secure, pegged firm, a maze of wire to be stretched around the fields and to encircle the wallows.

It was a great extended hollow tube of wire, a second twister. Dorothy's arms and chest were enmeshed in its embrace. She thrashed against it, arms working their way deeper into it. The mud pulled down. The wire held.

The twister wanted her. It roared in anger and pulled. Dorothy was snatched up. The wire sang. The wire extended like a spring; the mud pulled down. One end of the wire broke free. Dorothy found a fence post and grabbed it and held, and the loose spiral of wire turned around and around her, lashing her to the post, holding her to its wooden bosom as if to say, I will keep you, Dorothy, I will keep you in Kansas. The wire whipped around her, binding her tighter and tighter. The mud tried to pull her down. Overhead was the flock of sunflowers. They still giggled. Dorothy was held.

And in the dust, part of the dust, there was a nittering. Dorothy felt a cold wet nose. Toto climbed up onto her lap. She could feel his shivering warmth; she could feel his rough, loving tongue.

And the dress, the old dress slipped free from under her arm.

Dorothy blinked. How had it become so clean? It seemed to her that it was white, blazing white and covered in sequins. They flashed in the sunlight that peeked under the clouds. It ascended.

The dust was as thick as syrup and Dorothy had to close her eyes. Dust sizzled on her face like fat dancing on a hot, hot pan, and her skin was scoured. She stroked Toto with her raw hands; she could feel his fur like pine needles. You led me right, dog, she thought. The wire held her.

The wind shrieked and scraped. It passed singeing over her, enveloping her, brutalizing her with its love, like any love she could remember.

Then, as if something had popped, everything went still. Dorothy had time to open her eyes. In the center of the twister, the air was almost clear and everything was a beautiful blue. Blue Earth. Everything stood up straight, the grass, her hair, the wire, all hauled toward Heaven. She seemed to see buffalo, swirling up into it. All the extinct creatures had been pulled into Heaven. Dorothy had time to be glad. The twister drank the air out of her lungs. The Indians sang:

Wichita ta ta
to to
tot tot
ta ta

Then the singing stopped.

Waposage, Kansas

November 1956

The Wonderful Wizard of Oz *was kept off most public library shelves until the 1960s because librarians considered it hackwork. When Cornelia Meigs edited a 624-page Critical History of Children's Literature for Macmillan in 1953, there was not a single mention of Baum in the book. The Wonderful Wizard of Oz does appear in the fourth edition of May Hill Arbuthnot's Children and Books, revised by Zena Sutherland and published in 1972—but it does not appear in the first three editions, and in the 1972 edition, it is simply listed among "Books that Stir Controversy."*

> —ALJEAN HARMETZ,
> The Making of the Wizard of Oz

The hostility to the Oz books is in itself something of a phenomenon. . . .

It is significant that one of the most brutal attacks on the Oz books was made by the director of the Detroit Library system, a Mr. Ralph Ulveling, who found the Oz books to have "a cowardly approach to life." They are also guilty of "negativism." Worst of all, "there is nothing elevating or uplifting about the Baum series." For the Librarian of Detroit, courage and affirmation meant punching the clock and then doing the dull work of a machine while never questioning the system.

> —GORE VIDAL,
> in an essay, "The Oz Books"

Bill Davison had a few months to go before he got his draft notice, so he went to work in the Home. He was hired for his muscles. Bill Davison had been a linebacker on the school football team, had fairly bad grades and was generally recognized to be a nice guy. He was huge, happy and surprisingly gentle. Girls loved his gentleness. He was seventeen now and engaged to his girlfriend, Carol. He was a practicing Christian and had the bravery and confidence to be kind to his mother in public.

His father had been killed when he was six, during the Italian campaign. The experience had been terrible for him. He had needed and wanted his father, kept photographs of him in his uniform, had a map on the wall that traced with pins where his father was. The news of his death had been delivered personally by a friend of the family at the recruiting office. War had taken Bill's father away and would make of him a young man whose urges to violence were all sublimated into sports.

Bill's grades were bad—straight C's. Even so, people were surprised when he took on work at the Home. Who cared about grades? Bill was a presentable young man and could have gotten a good job behind a counter or in an office somewhere. Fat white women with too many kids ended up working at the Home, or blacks, or Mexicans. The Home was one of three state institutions for the mentally ill in all of Kansas. The citizens of Waposage were rather proud of their provision for the insane. They just didn't want to work in the place. Bill did.

He wasn't sure why. "Oh, I don't know," he would tell people. "I guess I just wanted a job helping people. The Home was nearby."

Since graduating in June, he had been working in an electrical supply store and showroom. It was run by Mr. Hardie. He was one of the many friendly older men who thought they had taken on the job of acting like a father to Bill.

"People in the Home can't always be helped," said Mr. Hardie, when Bill told him he was leaving the store.

"Well. They still need caring for," Bill replied.

"That's true, Bill, and it's a fine thought. But you still have got to think of yourself, and of Carol too. They won't be paying you much money for that job."

"Carol's got her job at the hairdresser's. And anyway, I got the Army coming up in a couple of months. It's just till then."

"From now on," said Mr. Hardie, "you got to be thinking of how you're going to set yourself up in life. You got to be thinking about what's going to happen after those two years. You find things are getting tight over the next few months, or you just want a change of scenery, you know there'll always be a job waiting for you here in the store. Need a fine young man like you."

Bill knew he was a fine young man—he had worked at it—but he wore his knowledge lightly. "Thank you, Sir," he replied.

Bill Davison started work in September 1956, in the geriatric ward. He would always remember arriving. On his first day at the Home, he was shown around by another orderly. The man's name was Tom, Tom Heritage. Tom was tall, plump, friendly, and had a very nearly invisible blond beard. He had been a truck driver until he lost his license for three years.

"First thing you do every morning is help wheel up the food from downstairs. Then, while they're eating, we change all the bedding. Some of them leak a little, so we just give them clean sheets. You make their beds for them, tidy up. During the day you help some of them around, maybe take them for a walk. If any of them get sick, you help them down to the infirmary."

"Anything else?" Bill asked, disappointed.

"What, you mean like try to cure them or something? No way, son. That's the Doctor's job."

Tom Heritage pushed against the swinging doors, and they walked into a ward of cots. The old people slept in cots to stop them from rolling out at night. Each one of them had a metal locker that doubled as a bedside table, and a chair to sit on.

"This here's what we call Heaven. It's where all the ones that don't give anyone any trouble are. The Angels."

One old man was still in bed, back turned to the door.

"Okay, Bobby," said Heritage, neatly flipping down one rank of blue cot bars. "It's time to get up. Breakfast."

The old man's face had fallen in on itself, collapsed, and he stared ahead with watery blue eyes. There was white stubble all over his chin.

"Sorry, Bobby, but we got to make your bed." Heritage gave Bill Davison a nod. Bill stared back. "Got to lift him out," explained Heritage. "You take the legs."

Heritage took the arms. Quickly, neatly, the old man was hoisted out of bed and lowered down into his wheelchair. He still stared. One foot began to jiggle up and down with nerves.

Heritage stood back and held up a greeting card from the table. The card had grown soft and worn around the edges, as if trying to grow fur. The corners were grubby. On the front there was a wide-eyed cartoon bunny.

"It says 'Get well soon,' " said Heritage, his eyes and smile just the slightest bit grim.

Heritage wheeled the old man off to his breakfast. All by himself, Bill stripped the beds. It was all so impersonal. The Angels of Heaven were bereft of possessions. Pajamas, a change of clothing, used handkerchiefs, a smell of weak and sweaty bodies. There would be nothing to move away when they died. Heritage returned with the sheets.

About eleven o'clock, they moved off toward the women's ward. From somewhere down the corridor came dim, echoing voices, murmuring or raised and querulous. They sounded like a choir that had not yet begun to sing.

"We treat the women just the same as the men, except that we come in after breakfast when we know they're all decent. Some of the old dears are a bit old-fashioned."

"Don't we do anything to help them?" Bill asked again.

Heritage gave him a thin-lipped smile and shook his head. "Nobody's going to help these people," he said. "Some of them been here for fifty years."

Some of the women sat beside their cots. One of them was making knitting motions with empty hands.

"Good morning, girls," said Heritage. None of them responded, except for one woman who looked up, very slowly, with round, haunted eyes.

Then, suddenly, someone spoke. It was a surprisingly smooth, polished voice, almost like an adolescent's.

"If you're through gabbing, you could get me up off this floor," said the voice. An outraged head reared itself up over the horizon of a crumpled cot.

It was a fine head, a noble head, something like a lion's, ringed with wild gray hair. The eyes were wild too.

Heritage closed his eyes and smiled. "Remember how I said none of them were trouble?" he said. He began to walk backward toward her, looking at Bill, talking to Bill. "Well. Meet trouble."

Bill Davison followed him, tardily. "Dotty," Heritage asked, "what are you doing on the floor?"

"I fell down!" she exclaimed, enraged. "Fell down and I can't get up!"

Tom Heritage had slipped his arms under hers and already had her on her feet when Bill finally arrived to offer assistance. He managed only to touch her elbow.

"Where do you want to be?" Heritage asked.

"Anyplace but here. In that chair."

She moved in tough little jerks, and she talked in tough little jerks. Looking at her, Bill thought: The West, the Old West. She had the tang of it.

"You miss breakfast?" Heritage asked her.

"Dang right," said Dotty. "That eggy stuff looks like cat sick. Can't stand it."

Heritage was smiling again. "Bill," he said, "this here's Old Dynamite. Dynamite Dotty. You want to help people, well this is one of our success stories. Used to take three big men to hold Old Dynamite down. Till she became an Angel and grew wings."

"I," announced Dotty, "always had wings." She began to stroke them, growing invisibly from her shoulders. She looked regal. "Hmmmph!" she said, and made a dismissive gesture.

"Come on, we got to make all these beds," said Heritage.

As they worked, Bill looked at Old Dynamite. A smile had grown on her face. It grew wide and joyous, and the eyes fixed on Heaven seemed to be full of light.

Bill stood and looked at her. He wanted to say to Heritage that she looked like something in a Sunday School painting. Heritage was rolling sheets, quickly, into loosely wound balls and throwing them into sacks. Dimly, Bill could hear her singing. She sang to herself. It was an old, grand song, some kind of hymn, but not one that Bill knew from years of churchgoing. But he did know it from somewhere. The words, high and thin, over and over, were "Hally hoo hah."

"There's nothing wrong with her," Bill said, later.

"Dot? Stick around," said Heritage.

*　　　*　　　*

Bill and Heritage wheeled up lunch in huge industrial catering tureens on carts. They boomed their way through swinging doors that were plated with metal. They themselves ate and then wheeled the tureens back down.

And after lunch, they stood watch over the men and women in the common room. There were wide windows looking over the lawns. It was cold and misty, and the landscape was in layers of misted silhouette. A row of leafless trees looked like charts of nerves.

There was nothing for any of the Angels to do. Some of them were playing cards. The cards were black around the edges. There was a chess set. Pieces were missing. There were a few deserted books, all of them left a quarter of the way through, facedown. And the constant murmuring, almost musical. The sound of the Angels.

"We call this the Pearly Gates," said Heritage.

Women sat mouthing the air or rocking the ghosts of children.

"It's so boring for them," said Bill.

"Used to be a radio, but they kept messing with the dials until it broke." Suddenly Old Dot loomed next to them. She was huge, almost as tall as Bill, and even now neither fat nor thin. She was very stiff on her pins, but that lent her a kind of creeping iron dignity.

"We haven't died, you know," she said, to Heritage. "Not yet, anyway."

Heritage leaned back against the wall and gave her an amused and crooked smile.

He feels superior, thought Bill. That's it. He's not mean or anything. He just knows he's farther up the scale, and he thinks there's nothing to be done. So he won't listen.

Bill thought he knew what the old woman meant. "So you think we shouldn't call this place Heaven?" Bill asked Dotty.

"But it is," she said, suddenly fierce, drawing up. "It is, goddamn it. Take a look! I don't know. You people!"

Old Dynamite turned away, shaking her head. Heritage gave Bill another crooked smile. You see? his raised eyebrows seemed to say. Very slowly Old Dot crept toward the window. From behind, she looked far more frail, bowed, her shoulders turning inward.

She stared out the window at the mist until it was dark.

* * *

Without realizing it, Bill must have said something to Mr. Hardie, because a few days later Hardie Electrical Supplies donated a television set to the Home. It was a great embarrassment. First, it embarrassed Bill, who had not asked and thought perhaps the Home would think he had been criticizing it. Second, it embarrassed the Home, which was overwhelmed by the generosity but was worried that one of the Angels would shove a fist into the vacuum tube.

When they tried to give it back, Mr. Hardie apparently suggested that Bill be put in charge of it, to change channels, to turn it off, to wheel it around, to guard its plugs and dials and glass face.

Bill was very wary of television sets himself. He had seen an accident. An assistant at Mr. Hardie's had been carrying two picture tubes, whistling as he walked, swinging them gently. The tubes hit each other, and there was a kind of popping sound, like small pistol shots, and a gasp. Glass had been sucked in and then spat out. The assistant stood surprised and startled, rivulets of blood trickling down his face and his arms. Slivers of glass had been driven into him all over his body. Like the wilderness, like a cyclone, televisions had a nothingness in their hearts.

There was some discussion among the senior staff of the Home. It was decided to allow television only at certain times. Late evening was forbidden in case the dependants of the Home got overexcited. News would be forbidden or any program with guns or violence. The children of the Home would be allowed *Captain Kangaroo* and *The Three Stooges* and the morning game shows like *The Price Is Right* and *Queen for a Day*. In the afternoon, they would be allowed soap operas.

Bill carried in the television the first day. He switched it on with trepidation and stood guard over it.

The first show the Angels saw was *Search for Tomorrow*. The title appeared over a picture of the moon in a cloudy night sky.

Bill waited for the reaction. There was none. At first the old, mad people kept staring somewhere else in their own private world. Then some of the women looked up, attracted by the sound of a young female voice and the sight of fresh makeup and nice dresses.

Brought to you by Procter and Gamble.

They scowled slightly, not sure they had the thing figured out. A kind of radio with pictures. They were only mildly bemused. The whole world had passed them by so long ago that nothing made sense. But they liked the sound of families, and breakfasts, and husbands being kissed goodbye, and the softened voices of women dealing with secret shame.

At night, it was taken away.

The next day, they clustered around it, a new hunger in their eyes. Inside that little box, children bounced in and out of living rooms or wept in their mothers' arms. Grand and powerful women schemed; husbands faced bankruptcy; toothpaste was sold. Gradually the nothingness sucked in the Angels.

Old Dynamite stood with her back to it, looking out of the window. Or she sat, staring somewhere else, her mouth creased around with smiles as if her face were a pond into which someone had thrown a stone. Sometimes her eyes blazed. Sometimes she sang softly. Bill found himself growing disturbed by her.

"Listen, Bill," said Tom Heritage, "the only way you can stick this job is to put it all to the back of your mind. You start taking it to heart, you could end up like them. Once I get my license back, I'm getting out of here, drive a taxi, anything. You should do the same, boy, I can tell you."

Forty years, fifty years, in this place, thought Bill. What a waste of a life.

In November, there was going to be a movie on TV. Networks did not usually show movies, so it was a special thing, a lot of publicity. It was a kids' movie, but a lot of the staff wanted to see it. A kids' movie would not have anything in it to rile the Angels.

So it was decided to wheel out the television from nine to eleven at night. The Angels, like children all over the country, were going to be allowed to stay up late to watch it. Bill, the gentle master of the TV, took the night shift for the first time.

The staff crowded in, the caterers especially, all the employees who were still too poor to own a television. They returned to the Home in their cloth coats. Some of them brought their kids. The children looked fat and sleepy and grumpy. A few of the Angels showed up too, drawn by the excitement and by the sound and sight of children.

The old people in their slippers shuffled up to the children, cooing, confused, wanting to warm their hands around young life, such as they had never had a chance to nurture. The children hated it.

Old Dynamite came lumbering forward too, like some stick insect on long prairie pins, in her Home pj's, smelling slightly of sweat and dry-cleaned sheets. She staggered smiling toward one of the children.

"Hello, hello," she said in a breathless but supple voice. "Hello children. Hello my little ones."

"Mo-mmmie!" wailed one of the children in fear, and turned her face toward her mother.

"I told you, Hattie," said the mother. "I said you was to be nice to the old people."

"Now aren't you the prettiest little thing!" said Dotty, with longing and bad breath. The child covered her mouth, shrank back into her mother's arms.

"Sunflowers," said Dotty. "You like sunflowers, honey?"

The child stared at her with sullen dislike.

"Well," whispered the old woman. "Their real name is moonflowers."

Bill smiled at the mother to let her know that nothing was wrong. "Come along, Dotty, it's just about to start," he said, across the room.

"Do you like Indians? I'll tell you a secret, honey. The Indians won. They're everywhere, but they're just invisible."

Bill walked among the old people, gently guiding them away from the children, into chairs. They should have realized the effect that seeing children would have. None of them had seen children in so long.

"And taffy apples," Old Dynamite was saying. "Oh, I used to like those. They pull out my teeth now."

Bill was next to her, lulled by the normality of her voice. Bill still thought normality was hardly to be breached. He touched Old Dynamite's arm, to lead her away.

The insanity came leaping out of her. Her face twisted up, and she hissed at him like a snake and threw off his hand with clumsy, sweeping strength. She staggered backward and nearly fell over. Bill felt something in him leap back with fear. Her back stiff with pride, Dynamite began to walk by herself toward an empty wheelchair.

The child's mother shifted her body and the subject, looking away from the old insane woman. "I don't know why they have to put on a kids' movie this time of night," she said to her buddy from the kitchens. She had been hoping all the Angels would be asleep, so her little

Hattie need not be frightened. She was bitter about being poor and what it cost her little girl.

That'll teach me, thought Bill. Looks sweet, but she's in here for a reason. I reckon Old Dynamite could still be quite an ornery handful. Some rough old pioneer lady who went mad.

They had their first bad reaction to the TV that night. Wasn't more than five minutes into the movie when Old Dotty stood up and shouted. "Who put this on?" she demanded. Bill moved quickly. He put a hand on her shoulder.

"Just sit still, Dotty," said Bill, trying to soothe her.

"How'd it get there?" she shouted, loud. "That's me. How did I get there?"

"It's just a movie, Dotty."

"Who said they could put me on that thing? They got it wrong! Wasn't like that. Only one room we had and couldn't afford no hired hands, I can tell you."

The woman from the kitchen made clicking sounds of disapproval. Did everything have to be ruined for her little girl?

"It's just a movie, Dotty," said Bill.

"What is that thing?" She pointed at the television.

"It's a TV. It's like a radio with pictures. You can show old movies on it. That's what that is, an old movie."

For some reason, that seemed to mollify Dotty. She dropped back down onto her chair, sulking, arms folded. "I ain't never seen a movie," she said, as though that might explain how she came to be in one. She sat looking merely disgruntled for a few minutes more.

Then the cyclone came. When the wind began to moan, Old Dotty began to shake her head from side to side, no, no, no. She looked confused; her hair was wild but her eyes looked frightened and lost. When she finally saw it was a cyclone, she shouted, once, very loudly, and covered her mouth. And when Judy Garland stepped out of Kansas into Oz, Old Dotty covered her face and wept. She pulled in breath with great heaving sobs. The little girl began to cry too.

"I want to go home!" said the little girl.

The mother began to gather up her coat in a rage. "Just for once," she muttered in bitterness.

"I want to go home," echoed Dotty, so softly that only Bill could hear.

"Come on, Dotty," he murmured. Experimentally he wheeled the chair around. Dotty did not fight. She had gone still and staring, her head hanging slightly. Bill wheeled her down the corridor to where the Angels slept.

"Here we are," said Bill. "Back home."

Old Dynamite didn't fight as he helped her up onto the bed and lifted her feet around, pulled up the bars of the cot. She turned her old seeping head with staring, watery eyes onto the pillow as he tucked her under the quilt. She's peaceful now, Bill thought. Getting her to go to the john will only rile her up. I'll clean her in the morning, before anyone sees.

"You just sleep now, Dotty," he whispered. He patted her arm, helpless to offer anything. He began to walk back quietly toward the lighted window in the door.

"Take me to the ocean," said Dotty.

Bill stopped and turned. Did she want to say anything else? He waited. There was a silence for a while. He was about to go again when she said, "I ain't never seen the sea."

"We're a long way from the sea, Dotty," he whispered back to her.

"I'd like to see the ocean," she said. "And then I'd like to die."

What could he tell her? That he'd take her there in the morning? That things were going to get better? That anything good was ever likely to happen to her now?

"They show the ocean on TV, sometimes," he said.

"I ain't no use to anybody. You oughta take me to the sea and drown me."

"I don't think that would be a very good idea."

Two beds down, old Gertie began to moan.

"If we keep talking, we'll wake everybody up. I'll come visit tomorrow," he said.

"It was about me," she whispered. "I really am Dorothy. Dorothy Gael, from Kansas."

The skin at the back of Bill's neck prickled. My, but that's spooky. That's what the character just said in the film.

Better say nothing, he thought. He walked out of the room backward. Better let her sleep.

He shuddered, involuntarily, and tried to calm himself. Whew. Must have been strange for her. Never seen a movie. Been in here since before movies. So she didn't know what they're like. So she sees an old movie that starts in Kansas about a little girl on a farm, must be like her own life coming back. He listened to his own footfalls, soft-shoed, on the corridor.

He went back to the TV, dreading that maybe someone had knocked it over and got hurt. Everything was fine. Bill leaned over to Jackson, the black janitor. He'd been working in the Home for an age.

"Jack," he said, "what's Old Dotty's real name?"

"Don't know," said Jackson. "Don't know their names, mostly. They got files on them all, though."

Wouldn't it be strange, though, if the names really were the same?

Bill drove the car home, and it all seemed to get stranger and stranger, the more he thought about it. Say she was about eighty. She could have been sent here when she was thirty and that would be about 1900. She could have been in here all that time. A whole world could have gone by. The Wright brothers, movies. And both world wars. It's like when they had Veterans Day parades, when he was a kid, and some old guys would come tottering along with their decorations, and they'd be decorations from the Spanish-American War. You had to pinch yourself to realize that there were people who could remember the Spanish-American War.

He needed to talk to Carol. He drove to her house, breathing the smell of the car heater. He parked and ran through the cold to the front door. Lights were still on downstairs. He rang the bell and waited, stomping his feet, waving his hands.

"Is Carol up, Mrs. Gilbert?"

"Why yes, come in, Bill. Anything wrong?" The door was speedily closed behind him.

"No, I'd just like to talk to her."

"Sure," smiled Mrs. Gilbert. It was hard for the young people when they were almost married to have to go bouncing back and forth between houses. "Carol?" she called upstairs. "Bill's here."

Carol Gilbert knew herself to be lucky. She had the boy she wanted. Everything about it was just perfect. Everybody thought so, even her parents. Even her mother, who left the two of them alone with a cup of coffee each in the living room.

He looked up at her and Carol reminded herself how good-looking he was, how reliable, how nice. He needed to talk, so Carol listened, like you were supposed to do. He talked to Carol about some old lady in the Home.

"You can't let it get to you like this, Billy," said Carol, stroking the hair at the back of his neck.

"It's just she's been in there so long. Can you imagine how strange that must feel?"

"You can't imagine how she feels and neither can I. It's sad, Billy, but she went mad and had to be put away."

"She asked me to drown her." Bill looked down at his big hands that could so easily kill.

He was so nice. Big and handsome and sweet. Carol took the back of his neck in both of her hands and pulled him to her and kissed him. She thought of the life they were going to have together. May not be rich, but we'll be happy. Why couldn't he just fix his mind on that?

"Anyway," said Carol, "tomorrow's Sunday. We can go looking for the house again."

"Oh!" said Bill, but it was a groan. "I promised I'd go talk to her tomorrow."

"Well," sighed Carol. "You got a choice. Me or an old mad lady."

He tried to smile and gave her a quick and slightly dismissive little kiss.

"How long you got before the Army?" she asked. She would hate being alone.

"Just a couple of months, I guess. Still haven't had my notice."

"Well," said Carol firmly. "We have got plenty to do before then." The wedding was going to be before then, and that too would be just perfect.

On Monday morning, Bill ran up the steps of the Home. He'd had an idea.

First he went to see Dotty. She sat in a wheelchair with her beautiful smile focused far away.

"Good morning, Dotty," he said. "This is Bill."

She didn't respond.

"Remember me? After the TV show?"

She began to hum nervously, in a high, frail, barely audible voice, shutting him out. That old song again.

Bill knelt by her chair and hung his head. A fine help you've been, Bill Davison. Between you and that television that got brought in here because of you, this old lady is worse than ever.

"I'm sorry, Dotty," he told her, whispering. He didn't want anyone else on the staff to hear. People had been fired for caring too much.

Then he went to see Gwen Anderson, in Admin.

Gwenny was one of his mother's many friends, a funny little widowed lady whose conversation Bill permitted himself to find tedious. It ran in a tight repetitive circle of cooking and homemaking. He had not visited Gwen since coming to work at the Home, and he felt bad about that. He felt worse now. He was going to ask a favor of her.

It was a bit better when he saw her. She let him off easy.

"Bill!" she exclaimed. "Hiya, honey. You haven't been to see me. I was just telling your mother."

"Oh. You know how it is. There's so much stuff to be done before the wedding and all."

Bill felt guilty again. He talked to her about the church's Christmas plans, and about the seat covers his mother was making for her, and how delicious her lemon sponge was. He also talked about the wedding, though he was surprised at how little he had to say about it. So was Gwenny. There was just a little lurch in her face as he ran out of things to tell her.

"Well, a February wedding will be such a treat," she said. "It'll come just when it seems that winter will never end. You must be real happy."

"Real happy, yeah," said Bill. "Carol's a good girl."

"I bet," said Gwenny. Her glasses seemed to smile for her.

And finally, Bill felt able to say, "Gwen, there's a patient here and I feel real sorry for her. Any chance that there'd be a file on her or something? I'd really like to know a bit more about her."

Gwenny was only too pleased to help. The files were supposed to be confidential but there wasn't an untrustworthy bone in Bill Davison's body. The file was big and fat. Bill could sit there in the office since the boss was late. Gwenny unfolded the wax paper around the white bread sandwiches that she took to work in place of breakfast. Breakfast made her feel sick. She ate daintily as Bill read.

Old Dynamite's name really was Dorothy Gale, or rather Gael. The spelling was different. That's what the latest reports said, but maybe they were wrong. Bill went all the way back through limp brown folders to the oldest layer of papers. There was a stiff shiny folder, with printed scrolls and lettering with leaves intertwined. Waposage Home for the Mentally Incapacitated, it said. There was a paper dated 1899:

Subject is well known to local people in the Abilene area under a variety of names and is a known vagrant thought to sleep in rough places including outbuildings or railway sheds. It is thought that she survives through petty theft from orchards and gardens, though it is thought she spent some years in and around Wichita. Records there do show a registration of a Dorothy Gael as a "singer" and common prostitute. She has shown belligerence and violence to officers of the law and is regarded by some people as a public menace. Apprehended in the course of a theft, she attacked a woman in Abilene and has been convicted of causing an affray in the same town. It was the recommendation of the judge that the woman be taken into state care for her own sake and for the sake of the community.

Subject shows some signs of religious mania. She frequently quotes Scriptures and sings hymns in a garbled and sometimes sacrilegious fashion. Her own hard experiences and corrupt nature make a bitter mockery of the sacred words, denying all comfort and salvation. Her oaths are such to blast the ear of the most hardened habitué of lowlife, entwining the Savior and lustful remarks in one evil net.

When not excited by theft or song, the subject is frequently to be found in a kind of trance that suggests alcohol poisoning or the more extreme forms of withdrawal noted in patients of this kind. In care she can sit without movement of any kind for hours. But do not be fooled, for she is capable of flaring up suddenly in a mighty rage, during which the stoutest men in the establishment have difficulty restraining her. Care will need to be taken to make sure the patient, whose hard life seems only to have served to make her physically strong, is kept under a degree of restraint.

She is a woman lost to the world, to sense, and to God.

Bill folded the file shut and sat and stared. Maybe, he thought, there are some things you can't go into too deeply. There's no help for them and no solace. Common prostitute. Blast the ear of the most hardened habitué. It was like staring into the pit. So where did the beautiful smile come from?

"Thanks, Gwen," he murmured darkly, and passed the file back to her.

"These people, Bill," she said, "they're like the rocks. You can dash yourself to pieces against them, and it won't help."

That's what everyone says, Bill thought as he smiled to Gwenny and thanked her. Everybody says don't get too wrapped up in them. But God, God commands us to love everyone. God says to find the lamb that is lost. And all these good people are telling me to forget, just close the file and put it away.

He went back to Dotty and pulled up a chair and sat next to her.

"You used to be a singer," he said.

There was a pause. "Yup," she answered him, abruptly.

A silence. Where to go from here?

"Where did you sing?" he asked, after having to think.

"Church," she said, and drew herself up and sniffed. Another long silence. "Nobody ever told me I could sing. Nobody ever asked me to sing. I just found out. So I'd sleep in one town and go to church in another. Sing in the choir. Till they found out who I was. Drove me out."

"Drove you out?" He was appalled.

Dotty didn't answer. Her jaw jutted out, and she jerked it in decrepit defiance. She pretended to brush something off her knee. "Couldn't have the likes of me singing in church."

Let those of you who are without sin . . .

"That wasn't very Christian of them," he said.

"Totally and completely Christian," she answered him. "Look what they did to the Indians."

He had a sudden strange feeling that Dotty had seen what had happened to the Indians.

"How old are you, Dotty?" he asked.

"Five," she replied. "Took a look around and decided to stay five. I just grew up five, and lived five."

The smile came flitting back across her face like a swallow over a cornfield. "I was a fairy," she whispered. "I lived in the fields, under the leaves. I had a laugh like broken glass." She nodded her head. Then she leaned forward.

"All of us here," she whispered, "are either Indians or fairies." She nodded again.

"Did you ever see any Indians?"

"Only good, Kansas ones. The ones that sleep all day drunk. Those are good Indians. The bad ones are invisible."

"What kind of house did you live in?"

"Underground. Wilbur lived underground, and he went first, and I followed him. We lived underground with the gophers. And Uncle Henry and Aunty Em, they lived in a cottonwood house that let all the wind in. It was better to live underground."

"What year was that? Do you remember what year?"

"No, I didn't know the year. That was why I felt so stupid. After that, I didn't need to know the year. Each year is the same year. All you got. Right now."

Crazy people talked crazy. It was like trying to grasp a handful of fog. You knew there was something there, but you couldn't feel it or touch it.

"And where was this?" he asked.

The stare had come back too. Old Dotty was looking somewhere else.

"In Was," she said. "It's a place too. You can step in and out of it. Never goes away. Always there." She smiled a moment longer and then suddenly said, "My mama died."

"How did she die?"

"I killed her," said Dotty. "I gave her the Dip."

The great stretch of the years.

"My daddy died," said Bill. "He got killed in the war."

"There you go," said Dotty, as if something had been proved.

"It can leave you pretty lonely." He was trying to understand.

"No it can't. People are the only thing that can make you feel lonely." He felt corrected. Loneliness had never been his problem.

"There's the China people," she added. "You got to watch out or they'll break. Crr-assssshhhh." She made a spreading, breaking sound.

"Are . . . are you a China person?" he asked.

Her mouth twisted around in exasperation. "Now do I look like it? I ask you!"

"No," he admitted cautiously. But he found he was smiling.

"I told you," she said. "I am a fairy."

Tom Heritage with the crooked smile happened to be passing. He grabbed Bill by the shoulders. "Well, he may not look like it, but he's a fairy, too, Ma'am."

Joke. Hah hah. "Thanks for butting in, Heritage," murmured Bill.

"He is not a fairy!" insisted Dotty, suddenly fierce. She looked like a wrinkled old snapping turtle. "He's a healer." She looked back at Bill. "Just like Frank was," she told him.

"Well, when you get through healing, Bill, we got us some beds to strip." Heritage's eyebrows were raised with meaning. But he walked on.

"I got to go, Dot," said Bill.

"I don't see what's stopping you," said Old Dynamite.

Bill stood up. "Who's Frank?" he asked.

"He was the Substitute," said Dotty, as if Bill should have known. "Frank Balm."

Heritage was at the door, holding it open. "Substitute for what?" Bill asked, walking backward. Her face had gone immobile. "Dotty? Substitute for what?"

She just kept smiling. She was gone. Bill was just at the door when he heard the answer to his question.

"For home," Dotty whispered.

Bill took all of this home to Carol, and Carol was disturbed. What she loved in Bill was his normality. She had been trained to confuse that with virtue. What Bill was involved in now was nothing to do with normality.

"I don't want to hear any more," she said, flustered. "It's a lot of babbling from some crazy old woman."

"But it's like it isn't crazy," he said. "It's like it makes a certain kind of sense."

"Oh, Bill! Can't we just forget it?"

There were so many things to be done. Christmas was coming up, and Mrs. Davison was going to spend it with Carol's family. After all, they were all going to be one family soon. And everybody in Waposage always had everybody else in for Christmas. That meant a cold hard clean of the house, and then Christmas decorations, and lights up along the eaves, maybe a Santa on the roof if you were really public-spirited, and taking relatives on long drives around the town and villages to look at the lights. And presents! Near enough everybody who came to the house had to have a present, not to mention all the stuff you had to get for Christmas morning. And after that, not two months later, there was the wedding.

So why was he getting all wrapped up in some old lady? Because he's a nice boy, that's why. But that kind of niceness could get you down, if it went on too long, and that kind of niceness opened up a door that led to God knows where. That kind of niceness scared Carol to death.

So they went about all their business, going from store to store, Carol's arm in his, finding presents for brothers and sisters and cousins. Bill got a bit worked up about what to get his mother. He felt bad because he was leaving her at home, well, he would have to once they were married, but he wanted to get her something especially nice. Carol helped. She especially devoted herself to finding Mrs. Davison the perfect gift. "I think I've got it," she said. "A home permanent kit!"

He was a man and didn't understand. "Look," Carol explained patiently. "She doesn't have one, and I know she likes going to the beauty parlor, she always just sits back and relaxes when she comes in. But every woman likes to think she can get her hair up for something special if she can't get into the parlor. And look, this is a real good one. Comes with full instructions, rollers, the whole bit."

Bill really didn't seem to understand what a great present it was.

"I'm just worried it might make her feel more alone," he said. "You know, staying in with her hair in rollers and no one to take her out."

"Look. We'll get her the home permanent and something else. Hey, wait, I got it. A new dress for the wedding! Mrs. Harris just made her one, didn't she? She'll have her measurements. Oh, come on, Billy!"

"Okay, okay, you win," he said, smiling and holding up his hands.

"Trust me," said Carol.

They picked up some stocking stuffers for the kids, and perfume for her mother, and went on to the hardware store for some new drill bits for Daddy. They passed the bookshop. "Hold on," said Bill.

"Since when," asked Carol, following, "have you been interested in books?"

Bill wasn't. In fact, he had never been in a bookshop and felt very uncomfortable going into one. But the book was in the window.

"That book in the window," he asked, after waiting for ages behind people at the counter. "Is that the book they based that movie on?"

"The one on TV? Yup," said the salesgirl and waited.

"Could you get it for me?" he asked, helpless.

"Um. It's just over there," she replied, pointing. "I got to work the cash register."

"Oh. Sure."

He really did feel out of place, but he found the book. Carol rejoined him, with a few books for the relatives and the kids.

"You're buying that?" she asked him. Her mother was a librarian. "That's supposed to be a real bad book for kids. None of the libraries will stock it. They don't even list it in the guides and things."

He turned the book over in his hands. "Is it dirty or something?"

"No. But the fantasy is unhealthy. Bad for the little ones."

"Well, it isn't a present for a kid."

"Who is it for, then?"

"It's for Dotty."

Carol felt fear. "You're buying that old mad lady a Christmas present?"

"Somebody's got to," he said.

He bought her *The Wonderful Wizard of Oz*. He looked at the name on the cover and felt that strange prickling again. Frank Baum. She had mentioned him. Did she really know him? Or was that too much of a coincidence?

"How's my girl?" Bill would ask Dotty in the mornings, when he arrived.

"Oh, just fit as a fiddle," she might reply. And then they would talk.

"I just realized," Dotty said one morning. "You boys call us Angels, don't you? I used to make angels. Wilbur and me."

He understood now that Wilbur was a childhood friend. He also understood that Wilbur was often with her.

"Has Wilbur come by again?" Bill asked.

"Oh he comes and sets a spell, just like you do," Dotty told him. "He used to set all day by the road, just waiting to see who would happen by. Sometimes God did."

Bill was thrown for a moment. He coughed. "Anybody else come and visit?" he asked.

"The Good Witch," she said. "And the Bad Witch."

He felt the prickling again. That was in the book. He'd read it. Most of it.

"They're the same person," she confided, in a whisper.

"Are you a good witch or a bad witch?" he asked.

"Oh, I'm not a witch at all. I'm Dorothy Gael from Kansas. And that's not East, and that's not North, and that's not South, and that's not really even West. Kansas is nowhere at all."

"Right where everyplace else meets."

"Meets right here," she said, and tapped her own head.

Bill found he was piecing her world together. She had at some point obviously read the book and found it so much like her life that it got wound up in the strange world she lived in. There was, as far as he could gather, this other place she went to when she got the stare. And in that place she was happy, with lots of old friends, all together there. She only got mad when someone tried to pull her out of it. He knew better than to talk to her if she was too far lost in the stare. Or if reality had been too far pushed under her nose, and she wanted to go back to the place she called Was.

And sometimes poison would jet out of her, as if from a wound.

He said hello to her one morning. "Why you talking to me?" Dotty demanded. "You must have something better to do." She shrugged herself deeper down into her own embrace.

"I'm just visiting."

"Go visit somewhere else. I know what you're after. All you men are just the same."

Then she said, "You'd pig-back Christ on the cross given half a chance."

"Dotty, there's no call to talk to me like that."

"You wanna see? You wanna see? You wanna have a good look?"

She said it in hatred. She started to pull her dress up. "Go on, then, have a look at a poor old lady."

Bill backed away. You had to make sure people saw you were nowhere near her. For legal reasons.

"You know you do it to children. Go on. Look at a poor old lady. You can't hurt her anymore with that thing of yours. Go on!"

Bill had to walk away. He knew his face was white and he could feel his hands trembling. He had been shaken in the depths of his purity. She had been made so bitter! Bill could not imagine what could make anyone as full of bile as that. Except that it seemed to him that it must have come from something terrible that was done to her.

The next day he saw her, and she laughed when she saw him and clapped her hands, like a child again.

"I baked you a cake," she would say. "A nice plum cake." And she would move the invisible cake onto her tray and pretend to cut it.

"How big a slice you want?"

"As big as you can cut it."

"Oh!" she said. "I know you! You'd have me cut just a teeny piece for myself and give you the rest. I don't know. Here you go."

And she passed him the cake on an invisible plate, and he would pretend to eat it.

Tom Heritage passed by the bed. "Watch it, Billy," said Heritage. "That's the first sign." He turned to Dotty. "How often does he eat cake that isn't there?" he asked Dotty.

"Only," she insisted, "since he's met me and I showed him how. Now he doesn't ever have to go hungry. Would you like a slice?"

"Uh. No thanks. Just had my invisible lunch," said Tom.

After Heritage had gone, Dotty said, with a sigh, "He'll never leave Kansas."

Christmas bore down on them like an express train, jamming all the days together. Billy put up lights on his mother's house for the last time. He and Carol were at a party every night, with relatives or friends. Their high-school class had a Christmas reunion party. Six months after graduation, everybody was pretty much the same, except for a couple of the brainy kids who went away to college. Muffy Havis was there.

Billy wanted to talk to her because she was studying psychology. He tried to talk to her about Dotty.

He loomed toward her. He and Muffy Havis had never spoken much. Muffy had grouped him together with the rest of the huge and popular athletes of the school. She called them the Dumb Oxen.

His hands did most of the talking, as if trying to pull words out of the air. He talked about some patient in the Home, a few scraps of her conversation; some problem she had with the television.

"What's the diagnosis been?" Muffy asked him. "Schizophrenic?"

"I don't know," he said, and smiled his big, dumb, sweet smile.

"It's a bit early in the course for me to give a diagnosis," she said wryly. She was amazed Bill Davison was interested. It made her feel on edge.

"What . . . what kind of things do you study?" Bill Davison asked her. "Do they help you understand people better?"

"No," admitted Muffy quite cheerfully.

Muffy Havis liked classical music and read all kinds of things and had not been terribly popular. She was hefty and pale and had her hair pulled back into a plain ponytail. Being asked unanswerable questions by one of the Dumb Oxen was not something she enjoyed.

"I sure wish I could understand Dotty better."

Really? Muffy thought. Or did you think everything would be as open and straightforward as playing football and getting drunk with your cronies? Muffy wished she had not come. She was tired of realizing that there was not a single person in her high-school class that she could call a friend.

And here came Carol Gilbert, blond hair, curls, bright smile; she's going to be oh so gracious and get him away from me. Oh, come on, Carol, this is Muffy, remember? You don't have to be jealous of me. Plain old Muffy. Aren't you going to pretend to be nice to me?

"What are you two finding to talk about?" Carol asked.

"Psychology," said Muffy.

"That's all he talks about these days since that job of his." Carol was smiling and dancing in place to get away.

"Maybe he should go into insurance," said Muffy, coolly.

"Something sensible like that," agreed Carol.

There are two kinds of stupid people, thought Muffy. The nice ones and the shrewd nasty ones. And both kinds come out on top.

Bill Davison murmured something. Muffy wasn't sure, but she thought it was "All-fired rush to be sensible."

"What was that, honey?" asked Carol, leaning forward. Oooh, thought Muffy. Trouble in the ranks.

Bill didn't answer. Instead he looked up straight into Muffy's eyes, big, dumb and not so sensible after all. "I'd really like to talk some more about this," he said. "Now's not really the time. Can I drop by while you're still in town?"

"Uh. Sure," said Muffy. What the hell, she thought, is happening?

"Maybe you could come out and see her."

"What? In the Home? Uh. Okay." Muffy looked to Carol, signaling: This is none of my doing.

"Give you a call," said Bill Davison. A football star, interested in me? Muffy maintained her quizzical expression.

"See ya, Muffy," said Carol, pulling at Bill's sleeve. She even gave her a dinky little wave with the tips of her fingers. Muffy gave her a dinky wave back. It's not you, Muff. It's that old woman he cares about. How strange.

People, Muffy decided. They really do grow up sometimes.

And, she thought, he really is sweet. Not to mention rather toothsome.

And sometime about mid-December, before Bill had a chance to call on Muffy, it snowed. A good hefty Kansas snowfall, in time for Christmas. It started about lunchtime. Bill was cleaning the tables and fixing trays. Some of the patients needed feeding. Dotty came running in. Her feet couldn't leave the ground, but she made a hurried, hopping motion with her hands and head.

"Billy. Billy," she said. "Come and see the snow."

She pulled him to the window. Great fat lumps of snow were falling like flakes of lard.

"God's dandruff," she announced.

Bill laughed out loud.

"Angel feathers. They're cleaning out the roost upstairs, making room for a few more."

"Dotty . . ." he said, shaking his head. He was going to say, You are out of your mind. It was what he said to anyone who made him laugh out loud.

"The snow's warm," she said. "The Eskimos make their houses out of it. They live in great snow cities, with snow skyscrapers, but nobody can see them because they mix right in with everything else. So the airplanes go over, and never notice. So it's all right. The Eskimos are safe. Nobody's going to touch them."

She gave her head a determined nod.

"Ride around on polar bears," she told him.

"Hell," she said, her voice suddenly different. "I used to sleep under snow six months out of every year. Snow's always been good to me. Let's go out."

"Can't, Dotty."

"Why not?"

"Rules," he said. "Besides, you haven't got a coat."

"You don't need a coat in the snow. I told you, the snow is warm!"

"Dotty. I can't let you out in it."

Her face went small and mean. She looked at him accusingly. "You're one of them," she said. "You're one of them!"

"Come on, Dotty, it's lunchtime. Let's have some food."

She snarled at him and threw off his hand.

"I'm not your servant," she growled. "I don't have to kowtow to the likes of you."

She held out her hand flat. "You can't do anything to me," she said. "Go on. Hit me! Hit me! You think that will stop me!" Her voice went down into a whisper. "I am the Happy One," she told him. "I come to avenge murder."

She walked away, flinging her hands around her head. "Hit me! Come on! Hit me! Doesn't hurt. Doesn't hurt. They make us tough. They make us tough in Kansas." She walked toward the doors shouting, outraged.

"They sport us till we're as tough as old boots. They'd stick their things up Jesus Christ Himself and make their wives lick off the holy blessed shit from Jesus's holy, blessed asshole."

The doors swung shut behind her. The tirade went on, echoing, horrible, down the corridor. Was it okay just to let her go?

"Then they stick their knives up our sweet little dewlaps and rip them open and hang them from hooks until we dry in the sun and then they call us beef jerky and we clack and clatter when we walk, gutless, flies in the intestines. Oh, no! It's not just enough to kill us! No! Never enough just to make us die."

It was the worst it had ever been. Behind the doors, a man shouted. Bill decided he better go see. He had to put down the trays first. He swung open the doors, following her into the corridor.

Dotty was in a fight with Tom Heritage. She was punching him in the face as he hugged her. The Angel had fallen.

Heritage seemed to have forgotten all his training. Don't come at them from the front, don't try to hit them, get them from behind and make them go still. Billy saw why he had forgotten. Tom Heritage was angry. He was trying to get a good enough hold with one hand, so that he could hit her with his right.

Bill slipped up from behind and got Old Dynamite in a headlock. He pulled back tighter, and she squawked and howled, her arms hoisted helplessly over her head. They waved in the air. She tried to kick backward, but her legs were feeble. Bill held off as long as he could and then swept her feet out from under her.

"Calm down!" he shouted at Heritage. Heritage swallowed blood and wiped his face. "Come on, Dotty, let's go sit down."

She howled in nameless rage and slapped the air and tried to kick. Heritage also slipped in behind, twisting one of her legs in front of the other so she couldn't kick. They lifted her up like a sack of potatoes. Both of them had been hired for their muscles.

Dotty began to sob "No, no, no," over and over. The Graveyard was near. Jackson the janitor saw them and pushed open the swinging doors and flipped down the side of her cot. By the time they had loaded her onto the mattress she had gone quiet. She shivered.

They stood over her. Heritage was nursing a split lip.

"Do you think you could see a way not to report it?" Bill asked Tom Heritage. He looked around at Jackson.

Tom Heritage glared back at him, working the inside of his mouth, tasting blood.

"It's only been this once. Only you, me and Jackson saw it. Please don't tell anybody, or they'll stick her back in the Pigpen. Please. It was my fault, I told her she couldn't do something and I should have just humored her or something. Please don't tell, Tom. Please."

"Okay, okay," said Tom Heritage, sounding bored. "I shouldn't have hit her anyway."

After lunch, Bill wheeled out the TV and stood guard over it. It was late afternoon by the time he got back to the Graveyard to see how Dotty was.

She was lying on her back, smiling the smile, singing to herself.

"Sleep well, Dot," he told her. "Have yourself a beautiful dream."

The next day he got to work late, and Jackson greeted him, wheeling out a tub of laundry.

"We've had a casualty," he said, his voice dark and laconic. Accusing?

"Who?" The old folks often passed away in the night or hurt themselves.

"Old Dynamite. They found her out in the snow. She'd slept out in it all night. She was lying on her back. She'd been making those angel things the kids make. You know, waving her arms up and down to make wings."

"Is she dead?"

"Near as, dammit. She can't breathe."

Bill started to move toward the Graveyard. "Not there," said Jackson, grabbing his arm. "Hospital ward."

Oh God, oh Jesus, please God, please Jesus. He said it over and over to himself as he walked. He got lost, found locked doors, heard strange cries, asked for help. "Why aren't you on duty if you work here?"

"The patient is a kind of friend of mine."

"We're not here to be friends of patients."

"She's ill. Can I see her?"

They'd strapped her to the bed as a precaution. There were tubes in her nose. Her breath came in wheezes and gurgles. Her eyes were closed, but she was smiling the smile.

"Dotty?" he asked.

"She's been unconscious since they brought her in. She's got pneumonia pretty bad. They call it the old man's friend. It is around here, at any rate."

"She doesn't want to die," he said.

"Really?" said the Nurse. "Why not?" She looked at him with a hard, straightforward glance that said, Are you kidding, with the lives these people lead?

"She's happy. Most of the time, she's really happy," he said. "The only thing that makes her unhappy is us."

He went out into the snow. The snow was still falling. It was filling in the angel she had made. It was a huge angel, with great sweeping wings and a head and a long, wide dress that she had made by moving her legs out and in across the snow. She had even scooped a halo out of the snow, around the top of the head. There were foot-prints all over the snow, big, heavy, booted footprints. But none of them led directly to the angel. They had hoisted her up out of it. That was the whole point. It had to look like an angel had gone to sleep there. And then woken up and flown away.

"It's the best angel, Dot," he said. "It's the best angel ever."

He knelt down and tried to brush away the snow that was falling into it, blurring the crisp, deliberate outline. As he brushed, his gloved and clumsy fingers broke the edges, blurring them. There was no saving it. Like everything else, it was to melt away into history. Like all of us, he thought as he stood up and walked away. Like that great muddy brown river. Like those broken stones. The names wear away. Like the log cabins and the rickety old carts and the sod-and-stick houses and the tent churches. Whole towns swallowed up, gone, lost. A whole America, he thought, it's going.

He went back to work. He worked with a vengeance, trying hard not to cry. It never occurred to him to think crying was unmanly. His mother had told him, when his father died, that it would be unmanly not to, because not to cry, to pretend nothing had happened, that was really cowardice. So you cry, son, she told him. You cry all you can. You do it in his honor. Bill wept now, for Dotty and suddenly also for his father and for the mystery of why all things had to pass away.

"Hard luck, Kid," said Tom Heritage.

"Yeah," said Bill, his voice thin.

"Kind of the end of an era, really."

"Yeah."

"Listen. Uh. I know I joke around and all, but . . . I really think you did the best another human being could do for that old lady. That was really good. You know?"

"Thanks, Tom." There was no consolation, because Bill found he blamed himself. "She said the snow was warm. She said she wanted to go out in it, and I stopped her, and so there was that fight." The conclusion was inescapable. "We should have reported it."

Tom just shrugged. Nothing for it.

Bill wheeled the TV out after lunch and listened to the soap operas. *The Guiding Light.* Brought to you by Ivory soap. The only wash-day powder that comes in flakes like snow.

The Nurse came in. "Mr. Davison," she said. "It doesn't look like it'll be too long now. Do you want to be there?"

Anything less would be cowardice.

"Yeah," he replied, nodding.

This time, led by the Nurse, it was a short walk to the hospital ward. Somewhere a radio was blaring. Voice talking. Music started up, some Christmas song or another, ghostly, echoing. It ended. The voice talked again, radio voice, soothing, phony. They opened the door.

Dorothy looked emerald green, and it seemed there was no breath at all.

"She's real weak," whispered the Nurse and left them alone.

Down the hall, the music from the radio started up again. Bill had heard the piece before. It was real old and sounded kind of creaky with just a couple of instruments and lots of people singing together.

Hallelujah. Hallelujah.

Bill had time to think: That's it, that's the song she sings all the time. Then Dotty was singing too.

Hallelujah! she sang. Only she pronounced it like a child.

Hally hoo hah! Hally hoo hah!

Bill felt his breath go as still as the air in the underheated ward. The voice was clear and strong, pure as a river, though her eyes were closed and tubes were taped into her nostrils.

She sang it over and over.

Hally hoo hah! Hally hoo hah!

Bill didn't know much about music, but he knew it was a voice that could have sung opera. Oh, Dotty, thought Bill. How could you sing like that and no one know?

They didn't ask me, he remembered her saying. And she seemed to go on to say, *You didn't ask me.*

One thin and withered arm was lifted up.

For the Lord God Omnipotent reigneth!

The Nurse came back in. "What is going on?" she demanded.

"She's singing," said Bill, helpless. "She used to sing in church."

The arm punched the air. Dotty was smiling as if in her sleep. The words began to weave back and forth, and Dotty lit on them where she would, like a bird.

> *The Kingdom of this World . . .*
> *For the Lord God . . .*
> *Hally hoo hah!*
> *Reigneth!*

"Do you believe in miracles?" asked the Nurse. Her face was hard, and she was chewing gum.

"Yes," said Bill.

"Well, you're seein' one. She shouldn't even be able to breathe hardly."

The arms folded themselves up like the wings of a scrawny chicken. Dotty kept on singing: *King of Kings. Lord of Lords.* Bill and the Nurse watched in silence. There was no one else to see or hear.

Bill took Carol to the service. There wasn't going to be one, but Bill offered to pay for it, and the local undertaker, inspired by his example, donated his labor. It was not held in the Home, but in the local crematorium. Bill's preacher, Reverend Carey, gave the sermon.

It was overheated to the point of discomfort. The mourners tried to slip discreetly first from out of their winter coats and then their sweaters. Tom Heritage brought some of the Angels with him. They shuffled along the pews looking utterly and completely lost. Heritage saw Bill, smiled, waved and ushered some of the old people to their seats next to Carol. They smelled of medicine and confinement. They saw Carol try to smile at them and saw her draw back, and they stared at her like frightened children, their jaws slack.

The Preacher told the story of Job, of faithfulness in suffering. Reverend Carey had listened to Bill and had understood that the old woman was in some way religious. Bill was trying to attend, but his mind kept wandering.

It had fallen to Bill to sort through Dorothy's possessions. She had two: the old green pioneer dress she was wearing now and another dress. At first Bill had not known what it was. It was tiny and crisp like an old leaf, brown, but made of lace. He had peeled apart its layers to find that it was a child's dress. It had once been covered in sequins. The child's dress was in the coffin with her.

So was the book. Bill had never had a chance to give it to her. Its ashes would now mingle with hers. It was just a kids' book, but Bill had read the first few pages and remembered them. There was so much in them that was like things Dot had told him about her life.

Dorothy lived in the midst of the great Kansas prairies, with Uncle Henry, who was a farmer, and Aunt Em, who was the farmer's wife. Their house was small, for the lumber to build it had to be carried by wagon many miles.

Dot had said they kept pork cool in holes in the ground, sealed in earthenware jars full of lard. They wiped the lard off and fried the meat in heavy skillets that were protected against rust by leaving on the fat. Women wore the same woolen dress all winter and just changed the apron.

There were four walls, a floor and a roof, which made one room; and this room contained a rusty looking cooking stove, a cupboard for the dishes, a table, three or four chairs, and the beds.

Airplanes, Bill thought, airplanes and radio and movies. She never saw anything like that come in. She was in the Home, instead. Like she was safe from it.

The Preacher was asking them to sing a hymn. There was a rustling of paper as people found it in the book. The music started too soon.

> Oh God our help in ages past
> Our hope for years to come . . .

The Angels looked lost. They couldn't find the place in the book— or even the book itself. Carol was trying to be nice and help one of them, her smile fixed and thin, but the old woman next to her had frail hands that mumbled the pages aimlessly while her eyes were fixed on the mystery of Carol's young face, with its short, slightly bouffant hair and its magenta lips. One of the male Angels was singing, very loudly, in a bellowing, tuneless voice:

Home, home on the range!

Bill thought of the book.

When Dorothy stood in the doorway and looked around, she could see nothing but the great gray prairie on every side. Not a tree nor a house broke the broad sweep of flat country that reached the edge of the sky in all directions.

Drapes were pulled back. The coffin began to move. People kept singing.

Even the grass was not green . . .

The coffin was swallowed up. Carol wasn't singing. Bill could tell from the rigid way Carol was standing that she was holding her breath. Bill felt sweat trickle from his ears onto his collar. The curtains closed. It's like the old days, Bill thought, like the old days were being swallowed up as well. Nobody knows.

When Dorothy, who was an orphan, first came to her, Aunt Em had been so startled by the child's laughter that she would scream and press her hand upon her heart . . .

Carol gave his hand a little tug, then a little shake. The organ finally stopped.

The old man kept on singing, *Home, home on the range.* Billy, knowing that Carol wanted to leave, strode toward the lectern. Carol hastily gathered up her scarf and coat.

It was Toto that made Dorothy laugh, and saved her from growing as gray as her other surroundings.

Bill went up to Reverend Carey, shook his hand, thanked him, and offered him a lift. "No thanks, Bill," said Reverend Carey, "came here in my own car." He said hello to Carol, and Bill thanked him again.

"I think Carol wants to go," he said, his smile edgy.

"Bill, I'm happy to stay," said Carol.

They walked in silence out of the crematorium. The corridor was the bleary kind of yellow or green that looks like vomit and there were echoes, of their feet, of dim voices, of the Angels being gathered up. The modern glass doors swung open and shut, and the air seemed to blast into their faces, tingling and cold.

"Uhhhhh!" sighed Carol. "Feel that good, night air!" She smiled, bright-eyed, trying to be pert and full of pep.

They drove home. Bill's knuckles were white on the steering wheel and he couldn't think why. Carol was silent and looking out the window.

"I'm going to have to do something about all of this," he said. It was a warning. He was saying: I will be going to work in places like that in the future.

"Like what?" said Carol, in a tired voice. She still looked out the window at the snow. "What are you going to do? What can anybody do for them?"

"I don't know," Bill said. He wanted to say something like: Make sure that they know somebody loves them. But he found he couldn't say something like that to Carol.

"Like maybe go to school or something," he murmured.

"You just got out of school," Carol said, lacing the words with scorn. Going back to school of any kind would be to surrender adulthood.

"I mean, go to college or something. Study nights or stuff."

"Oh, that's just great," said Carol miserably.

What am I supposed to do? Carol thought. Work my butt off in some beauty parlor while you hang around with a bunch of creepy college kids like Muffy Havis? And then what? Then I'd have to spend my life with people like in there this afternoon. But Carol couldn't say that to Billy.

None of this was normal. Maybe she wasn't normal. Carol knew what was normal in situations like this. You were supposed to be warm and helpful and understanding and talk sensibly about how they could get by while he studied. She should be telling him how proud of him she was. She wasn't proud of him. The life he was offering would choke her.

"Why can't you just go and get a job at Mr. Hardie's?" she asked him, pleading. A job like everyone else. "What's wrong with staying in the Army, like your father?"

People like you and me, Carol thought, we're better off in something like the Army, Billy. I can see you in the Army. I can see me there with you.

"There's nothing *wrong* with it." Billy looked impatient. There was a kind of light in his eyes that Carol didn't like, couldn't trust. "But I'd like . . . I don't know. I'd like some kind of qualification."

Big heart, thought Carol. If you've got such a big heart, what about saving some of it for me?

"What about us?" she asked him. She thought of white gloves, light pink fabrics, beaded purses, the smell of new hairdos. She thought of home.

"It shouldn't make any difference," Billy said.

It shouldn't, it shouldn't, she knew it shouldn't. But it did. The car was warm now, and the hot air coming through the heater smelled of something harsh and itchy. It made the back of their throats go dry. Billy coughed. Carol said nothing. There was something dry and hot and dark between them. Finally it was Billy who said it.

"Maybe it's a mistake getting married this young," he said.

A pause. There was such a slender bridge leading out into the darkness, and Carol saw herself on it in high heels and a black cocktail dress. Black for mourning. Nothing she had been taught was adequate to deal with this. She felt dirty somehow. She felt defenseless.

"Maybe so," Carol whispered, admitting defeat. She dreaded the shame that was to come, and the embarrassment of telephoning friends, of telling her aunts. She contemplated her coming freedom as well, with a lightening of the heart.

"Maybe, you know, it's just a bit too soon, what with the Army and all," said Bill, and coughed again.

That's what they would say to everybody, that they felt they were rushing into things because Billy was about to go off into the Army.

She could say that they just felt maybe it was better to wait awhile. Carol could live with that. People would say how sensible they were being. They would know what was going on, but that wouldn't matter. The date for the marriage would be postponed, to some dim future, in some other life.

Goodbye, Billy, she thought. She saw autumn leaves in her mind. That's what he said, when he kissed her goodnight on her chaste doorstep. Goodbye, with something in his voice that had no promise of tomorrow.

About four months later, in the spring, Bill's church started a drive to collect funds for the Home. The Preacher knew what he was doing. The sight of some big ordinary kid like Bill in his Army uniform would be worth ten preachers.

There was a launch party with banners and free punch. Bill gave a speech. He kept it simple and short.

"It says somewhere in the Bible," he began, "that to approach Jesus you've got to be like a little child. Well, that's how some of the people in the Home are. I don't mean that some of them aren't unpleasant or even dangerous, because they are. But they see things differently than we do, and not always in a bad way."

He told the story, as best he could, of Dorothy Gael of Kansas. He told them what he knew of her childhood long ago amid the steam trains and peach orchards and school stoves that smoked and how she had stayed a child. He told the story of how she had died making angels in the snow, and how she went out singing hallelujah to the God she had cursed.

"You see something like that, you know we've all got something inside us," he told them, eyebrows slanting with pained honesty under his tiny Army hat. "We've all got something of worth, even those people in the Home, and they deserve just as good as we can give them."

Money? There was an avalanche of it. Turned out that Bill Davison had a talent for money as well.

Part Three

Oz Circle

Santa Monica, California

September 1989

Now we can cross the Shifting Sands.

—L. FRANK BAUM's last words, May 6, 1919.
The Shifting Sands border the East of Oz.
Baum was seeing himself traveling westward toward it.

Years later, Jonathan was sitting in Bill Davison's office looking at photographs of athletes on the wall, and thinking of horror movies.

Jonathan starred in horror movies. The fear they generated seemed small and mean now, next to the real thing. You could only enjoy horror movies, Jonathan thought, when you were young and well and your fears had no name. Jonathan had a name for his terror now. He was dying.

The athletes in the photographs beamed at him, football players framed by a hunch of padding, hockey stars with missing teeth. They looked like gods of wholeness, gods of health.

Except that each of them had needed a psychiatrist. Bill Davison had made a fortune counseling athletes.

Football players who developed a terror of falling on Astroturf; baseball players who kept throwing out a knee, a knee that was medically perfect; rookies who developed such stage fright of crowds that they could not play. The photographs were signed with thanks.

Outside Bill Davison's office, Los Angeles gleamed. It was blue and white, blue with sky and smog, white with sunshine, white as bone. Both Jonathan and Bill were a long way from home.

Bill Davison was leaning back in his chair and regarding Jonathan with narrowed eyes. It was toward the end of their session.

"Right," he said. He rubbed the palm of his hand across his face. "Jonathan, I want you to try something new."

Bill Davison was nearly fifty, still handsome and broad-shouldered, though his face was creased and puffy and his chest sagged. His crewcut had been modified to suit later fashions. He wore a blue Lacoste shirt, casual and short-sleeved, that showed his football-player arms. Jonathan was rather in love with him. Counselor Bill, Jonathan called him, as if the whole sad business were a summer camp. It was appropriate. Jonathan had always hated summer camp. And loved his counselors.

Counselor Bill leaned forward on his desk and steepled his fingers. "I want you," he said, "to think of the place where you were happiest."

Jonathan did not try very hard. "I can't think of a place," he replied.

"Okay. Just think of something that you like, and try to remember where it happened."

Jonathan's thinking came slowly these days. Part depression and part drugs and part disease.

"I'm sorry, I just can't," he said.

"Where's home?" Bill Davison asked. His face looked very serious.

"Canada, I guess."

"Okay, Canada. Were you happy there?"

In school? As a little boy tearing up sheets? "How is this going to help the AIDS?" Jonathan asked.

"Maybe it won't help the AIDS, but it could help you."

Bill Davison had a direct approach. There was no time in the business of sports for psychoanalysis. In sports, with contracts worth thousands of dollars at stake, you had to intervene. Jonathan had read articles about Bill Davison. Bill would say to black tennis players who felt themselves adrift in a white man's world, "This is your game. This court here is your neighborhood. Think of it as your own street."

To football players who had suddenly grown angry at the ball, he would say, "Think of it as a woman. Imagine that it's the sweetest, kindest woman you ever met. Think of someone you knew. If it ended badly, then make it up to her this time. Catch the ball gently."

It worked. He had been criticized for merely treating symptoms.

"I can read *The Power of Positive Thinking* myself without Dr. Davison's help," one psychiatrist had said. It turned out that Bill Davison was using visualization techniques fifteen years before anyone else. When the chemical pathway between conscious thought and the triggering of immune response was traced, it became, as they say, a whole different ball game.

Jonathan looked at Bill Davison and thought: You've been happy everywhere. What do you know?

"I don't know, on stage maybe, when I'm performing." Jonathan thought of the last play he had been in. "Oz," he said. "I was happy in Oz."

"Go there a lot?" Bill Davison asked, beginning to smile.

Jonathan remembered. "I used to. When I was a kid. Used to take my summer holidays there."

"Okay. I want you to pretend to yourself that you're in Oz."

"You're kidding," said Jonathan.

"No, I'm not kidding. I want you to think of yourself in Oz, all the time. You step out of here, and you're in Oz."

Jonathan closed his eyes and gave a weak little laugh. Jonathan and Bill had a contract: to do whatever Bill asked.

"We're fighting, remember?" Bill said.

"Yeah," said Jonathan. He had thrown up breakfast. He had thrown up lunch. "What's the point of doing this, Bill?"

"I think it could help you feel more at home," said Bill, shrugging as if it were obvious. "You're not. At home."

"I'm in Los Angeles," said Jonathan.

It was time to go. Bill would have another client waiting. Jonathan stood up. His good behavior ran on automatic pilot.

Bill shook his hand. Bill always did that to show Jonathan he didn't think of him as being different from anyone else. It was like the visualizations: Jonathan was aware of everything that Bill Davison was doing. He was still surprised when it worked. He was still surprised by the softness of Bill Davison's hands.

He was surprised by the face; swollen by age, with hatchet marks around the eyes. The teeth grinned out at Jonathan, part of the skull peeking out. Hi, there, the skull seemed to say from underneath its temporary flesh. I won't go away.

"Anyway, see you later tonight," Bill was saying, still alive.

Jonathan's mind went blank. He still saw the skull.

"You're coming to our place for dinner, remember?" It was yet another way in which Bill Davison was unconventional. He was a psychiatrist who invited his clients home.

Jonathan stepped out into the hot white vastness of Wilshire Boulevard. He felt exposed and alone. The traffic roared past, impersonal, as if the cars carried no people in them. There was no one else on the sidewalk, all the way down from Barrington to Bundy. The lights changed; Jonathan began to cross and the traffic still advanced toward him, crawling to a stop, like bulls with their heads down. Jonathan found himself scurrying to get out of their way, even though the lights were still with him.

Jonathan sat down on a bench to wait for a big blue bus. The backrest was covered in a painted advertisement for a funeral home. Gleeful, thought Jonathan, but at least my back is toward it. He looked at the shadows cast by the giant buildings. They marched in rows like morons and gleamed like glaciers. Poor old silver-coated Barrington Plaza looked ancient now beside them. When Jonathan had first come to Los Angeles in the early seventies, the Plaza had been the biggest building all the way from the ocean to the Veterans' Hospital. Jonathan could see the ocean, four miles away at the end of the wide straight road. The sea sparkled in sunlight. Everything was blue with fumes.

Jonathan remembered his contract.

Okay, he told himself, I'm waiting for a big blue bus in Oz. The sidewalks are perfectly laid, because if someone is dumb enough to trip on the edge of a paving slab, they can sue the city. Because the paving is perfect, people roller-skate to work. They wear shorts and shades and a Walkman.

Can I imagine Munchkins here, little people flooding out of shopping malls and insurance offices the size of mountains? Do Munchkins wear mirror shades now? If this is the Emerald City, then the towers are tall because of the value of the land underneath them. And all the windows and doors are sealed because the air inside them is temperature-controlled. If Dorothy and the Scarecrow and the Tin Man went tripping by, no one would notice. They'd think they were high.

It was a twenty-minute wait for the big blue bus. Jonathan read a free paper. It listed courses in adult education. On the cover an attractive woman pouted in a leotard and tried to look as though she were selling fitness courses and not sex. RELAX, said the headline, IT'S SO EASY.

There were courses about making money. How to Sell Real Estate in Your Spare Time. How to Make $ in Catering. How to Get Credit Cards.

And there were courses in Self Discovery Through Metaphysics. Coming Alive with Love. How to Flirt and Not Get Hurt. Courses in counseling or shiatsu or how to begin a conversation.

And there were courses that were an odd mix of the two. One offered instruction in Interviewing Techniques for Selecting a Husband:

> Dating is time-wasting and inefficient. Before accepting that time-consuming invitation to dinner, you need to apply the techniques of market research to discover if the man is really interested in marriage. Manipulative? Yes—and we make no apologies for that. If you change your makeup and put on a nice new dress for a date, then you're manipulating. This course will simply help you to LEARN TO MANIPULATE FOR SUCCESS.

And I was thinking of learning Spanish, thought Jonathan.

He thought of bars where the men all wore nothing but leather harnesses or Dodgers T-shirts, baseball caps and jockstraps.

Oz, he reminded himself, I'm supposed to be in Oz.

HOW TO FIND A LOVER OR A LOVING PARTNER

> A solid, proven system for finding that special someone who's fun to be with, able to carry on a sparkling conversation, financially stable—maybe even rich.

Which, thought Jonathan, is why they haven't found love. And never will.

The bus finally came, and Jonathan got on it, wrestling with coins. He had never, in all his thirty-eight years, learned how to count out change quickly. The door whooshed shut; the bus lurched; the driver said nothing, his face blanked out by sunglasses.

Jonathan sat in the back, where he always did. He tried to pretend the bus was full of Munchkins, all of them talking in speeded-up voices. The bus was full of Angelinos instead. Angelinos have never met each other and cannot trust each other. They suspect each other of carrying murder weapons, possibly with some reason. Angelinos sit alone, in silence, no one next to them. As Jonathan was doing.

On the seat in front of him, a very fat man in dirty shorts sat reading the Style section of the *Los Angeles Times*. The person across the aisle from Jonathan stood up and moved two seats farther back, to be more alone. He was reading *People* magazine. He was thin and smelly, in what looked like standard-issue Veterans' Hospital couture—a tartan shirt with rolled-up sleeves and khaki trousers. UNITY BY THE SEA, said a passing billboard, JOIN US FOR A LOVING EXPERIENCE.

The bus stopped with a slight squeal of brakes. The squeal came and went with the rhythm of a kiss. An old man got on. He was very thin, very brown. His skin was somehow translucent and splotchy. He stumbled unsteadily toward his seat, and when the bus lurched forward, he fell into it, swinging around one of the support poles. The old man was almost too frail to walk, but he wore a jaunty tracksuit. A yellow plastic Sony Walkman whispered disco music into his ear.

Lighting-fixture shops and banks passed by, with acres of parking in the back. Beside a large drugstore, a sign said PARKING FOR PATRONS ONLY, in lettering that imitated nineteenth-century script. Jonathan loved that word "patrons" and that word "only." An old-time, old-fashioned drugstore with an admissions policy?

At the next stop, a middle-aged woman got on with a boy. Her hair was yellow and she wore black tights that showed how far and loose her hips had spread. The boy was about seventeen and wore long, boxy swim trunks and a vest and a bomber jacket. His upper lip was trying, and failing, to grow a moustache. They sat down just in front of Jonathan. The jacket was shrugged back and the woman began to peel sunburned skin off the boy's back. The windows of the bus were open. Patches of skin were caught up in the wind and were whirled about like snow.

A few moments later, the boy got up and started to ask people for money. "Don't have any, man," said Jonathan, wondering if that was how seventeen-year-olds still spoke. He went back to reading about adult education. If this is what they teach adults, he thought, what are they teaching the kids? He finally found his course in Spanish. It was opposite Hot Air Ballooning.

He got off the bus at Fourteenth Street, and across Wilshire Boulevard there was a billboard, an ad for chocolates. IT'S NEVER TOO LATE, it said, TO HAVE A HAPPY CHILDHOOD.

Jonathan lived on Euclid—Thirteenth Street, except that people were too superstitious to call it that. Euclid Avenue was tree-lined and residential and quite pleasant, but it was as if the shrubs and the flowers and the sprinklers and the sunlight and the glimpses of the Santa Monica mountains were all lying. They could bring no real comfort.

Jonathan's property was quite extensive. There were two bungalows in front that he used to rent out in his days of relative penury as an actor. Behind them was his garden, and backing the property, a two-story house for him and Ira. Downstairs were the garage and Ira's office. Upstairs was the house itself. Jonathan trudged wearily up the steps and pulled out his keys.

The key for the house wasn't on it.

What? Jonathan tried to remember what he had done with it. Who could he have given it to? He had his car keys. What could he have done with the key to his house?

It had been happening a lot lately. Forgetting things. Jonathan climbed back down the steps. Well. It was three o'clock. He would just have to wait until Ira got home. He slumped down into his chair, in the garden by the pond.

Jonathan did not want to sit in the garden. It made him feel vulnerable, as if his back were unguarded. He wanted to sit in the house, on the couch just behind the stained-glass window, sheltered in his own little nook, hidden away from people. He wanted to listen to National Public Radio.

Funny the things that kept him going now. NPR saw him through the desolate afternoons like a friend. The music, the features, reassured him that there were other people who thought like him.

Downstairs, outside in the silence, he sat so that no one could see him from the street, and he began to feel a sick and creeping fear crawl up over him. He was going to die, and no sunlight and flowers, no songs, no prayer, could save him. He tried to look at his garden.

He looked at the base of the palm tree. The roots reached down like sinuous worms into the earth. He looked at his ornamental pond and the lilies growing out of a tub under the water. Jonathan remembered. He remembered the party they had held to dig the pond. People had got carried away and dug it so deep that it had to be partially refilled.

What happens to a garden, he wondered, when its owner is gone? Ira had no time for gardening. Would the world, heartless, kill the little blue flowers, the succulent ground cover? Would the dry dead stems haunt Ira, like ghosts? Or would he dig the garden late at night, to keep it going, out of love, for the memory?

Fear was a chill light sweat on Jonathan's forehead. Upstairs the telephone began to ring over and over.

Jonathan remembered the day he had been told he was ill. He had spent an eternal, twisted afternoon waiting for Ira to come home. He had paced the floor, weeping, chewing on his fingers, unable to quell the horrible, quivering animal panic that made him want to run and hide. Then Ira had come, and Jonathan had collapsed against him and told him, and the terror had abated. Ira took the terror away.

"The first thing," Ira had said, "is that we both go into counseling. Did they tell you where to go?"

Jonathan nodded. "They gave me a name. Some hotshot psychiatrist who volunteers."

"Did you get in contact with him? Her?"

Jonathan shook his head. "Not yet. Dr. Podryska had a long talk with me anyway. She gave me some happy pills."

"Did you take them?"

"No. I thought they might be bad for me."

"Stress is bad for you. Take the pills."

"I'm worried about you too, Ira."

Ira sighed and shifted in his smart lawyer working clothes. "It's not your fault. It's not anybody's fault." Ira was puritanically insistent on good behavior.

"You'll have it too."

"Probably," Ira admitted.

"I'll be careful around the house and things." Jonathan meant he would mop up his own blood. He meant they would stop having sex. What he felt was immense relief. Already he knew that Ira was planning to stay with him.

Ira's body jerked with rueful, silent laughter. "You mean you'll eat with a separate knife and fork? Use a different toilet maybe. Maybe I should put some black insulating tape around the handle of your toothbrush. Good thing you have your own electric razor, huh?"

They both looked at each other. Jonathan knew he was in danger of saying something stupid. Stupidity made Ira cross.

"It's a bit late for precautions, Baby," said Ira.

Jonathan retaliated with a practicality. "You should take the test," he said.

"I'm not taking that test," said Ira. They had had arguments about it before.

"Because you said that whatever the result, you had to do the same thing. No casual sex and look after your health. No point taking it, you said, unless you would do something different depending on the result. Well, if you take the test and by any chance you're negative, then we both will have to be a lot more careful, huh? That's a good reason for you to take the test."

Ira was trapped. "Maybe," he said, and he shrugged his beefy arms, convulsively, as if trying to break his way out of his business jacket.

Jonathan knew Ira didn't want to take the test because it would mean coming out to his doctor. Ira's doctor did not know he was gay. Ira was a curious mix of decency and misplaced self-respect. He thought the people where he worked had not noticed that the company lawyer was unmarried and living with another man. Jonathan didn't push any further. He knew that he was right and that Ira would force himself to be logical, force himself to take the test. Talk about the English having a stiff upper lip. Ira forced a set of strictures on himself that were wholly his own.

They had met at UCLA. At twenty-eight years of age, after eight years of professional acting, Jonathan had gone back to school. He studied history. In some quiet place in his actor's soul, he found something very mysterious and soothing in studying the past and in recovering it.

There was a great weight of things that had been lost. Pioneers made houses out of earth and withstood plagues of locusts. The ancient Assyrians left behind them treasure troves of family letters baked in clay. Jonathan's family name was in the Domesday Book. The name meant Dweller by Low Water. They had been a marsh people, farming for their master and hunting birds in the reeds in what was now the county of Hampshire in England.

Ira's people had been Russian Jews. Jonathan met Ira in one of his history tutorials. Ira was huge and jovial and bound for law school, after an improving degree in history. When Ira suddenly invited him to lunch, Jonathan was pleased. It was not always easy to meet people at UCLA. Jonathan was pleased when Ira invited him to play a game of tennis. Jonathan had always found sports easy, though he made no effort at them. Ira beamed back at him, hot, sweaty, his tummy bulging over his immaculate white shorts. What a decent fellow, thought Jonathan. Ira, it turned out, lived at home. His parents seemed to want to protect him from corruption. He was a strange mix of the deeply worldly—he talked about stocks and shares, and the details of Democratic Party politics—and bestilled innocence. At age twenty, Ira lived in the world of a bright seventeen-year-old.

Ira invited Jonathan to an evening of Israeli folk dancing. It did not occur to Jonathan that Ira was doing all the work. Jonathan was amused. Someone else had thought he was Jewish. People usually did. Maybe it was his mother's side of the family, his Cornish ancestors with their black curly hair and Mediterranean complexion.

The folk dances were held in a hall near UCLA. Jonathan had learned all kinds of dancing as part of his training as an actor. He danced with real flair, feet crossing each other, arms outstretched. He danced, his arms around Ira's shoulders. There were bands of muscle from shoulder to shoulder, across the back of Ira's neck. Ira asked Jonathan if he had ever been to Israel.

"No," said Jonathan. "I wish, but I've never really been abroad. My folks live in Canada, so if I have any money, I always end up spending it to go and see them."

"Funny. You don't look Canadian," said Ira. Jonathan did not understand.

"What do Canadians look like?" asked Jonathan.

Ira looked about him in mock secrecy. "They don't know it," he said, "but they look Jewish."

Jonathan was taken aback. Ira touched any area of tension with a joke, to relieve it. Jonathan began to sense a powerful personality in Ira, somewhat obscured by youth and inexperience. There was an imbalance of personal power between them. If they had both been the same age, the imbalance would have destroyed the friendship.

But it was easy for a twenty-eight-year-old actor to appear somewhat exotic to a sturdily conventional undergraduate. Jonathan got Ira into one of his plays for free. The play was a joky rewrite of stories from the Old Testament. The author had written it for children. When she couldn't get it produced, she added a few satiric references and pretended that it had always been for adults. She sat in the tiny audience every night and laughed long and hard at the same jokes, her own jokes.

Jonathan played Adam. Adam made his entrance holding a bath towel around his middle. The serpent was played by a dotty lady wearing a huge red bow tie. Her tongue flickered beautifully. Ira got to meet them all afterward. His cheeks were bright red, his smile wide, his eyes gleaming. He was impressed. That did not stop him from insulting the author.

"Oh, that was you laughing at all the jokes!" Ira exclaimed. "You really sounded like you thought they were funny!" Then he said, still smiling, "You should be an actress." Her smile went thin and tense before she moved on to someone else.

Going home in the car afterward, Ira said, "Hey, you know, that was a really good play." Jonathan wasn't sure to what degree he was being sarcastic. Neither was Ira.

Ira invited him to the sauna that was meant only for teaching staff. They pretended to be staff and sat in the tiny box, naked under towels. They had seen each other naked, and they sat, knees touching, the air thick with some kind of tension. Ira kept wiping his face and shifting and avoiding Jonathan's eyes. It was Jonathan's turn, now, to be innocent.

Then Ira invited him to his synagogue in West Hollywood. He looked awfully solemn as he asked Jonathan, his arms folded. Jonathan began to tease him. "No engraved invitation?" Jonathan asked. And Ira scowled with confusion.

Ira was still tense and anxious as they arrived. He sat stiffly on the bench, his cheeks puffed out, not looking at Jonathan, and Jonathan very slowly realized that all the couples were of the same sex. He began to take in what some of the notices on the wall were saying.

It was a gay synagogue. Beefy, thick-necked Ira was gay. This was the only way he could think of to tell Jonathan.

Outside, in the dark, after the service, Ira stopped and turned around. "So," he said. "Now you know." His eyes had been looking at the ground. Now they looked up at Jonathan, waiting for an answer.

"Yup," was all that Jonathan said. Jonathan was touched when Ira began to look worried. Jonathan found it endearing. Jonathan prolonged the suspense.

Ira's arms made a sudden convulsive movement, the involuntary shrug. "My parents keep asking why I don't go to their synagogue in Burbank," he said.

"I guess they do," said Jonathan.

Ira suddenly smiled, but his lips were turned inward, taut, and he very lightly hit Jonathan on the shoulder. "Well?" he demanded.

"Well what?" Jonathan made himself look innocent.

"What do you think!" bellowed Ira.

"I think it's very nice that you're so religious," replied Jonathan.

"What else?"

"Are you asking about my religious beliefs?"

"I'm asking about you," said Ira, grinning, aggressive, voice low.

Jonathan decided it was time to be serious. He found it was difficult for him to talk straightforwardly. "I'm . . . I'm kind of hazy about all of that," he said.

"Hazy. What does that mean?"

"It means I don't know. Either way." Jonathan made an embarrassed wiggle with his hand. "I guess I'm waiting." He sighed. "Waiting to be persuaded."

There was a blankness in his sexuality. In a society that valued sexual athleticism, he felt himself at a disadvantage. He had a putative girlfriend, and they saw each other once a weekend for a cuddle and a cultural event. She was a well-known performance artist. She swallowed canned peaches whole while gargling the theme song from *Dr. Zhivago*. She looked like a librarian, which was perhaps one of the reasons people laughed. She was serious.

"Do you realize," she had said once, to Jonathan, "that there are more artists living in Los Angeles now than did in all the rest of history?"

Jonathan didn't. "It might depend on what you call an artist," he answered her.

What the girl made of their affair, Jonathan did not know. It was part of the blankness. Maybe she was waiting too. It suddenly didn't seem fair to make her wait any longer.

"Are you going to invite me home?" Ira asked. Virginity hung heavy and embarrassing like something around his neck, to be discarded. Ira lived at home and had nowhere to go. Jonathan began to understand the weight that the boy carried with him.

Ira had taken so many risks. He was frightened of himself and of Jonathan—Jonathan might have been shocked or angry or answered with his fists. Ira's eyes were round, watching, hopeful, sad.

It was time for Jonathan to take charge.

"If I said no, just for tonight, would you stop asking me?" Jonathan asked, and quickly added, "Because I don't want you to stop asking."

Ira said nothing. He looked very young, very disappointed.

Jonathan sighed. "It's just that if we did anything now, I'd feel slightly railroaded."

"You're a nice boy and don't do it on the first date," Ira murmured miserably.

"Something like that."

"If you mean no, just say no."

"I don't mean no."

"I'm supposed to show up with my car on Friday nights with a bunch of flowers?"

"That would be nice. Only no flowers. The neighbors might think I was queer or something."

Ira looked so dismayed that Jonathan felt compelled to kiss him, on the cheek, under streetlights. "Bring chocolates instead."

Ira broke into a terrible sweat. It trickled down his forehead and soaked in patches through his shirt. His conventionality had been taxed to its limits. "Well," he said. "I guess I always did believe in long engagements."

Jonathan drove him home. "Ease up, guy," Jonathan said, temporarily sounding American. Somewhere on the San Diego Freeway, Ira suddenly understood that he had won.

Ira became boisterous and bounced up and down on the car seat in time to the radio. He began to sing. He looked younger than ever. From the front porch of his parents' house, he turned and gave Jonathan a wave. For some reason, it was that wave that made Jonathan finally decide. Jonathan could still see Ira, ten years ago, standing and waving and smiling. Ira was history, too.

Jonathan woke up in his garden. It was bleary with sunlight. Oz, he reminded himself. I'm supposed to be in Oz. And as he awoke he seemed to hear laughter, high childish giggles of something hidden under leaves. Or was it only the last of the telephone, fading away?

His mother was there.

She was wearing her mink stole and narrow tartan trousers, blue and green, and little elfin bootees. She also wore sunglasses and was surrounded by a blaze of sunlight.

When had she last dressed like that?

"Mom?" he asked, sitting up. He was horrified. How long was she going to stay? How long was he going to have to pretend to be well? Already, with actorish skills, he was firming up his eyes and straightening his back. He stood up, with a spring in his step. It was like watching a very aged actor trying to be sprightly. Jonathan could see himself move, very plainly, though his limbs were weighted to the chair.

His mother backed away from him. "I'm all right. You keep sitting," she said. Vapor wreathed out of her mouth, like steam. She found her way to another garden chair, uncertainly, nervously.

At first Jonathan thought it was cigarette smoke coming out of her mouth. But then he saw that she was sitting in a field of snow. Sparkles of sunlight blasted back up from it, like sand in his eyes. It was cold, where his mother was.

She leaned forward, uncertain how to begin. This was not the confident businesswoman that his mother had become. Now in her sixties, Jonathan's mother had lost all sense of fear and, because of that, all sense of style.

This was his young and insecure mother, who had no assurances how well her life would turn out, who wanted everything to be new and modern, who threw out anything old, who was a model but who still did not believe she was beautiful. This was his mother when she was younger than he was now. Poor ghost.

Are you a good witch or a bad witch?

"Did you ever notice," she began, hesitantly, "how in biographies they never tell you much about the adult's relationship with his parents?"

"Yes," said Jonathan. Indeed he had, being interested in history. The words flowed out of his mouth slowly and messily like molasses.

"It's because people are embarrassed by it," said his mother. There were no creases in her cheeks, no patches of scaly skin on her wrists. Her lipstick was ruby red and her hair black.

"It's embarrassing for everyone. Embarrassing for the child who needs to become independent. How can you be independent when there is someone who still calls you their child? For the parents, it's a constant reminder how old they are and how strange life is. They look at the face of a forty-year-old man and say, I gave birth to him. I held his hand as a baby."

Jonathan couldn't see what was happening behind the snow-blind sunglasses.

"When you were first born," his mother said, "I took you out into a field of snow, like this one." She held out her hands, and showed him the Canadian field. "I held you up against my cheek and it was as though I were launching you into the future. It seemed to me you were like a branch, that would grow into the year 2000."

Somehow they were back in Los Angeles.

"You won't see the year 2000, will you?" his mother said.

"No," whispered Jonathan.

"I used to think there was some compensation," his mother said. "When you were a baby, and I realized there was something wrong with you, when you rocked and wouldn't speak, when you tore things up, I asked everyone what I had done wrong. Then I saw. You could draw. You could make those heads out of clay. And I thought: There always is some compensation. When you quit university the first time, and I saw you act at Stratford, I thought: There's the compensation. Even when you left me, left all of us and came here to do whatever it was you did in all those bars, I thought: He's got to be there to make it. He's got to be there for his profession."

She looked around at his garden, at the L.A. sun. "But there's no compensation, Jonathan. There's no one to pass anything on to. You'll die, and the future will be only silence. You'll die and there won't be anything left."

Somewhere there were birds singing in bushes.

"I went back to our old house. The one your father built. It has had eight owners since we left. I walked through its rooms. Everything had been torn out, replaced. Even the stone fireplace your father built.

Even the tree we planted that had your name. The shoebox at the end of the hall, even the patio out back."

"What?" Jonathan began, words trailing limply. He meant to ask, what did the owners think, with you wandering through their rooms.

"They didn't see me. I wasn't really there." She admitted it, shyly, with a sad shrug of her shoulders.

"You never told me," she said. "You never told me anything about yourself. You shut me out. You were embarrassed. You should always pay attention to embarrassment, Jonathan. It means there is something too tangled to deal with. And humor, when people turn things into a joke. Or when they make them weird or spooky. It means that there is something people cannot face."

She took off her sunglasses, and looked at him directly.

"Have you ever noticed, Jonathan? Being an actor. Has it ever occurred to you that there are only two genres that can deal with family life? One of them is comedy." She smiled ruefully. "And the other is . . ."

Her voice went rough and deep and harsh and menacing, and her face blossomed out like a flower in time-lapse photography, burst out in an eruption of scar tissue and deformation, marks where knives had passed.

"The other is horror!"

Jonathan howled and threw himself back in his chair, nearly knocking it over. He lost all of his breath, he couldn't pull in air, and his heart was thumping.

He looked around his garden, and there was no one there, and it was dark. When had the sun set?

I was dreaming, he told himself. That was all; I was dreaming.

But he knew his eyes had been open, and he knew he had been awake. He knew his mind was beginning to go. He didn't have as much time as he had thought.

Behind the locked door, the telephone began to ring again, over and over.

Finally, in 1981 when he was thirty years old, Jonathan had been offered a leading role in a film.

It was a horror movie. His agent described the script, euphemistically, as "powerful." The character was so disfigured that Jonathan had assumed no one would know it was him under the makeup.

The film was called *The Child Minder*. Jonathan played a character called Mort. Mort's face had been slashed by his father when he was a child. The face looked like a crazy quilt, all swellings and stitches. The character Mort loved children, and he loved killing them.

Mort hung them from meat hooks. He pressed cheese-cutting wire through them. Mort kissed them as he killed them and called them "my sweet baby, my sweet child."

Jonathan needed the money. It was with a sense of dread that he showed up at 5:00 a.m. in the scanty little trailer on location in Santa Monica. He assumed he would dry again. He often did, without warning. Despite his reputation for brilliance, Jonathan would sometimes unaccountably be unable to act. It was unaccountable even to himself.

Ira had read the script and described it with one word: pornography.

But as the layers of latex accumulated, destroying his face, Jonathan found he began to feel pity for the character he saw being built up in the mirror. Jonathan found a voice for him—desperate, wild with sadness and humor and betrayed good grace. His voice would be cultured, his laugh hysterical and poisoned. There was something solid there, as solid as history, that Jonathan could grasp.

Jonathan stepped out of the trailer into a gray California morning. He walked toward the lights and stepped into their magic circle. Jonathan spun on his heel once, and something alive reared out from him, took over his face, took over his voice box and his cheek muscles. The latex on his face was as unresponsive as scar tissue. That was right, too.

Children. What the world does to children. Cuts them, scars them, imprisons them, destroys them. It was all so terrible as to be a horrible joke, an embarrassment, a subject for comedy, comedy or terror.

They filmed the last scene first.

"Hey," said the director, a beefy, forty-year-old ex-cameraman. "You know, that's really good." He was surprised. They were on to something.

MEET MORT, said the billboards. HE LOVES KIDS. TO PIECES.

The Child Minder was a monstrous success. For some reason, young teenagers were willing to pay to see people their own age tortured and killed in various ways. Market research showed that many of them went to see *The Child Minder* two or three times.

Ira never went to see it at all. "I just think it's a terrible shame that the only thing this society can find to do with your talent is that garbage."

Jonathan disagreed. There was something to Mort, something he couldn't define. Mort meant something.

There was a sequel. Mort had died at the end of the first film. *Child Minder II* resurrected him in a studio-bound hell.

Hell was full of the souls of children. They were made to sing merry school songs, chained to desks. They were drilled by tormenting demons in gray clothes with spectacles and fangs and rulers that beat wrists until hands dropped off.

There was a race of dwarves in Hell. They wore black leather harnesses, just like in certain L.A. bars. They had interesting deformities that took the better part of a day to create in makeup, and they flayed people alive. They sang and danced as they worked, like a Disney movie played backward. At the climax, Hell was harrowed by a visiting priest, and Mortimer escaped in a blaze of fire, out into the real world, an eternal spirit, to kill again and again in a chain of sequels. Mort was the wounded spirit of the eternal hatred of children.

In each of the films, all of the adults were either fools or drunks, wrapped up in work or sleazy sex. They had failed their children utterly. The children were left to defend themselves.

Mort materialized out of their parents. In sequences of special effects, he slimed his way out of parents' sleeping, snoring mouths. Mortimer was wept out of their eyes, to coagulate on the floor. He climbed out of the television set as adults watched the news impassively. The news, in the form of armed alerts, terrorism and serial murders, continued to flicker on Mortimer's face. The children died, slowly, horribly.

Market research showed that there had to be a murder every ten minutes or the audience got bored. In each ending, virtue triumphed in a blaze of light, and another generation would be left to grow up in peace. Except that as each sequel ended, Mort's face would be glimpsed, reflected in a pair of adult sunglasses or waiting for a bus, reading a newspaper. CHILD MURDERED, the headline would scream. With each return, Mortimer made more money.

Jonathan started to get letters. Many of them were from boys, wanting to know about the makeup and the special effects. Some of the letters were from girls who wanted to know about his emotional life. Was he as lonely as he seemed in the movie? Did he have someone to love him? One letter was from a woman who claimed to be a vampire. Was he one himself? Did he want to become one?

Jonathan became a star interview, in a certain kind of magazine.

In full color, the magazines showed how rubber bodies were made so that the skin and flesh could be pulled off in realistic detail as the arms writhed, as the arteries pumped out jets of blood. There were faces of women, with tiny pig eyes and huge mouths the size of footballs full of teeth. The center-page spread would be of Jonathan as Mort, his face in healed sections.

Jonathan endeared himself to the market by showing in the interviews that he had once been a fan of horror movies himself. He would lapse into lines of Bela Lugosi's dialogue. He would pay tribute to the grand old Gothic tradition. He might allow himself a touch of yearning for a time when fear was achieved through suggestion rather than bloody detail. He tried to explore what he thought he saw in the character of Mort. The audience found all of this flattering.

Jonathan was invited as Guest of Honor to something called a Con. It was a convention for fans of what was described as dark fantasy. Darkcon it was called.

Darkcon was held in Baltimore. Jonathan had never seen Baltimore. He spent three days in the city and still didn't see it. He saw the inside of the convention hotel instead.

It was a large, modern facility, with polished corridors and carpets and polite young women in orange jackets wearing name-tags. They smiled behind desks. The smiles grew uneasy as men in long hair, beards and black T-shirts began to take over the hotel.

Jonathan was welcomed by the Con committee and given a pack of publications—program books, more magazines. A plump, fresh-faced young man called Karl had been assigned to him. Karl was in charge of Guest Relations. He took Jonathan on a tour.

The Con had a bookroom, full of paperbacks in black jackets. Just inside the entrance there was a row of realistic, severed heads, caked in blood. Outside the bookroom, a little child was screaming, being pulled inside by her mother. Behind the severed heads, the book dealers were chuckling.

The Con had an art show. Its largest piece consisted of five realistically re-created nude corpses, hanging from hooks over a fan of rusted, bloodstained buzz saws.

Jonathan stood before it, with an expression of rapt and dazzled wonder.

"Toto," he said, in a little girl's voice. "We must be over the rainbow!"

As a Canadian, Jonathan seemed to spend half his life signaling Americans that he had told them a joke. He wiggled his eyebrows and leered at Karl. Karl suddenly grinned and covered one eye with a hand. "Oh, I get it!" he said. Karl's skin was brown, but his cheeks were very pink and his thick eyebrows almost met. Jonathan found himself feeling tender toward him.

A tall, thin woman approached them, all angles. Her hair flew everywhere, and her eyes were bright, and she was the same age as Jonathan. He placed her perhaps a bit too quickly. An ex-hippie, he judged, one of his own kind, a kindred spirit.

"I did the metalwork," she announced, pointing to the buzz saws.

"I'm . . . impressed," said Jonathan, choosing his words carefully. "You've put a lot of effort into it." Looking again, he had to admit that the metalwork was beautifully done. He suddenly saw the woman in his mind, slim in overalls, with a blowtorch.

"This is Moonflower," said Karl, coughing, shuffling. "She's famous," he added. "She does my fanzine."

"How . . . This is a strange question. You're obviously talented."

"I usually draw elves," Moonflower said. "And seagulls and stars. Stuff like that."

"Right. So where do the corpses fit in?"

"You're asking me that?" Moonflower seemed surprised. "The elves and this. They're the flip side of the same thing."

Karl and Jonathan had lunch together in the Con buffet. Eye of Newt was on the menu. Karl was obviously starstruck by Jonathan. Jonathan found this charming. To please Karl, Jonathan found himself becoming Mortimer.

"So charming to have lunch with you," he said in Mortimer's voice. "Are you often on the menu?"

"Uh-oh," said Karl, in something not unlike real fear.

"Joke," cooed Mortimer and batted his eyelashes. "People do say my humor slays them."

Mort was a pastiche of different acting styles. Mostly he spoke like a slightly camped-up Boris Karloff.

"Yup, really kills me," said Karl, wincing with anticipation.

"Is that an invitation?" said Mort.

"Ew!" said Karl in delicious discomfort. "Ew! He's doing it! He's doing it!"

The fans didn't know Jonathan's face, but they recognized the voice. They looked up from the tables. They put down their trays and began to gather around.

Jonathan played with Karl's hair. Karl stood, eyes closed, bearing up like a child determined to resist a tickling.

"My little baby," said Mortimer in a greasy, singsong voice. "He's rigid with embarrassment. You might say Mort-ified. Shall we play a nice little game?"

"Eeek," said Karl in a tiny voice. There was an appreciative murmur of laughter. Laugh at me, will you? Mortimer thought. Laugh? Then listen to this.

And Mortimer threw himself from side to side in the chair, possessed by laughter, shrieking with it, loud and piercing as a knife.

"Ooooooooo!" breathed out the audience in fear. It was the laugh of the Wicked Witch of the West.

Later that night, Karl came and drank whisky in Jonathan's room, and slept with him, even though, as far as Jonathan could determine, he was heterosexual. Karl's last name was Rodriguez. Karl Rodriguez. Jonathan kept saying the name. Could you fancy someone for their teeth? Karl had a huge grin full of large bright teeth. Karl's parents had come to the north from Mexico.

The next day, Jonathan was interviewed in front of five hundred people. He sat behind a folding table, next to a scholarly looking woman with plain, pulled-back hair and glasses.

"What's your worst nightmare?" she asked.

"Waking up to find I'm in *Child Minder Fifteen*." There was laughter. The laughter was uneasy.

"Do you sometimes find the violence hard to take?" the interviewer asked.

"Oh no. I can't see all that meat and blood," said Jonathan. "I can't see red. I'm color-blind."

And he thought: I've got, I've got to find something else to do.

There was to be a charity performance of *The Wizard of Oz* in the Hollywood Bowl. Dorothy was going to be played by Cher. Nick Nolte was the Tin Man. Sam Shepard was going to play the Scarecrow, but had to pull out.

For the first time in his life, Jonathan hustled. Ambition alone could not have made him do it. Only an overwhelming urge to play the part could have driven him.

He went straight from reading *Variety* to Aaron Spelling's office. Aaron was producing; Jonathan had appeared in "Dynasty," another one of his tormented character roles, a priest in love with Joan Collins. The character had not been popular with audiences and was speedily dropped—but Spelling still had some time for Jonathan.

Jonathan simply told him the truth. He was the only man in L.A. who could still play the Scarecrow. To prove it, he sang "If I Only Had a Brain" right in the office. He ran full speed at the wall and did a backward somersault from it. Jonathan shook his head like a saltshaker and knew that he was sprinkling from it something he could only name but not describe. The something was Ozziness, the quality of Oz.

Spelling chuckled and shook his head. "Okay, okay, you sold me." Maybe he needed to fill the part quickly, maybe it didn't matter with all the star names on the bill. There were a lot of maybes.

But word soon went around town that some horror-movie star was playing the Scarecrow. The buzz was that the horror-movie star was wonderful.

"Well, he's always been a brilliant actor," said those who cared to remember the little theaters, his TV psychos, his TV academics.

Jonathan found himself having lunch with Cher. She seemed to take a kind of rueful, maternal interest in him. He told her about his researches into Baum, into Kansas, into Oz. He told her about his visit to Lancaster, California. She changed the subject.

"This show could do you a lot of good," she said. "This show could really break you."

Jonathan was dazzled. Something alive seemed to stir in him, made out of joy. With a kind of twist and a flip of his hands, he folded, out of the corner of the tablecloth, a dog's head. It had little knots for ears, a snout, and a punched-in, toothless mouth.

"We're not in Kansas anymore," said Jonathan, stroking the dog's head. The dog turned around and looked at Cher and cocked its head with curiosity. Its ears rose up, attentive. The dog was alive.

"That's terrific," said Cher.

"I only wish I would stop losing all this weight," Jonathan said to Toto.

A week or two later, he went in for tests.

Ira didn't show up. Jonathan hated driving now, but he drove to Bill's house by himself anyway, alone in the dark, and got horribly lost. He missed the exchange onto the freeway, and he missed the turn off the freeway, and then he wandered aimlessly up and down Topanga Canyon. The roads on the map wriggled under his eyes like worms.

He arrived in a panic, sick at being lost and alone, horrified at how fragile his illness had made him.

"I drove round and round for hours! I couldn't find where I was!" He was sobbing. He had to sit down.

"Muffy, get a whisky, could you?" asked Bill.

Bill took Jonathan in his arms. It was a great comfort to be held. But it was an enfeebling comfort. Jonathan had been reduced to needing to be hugged after a simple drive in the car. Jonathan wiped his cheeks and tried to pull away, patting Bill on his great bare arms.

"There you go, buddy," said Bill, and let him go.

And Bill's wife Muffy was there, holding out a glass of whisky. A glass of whisky in Waterford crystal. Jonathan was terrified he might drop it.

"You must think I'm a real wimp," he said.

"I think you're scared," said Muffy. "It's not pleasant, being alone and lost."

It was alarming how people were the only island of safety he had against terror. As soon as he was around people, the fear went. Most of the time in L.A., he was alone.

"I couldn't read the map," he said, gulping whisky and snot.

"Let me show you around the house," said Bill.

The house was a museum. It was a great old farmhouse from the days when L.A. was a Western settlement of farmers and fruit trees. There were huge wooden spoons on the wall that had been used for stirring vats of lye soap. There were old homemade candles. There were shoes people had made themselves out of hides. There were family Bibles, with names of parents and grandparents.

"Look at this! Look at this!" Jonathan exclaimed. "I didn't know you were into all of this!"

How can you cover so many bases? Jonathan thought, looking at Bill Davison's face. You can talk shop to a ball player, history to a historian. With a face like yours, you ought to be some Reaganite businessman in favor of defense budgets. With money like you make, you ought to be slick and sharp and spouting horrible, phony relation-speak.

"All these things," said Bill Davison. "They're from Kansas. I kind of collect them."

"I only take photographs," said Jonathan.

Muffy walked with them, commenting quietly on the implements. "That object there is for firing pills down horses' throats." There was something European about her. She was plump and pale, with undyed hair, no makeup, and yet there was something forcefully sensual about her. Even Jonathan felt it. Her breasts hung loose, her hips wobbled under the peasant dress. Jonathan found that he was glad for Bill, glad that he had a wife who was his match.

Muffy had gone with Bill on his expeditions to Kansas. She talked about the samplers on the walls. She knew about the people who had made them. One of them had been singed in the fire at Lawrence. Made by Millie Branscomb, aged eight.

"This is the strangest thing," Muffy said. "When we researched this, we found out it was done by the mother of someone Bill knew."

"The mother of a patient of mine. My first patient, you might say," said Bill. "It's all very strange. I got to know a woman about eighty-something. She was living in a Home. She thought she was Dorothy Gale."

It took a moment. "From Oz," said Jonathan.

"Turned out," said Bill, "that she was. She knew Frank Baum."

There was that icy vapor again, from the snow, from the cold. It rose up from the floorboards. Jonathan saw it at his feet.

Later, when Muffy was in the kitchen, they sat at the table and Jonathan said, "I'm having visions, Bill."

"What?"

"I'm seeing things. I'm hallucinating. You're a psychiatrist. You tell me what that means."

Bill went very silent. In front of him was a rush place mat. He traced its spiral pattern with the blade of a knife. "It all depends," said Bill Davison, "on whether the visions are true or not."

Jonathan thought a minute and then said, "I think they are."

Muffy had cooked a Turkish meal. The main course was made of egg-plants and onions. They waited awhile before dessert, hoping that Ira would come. Drinking whisky had been a mistake. Jonathan felt himself go quiet and slightly confused. He listened.

Bill talked about the history of Kansas. The Old West, he said, had stringent gun-control laws. You checked your firearms before you came into town. Wichita, Kansas, was the town of Wyatt Earp, of Bat Masterson, the town of all those TV shows along with Dodge City, also in Kansas. For the whole decade of the 1870s, when Wichita was one of the wildest cowtowns, the total number of people murdered in it was four. Four people killed in ten years. In Los Angeles, it was four a day.

"It was the cities Back East that made up the Wild West," said Bill. "The penny-dreadful magazines, and the movies after them."

"What about Billy the Kid? He was real."

"Looks as if he may have been born in New York City."

Jonathan began to hear cattle lowing, somewhere up the canyon perhaps.

"Tell me more about Dorothy," he said.

"She was from a farming community called Zeandale, near a place called Manhattan, Kansas. Its other claim to fame is that Damon Runyon was born there."

"What was she like?"

"Well," said Bill, looking into his wineglass. "It was as if she lived in Oz all the time. She lived in a world of her own. Maybe that was what Baum saw in her, maybe not. I wrote to the Baum Estate to find out more about it. All they could tell me was that Baum had been a substitute teacher there for a short while. They thought it more likely that the character in the book was named after Baum's niece."

He told Jonathan the story, as much as he knew. He told him how Dorothy had died. The room seemed to fill with the low smoky light that comes on winter afternoons, sun through silver mist.

"One day," said Bill, "I might just go to Manhattan and see what else I can find out about her. Speaking of which, how are you and Oz getting on?"

"I beg your pardon?"

"Oz. Remember our contract?"

Jonathan had forgotten.

Ira finally arrived in his own car. He was gray with fatigue, and he stared coldly at Jonathan.

"I rang and rang. Where were you?" he asked, as he sat down.

Jonathan's eyes were round, unblinking, feverish. He didn't answer.

Ira turned to Bill. "I'm really sorry, Bill. I wanted to call and say I was going to be late, but I didn't have your home number."

Bill explained. "That's okay. Jonathan told me he was locked out of your house. He couldn't answer the phone."

"I've lost my house keys, Ira," said Jonathan. The room glimmered, as sunlight sprinkles snow with stars. Someone was trying to walk toward Jonathan through the mist. All Jonathan could see was a dark shape, lumpy, in dark clothes. Light came in rays from all around it, cutting through the mist, casting shadows.

"I'll need sunglasses," said Jonathan and grinned and grinned.

Muffy came in, carrying the dessert. To Jonathan, the dessert looked like a chocolate pudding.

"I made this specially for you," Muffy said to Jonathan.

Jonathan imagined how smooth the chocolate pudding would be. He picked up the serving spoon and plunged it into the dish, and then, confused, pushed it into his own mouth.

"Jonathan!" exclaimed Ira and thumped both hands on the table. The pudding seemed to turn into dust in Jonathan's mouth. It was chestnut pudding, bland and with a kind of powdery texture underneath.

"It's okay," said Muffy. "I'll get another serving spoon."

As she left for the kitchen, Jonathan thought: She made it for me, and I don't like it and that will hurt her feelings.

I know. I'll eat without chewing it, so I won't have to taste it. There was silence at the table as he gulped it. He took another serving spoonful and swallowed again. He made a noise like a frog.

Muffy came back out. One more mouthful for her. He stuck the spoon in and swallowed it whole, raw.

"Very. Good," he said.

Then he stood up and shambled into the kitchen and threw it up, into the sink, over the draining board.

"Oh God! Jonathan!" shouted Ira.

There was a kitchen chair. Jonathan slumped helpless onto it, otherwise he might have fallen.

Ira was in the kitchen first. He picked up a towel. It was a good dishtowel, too good to use.

"Oh Jesus, Jesus, Jesus," he said and flung the towel against the wall in rage. Muffy came in.

"I'm so sorry," said Ira to her.

"That's okay. I can clean it up," said Muffy. She did not sound cheerful, but managed to be reasonably businesslike.

"No. You will not. That is one thing you mustn't do," said Ira. There were wispy trails of blood in the pudding.

Jonathan had begun to realize exactly what he had done. He wished he was dead. Then he remembered that he would be soon enough. "I'm sorry," he said, in a voice perhaps too low for the others to hear. Jonathan tried to get up and found that he couldn't. "I'll clean it up," he said. Again, no one seemed to hear.

Muffy flashed rubber gloves. Ira took them from her. "Really," he said. "I'd rather you let me do it."

"Okay," said Muffy. "Jonathan, would you like to go outside for a walk?"

What?

Then it was a minute or two later and Muffy wasn't there. Ira was scrubbing, his back to Jonathan, pouring bleach on the draining board.

"Ira? We were talking about Wichita," said Jonathan. "And Wyatt Earp. He wore a policeman's uniform. Mostly he just took in stray dogs. His sisters were registered prostitutes."

Ira did not answer.

"I'm sorry, Ira."

Ira still did not answer. When he was done, he seemed to sag in place. He pulled off the gloves and let them soak in bleach, and he washed his hands, and he turned around, and his face was white like a fish's belly and stubbled with blue-black beard. He looked fat and haggard at the same time. He had been working until nine o'clock. He had been working a lot lately.

Ira walked out of the kitchen and left Jonathan sitting there.

And there was the mist again, and there was someone walking through the mist, out of the midst of the dishwasher.

"Squeaky clean," said Jonathan and grinned.

Whoever, whatever it was drew back as if afraid. Was it wearing a dress?

"No, no, don't be afraid," said Jonathan. It seemed to come back.

Sometime later, Bill was leaning over him, arm across his shoulders. "Who are you talking to, Jonathan?"

"I beg your pardon?" Jonathan replied, on automatic pilot. There was nothing in the kitchen except for the stove, the sink, the dishwasher.

"You've been talking to someone out here for quite some time."

Jonathan didn't remember that at all.

"Who to?" Bill asked.

Jonathan wasn't quite sure, but he could hazard a guess. "Dorothy," he replied.

Ira drove them back home in silence. They had had to leave Jonathan's car behind. Muffy said she would drive it home for them the next day while Ira was at work. "I'll stop in and see you," she said to Jonathan.

Jonathan realized later that he had not answered her.

It had drizzled during dinner. The streets were greasy with rain, slick and shiny. The colors swam in Jonathan's eyes.

"Snakes," he said. "Snakes on the road." He meant that the lights seemed to move. He did not mean that he was actually seeing snakes. Ira's eyes were as hard as the lenses of his glasses.

Getting back to the freeway, they passed an old-fashioned shopping plaza. There was a long low blank white wall, with a row of poplars in front of it. It glowed in blue-white strip lighting, and Jonathan blinked.

The wall looked to him exactly like the face of a faraway hill. He began to see the evergreen trees in its blue mistiness. There must be a deep gully, a valley between him and the slope. He smelled water. A river too, full of cool spray.

"I didn't know there was a valley with a river here," said Jonathan.

"What?" asked Ira. His knuckles on the steering wheel were white.

"There, the valley over there, with the river." Jonathan pointed at the shopping plaza.

Ira was sweating. He kept looking over at Jonathan, and pushing his glasses back up his nose.

"We need some gas," Ira muttered to himself. He signaled and pulled in, under a bright canopy with Coke machines and the glimmer of piped music. A Mexican strode over to the car and saluted them. He held up a bottle of wine. He smiled, face creased, some of his teeth outlined with gold. He held the bottle out to Jonathan. Jonathan smiled blearily back and took a swig.

Ira came back to the car after paying.

"That will be some surprised Mexican if he finds out he's HIV positive," said Ira.

Jonathan suffered a moment of clarity. "It doesn't spread that way, Jo-Jo." Jo-Jo? He had just called Ira by his own nickname.

"You've got bleeding gums," said Ira, succinctly. He turned the car key with a wrench and the engine made a grinding sound. They pulled out into the wide boulevard, toward the on-ramps.

Very suddenly, in the middle of the road, Ira stopped the car. He threw off his glasses and covered his face and sobbed, and wiped his eyes with the heel of his hand.

"I don't think this is a good place to stop, Ira."

"Oh, shut up!" said Ira.

A truck howled in alarm behind them, swerved onto the wrong side of the road and, blaring hatred, roared past them.

"You used to be a pretty bright guy, you know?" said Ira quietly. He put his glasses back on and started the car and crept carefully forward.

"I get confused, Ira. Ira?" Ira didn't answer.

Jonathan needed Ira to take the terror away. Jonathan shrank down very small and quiet in a corner of the car, so that Ira would not be angry. So that Ira would not go away. The freeway, the Santa Monica hills, sped past in the darkness.

Jonathan began to sing. He was not aware of it.

> I would wile away the hours
> Conferring with the flowers
> Consulting with the rain.
> I would dance and be merry.
> Life would be a ding-a-derry
> If I only had a brain.

"Don't sing that," said Ira, teeth together.

Jonathan shrank even smaller.

The car pulled into the garage, a reassuring throb of engine bounding back from the narrow walls and a smell of gas and the settling down of light and noise when the engine was turned off. The sensations of coming home.

They walked around to the front, into the garden, and then Ira pitched himself forward. It was Ira's turn to be sick.

"Ira? Ira?" Jonathan's hands danced like butterflies.

Ira rolled sideways and sat in a garden chair, head in hands, glasses dangling.

"Are you sick?" The prospect of Ira being ill too filled Jonathan with alarm. "Let me get you a drink or something."

"I don't want anything." The garden floodlights made Ira look blue-white. He sat still with his eyes closed. "I'm very tired, Jonathan."

Jonathan had to say something. He found that he was fighting. "Maybe we could, maybe we could arrange like a holiday for you."

"Juh!" said Ira, turning away, eyes still closed. With a great effort he stood up and began to walk up the steps.

Jonathan followed him, his head wobbling like an Indian dancer's. Everything felt loose, as if his ligaments had come untied. "You. You could stay at Jenny's for a few days, Ira, in the hills. I'll be okay, I can stay here, maybe see a few people, go out for dinner. You're very tired, Ira, I can see that, I feel real bad about that, I know I make you do everything . . ."

I leaned on you too hard and you broke.

Ira stopped in front of the door and turned. "Do you think I want to go through all this twice?"

Ira wanted to go away.

"No, no, of course not, that's why I said, maybe a break would be a good thing." Jonathan followed Ira across the darkened living room, into the kitchen. "Maybe the time has come to get a cleaning lady or something or a nurse or something, you know, just to take some of the strain."

Ira was greedily drinking a glass of water straight from the tap instead of the filter. The freezer buzzed, where Ira kept the coffee beans frozen until they were ground. So it would be healthier. Ira turned and looked at him solemnly, heavily, like stone. Jonathan looked at him.

"Please don't go, Ira."

"Where the fuck can I go?" said Ira. He walked with his tumbler of water into the bedroom. "I carry it around with me."

"You're working too hard."

"I'm working too hard to keep away from you," said Ira. He began to undress. He kicked off his trousers, leaving them discarded, twisted. He really was getting very fat. His body was familiar, like an old pillow.

"That bad, huh," said Jonathan.

"That bad. Now if you don't mind, I'd like to get *some* sleep."

Jonathan stood helplessly in the middle of the room. They slept separately now; sleeping next to Jonathan was unpleasant; he knew that. He shivered, he sweated, he got up. He didn't expect Ira to sleep with him, but he did want to be touched, he did want to be held. He wanted to be comforted.

Without saying anything, Ira began insistently to push him back out of the room.

Jonathan panicked. He began to gabble as he walked backward, as if a tape were being rewound. "Ira. Don't go, huh. I'll ease up, I'll do anything, I'll go away and come back, I'll do anything, only please, Ira, please don't leave me alone!"

The door was closed. He stood looking at it.

"Oh, God," said Jonathan, to the ceiling. What do I do now?

You try, said a more sensible voice, to get some sleep. You try to get yourself calm and try to sleep. You've got a disease to fight.

Even if I want to die?

The room was spinning anyway. Oh God, Jonathan felt himself surrendering the world from exhaustion. He stumbled toward the big easy chair.

In something like sleep, he dreamed. He dreamed he had played the Scarecrow after all. He was swept up in the magic circle of light, and gave the performance of his life. The Scarecrow was goofy and brainless, at war with the physical world, possessed of imagination, another kind of intelligence. He was more magical than the Wizard, kinder than the Tin Man, braver than the Lion. The Scarecrow was the favorite. He and Dorothy danced around and around in circles like a cyclone, filling the vacuum at its heart.

He woke up and knew what he had to do. He did not have much time.

He stood up and emptied his pockets. The garage keys, the bungalow keys, he left on the table in his little niche with the stained-glass window. He didn't want to die in L.A., alone, listening to NPR, waiting for someone, anyone to call. He didn't want to bother Ira, torment him, make Ira take care of him and make himself sick. Jonathan wanted to disappear. He wanted to make one last visit to Back Then.

He left his keys, but no note. He took his little purse, with notebook and credit cards. He smiled. An adventure. What do you want to do? people always asked him when they found out, meaning, Do you want to write a novel? Travel? I want, thought Jonathan, to do this.

He closed the door behind him. It was locked. He could not go back. He went down the steps. There was a silver hint of dawn in the sky. He would catch the blue bus on Wilshire and then the blue bus along Lincoln. He would take the big blue bus to Oz.

After Ira and Jonathan left, Bill had climbed up the wooded hill in back of his house. He looked down on the City of the Angels, at its rivers of moving light. He felt wonder at the world. Unaided by faith or meditation, a visitor to his house was having visions, like a medieval monk. Bill Davison was going to pray to the blank yellow-gray sky, to the lights, to the God that drove them all. He suddenly found that he couldn't.

Manhattan, Kansas

September 1989

"BREAKING THE WILL"

This phrase is going out of use. It is high time it did . . . But the phrase is still sometimes heard; and there are conscientious fathers and mothers who believe they do God service in setting about the thing.

I have more than once said to a parent who used these words, "Will you tell me just what you mean by that? Of course you do not mean what you say."

"Yes, I do. I mean that a child's will is to [be] once for all broken!—that he is to learn that my will is to be his law. The sooner he learns this the better."

—The first paragraphs of a front-page article on child raising from the Manhattan *Nationalist* of Friday, January 15, 1875. The article goes on to describe, as an example of *good* child-raising practice the case of a four-year-old boy who was subjected to a two-day campaign to get him to pronounce correctly the letter G.

Jonathan's Canada had disappeared. It had been there when he left in the earliest seventies. By the late eighties, Corndale had been swallowed up by an administrative fiction called Missasauga. It was another Indian name, another vanished tribe.

Missasauga was a sea of subdivisions. Corndale's nearest neighbor, Streetsville, was solid, stolid housing as was Corndale itself. The two realities met as fiction. The farms on which Jonathan had seen running deer as a child had disappeared. When he visited Corndale now, he got lost in the bewildering meander of streets designed to stifle speed and protect children. It was all about land values and Toronto airport and Highway 401. Urban foxes, urban raccoons were rumored to rummage through trash cans at night.

So where was home?

Jonathan pulled the gray Celebrity out of the parking lot of the airport of Manhattan, Kansas, and suffered a delusion. Outside there were wide green fields, and huge trees the like of which he had not seen since the elms in Corndale had been cut down after Dutch elm disease. He thought he had finally, somehow, found his way back to Corndale. In particular, he was driving along the number 10 highway, the road that led from Brampton.

This made him very happy. This made him feel that suddenly everything had gone right with the world, even though there was for some reason a puddle of blood and stomach juices on the back seat. It seemed to him that he recognized the road signs, the chalky limestone through which the road had been cut. He recognized the huge, 600-acre farms. He wondered what had happened to his childhood friends, and if he could visit them now.

Then suddenly, instead of blood on the back seat, there was a visitor. Oh dear, thought Jonathan. Why did I bring him along?

On the back seat sat Mortimer.

It was going to be terribly embarrassing taking Mort home, because he was in full drag. Perhaps he had come fresh from some Halloween parade. He was dressed as Dorothy.

He had pigtails and a checked apron and balloon sleeves and white surgical gloves. For some reason he was also wearing a bandito hat and was holding maracas. His face was in sections like a quilt.

Mortimer gave the maracas a shake. "Hola!" he cried. "Que tal!"

Spanish? "Bee-ba Meh-heeko!" he cried, lips thick with red lipstick. Jonathan was mildly surprised to see red, but could not remember why.

"This *is* Mexico, isn't it?" Mortimer was not sure.

Jonathan couldn't remember.

"We're in *Kansas?*" said Mortimer as if he had stepped in something. The maracas sank to his lap. The surgical gloves were blood-stained. "What the fuck are we going to do in Kansas?"

I don't know, thought Jonathan, still driving.

"I thought you wanted to go to Mexico! That's why you were going to learn Spanish." Mortimer gave a showy sigh. "And I so wanted to go abroad." Mortimer giggled. "Who knows, I might have come back a lady."

Jonathan had never realized just how camp Mortimer was. Jonathan hated camp. Where, Jonathan asked Mort, do you come from?

"From you!" said Mortimer, pointing. He smiled and gave his nose a wrinkle.

I'm nothing like you.

Mortimer pressed his spongy, latex face against Jonathan's sweaty cheek. In the mirror of the visor, Jonathan saw the same blue eyes staring back at him.

"See the resemblance?" Mortimer whispered in his ear.

How? That face? Jonathan thought.

"Daddy sliced it."

My father was good and kind, thought Jonathan. He was an athlete. He wanted me to be an athlete, but he never pushed me. He only hit me twice, once when I had hit little Jaimie Cummings and when I'd stained his walls with berries.

"He only hit you twice!" exclaimed Mortimer and clapped his hands together as if in admiration. "*What* a sweetie. Did you ever hit him?"

He never deserved to be hit.

Mortimer lounged back in the seat, smiling as if his lips were full of novocaine.

"Did he die or simply ascend into Heaven?" Mortimer asked. "Making a noise like a dove, perhaps. Whroooo!" Mortimer blew on the palm of his glove and white pigeon feathers fell in the car like snow. "And dropping doo-doo on people underneath."

He was killed in a car crash, thought Jonathan, bitter with grief, as if it were some kind of vindication. Mortimer grinned back at him. Jonathan searched his mind and really did find his father without blemish.

"He never did anything wrong!" Jonathan was shouting aloud.

Silence, and a numb smile.

Jonathan muttered, "How else are you supposed to discipline kids?"

"Oh! I am in complete agreement," said Mortimer, hand on breast. There was an instrument of torture, rather like a corkscrew, on his lap. "In fact, the differences between me and your father might be less than you think. Do you like my dress?"

Mortimer batted his eyelashes.

Go away! thought Jonathan.

Mortimer's eyes went evil. "I thought you wanted to see Kansas!"

He pressed his face against Jonathan's again and grabbed Jonathan by the chin and made him look in the rearview mirror.

"This face is Kansas. A country is like a child. Smooth and new and virginal until Daddy slashes its face."

Mortimer fell back into the rear seat. Jonathan felt Mort's sweat still on his cheek. Mortimer was opening the back door. "Don't kill any babies," he warned, and launched himself out of the moving vehicle under the wheels of a truck.

Jonathan swerved violently as the truck roared past, horn blaring. Jonathan pulled over onto the soft shoulder and stopped the car, his hands weak, his heart pumping. In the side-view mirror, Mortimer lay on the road like a prairie chicken. A loose, broken wing stirred in the backwash of air from other cars.

Jonathan sat shivering in the front seat.

My God, he thought, my mind is going. I really am going crazy. I shouldn't be let loose, I shouldn't be driving this car. I don't even know what country I'm in, and I haven't been able to keep anything down, even water, since breakfast yesterday. What am I going to do in Manhattan, Kansas? He ran a hand across his damp forehead.

There was nothing he could do, but press on.

Kansas, he told himself, as with extreme caution he moved the car back out onto an empty stretch of highway. I'm in Kansas. God knows why.

Then he looked up, across the road into the fields, and he thought he was having another vision.

Some way back from the road, there was a white schoolhouse. It was one-roomed, immaculate, blazing white, with a blazing white bell tower. It was nestled in trees. Beside it, sitting in a field of autumnal red sorghum heads, was a two-story frame house. The windows were not set square in it. There was a porch. Behind it there was a windmill.

Jonathan pulled the car over once more. He reached over the back of the seat and pulled out his new camera. He had bought it, credit card once again, at St. Louis airport. He had read the instructions on the airplane.

He began to feel his old hunter's urgency. PRIVATE, said a sign. That's okay, he told the sign, I'll photograph it from here, safe in my car. Hands in a tumble of nerves, he pulled off the lens cap and looked through the viewfinder.

1000 1000 1000, blinked the camera, over and over. It was saying the vision was too bright.

Scowling, hands still trembling, Jonathan took out and reread the booklet. Yes, his new camera was on automatic, and yes, a flashing thousand meant too bright, okay, yes, so what do I do about it?

Anyway it was only sunlight. How could ordinary sunlight be too bright?

1000 1000 1000.

He took the picture anyway. There was something dead in the way the shutter clicked.

Suppose, he thought, suppose I hit it in one, right the first time? Suppose this was where Dorothy lived?

He held the fantasy glowing in his mind for a moment. It was enough to comfort him.

Time to move on.

Jonathan got lost. There were interchanges, small cloverleafs, and signs giving highway numbers and town names that meant nothing to him. Jonathan did not have a map. He found himself driving on a wide, sweeping dirt road, between balding hills. They were dotted with small evergreen shrubs. He stopped the car, and got out.

Crickets were singing. At first he thought they were birds, a flock of them, the sounds they made were so loud, so sweet. But the sound was too mechanical, too regular. He looked down on a valley full of trees and white modern houses. In the far distance was a rounded white water tower, stranded alone, it seemed, in a forest. Where was the town? Why hadn't he asked for a map at the airport?

There was a rumbling sound, like thunder, as if thunder had giant hollow wheels and were driving over the hills.

"Rain," said Jonathan. He wanted an umbrella, and he turned and looked at the empty prairies. No rain. Only sunlight.

He got in and drove down the hill. MANHATTAN, said a sign, and as if someone had switched on a light, the road was paved. At the first cross street, Jonathan turned right, and down.

He was very tired. He forgot where he was again. Confused, he thought he was lost in some suburb of Los Angeles. He passed one crossroad, scowled and stopped.

He got out. There was a low modern house, with a long sloping sunroof, and some kind of wooden jungle gym for kids to play on. Jonathan heard the rumbling again, perhaps a bit different in sound.

It was definitely Los Angeles, somewhere out in the Valley. The sound was coming from a wooden ramp built in a driveway. A kid in a bicycle crash helmet was practicing on his skateboard. He rumbled up and down the ramp. The houses had no fences, but stood isolated amid stretches of immaculate, featureless lawn. There was a low hill behind, with many trees, and some rooftops with satellite dishes.

"Where am I?" Jonathan asked.

A little girl answered him. At least, it was a little girl's voice. "Look at the sign," the voice told him.

Attached to the telephone pole were the words LITTLE KITTEN AV. At right angles to it, another sign said OZ CIRCLE.

"Oh," said Jonathan. It made perfect sense. A sign, if you like. He felt quite contented. For a moment he thought that he had somehow managed to drive from Santa Monica to Manhattan, Kansas. Then he remembered the airplane trip.

I have to get to a bank, he thought. He had no money. I have to find a place to stay. He was happy again.

The rumbling went on. It was from the Drop Zones, the Artillery and Mortar Impact Area. The crickets sang, like metal warbling on metal.

Manhattan seemed to writhe its way under his fingers, in sunlight. He drove in and out of shade, turning left, turning right. He passed shopping malls and Texaco gas stations. He was sure that he had dreamed the medieval amphitheater of white limestone. It had crenellations and huge overhead lights. The sky rumbled. Was this Los Angeles having its earthquake? He was elated.

Then the car seemed to plunge into permanent shade. Huge trees sheltered the roofs. Who had had the wonderful idea of building a town in a forest?

And he was there, Back Then. The white frame houses had

French-looking, sloping tile roofs and front porches with pillars shaped like Greek columns. There were white trellises and window frames that were not quite square and painted dark blue or khaki. How old? How old? Jonathan's internal clock answered. 1896. 1910. 1880. 1876. He kept stopping the car and fumbling with the camera. Other cars growled behind him, drove around him, beeped their horns. Jonathan thought they were Santa Monica friends, saying hi. He beamed and waved.

30 30 30, said his camera. Too dark. Too dark.

A beautiful girl sat on a porch eating ice cream.

"Whatcha doin'?" she called.

"I'm in love with your house!" Jonathan cried back.

"Well you can't have it!" she answered.

"I can't even photograph it!" said Jonathan, holding up the camera helplessly.

"Oh yeah? Lemme look."

Seventeen and fearless, never having had to be afraid. She wore white trousers and a fawn sweater. She took hold of the camera and looked through the viewfinder.

"The flashing numbers mean something's wrong," said Jonathan.

"Well, s'okay now," she said, mystified. She took a picture. "Here you go. Hope you find a house. This one's not for sale." She strode off. Jonathan looked through the viewfinder. This time a lightning bolt flashed inside it. That meant the flashlight was attached. It wasn't. Jonathan turned to ask her where there was a good place to stay. He saw the screen door swinging shut.

The car nearly lost its oil pan driving over an intersection. The cross streets had high humps and dips for drainage. BLUE MONT, said a drive. Jonathan turned right, and beyond a confusing series of traffic lights and franchise restaurants, there was another sign.

BEST WESTERN.

It was the name that drew him. Jonathan was chorused with car horns as he drove straight through two sets of lights into what he thought was its parking lot. He showed his credit cards at the desk and signed.

Was it the same girl behind the desk? She chewed gum and gave him a map.

"I can't read it."

"I know," she sighed. "Nobody can. The whole town's run out

of maps. Everybody just keeps photocopying the old ones, till you can't read them. Anyway they're all so old none of them show the new town center or any of the new shopping malls."

She tried to tell him about the shopping malls and the cinema complexes.

He asked her where the Registry Office was. He asked about historical museums.

"You go up Blue Mont, only you can't read it, and turn right on Denison onto Clafin, only you can't read it."

"What time is it?" Jonathan asked.

"Three-fifteen."

"What's your name?"

"Angel," she said, smiling. "Dumb name, huh?"

It's the right name, he thought he replied. Only he didn't speak. Outside there was the rumbling in the sky. Gosh, that skateboarding is loud, thought Jonathan. He went hunting.

The Registry Office was in the new county offices. Like everything else in Manhattan, Kansas, they were lost in trees. An old limestone tower rose above the new civic space. 1900, said Jonathan's inner clock, of the tower. 1976, it said of the offices, because the building was still square and flat. There were no postmodern gewgaws, no turrets, triangles or circles. There was a three-story-high portico outside it with three-story graceful pillars. The pillars were rectangles too.

The offices were air-conditioned. There was a mural over the reception desk, but it looked to Jonathan's fevered eyes like a video screen seen too close: the image dissolved into lines.

The Registry Office itself was up one flight of stairs. It was full of desks, slightly outdated equipment and enthusiasm.

Jonathan kept himself standing straight behind the counter. "I'm trying to find someone in the past," he said. He was maintaining, in the way someone on drugs maintains, by conscious focus.

"Okay, we'll do what we can for ya," said one of the women at the desks. She was about Jonathan's age, well groomed, bronzed hair cut short and swept up. Her name was Sally, and she invited Jonathan into the tiny back rooms where records were kept. The first small room was lined with shelves on which thick volumes lay flat.

"How long ago ya talking about?" Sally asked him.

"Eighteen seventies."

That did not surprise her. "Uh-huh. Do you know what section or range the people lived in? Township would help."

Jonathan didn't. He gave her the names, spelled them for her. G . . . A . . . E . . . L. Branscomb. Sally wrote on the sloping surface of a kind of house for records that stood in the middle of the room. Jonathan looked at the walls, at the books. *Mortgage Record, Riley County, 217*. Record of Military Discharge *3*.

More huge books lay suspended under the roof of the little house. On the walls were maps, in colored sections.

"Now," said Sally. "Let me show you what the problem is." She led him to one of the maps and pointed with perfect, frosted fingernails. There was the Kansas River. There was the land, divided into squares which were divided into further squares.

"If you knew the township, we could then start to look for what sector they lived on. You see, when the land was settled, each township and range was divided up into these sectors. And each sector was divided up into quarters, Northwest quarter, Northeast quarter. Sometimes they were divided up even further."

Sally turned and reached under the roof, and with a grunt pulled out one of the huge books. Laid open, it consisted of a page to each half sector. Names and dates were written in lines.

"This tells us who had what sector when and how it changed hands," she said.

Jonathan read:

4-1-72 / Webster J.M. to Louise R.B. Rowe / Book B /
       page 308

"That tells us where to find the deed on microfilm. And that can tell us all kinds of stuff."

Jonathan scanned the page. "But I've got to know where I'm looking first."

"Yup," she said with a sigh.

The dates were out of order. The land seemed to change hands every two years.

"You can see how tough things were for them," said Sally. "They mortgaged the land, then sold some of it off, then bought it back, then mortgaged it again. It sure gets confusing. The deeds are great; you find out that someone couldn't pay his taxes, or someone else has been jailed."

Jonathan looked up. "That must be great."

"Oh, listen, the stuff you find out," she agreed.

Jonathan paused for thought. "How about school records?" he asked.

"Hundreds. Thousands. But same problem again, we got 'em for the whole county. I can show you."

She led him into a second room, even smaller. Jonathan suddenly saw it had a metal door. It was a safe.

Another grunt and a groan and another huge, beautiful book in leather with marbled endpapers was laid open. A sticker said: Grant and Burgess, Blank Book Manufacturers, Topeka, Kansas.

There were hundreds of schools, recorded by number, and lists of schoolteachers for each year and how much they were paid, fifty dollars a month. Jonathan looked at the tidy, scratchy handwriting done in nibbed pen. The ink had turned orange with age.

"And up there," said Sally, pointing. Along the top of the shelves ran a line of blue-bound papers. "We have everybody's school reports. I even found some of mine up there. And my mother's. But we do not have much before 1903. You see, before the levee was built, we used to have real bad floods, and almost everything was lost in the 1903 flood." She shrugged and held up her hands. "We might have some older records down in the basement."

"I've got to know where she was," said Jonathan.

"Unless you want to look through everything for the whole county. Got a month or two?"

Jonathan stood, eyes closed, thinking. "Do you keep the census records too?"

"Good," said Sally and pointed at him. She had a hunter's look as well. "But we don't have those. Hold on a sec." She leaned into the outer office. "Betty? Sorry, excuse me. Where would census records be for the 1870s?"

"Oh," said her boss, coming in, a hand lightly across her forehead. Her boss wore a suit, blue jacket, blue skirt, blue ruffled shirt. "Let me think." She looked concerned, helpful. "I think that would be the historical museum."

She even gave Jonathan a slightly better map.

*   *   *

Just inside the door of the Riley County Historical Museum, there was an old ship's bell on a plinth. There were some publications for sale, about the Old West. A pale young man in a nylon shirt with pens in the pocket was stapling papers together by a reception window.

"We'll be closing soon. Can I help you?" he asked.

"I," began Jonathan and found his mind had gone blank for a moment. "I'm doing some research. I'm trying to find a family who lived in this area."

The pale young man sighed. "You've only got half an hour."

"I don't have much time anyway," said Jonathan, hunter's urgency upon him. "Can I start?"

"Okay," nodded the pale young man. "Look, things are a bit of a mess. What do you need?"

Jonathan's mouth hung open. Come on, Jonathan. You have a degree in history. You know how this works.

"I need the census. Do you have a census?"

A wisp of a smile on the pale face. "I'm afraid you'll need to be a bit more specific."

No place like home, Jonathan remembered, *Millie Branscomb, aged 8,* 1856.

"Eighteen sixties. Eighteen seventies."

"Sure. You might as well come in," said the young man.

There were rooms to the right and left, darkened, full of displays of furniture and clothing and blown-up photographs. Jonathan and the librarian passed beyond those into a large room lined with old bookshelves of varying heights. There were tables littered with books and files. On the walls were giant maps of the county and aerial photographs of the airport. There were filing cabinets, giant staplers and a statue of a Paul Bunyan figure with a scythe instead of an ax.

"Jeannie and I have been trying to file all this stuff," said the young man.

"All what stuff?"

"Oh. Everything," said the young man. "We got all these memoirs to file, old photographs, things like that. Have a seat, I'll find you a copy of the 1875 census. It isn't all that long."

Jonathan sat down, shaking. There was a smell. A smell of pancakes. Very hot, slightly charred. Was that wind stirring his hair?

I am losing my mind, he thought.

Very gently, in the distance, he heard cattle lowing. He wanted to weep, but not from dismay. He wanted to weep from yearning. For grass and huge buttercups and the sound of air moving across distances.

"It was, uh, it was retyped," said the young man.

I'll just look her up. Here. I'll find her. Jonathan held a sheet.

EXPLANATION

In 1875 the townships of Riley County were Ashland,
Bala, Grant

That's right, Bill said she didn't live in Manhattan. She lived near it. Where did Bill say?

Madison, Manhattan, May Day, Ogden and Zeandale

None of it rang a bell. There was still the sensation of moving air. Jonathan felt sick. His throat clenched and there was a nasty taste in his mouth.

"This will be fine," he said, his voice clenched. He needed air. "Can you Xerox it for me?"

"We have to charge," said the librarian's assistant.

"Okay. Anything else?"

Dear God, stop me being sick. I can't be sick here.

"Some of those memoirs. One of those memoirs. I can read it tonight." Jonathan clutched his throat. He could feel the ribs of his voice box.

"I need some air. Could I step outside, please, while you Xerox them? I'm terribly sorry. I don't feel well."

He could feel his face coated with sweat as if he had smeared Brylcreem all over it.

The librarian's assistant was concerned. "Listen, give me a couple of minutes and I'll have these ready for you. You step outside, sure."

The Riley County Historical Museum was made of plates of limestone, laid flat into the wall. It was set on a green slope, and halfway down that slope there was a barn and an old house.

1850s, said Jonathan's clock.

Breathing in sunset shadow, calming his stomach and his killer instinct, he stumbled down the hill toward the house.

It was made out of stone, obviously having grown in extensions from a smaller core. A large wooden room had also been added about the same time, now painted orange with green shutters. Another young person was climbing out of it, with a key.

"How old?" asked Jonathan. "How old is it?"

"The first rooms of the house were built in the 1850s. Do you know about the Goodnow House?" The delivery was practiced, polished.

"I'd love to," said Jonathan.

"Well, okay. The first rooms were built in 1855 when Isaac Goodnow and his wife, Ellen, came to live in Manhattan. It was called Boston at the time." She smiled. "Isaac Goodnow was a staunch abolitionist and a friend of Abraham Lincoln's. I'm afraid the house is closed for the afternoon, otherwise I could show you the envelope we have addressed to Professor Goodnow in Lincoln's own hand. The house is fully furnished with pieces either belonging to the Goodnows or to the period. The Goodnow furniture came to us through Harriet Parkerson, one of the Goodnows' two nieces who came to live with them."

"Why are there so many nice young people here?" asked Jonathan.

"Uh?" said the girl. "Oh, that's because of KSU."

It sounded like a symptom.

"Kansas State University," she giggled and made a helpless gesture. "That's where I'm studying. Um. In fact, KSU was founded by Isaac Goodnow. It started out as an agricultural college. Blue Mont College."

"Why is there brick in the wall?"

He was confusing her. He pointed. The limestone wall had a snake of brick down its front.

"That's the chimney. You see how it curves around the window? Well, that's because Mrs. Goodnow wanted to have a window there and they had to build the chimney around it. That room there is where one of the nieces slept. She was Etta Parkerson and she worked for the Goodnows. Um. We actually have her diary from that time, with photographs of the house and family. Would you like to purchase a copy?"

"Oh, please," said Jonathan, in a voice like the wind.

The girl stared at him for a moment. "Okay."

Without moving otherwise he passed her his credit card. He was leaving a trail of numbers behind him.

Then he tried to photograph the house.

30 30 30. Too dark.

"You're going to have to do it without the camera, this time," said a voice.

Jonathan thought it was the KSU student. He turned, but she was gone. There was no one there.

"You'll have to do it for yourself," said the child's voice.

The student came back with books, and Jonathan held out the camera bag toward her.

"Here," he said. "Take this. Keep it."

"I can't take this, this is an expensive camera."

"I can't use it," said Jonathan.

"Look, it's got a book of instructions."

"It will just be a burden," said Jonathan, and cast off one more thing. "I think it will keep me from seeing."

The room at the Best Western was exactly as Jonathan had hoped it would be, clean and anonymous, with a patterned quilt over the bed, and ornate lighting on a brass chain and cable TV. It was stuffy, though. It only had a huge French window that would let in both air and burglars. Jonathan had developed an unreasoning fixation about being burgled. He did not open the windows.

The room also had two doors, one leading out to the pool, the other to the parking lot. This confused Jonathan. He chained and double-locked the door leading to the pool. He went out through the parking lot door to get a Coke. He tried to get back in through the wrong door. His key didn't seem to work. He tried the key in several different doors. This caused nervous women to cry out, "Who is it?" He asked for Angel's help. "Which door did you come out of?" she asked, finally.

Back inside his room, he went to work, sipping a Diet Coke. He still thought that he needed to lose weight.

There was no Branscomb listed in the census.

There was a Bradley, D. W., blacksmith, twenty-six years old, white male, from Illinois, living in Manhattan City. Married to

C. W. Bradley, twenty-four, and living with L. H. Bradley who appeared to be both five and twelve years old.

Same ages as Dorothy. Five in the book, twelve in the movie.

There was Brady, Susan, forty, white female, seamstress, from Virginia, Manhattan City. She lived with Lewis and Betty, eighteen and fourteen respectively.

A widow?

Jonathan saw her in his mind, as if in a photograph, wide gray dress with neat black trim and neat black hair pulled back. Susan Brady had an earnest, slightly smiling, honest face.

Then came Breese, a farmer from Indiana, with lots of children.

No Branscomb.

So he looked for Gale. He hit pay dirt.

There it was; he had found her; there was an H. S. Gale, from Iowa, living in Zeandale. Thirty-three years old, born in New York State. Twenty-eight-year-old wife from Pennsylvania, with four children. Only one of them was a female, twelve years old in 1875. Would that be about right? Initials A.L. Anna Louise? Not Dorothy.

But maybe that was where Dorothy came to stay.

Grow, Guduhan, Guinn, Gulch . . .

Maybe not.

What now? Bill had said she lived near Manhattan, but that could mean anywhere in hundreds of square miles. Jonathan had another thought: Oh, Lord. What if she went to stay with her mother's sister? If she had married, the name wouldn't be Gael or Branscomb. It would be another name altogether.

"Fool's gold," he murmured.

He took out the Xeroxed memoir.

In the upper right-hand corner there was dim Xerox pencil writing: *Donated by Annie Pratt, copied by her from papers written by author.*

It was typed, in a very old-fashioned, heavily serifed face.

"Pioneer Beauty," it said, without further accreditation.

We came to Manhattan in the fall of 1857 because of the first sacking of Lawrence the year before. We were hardened to pioneer life by then. Manhattan was even then a sizable place, not too unlike Lawrence.

We had nothing to start with except our hands and feet

and some land the good Josiah Pillsbury let us have on very reasonable terms. The land was heavily wooded, and so with the help of the Pillsburys and Mr. Monroe Scranton, we soon had a house.

Out on the wild hills, the grass was taller than a man, and my little sister and I used to walk through it back to back because it was said the wolves would not attack if your eyes were upon them. We called them wolves because of the howling. They would be recognized as coyotes now, but they seemed no less threatening because of that.

Sometimes we could see the wild deer ranging on the bare hillsides. Sometimes we could see the wolves basking in the sun after getting all they could eat.

There were many Indians in those days. They used to pass by our house en route from the reservation near Council Grove to cross the Kaw to get to hunting grounds or to raid the Pawnees.

They would come to our door, wishing to trade venison for some bacon or cornmeal. They would visit for an hour or so and piece quilts. They were very friendly and inclined to be neighborly, to our family especially. My father Matthew was an abolitionist and journalist and took the treatment of the Kansas very much to heart. Already squatters were flooding their reservation. Demands were being made to President Buchanan to reduce its size. The stated intention was to remove them from the land altogether! And yet, years later, these same Indians were to be drafted into the Union Army!

My little sister seemed to be their particular delight. She was nine years old and had long blond hair which the Indians found fascinating. They would sit at our table and tell us stories in halting English of the hunt and their great seasonal treks. At this stage, the Kansa tribe still wore Indian dress, headscarves and leather trousers. At first I felt a great deal of concern over their presence. At sixteen, I was able to leave them with the impression that I was the lady of the house, a married woman, which I felt gave me a measure of protection. I was worried about little Millie, but I need not have. First, Millie, as always, seemed to dance over any difficulty. Secondly, the Indians themselves were as far as I could see a peaceable people, interested mostly in trading and the conversation which accompanied it.

Millie soon learned their language. I also picked up a few words, and it is now the most bitter sadness to me that none of us had time to write them down. I am told there is now no record or lexicon of their language—the Indians who gave their name to our state.

Sometimes odd words come swimming up to me as if from the bottom of a creek.

"Caye" meant chief. "Pi-sing" meant game. I know that "zetanzaw" meant big and "basneenzaw" meant little, which is what the Indians called my sister and myself: Big and Little.

I can remember walking with them to the river. It was not unusual in those days to see two or three hundred of them crossing the Kaw. When a party of Indians arrived at it, the men would throw themselves down onto the grass and spend the time in talking and games while the women prepared the meals and fixed things for the crossing.

I remember Millie being able to ask them in their own tongue why the men did no work, and I remember being able to understand the answer: "Big braves do not work."

The women would unpack the bundles and spread out on the ground large buffalo skins. They would then cut themselves lengths of small bushes or hickory about five or six feet long. They would use these as the frames of small boats, bending them across each other and stitching the skins in place, to make a rudderless, prowless square craft. The women would then pile into them the corn and the reed bowls and the naked children.

Then a woman would get her pony and drive it into the river. She would hold on to its tail with one hand, and the boat with the other, and in this way pull life and property across the current. The men simply swam.

I remember one night my father, my sister and I camped with them overnight. I remember the moon. I remember the smoke from the fires and from the pipes. I remember women sharpening knives and feeling no apprehension. I remember we ate a fish caught fresh from the river, a giant channel cat that must have weighed all of forty pounds—or so my father declared.

There was no whisky among them. This may have been unusual. At least my father was not supplying them with it. I remember him picking his teeth with a fishbone and trying to explain mortgages to the Kansa men, who roared with laughter.

My father was always a hero to me, but the next day, he became a hero to others. It was at the time of the June rise and the river was full to the bank. My father and I were up early, to begin the trek home. It was first light, and the women had already begun their crossing.

My father noticed one horse, with woman and boat, pull away from the crowd and start downstream. I think most of the men were asleep, and most of the other women were wrestling with the strong current, for it was my father who ran down the bank and plunged into the water. I saw him swim toward the woman and catch her by the hair, just as she went under. He pulled her back toward the bank, into the arms of some of the women. The boat went spinning downstream, a child wailing on top of it. My father went after the boat as well, which tangled with some branches overhanging the stream. By the time he had rescued the child as well, the entire camp was aroused. I can still remember the gratitude on the faces of the braves. The pony was swept away and drowned.

I grow confused in time, which seems to me to be like a river. Trying to remember is like trying to hold on to the current. It does seem to me that my father was marked for good things by the Indians because of that incident, so I think that my other memories of them must follow this incident.

To this day I think of Indians and my father in "one breath." Neither of them worked and both of them drank whisky and both of them were robbed of their birthright. In the end, both were wretched and miserable. In 1873, Congress finally took the Indians' diminished reservation, and the Kansa tribe was forced to march away from the state that bears their name. My father died the same year.

The air conditioner was clanking.

Jonathan woke up on the thick patterned coverlet of the bed, leaves of Xerox scattered all around him. His throat was horribly sore. Sitting on the chair by the desk, a plump young man looked at him. Jonathan knew his face, but from where?

"It sure is stuffy in here," said the young man. "You ought to go outside for a while."

It was the kid from the Con. "Karl," said Jonathan, sitting up.

"Hi," said Karl, grinning with his huge white teeth. "How are ya?"

"I'm not well," croaked Jonathan.

"Yeah, I heard." Karl's eyes were downcast.

Jonathan remembered and felt a flood of misgiving and guilt. "And you. Are you okay? I mean, are you well?"

"I'm okay," said Karl. "When I heard about you, I took a test. Nothing. We didn't do that much, remember?"

"Yes, yes, that's right!" Jonathan settled back onto the bed with relief. "We didn't, did we?"

"I thought you might like to know that," said Karl. "Come on, there's somebody wants to see you."

He helped Jonathan to his feet, and Jonathan fumbled woozily with the locks on the door. Outside the air was cool and sweet-smelling and seemed heavier, as if it contained more oxygen. White light glowed inside the blue swimming pool. Worms of light wriggled over the walls of the Best Western.

And Moonflower walked toward them. For some reason she was wearing a 1930s evening dress, white satin with a long train. Her small breasts hung unsupported within it. Her hair was still wild, uncombed.

"We were all real upset when we heard about you," she said.

"All of us fans," said Karl.

"Some of us used to talk to you when you weren't there," said Moonflower.

Jonathan held up a hand. "It was just a part. All you could see was the makeup."

"You became," said Karl, "an icon. We saw your picture so much, you moved from the right-hand side of the brain to the left. You stopped being a visual image, you became more like a word sign. You became a meaning."

"That's the trouble with you intellectuals," said Moonflower. She slipped the satin dress off over her head. "You always stare at the images and tell us what they mean to you. You should ask us what the signs mean. We're the people who use them. You should be doing scientific surveys, not staring at your own belly buttons."

She walked away, naked. Her legs and arms were thin, her hips and stomach already settling down with age. Seagulls in the blue light played about her hair.

"You also ought," she said, "to go swimming." She dived into the pool and disappeared amid a flurry of bubbles, white like pearls.

"Let's get some chow," said Karl. "You haven't eaten anything since Bill's last night, and you lost that."

For some reason, Jonathan already had the car keys in his hand.

The new town center was a huge shopping mall that covered the end of Poyntz Avenue, where the bank of the Blue River had once been. Jonathan walked inside and his breath was taken away.

It was glass-covered like a train station, with huge hoops of light in a row along the ceiling's pinnacle. The floor was made out of brick and there were tall fountains and shrubbery in pots and walkways leading off down avenues of shops to the closed and darkened caverns of department stores.

Jonathan walked forward with tiny, almost fearful steps, looking about him. It was late and the mall was just as deserted as the rest of the town center had been in daylight. Somewhere, echoing overhead, were the disembodied voices of children and the imprecations of adults.

He tiptoed down the main corridor, where it was narrowed by flanks of white columns, and out into a wider space. There was the sound of splashing water and emptiness. A sign hung over it. PICNIC PLACE, said the sign in neon.

In the center of Picnic Place was a black, convoluted, and somehow Italian fountain, surrounded by palm trees. Empty tables were rimmed around it. Along the walls were franchises for Mexican or Italian fast food, and for something called runzas. The voices overhead still had to find bodies. An Asian Indian woman strolled past him in a purple-and-silver sari. Her sandals made a flapping sound.

In the far corner there were double doorways that seemed to promise a more substantial restaurant. CARLOS O'KELLY'S MEXICAN CAFÉ, said a sign. Jonathan seemed to waft into it. Suddenly he was standing before an empty front desk. No one came to help him. He felt foolish. He walked past a kind of structural screen of plaster, meant to suggest a Mexican building.

The place was a confusing welter of decor—stuffed foxes, Pepsi signs, cow horns, old tin advertisements of women who raised fringed skirts like theater curtains over their thighs, antique (perhaps) mirrors. A table full of male students as big as sides of beef roared with laughter. Jonathan jumped as if they were laughing at him. A waiter finally came up, apologizing. "Sorry, it's kinda late, I'm the only one here," he said. For some reason he had a flapper haircut, like a woman from the 1920s. He wore very baggy shorts almost to the knee. He sat Jonathan at a table and passed him a large menu encased in plastic sheeting.

Chimichangas, thought Jonathan. They had not existed a decade before. In the 1970s, you sat down to beans, enchiladas and chile rellenos. Who invented chimichangas? Were they authentic? If not, how long did it take for something to become authentic?

Time seemed to be leapfrogging over itself. Parts of it were missing. The sides of beef had been laughing so long and so hard they couldn't stop and one of them was in danger of choking. He made squeaking noises like a mouse. Jonathan felt distant from them, and sour. How did they get so big, so strong? He didn't want to eat. The waiter came, bringing him a microwaved chimichanga. When had he ordered that?

Jonathan was used to being friendly and tried to talk to the waiter. Was he a KSU student? How did he find time to do this and his homework? Jonathan was losing his conversational touch—university studies are not called homework. Jonathan felt like one of those plastic fairgrounds smiles had been stuck on his face. It was held in place by biting down.

What was he studying? The answer flattened the conversation like some pathetic animal run down on the freeway. The young man was studying the marketing of new textiles. Uh. Did that mean he researched what kinds of new fabrics people wanted?

Not exactly. It was more to do with pricing strategies. "Only people are beginning to tell me the market is bottoming out and I don't know if I'll stay in it." He had a pleasant, intelligent face, a hooked nose. He was enthusiastic when he found out Jonathan was from L.A.

"Oh, I love Los Angeles!"

"I love Manhattan," said Jonathan.

"How come?" the young man was mystified.

"Its history."

"Manhattan has a history?" The young face was crooked.

"Got more history than Los Angeles. Los Angeles, they just bury it under the freeway."

"Oh but the shopping is wonderful!"

Jonathan looked at his pleasant, intelligent face and said, "Your values suck."

Had he really said that? The young man was no longer there. A cold chimichanga was half-eaten on his plate, and Jonathan's throat and gut felt like a wall from which paint was peeling. He coughed slightly, and something really did seem to come free. He swallowed it. The stuffed fox, the orange lights, the drifting beer signs swam inside his eyes.

Jonathan got up to go. He forgot to pay.

Outside, there were humps in the parking lot, like that designer supermarket where there were buried cars for a joke. Knees jiggling uncertainly, as if he were trying to be hip, Jonathan walked forward.

Which car?

He found he couldn't remember the make or the model or the color. He was color-blind, and in this light, they would all look the same. He walked down a row, looking at license plates. He wouldn't be able to tell.

He panicked again. How am I going to get back? he wondered miserably. How will I ever find the car again, how will I get it back to Hertz? Jesus, I can't even go to a restaurant and park a car anymore. It was dark and traffic whined past on the big blue road around Manhattan where the river had been. Trucks, the odd car, wind, emptiness.

What am I going to do? he wondered.

Then he saw the sign, glittering on down the road. BEST WESTERN. Maybe a mile away. He began to walk.

There were ditches and treacherous green humps of manicured grass. Jonathan kept stumbling. He made a sound over and over, like he was about to sneeze. He was dimly aware of it. It was just how he breathed these days. When he was in trouble.

There were train tracks underfoot, hard metal, and splintering ties, and he kept stumbling. Why were there humps and train tracks? Would he get flattened by a train, or would he hear it first? And where was the other river, why was there only one river now?

A child's voice whispered to him: "There was a flood and the river moved."

Very suddenly, everything spun up and under and away from him. Jonathan lost his balance and fell onto the train track and felt the earth spin and his dinner pour back out of him. It hurt, as if he were vomiting up raw sand.

"I can't keep down my food," he said, feeling weak and a little bit tearful. His own body was something precious that had been lost.

It was the beer, he shouldn't have drunk that beer with the chimichanga. Remember, he told himself, no more alcohol anymore. Say goodbye to beer. He managed to reel up to his feet and stagger on along the train track. The train track ended suddenly, no longer wanted. Jonathan veered right and slipped down into a dry, lawn-mowed ditch. Huge trucks buffeted past him, coughing over him. To his left were a Wendy's, a Pizza Hut, alone, isolated and empty, the lights still on.

Ahead was the office of the Best Western, and he could see through its glass walls that it was lit, with a television on. He felt calmer.

Inside, the office smelled like some particularly fruity flavor of bubble gum. Jonathan wiped his face on his sleeve. Angel came out of the back office.

"I'm sorry," said Jonathan. "I can't remember my room number."

He thought he managed to say it very well, with just the slightest catch of tension in his voice.

"Dontcha have the key?" Angel asked, pulling her pallid hair back from her face.

"I forgot it," he said. He made a joke of it. "But I can just about remember my name still, so if I tell you that, will you tell me the room?"

"I'll have to open up for you as well," she said, looking over her list. She glanced up.

"Are you all right?" she asked.

What could he tell her? Yeah, I feel great? He felt like mist about to be blown away. "I'm not too well," he admitted.

She waved toward herself. "Lean forward," she told him and felt his forehead. "You got a fever. You want me to drive you to the hospital?"

"No!" he said, too abruptly. He modulated. "No, no thanks, I just want to sleep."

"All righty. Let's get you all tucked in." The keys clinked pleasantly.

As soon as they stood outside the door, Jonathan remembered the room number: 225. The lights were still blazing. Angel opened the door, and everything was just as he had left it: sealed. The room smelled like a headache.

"There's some aspirin in the medicine chest," she said. "If you need anything, just press nine." She pointed to the telephone.

Jonathan couldn't make sense of the words, so he nodded and smiled. Oh, yeah, I'll be fine, he thought he had said. She nodded and closed the door and Jonathan went into the bathroom and retched blood. The droplets spread on the surface of the water of the toilet bowl like stars spinning away from galaxies. Jonathan drank some water from the cold tap of the basin and that promptly bounced back out like sheet rubber.

I can't keep down water, he thought. His stomach burned. The tips of his fingers buzzed. Shivering, he peeled off his clothes. There were patches of sweat on them. The stale, warm air made his tender skin rise up in goosebumps. The sheets felt freezing and he curled up on them, his bones quaking in spasmodic jolts.

There was a knock at the door. "Can I come back in?" Angel asked.

She unlocked the door and looked at him. "Do you want someone to sit up with you?"

Jonathan couldn't answer the question. He didn't know.

"I just thought maybe it would help you sleep if someone read to you."

Jonathan thought that sounded pleasant. "You don't have to."

"It's okay. I got to be on call, kinda, anyway."

"Thanks," said Jonathan.

She sat down primly on the chair by the desk. "What you want me to read?"

"I have some photocopies," he said, trying to think where they were. He had left the papers somewhere on the bed.

"I don't see any," said Angel, leaning forward on her knees.

"That's funny." Jonathan sat up, holding the sheet modestly in front of himself. He didn't want her to see his ribs. Dismay came. "They were just here!"

He went weepy. "They were just here!"

"Ssh ssh ssh," she said. "It's okay, I got them." She coaxed the papers out of a fold of the quilt, thrown on the floor. She tapped them neatly back into order on the desk. "Righty-ho," she said, lightly.

"I'm losing everything," said Jonathan, lying back down.

He told her where to start reading. The memoirs began again. "Pioneer Beauty."

It seemed to him that he was not being read to. It seemed to him that the author of the memoirs was speaking to him with her own flat, plain voice. He thought he heard the crackle of a fireplace.

" 'In those days,' " she read, " 'Manhattan was abolitionist, but St. George was pro-slavery. There were rival gangs, many of them from far afield. Once my father was traveling to Topeka to bear witness to the treatment of the Indians on the Council Grove reservation. He agreed to travel for part of the way with a friend who had an ox team. The friend assumed that my father would travel faster than himself, and so left early, the plan being that my father would catch up with him on the road.

" 'On the road, my father was stopped by a gang of men. Judging them to be from Missouri, he told them he was from near St. George.

" ' "Well," the ruffians replied. "It's a mighty good thing you are from St. George or the same thing would have happened to you as happened to that damned man from Manhattan." The gang let my father have his freedom. Further along the road to St. Mary, he found what he was dreading, the body of his friend. He had been murdered and his team stolen.' "

The author remembered orchards of cherries, crab apples and winter apples. She remembered the more uncertain crops of peaches, plums and pears. There were native plums as well, and wild grapes in tame arbors. The fruit had to be canned or dried. Jellies and pickles were made. Paper coated with white of egg would be laid over the contents. Pickles were put up in earthen jars or crocks with a large plate inverted over them and a scrubbed stone placed over each plate for weight.

Jonathan saw woodpiles. Cottonwood, cobs, chips for a quick fire. Blackjack for a steady burn. He smelled apple-scented carbon dioxide, exhaled from fruit in barrels.

Suddenly he was awake. Angel was at the door.

"Oh darn, you were asleep, I'm sorry."

"Stay," he croaked. He was scared. He felt very odd indeed.

"I can read you some more."

"I can't follow it," he said. "Just stay with me."

She sat down again. "So why don't you tell me why you came to Manhattan?"

He told her he was looking for Dorothy. Dorothy of Oz, she had really lived, she had lived near here, she knew Frank Baum.

"Really? Wow," Angel said lightly. "I mean, everybody knows Baum came here once. That's why they named some streets after the movie."

"I'm trying to find her house. I'm trying to find where she lived."

"Why? So you can get to Oz?" A smile.

Jonathan paused. "It's that dumb. Yes." Something seemed to swell in the air between them. "I haven't got that long," he said.

"Oh," she said. "I see."

"I'm dying," he said.

"Mmmm hmmm," she said, pressing her lips tightly inward.

"And," he said with a singsong sigh, "I don't know that I'm going to find her. But I do reckon that I might stay here."

"In Manhattan. How come?"

"I don't want to go back to L.A.," he said, and started to tell her about NPR, and a British pop group called It's Immaterial, and how he loved their single, "Driving Away from Home." He told her about Ira, his friend, how they had lived together for years, and then had a fight. Dimly he realized that she might guess what he was dying of, but he didn't care suddenly. He felt like a scarf tied to a fence post, blowing in a hot wind. His words were hot.

The scarf came untied.

"It's like Gilgamesh," he said. "She goes to find the Wizard, like

Gilgamesh tries to find . . . find . . . this Noah character and . . . and . . . and the Wizard is like a king because he and the land are the same thing, Oz and Oz, they have the same name and when he leaves in a balloon it's like his big bald head, and the land dies, and . . . and . . . and Dorothy is . . . goes to the Netherworld to find life. She goes to the Land of the Dead."

He was raving. It felt good to rave. He finally found words. "She goes to the Land of the Dead to find Life. Isn't that dumb? Why can't we find it here?" It seemed to him a very reasonable question, asked in the spirit of inquiry.

"You're scaring me," said Angel.

Jonathan seemed to settle back. He touched his own forehead and it felt burning even to him. "Sorry," he murmured.

"Maybe if I read to you some more?"

Angel rattled through the pages. The plain Kansas voice spoke.

" 'My sister would never be held down. She was small and pretty, like something in a music box. People were always asking her to sing. I remember that if she liked something, she would try to give it away. She would wrap it up, sometimes even with her best hair ribbons and give it to me, or Father, or the neighborhood gals. And she'd wait and watch as we opened up her gift.

" 'The life of a farmer's wife would never have suited her. I know my father wanted her to be a schoolteacher. When she ran away to St. Louis, he was very unhappy. He need not have been. She became, I am informed, even more beautiful. How I wish now that I could have visited the refined places in which she performed, to see her success, to hear the fine gentlemen, the appreciative ladies, applaud.

" 'After the Angel of Death descended, an exhalation of my sister's perfume was sent to us, a sweet child, her daughter, Dorothy.' "

Jonathan went still on the bed, unable to move.

" 'This little girl became a new source of happiness to us. I learned then what I know now, that childhood is the source of all happiness. We remember joy when reminded of our lost years.' "

"Where?" whispered Jonathan. "Where is she?"

"Oh," said Angel and stopped. "You think it's her?"

"What's her name? The name of the author?"

Angel turned the wad of papers over in her hand. No name on the front. There was handwriting at the end of the manuscript.

"All it says is that this was retyped, but that most of the papers were lost in the 1903 flood. But, here, at the back it says the author was E. A. Branscomb."

"That's her, that's her." Jonathan nodded. He looked at Angel. "I'm not making this up, am I?"

"Don't think so," she said and passed him the papers.

He flipped through them, scanning. "Do you remember her saying anything about where the farm was?"

"She mentions the Kaw." Angel shrugged.

"She's got to tell us where she lived!" he exclaimed.

Something stopped him dead on a page before he knew consciously what he had seen. He stopped dead, and seemed to see the word "School" and then read:

I felt as blessed as my little charge to have had Miss Ida Francis for a schoolteacher, and Sunflower School so close at hand.

"I got her!" whispered Jonathan.

And then there was a knock, and Bill Davison came in.

"Hello, I saw the note in the office," Bill began, to Angel.

"Bill!" Jonathan shouted, not at all surprised to see him. "Bill, I got her!" He shook the papers at him.

Bill stood stunned for a moment.

"I found Dorothy!" Jonathan said.

Bill answered him. "That's why I'm here," he said.

After they had talked for a while, Bill gave Jonathan something to help him sleep. Jonathan crept back to bed in a darkened room, and found Karl waiting for him there. Karl's body was smooth and cold. He kissed the tip of Jonathan's nose and asked the question that everyone asked.

"What," Karl asked Jonathan, "do you want to do?"

"I want to stay here in Kansas," said Jonathan. "With you."

Manhattan, Kansas

September 1989

"*Öz Ev*"

"Real Home"—a motto on many trucks in Turkey, usually accompanied by a painting of a white house in green
fields by a river

In the morning Jonathan wasn't in his room.

Bill walked out into the parking lot. There was a low, golden light pouring across Highway 24, the trucks tirelessly rumbling past. On the other side of the road there was a warehouse made of aluminum sheeting with an orange sign—REX'S TIRE C. Above that there was a rise of large trees, like clouds, up a slope to a deliberate clearing. MANHATTAN, said giant white letters. On the top of the hill there was a water tower, like a white upside-down test tube. There was an apple painted on it. MANHATTAN, said the water tower, THE LITTLE APPLE.

Bill saw Jonathan walking out of the shrubbery. Jonathan was walking backward. A newspaper was curled up and held firmly under his arm.

"There you are," said Bill. "I was getting worried."

Jonathan answered with his back toward Bill. "The river moved. I was trying to find it."

"By walking backward? Come on, Jonathan." Bill tugged Jonathan around to face him. Jonathan was grinning. As soon as Bill let him go, like a door on a spring, Jonathan spun back around.

"Jonathan, turn around, please."

"I could walk into the river backward," he said.

"We're going to have breakfast. Are you up for breakfast?"

"Oh, yeah, I could eat a horse."

"Good, then let me look at you." He pulled Jonathan back around. Jonathan was still grinning. Bill held him in place and peered into his eyes, which had gone yellow.

"What color is your pee?" Bill asked.

"Bet you say that to all the girls."

"Come on, just tell me what color it is."

"How should I know? I'm color-blind!" Jonathan replied.

"Open wide." Jonathan stared back at him like Groucho Marx. "Your mouth, not your eyes."

Beginning at the back of Jonathan's throat there were ulcers, patches of yellow in pink swellings.

"Can you hold anything down?"

"Not even a job." Released, Jonathan spun around again. "If I walk backward, I'll go backward. Maybe I'll disappear."

"Jonathan," said Bill, to his back. "Do you want to find Dorothy?"

Silence.

"If you keep acting up, I'll have to take you straight to the nearest hospital. So turn around. You can turn around."

"Nope. Can't," said Jonathan, and turned around to face him.

"You're jaundiced, Jonathan. You may have something wrong with your liver. And you've got something very nasty down your gullet. You should be in the hospital. Now. I can give you today, Jonathan, but by evening, I want you in the hospital."

"Sure, Ira," said Jonathan.

There was a steakhouse next door to the Best Western, next door being about a fifth of a mile away. They walked across dirt to a breeze-block bungalow. The floor was made of tiles designed to look like blocks of wood. The Formica tables looked like wood. The food looked like wood. The hash browns looked like sawdust, the egg like putty. Breaded mushrooms steamed in tin basins like wooden knobs. Caterers had finally found a way to bottom-line breakfast.

Jonathan stared at the buffet, looking ill.

"You could try some bacon," said Bill. It looked purple and soggy. Jonathan very firmly shook his head, no.

"Jonathan, you've got to take something. How about some coffee? Tea?" Jonathan just kept shaking his head.

Bill's heart sank. The physical symptoms were bad enough, but it was the presenting behavior that was really worrying him. "Okay, let's sit down. Do you think you could swallow some soup?"

Jonathan's eyes moved sideways, terrorized by the prospect of food. He nodded yes. Bill took him by the arm and led him to a table.

A waitress came up to their table. "Coffee?" she asked. She had brown circles under her eyes and slightly hunched shoulders, but she seemed cheerful.

Bill said yes, and she poured coffee, not from the spout, but from the side, over the edge of the black-rimmed glass container.

"Did you catch my awesome backhand?" she asked.

Jonathan was staring up at the lights overhead. They were imitation oil lamps, with pink roses printed on them. Bill could see the dots.

"Are those old?" Jonathan asked the waitress.

"I don't know, we just got them in last week." The waitress giggled. "I'll come back for your order in just a sec." She waddled up to the next table and gave a gladsome cry. "Hi, Horace, how are you?"

An officer of the law in a brown uniform placed his cowboy hat on the table. "Well how you doing, boss lady?" he boomed.

"How was Ira?" Jonathan asked.

At last, a sensible question. Bill almost sighed with relief.

"He's hysterical," said Bill. "He blames himself, he's full of worry. He thinks you can't cope on your own. I told him how you'd used the credit cards to buy a ticket and rent a car and said it didn't sound exactly helpless to me. I—um—told him it would probably be better if he didn't come along."

"He told me to go away."

"He may not have meant that."

"I don't want to go back."

"Okay. But do you think you could write him a card or something?"

Without looking at him, without saying anything, Jonathan took the newspaper out from under his arm and gave it to Bill. It was a local newspaper, and the edge was ringed around and around with Jonathan's handwriting. It was a letter to Ira.

The waitress was back with them, breathing good cheer, perfume and sweat. "Right, gentlemen, what will it be?"

"Do you cook any breakfast fresh?" Bill asked.

*   *   *

They found the car. Jonathan had the keys, and they had a plastic tab that said the license number, model, color.

They drove it to the Registry Office. Jonathan's knees jiggled with nerves, and he hummed to himself. In the office, Sally greeted them.

"Sally, Sally," he said, bobbing up and down. "I found the school!"

"Great!" she said. "Which one is it?"

"Sunflower School?" he asked.

"We'll find it for you. Who's your good-looking friend?"

"This is Bill," said Jonathan, rather proudly. "He's my psychiatrist."

Sally shook hands properly. "You think he could be my psychiatrist, too?"

"Sure," said Jonathan in a faraway voice. "But you have to be sick like me."

Her smile faltered for a second. "Right," she said. "Let's check out that school."

In the safe room, the big book was taken out, and Sally's metallic pink fingernails raced across the pages. "We need its number," she said. "Here we are. Sunflower School, number forty-three. It's Zeandale Township but where exactly . . ." Scowling slightly, she went to another book. "Uh. Okay. I'll show you where that is."

She led them out of the main records room to the map on the wall and pointed. "That's it, there, Zeandale Township, smack dab where Sectors 23, 24, 25, and 26 all meet." She stood back and with a hooked finger delicately rubbed the tip of her nose.

Both Bill and Jonathan crowded around the map. Beside the main road was a tiny square with a number. It was near the Kaw, not far from the main road.

"So we've got about eight big pages to look through. What were those names again?"

"Branscomb or Gael," said Bill.

"That's right, or another name if there was a marriage."

Another huge book thumped down on the sloping desk, and Sector 25, Township 10, Range 8, was found, northwest and southwest.

"Pillsbury, Lewis, Long and . . . Monroe Scranton," she murmured.

"Monroe Scranton?" said Jonathan, leaping forward, slightly frog-like. "He was hung for stealing Ed Pillsbury's horses!"

Sally looked up. "Really? How do you know that?"

"I read it last night."

"Well I'll trade you. This guy Lewis here was jailed for theft. And this guy Long lost the property because he didn't pay his taxes. So this was kind of the bad corner of Zeandale. But . . ." she scanned the page. "No Branscomb or Gael."

She turned the page. "Look at this. This is why we have so much trouble. You got L. H. Pillsbury deeding this quarter to Minerva Wiley in April '82, and then it goes in reverse in the same month—well, she mortgages to him. But then in September '82, you got George Pillsbury giving it to L. H. Pillsbury by relation—but it just doesn't show how George got it. Then in '83 the District Court is giving it to Minerva. Oh, I get it! They've divided the quarters into halves. And I bet that court deed is a divorce."

Jonathan was making a rapid hissing noise through his nostrils.

"Jonathan," asked Bill, "are the tips of your fingers buzzing?"

Jonathan looked around at him in woozy surprise. "How did you know?"

"Because you're hyperventilating. Just breathe slowly, calmly." Bill's hands and chest moved outward, slowly, showing him how to breathe. "Relax. We have all day."

"We only have today!" said Jonathan, in sharp dismay. His face crumpled up.

Sally ignored it. "Right, next page," she said lightly, and looked up and around, still smiling. "Sorry, I just find all of this so much fun, I get distracted."

And her glance caught Bill's as she looked back to the pages.

I wonder how far you've gotten, Bill thought. He watched her scanning the pages. I would say you've probably decided that Jonathan is not exactly a mental patient. You've probably decided there is a physiological element. You're used to puzzles. I wonder if you've worked this one out.

"Here we go," said Sally. "Branscomb." She stepped back and tapped the place with a fingernail.

"You found it?" Jonathan's voice rose high and thin.

*　　*　　*

The farm was listed in Sector 26, southeast quarter. It passed from J. Pillsbury to E. Pillsbury to Branscomb, all in 1857. They were listed out of date order, widely separated by other sales or mortgages, mostly in the early 1900s. The next entry by date was in 1890—a deed to J. Pillsbury from the government.

"That will just be a late copy entry," said Sally. "I bet when we look at it, the deed will be typed, with a typed signature of Abraham Lincoln."

"So what's the story?" Bill asked.

"Matthew gets in it 1857 . . ." Silence. Sally read, chin resting on her hand. "After that, I don't know. In 1890 it passes from the Pillsburys to the Eakins. So maybe it did go back to the government and then to the Pillsburys."

"That is the farm, though," insisted Jonathan.

"We don't see it passing from Matthew to anyone," said Bill. "Not even his daughter?"

"They should show it passing by relation, but they don't." Sally lifted her hands up and let them drop. "Sometimes they didn't."

"What we're looking for," said Bill, "is the farm going to Emma, and then from Emma to her husband. That way we would know her married name."

"That is the farm, isn't it?" Jonathan's voice rose.

"Unless Matthew had some land somewhere else as well," said Sally.

"That's not the farm?" Jonathan danced with confusion.

Sally looked at him. "Oh, we'll find it. We know it's somewhere around here."

They skimmed the other pages. There was no other entry for Branscomb.

"Okay," said Sally, still cheerful. "That means that must be the farm. Come on, I'll show you."

She walked to the map. "There it is," she said, pointing. The sectors looked dead and cold.

"Could we find the farm from this map?" Bill asked.

"Sure! Sure we could!" exclaimed Jonathan. "Couldn't we?"

Sally's boss came in. "Excuse me. Sally, there's a call for you about those mineral rights in Ogden. I'm sorry, gentlemen."

"I don't know how these sector maps relate to the roads. What I suggest you do," said Sally, talking quickly, "is find that schoolhouse.

Get hold of a plat book or something and use the schoolhouse to orient yourself."

"Sally, I'm sorry, they're holding on."

"Okay," said Sally. "Let me know what happens, huh?" She backed away, toward the outer office. She looked directly at Bill and said, "Take care of him."

"Back so soon?" said the pale young man at the museum.

Jonathan seemed to blurt his way through the door, like an unintended remark. He did not wait for the young man to step aside from the entrance and jostled into him. The young man's lips went thin.

"We got it," said Jonathan. "We found the farm!" He was as awkward as a newborn colt. "We know the school she went to, so we can find the farm from that. Zeandale Township, Sector Twenty-six."

"Hold it. Hold it," said the young man.

Jonathan wavered in place, unable to understand why the librarian didn't show more enthusiasm.

"What would you like to look at?"

"Hello," said Bill. "We need to find a particular schoolhouse and farm in Zeandale. Basically, I think if we had a plat book for the 1870s, 1880s, that would help."

The young man breathed out. "Do you mind telling me what this is for? Is it a research project? Is it connected with KSU?"

"It's only a personal interest," said Bill. "We'd be happy to talk to somebody if that would help."

The young man sighed. "Our director is Kathy James. She'll be in about ten today. If you wouldn't mind talking to her."

"Thank you, I'd be happy to."

Back in the big, book-lined room. Hole punches and paper cutters, index printouts, stacks of wooden drawers out of their chests, cardboard tubes with maps inside, globes of the world.

"We've got a very good plat book for 1881," said the young man. "It has engravings of local farms, shows the railways, has a list of businesses."

"Perfect. Thank you," said Bill.

"Your friend owes us ten sixty for photocopies," said the young man. "He left without paying."

"I'm sorry," said Bill. "He's very ill."

The pale young man walked around to the front of the filing cabinets. They faced the wall. Bill sat down at the table, opposite Jonathan.

Jonathan's knees bounced up and down, and the rims of his eyes looked almost brown. He had thrown up his breakfast soup.

"How ya doing, buddy?" Bill whispered.

"I'm going to ring the church bell," answered Jonathan.

"Which church bell?" Bill asked quietly.

"The one in the little tower. In the school."

Then Jonathan looked up in the direction of the doorway and beamed and greeted someone. "Hello," he said.

Bill turned around in his chair. There was no one.

"Who's been visiting?" Bill asked.

"Ira was standing beside the Coke machine," said Jonathan.

"Was he?" said Bill.

"He hadn't graduated yet."

There was the sound of a filing cabinet rumbling shut.

"This do you?" asked the librarian.

He passed Bill a Xerox. It showed a sweep of river in flowing curves and centipede lines of railways. Manhattan the town was blanked out by corduroy lines. At the bottom of the page there was a very fine, tiny engraving of a man on horseback looking at a distant train.

Jonathan stood up and rested his chin on Bill's shoulder, as if it were a pillow.

There was a little square marked "No. 43." It was on the corner of the main road and a lane that ran south toward hills. There were the sectors and quarters with names.

"It says Gulch," said Bill. "Is that a name or a geographical feature?"

"I don't know," said the young man. "I also had this."

He tossed down onto the table a Xerox of a photograph.

It showed a white, one-room wooden building with two windows on either side of a narrow roofed porch. The building also had a small bell tower.

Lined up outside it were about ten children in gingham checks or knickerbockers and a woman. She stood very stiffly, hands behind her back, smiling and young in a long, dark skirt and white blouse with mutton sleeves. In crabbed handwriting were the words "Sunflower School."

"That will make it ten seventy for copies," said the young man.

"Oh golly. Oh golly," said Jonathan. "What if it's her? What if it's her in the photograph? Huh? Huh?"

The pale young man looked at him. "Whatever it is you're looking for," he said, "you're not going to find it in an old photograph. It's only history, you know."

They drove. Bill had great difficulty finding Highway 18 out of town—the on-ramp rose out of the old streets that had not been razed for the shopping mall. Then very quickly they were passing over the levee, a great hump of green grass, then trees, and then they were driving over the Kansas River on a narrow bridge with narrow railed walkways. There were sandbanks in the river and the concrete supports of another modern bridge, crossing diagonally under them. It had been washed away.

Then the river was gone in a flurry of leaves. The highway divided. ZEANDALE, said a sign to the left. The road eased itself up a slope and down again. On one side there was flat, open farmland, on the other steep shaded woodland.

"Look at it!" said Jonathan. To the left were wide fields of almost orange sorghum, the heads in thick clumps. There were windmills far away and old farmhouses surrounded by beech and walnut that had been planted a hundred years before. Trees in a long line marked where the river flowed. Running parallel to the road, through hedges and fields and shrubbery, there was a gap where the railroad once had been.

"Clop clop clop," said Jonathan, very faintly, transfixed.

Bill balanced maps and photocopies on his lap, glancing down. "The river curves in again close to the road just before we get to the school."

"Fwoooo whooosh," said Jonathan. "The river moves. It rolls over in its sleep."

The papers fluttered.

The woodland left them, moving south. There were fields on either side now, flat, rich, and the road was straight for miles. Zeandale village was a blur ahead of them, blue with distance, wavering with rising heat. There were lanes to the right. Bill slowed. PLEASANT VALLEY CEMETERY, said a sign pointing right. They passed another lane, with a clump of trees.

"It's supposed to be on the right," said Bill. They both grew more anxious, leaning forward, peering.

"That's it," said Bill suddenly, flicking on the turn signal and pulling over to the right, the sound of dust under tires.

On the wrong side of the road was the schoolhouse. It had been painted gunmetal blue.

"That's not it," said Jonathan, very quickly, very firmly.

"I think it is," said Bill, and got out. Dust from the soft shoulder still drifted across the road. The silence was very sudden, very complete. Their footsteps sounded very clearly as they crossed the road.

As they neared the old building, a droning noise started. It was as if a hollow tube were being whirled over their heads. Locusts.

"It's the same building," said Bill, holding the photograph.

The front porch had been turned into an extension, its door turned into a window. There was the bell tower.

"That's not it," said Jonathan in a wisp of a voice.

Bill chuckled a bit with exasperation. "It is. Look, everything's there."

Suddenly Jonathan was shouting. "It's the wrong goddamned side of the road!" He ran out of breath. He began to make noises as if he were about to sneeze. "Huh ahuh ahuh ahuh."

"Breathe slowly," Bill said. Jonathan knocked away his hand.

"The memoirs say it's on a lane! Ahuh ahuh. The plat book says it's on a lane!"

"Roads move."

"On a lane that leads to the hills. Where are the hills? A big, bald hill where Dorothy made snowmen!"

Bill went still and cold. That's what the old lady had said. Snowmen, with Wilbur, on a hill. Angels in the snow.

"It's on the wrong side of the road, it's pointing the wrong way. It's the wrong goddamned schoolhouse!"

As if clubbed, Jonathan dropped. He sat down in the middle of the road.

"Jonathan, that's kind of a dumb place to sit." Bill tugged at his arm. Jonathan started to cry with frustration.

"That place was built about 1890!"

"Look, it says Sunflower School. Stand up, Jay, out of the road."

"It was rebuilt in a different place!" Jonathan had flowered into full tears.

"How do you know it's 1890?"

"My clock. My clock is never wrong. Look, the teacher's wearing mutton sleeves."

"Jay, get out of the road!"

"It's my last day, and we haven't found it!" He pounded the asphalt with the flat of his hand. "We've fucked it."

On the horizon, a car was coming.

"Jonathan. Please stand up."

"What for?"

"So we can keep looking."

The car was shimmying like a dancer.

"I just want to stay here. I don't want to go on."

Bill leaned over. "Jonathan. You know what we're going to do? There was a sign back there for a cemetery. Remember? We're going to go to the cemetery."

"What good is that going to do?"

"You're asking me? What are cemeteries good for, Jonathan? Names. Names and families."

Jonathan looked up. "Yeah," he said.

"Come on, let's get up."

The other car began to flash its lights.

The road to the cemetery went up the hills to bald grassy slopes and down again through thickly shaded ravines, over shaded rivulets, toward a place called Deep Creek.

Jonathan snored. His whole face was going an unnatural brown, as if he had spent his life under a sunlamp. Beads of sweat were trickling down him, as if he were melting. Bill felt guilty. I should have taken you to the hospital, he thought. I know better. He promised his profession: Jonathan, I get you back into care by four this afternoon.

Under the blue sky, amid the brown grass and the passing shadows, Bill felt alone. He looked back at the mask that was Jonathan's face and spoke to it.

"I don't believe in God anymore, Jonathan," said Bill. "My faith has gone. I think . . . I think I need some kind of sign. You have visions, Jonathan. Do you have visions of God?"

Jonathan didn't, couldn't, answer.

Pleasant Valley had a chain-link fence around it and a big metal gate with upright bars and letters cut clean through large metal plaques on either side of stone gateposts. PLEASANT, said one side. VALLEY, said the other. A dirt driveway led between two conifers and circled through the tough little oaks of the cemetery.

It was on a hill far from anywhere. Jonathan and Bill left the car parked in the lane near the gates. The sound of crickets was high, strong, sweet. The air was surprisingly cool, and there was a strong wind, as if the Spirit were moving. Jonathan's eyes were yellow and feverish, and he looked distracted. He blinked and stumbled up onto a concrete platform, with a gravestone at its head like a pillow. At its foot, planted in the concrete, was a rusty old hand pump.

Jonathan played with the pump's long wooden handle. "Can you imagine what a water pump must have meant to them? No more buckets hauled up from the well. I bet this was some old guy who finally bought a water pump. And he was so proud of it, they used it for his gravestone."

They wandered between the stones. The names carved into them were already familiar. There were Pillsburys scattered everywhere.

FAREWELL, said a scroll over a carving of a man's and a woman's clasping hands:

ANNIE J. PILLSBURY

WIFE OF

B. MARSHALL

DIED

FEB 26 1857

AGED

27 Ys, 7 Ms, 27 Ds

Down the row from that there was an obelisk:

MARY ANN
REED
PILLSBURY

BORN
JULY 21 1826
DIED
JAN 1 1892

There were more humble stones, small, laid level with the ground. Bill leaned over to read them.

MOTHER
HELEN EVA
MAR 14 1869 FEB 12 1937
LIVED ON PILLSBURY HOMESTEAD 58 YRS

Side by side.

FATHER
ELLERY CHANNING

APR 5 1850 JAN 6 1933
KANSAS PIONEER OF 1862

Jonathan began to sing, amid the sound of crickets. His throat was raw, his voice cracked, harsh, tuneless:

My eyes have seen the glory of the coming of the Lord!

Bill looked up to see Jonathan staggering up the hill. His singing grew louder. He looked like something that had climbed out of the graves, long legs, skeletal arms flapping wildly.

He is pressing out the vintage where the grapes of wrath are stored!

Oblivious of the gravestones, Jonathan marched up the hill, out of the cemetery.

"Jonathan!" called Bill. "Where are you going?"
The voice went wild, loud, screeching like a hawk.

Glory, glory, hallelujah!

Jonathan was marching out toward the prairie, into the high, crackling grasses. There was a barbed-wire fence on top of the hill. Jonathan stumbled into it, entangled, holding out his arms like a scarecrow.

Bill ran after him, puffing up the slope. Fifty years. The grass streaked with blue and purple slashed his ankles.

On the hill someone had lashed together a crucifix of branches, barkless and polished by the weather. Jonathan howled, arms waving as if blown in the wind:

His truth is marching on!

Like a rag wrung dry, the voice gave way. Panting, Bill stopped running and pushed his way up the hill, hands against his knees.

Jonathan was standing, staring, mouth hanging open. His teeth showed, and his gums, and his staring eyes watered. Bill turned and saw the valley, with its one straight road, its large fields, some of them harvested and plowed under, some left browning. There were woods in bands every mile or so, across the valley, to the hills, piebald in blue and gray.

"Come on, Jonathan," said Bill and took his arm and led him down the hill. Jonathan didn't say anything. Bill could feel the weakness in Jonathan's knees. He trembled, hot, like a trapped bird.

The time was twelve-thirty. Please, Lord, give him three more hours. Three more hours is all we ask.

Back among the dead, Jonathan seemed calmer, more focused. He blinked, and his eyes and head began to move, looking around him. Very suddenly, despite Bill, he knelt.

"Look," Jonathan said, very gently.

There was a low flat grave. He pulled grass away from its face.

HENRY

GULCH

1831–1888

HUSBAND OF EMMA ANGELINE

BRANSCOMB

"A name," whispered Jonathan. "Or a geographical feature."

They headed back toward Zeandale. After they had turned out of the gate, Bill asked Jonathan, "Why were you doing all that singing back there?"

Jonathan looked around in mild surprise. "Was that me?" he asked.

They eased down into the valley, passing a road on the left. AIKEN'S LANE, said the sign in green.

"Turn there," said Jonathan.

Bill stopped the car with a very slight skid on the dirt, and backed up. Aiken's Lane hugged the side of the hill. It passed farmhouses. One of them had walls covered in roof tiles. Another was white frame, with awnings. Old houses no longer seemed to interest Jonathan much. He turned away from them toward the fields.

They drove over a ditch. The bridge was made of wooden beams. Reeds and flowering plants grew along the banks. The ditch's bed was smooth, damp, cracked. It ran off into the silent fields and was lost among them.

They came to a house where one wooded slope dipped down and another rose up, a gentle cleft in the hillside. The house had a blank stone front with some kind of ivy growing up the side and along the eaves. The roof had new, smooth tiles and small skylights and a TV antenna.

In the front garden, a woman in a blue tracksuit was pushing a hand plow through a vegetable patch.

"Stop," said Jonathan.

He got out of the car and drifted toward her. The light was so fierce, he was so thin, he seemed translucent. The woman looked up as he wavered toward her.

"I'm sorry to trouble you," said Jonathan in his faraway voice, the one that made him sound like a child.

"You bet," said the woman. She meant it was no trouble.

"I'm trying to find Sunflower School," he said.

"Well," she said, wiping her hands. She was rather old, rather plump for hand plows. Her blue-white hair was tied up in a scarf. She wore running shoes.

"Why sure. You can see it from here." She pointed toward the gunmetal-blue house, across the valley.

"Was there another Sunflower School before that?" Jonathan asked.

"I wouldn't know. But my husband might, and he'll be in for lunch soon."

"I'm very, very thirsty," said Jonathan.

"You're dead on your feet as well. My name's Marge Baker. Who are you?"

"I'm Jonathan. This is my counselor, Bill."

Bill stepped forward. "I would be very grateful if you could give Jonathan a drink," he said. "He's not well."

"I can see that, too," said Mrs. Baker. "Come on in and I'll give you some lemonade." She began to walk toward the house. The front porch had white metal railings around it and wind chimes that tinkled. A Dalmatian stood up in his cardboard box and barked and barked.

"Oh now, Rex! He's not used to visitors."

"Tell me," said Bill. "Did this farm used to belong to people called the Gulches, or the Branscombs?"

"I'm not from around here myself. I just came here to teach school and ended up marrying a farmer. Come on in."

They went through a side door into an extension, a kitchen, with wooden wainscoting and wooden floors, a rainbow rug, made of thick, braided, concentric circles of color, reds and greens and yellows. By the door, there was an old cabinet. It was thick and lumpy with generations of white paint. Inside it was a host of tiny oil lamps.

"Oh I collect those," said Mrs. Baker. She opened up the cabinet for them. She took out one with a blue glass base. NUTMEG, it said in embossed letters.

"Back then people used to buy spice in them. Now mind, these wouldn't be parlor lights. They would be little nightlights for children."

Very carefully, she put it back. "I said I would get you some lemonade, didn't I?"

"I'm sure it's delicious," said Jonathan. "But I think it might burn my stomach. Could I just have a glass of water?"

"Nothing simpler," she said. She poured a tumblerful from a new mixer tap.

"I'd like to look at your shed," said Jonathan.

He wants to get outside, thought Bill, in case he's sick.

"It is quite a feature," said Mrs. Baker.

Bill had not noticed the shed. It had been half-hidden beside a newer outbuilding made of corrugated iron.

It was a log cabin.

As they approached, a cloud of crickets jumped up from the grass. The cloud swirled, thickened, thinned again, with cries like windup birds. Bill was pelted by them. They flew into him, their wings throbbing against his chest.

"Hello, Mary Ann," Jonathan whispered to them. "Hello, Ellery."

Mrs. Baker affected not to notice. "This is our storm cellar," she said. There was a doorway into the ground. It was made of wood, framed with limestone, and along the frame was a line of old stoneware jugs. Jonathan was running his fingers through the leaves of a tree. "What kind of tree is this?" he asked.

"That's a hackberry bush," said Mrs. Baker. "You can't do anything with the fruit, but the birds love them."

"What kind of birds?"

"Chickadees," said Mrs. Baker, and she and Jonathan shared a smile.

They walked on, toward the shed. It was tiny, square. A thick limestone chimney rose up one side of it, supporting a vine. The frame of the front doorway was jammed up hard against the frame of a window. There were thick beams holding the whole structure off the ground.

"We have a lot of people asking to see this," said Mrs. Baker. "This is an original pioneer dwelling."

She and Jonathan walked around to the side.

"They were embarrassed," said Jonathan. Bill came around to join them. From under the apex of the roof, flat planks of wood covered part of the log walls.

"See? They didn't want anyone to know they still lived in a log cabin, so they covered it with clapboards," said Jonathan.

There was another door on this side of the cabin. "Why two doors?" Bill asked.

Jonathan touched an outline in the ground with his foot. "There was an extension on this side," he said. "I bet it was a summer kitchen."

"I bet it was too," chuckled Mrs. Baker. "It would get awfully hot without one."

Farther up the hill, there was a 1940s car. Jonathan walked on toward it, more crickets jumping out at him. The car had a long sleek hood, a short rounded trunk. Its paint had faded and rusted.

"That's my grandson, Paige," explained Mrs. Baker. "He collects old machines. Tractors mostly. Some of them you have to crank up to start. He even has one that runs on butane. They're in the other building, if you would like to see them."

Jonathan looked at the car in silence.

"Paige wants to be a farmer. We know there's no future in it. But we just have to hope he sees that for himself. Do you know, they are bulldozing some of the old farmhouses?"

Jonathan's smile was fixed, his eyes unfocused.

There was a rumbling of a tractor up the road. "Well," said Mrs. Baker. "Here comes my husband. I'll just go down and check the oven, if you want to come along presently."

"Thank you very much, Mrs. Baker," said Bill. Jonathan did not move. Mrs. Baker walked back down the hill toward the wind chimes.

Jonathan was holding his breath.

"Breathe, Jonathan, slowly and deeply."

"It's green and red, isn't it, Bill?" he said, without breath.

"What is?"

"The car!" Jonathan was smiling in wonder. "It's green and red, very pastel in patches, like someone had airbrushed it. Very light, very metallic?"

"I'd say that's a pretty good description."

Jonathan turned toward him, still smiling. "I'm seeing green and red," he said, and clenched Bill's arm. "I'm not supposed to be able to. I'm supposed to be color-blind.

"And the trees," he added. "And the crickets, in a flash."

Bill looked at his watch: quarter past one.

Jonathan leaned over and lost all the water he had just drunk. Bill stroked his back.

In the driveway, Mr. Baker was patting the Dalmatian's head. Mr. Baker wore dungarees. He was a big man, but faded, with watery blue eyes and blue veins in pale skin. He held a clean new straw hat in one hand. His wife came out of the house.

"Vance," she said. "These two gentlemen came to ask me about Sunflower School." She introduced Bill and Jonathan. Vance shook their hands and smiled with perfect false teeth.

Jonathan showed him the photograph.

"Well, I'll be," said Mr. Baker. "That's my sister!" He pointed to a little girl in checked gingham.

"And that will be Miss Soupens, the teacher."

"Was there another Sunflower School? One before that?" Bill asked.

"Why yes, there was."

"Where?" asked Jonathan, his voice rough.

"Stand over here, young man," said Mr. Baker. He leaned over Jonathan's shoulder and pointed. "See that hump of trees there? That's where it used to be. You see, the Worrells wanted to be able to say they were helping everybody so they built a new schoolhouse and paid the teacher. But the old schoolhouse was there until, oh, 1961. Thereabouts. Old Paul Jenkins lived in it with his mother. I think he set it alight when she died."

"Yee hah!" Jonathan screeched. His voice gave way, and he began to cough.

The Bakers smiled a bit nervously, and Mr. Baker stepped back. "Well, I'm pleased to have been able to help," he said.

Jonathan kept coughing, unable to speak. He doubled over, hand over his mouth. He danced in place, still happy.

"Thank you, thank you very much. It really means a lot to him," said Bill.

"Well, you're both very welcome," said Mrs. Baker. Jonathan was still coughing, smiling, shaking his head.

"Now, if you'll excuse us, my husband needs his lunch," said Mrs. Baker. "Then he'll go lie down. I'm afraid he's not very well either."

The Bakers walked back to their house, arm in arm.

"We did it," croaked Jonathan.

They drove on down the lane, through fields of plowed, rich, brown-black soil. Off to the right, far away on the horizon, there was a slight rise of trees, with a white, test-tube tower. It was the hill over Manhattan.

"Stop," whispered Jonathan, his voice gone. He patted Bill's arm. Ahuh ahuh ahuh.

Bill eased the car to a stop. One-thirty.

"The hill," whispered Jonathan, and pointed to the left. His skeleton hands fluttered against the window.

There it was in bald ziggurat layers. Dorothy's hill.

"It's around here. It really is!" chuckled Bill.

"Hurry," said Jonathan.

As Bill drove, Jonathan seemed to fold up smaller and smaller on the front seat. He leaned back, mouth open. His lips were cracked. As the car bounced up onto the main road, he began to talk to someone.

"Sure they will be. I know they will be," he said, hoarse. "They'll be there."

Then Jonathan paused, as if listening.

"But you didn't die," Jonathan answered. "You grew up. Into me."

They came to the lane. ROCK SPRING, said the sign. The clump of trees was at the crossroads. Bill turned right and parked the car. The lane was unpaved, white gravel, and it led in a straight line to the ziggurat hill. A row of old-fashioned telephone poles ranged along it on the left, like a line of crucifixes. Two huge farm machines stood some way away amidst the sorghum. On the other side of the lane, the field was harvested, bare earth, thrashed stalks. Everything was seen. Everything was visible.

Quarter to two. We've done it. Thank you, Jesus.

Bill patted Jonathan's knee. "Come on, kiddo," Bill said. "Let's go see it."

Jonathan still smiled. He didn't move.

"Come on, Jonathan."

"Yes, Daddy," he answered in a whisper. He stirred slowly.

Bill helped him out of the car. Bill got out the plat-book map and turned it upside down, south on the top.

"You're not going to believe this, Jay," said Bill, with a nervous chortle. "The Bakers' farm? That was it, Jonathan. That cabin. That was the house. That was where she lived."

Jonathan moved as if he were on a ship at sea. His smile was fixed. Did he even understand?

"Let's go have a look at where the school was," said Bill. There was a collapsed fence of barbed wire that he had to hold down and a ditch beyond it that made climbing over the wire difficult. They had to duck under and around small conifers or larger ash trees. And then, unmistakably, there was a clearing, a clearing where a building had been.

Jonathan stepped into it and smiled toward one end. "Hello," he said. He stood still in the low grass with its purple heads.

"This is where the school was," said Bill.

Or maybe not. In the midst of the thicket there was another building, gray and parched.

"Let's go and have a look at that there," said Bill. He fought his way through leaves and whiplike branches. He swept them away from his face. He saw a window, some kind of shed or outbuilding perhaps.

"Wait for me," he heard Jonathan whisper behind him.

"It's okay, you can get through," said Bill, distracted. Elbow across his eyes, he stood up. There was still glass in the windows, and a glass jar on one of the windowsills. There was a paintbrush in it.

"Wait for me!" Jonathan screeched.

Bill turned around and shrugged his way back through the trees. The clearing was empty. There was the sound of the car starting.

"Jonathan?" shouted Bill.

He heard the car pulling away, dirt spurting out from under the wheels. Bill sprinted across the clearing. Through the trees he could see the gray car accelerate, swerving. Bill got caught on the barbed wire. He slipped down the grass in the ditch. His trousers tore. He pulled himself back up and over the fence, into the lane.

The car had stopped. Dust still rose from it. The driver's door hung open. Bill broke into a run, down the row of telephone poles toward the hill. He got to the car. Its engine was still running. The key was still in the ignition. It swung back and forth like a clock.

Bill looked around him, shouting "Jonathan!"

On the right, bare and harvested, there was no one.

"Where are you?" Bill started to run across the fields, toward

Dorothy's farm and then stopped. This is crazy, he thought. There's nowhere to hide. If Jonathan was ahead of him, he would see him, running. If he had fallen over, he would still see him, there was no cover, Bill could see every clump of dirt.

Bill turned and pelted back toward the car, up and over the lane and down into the other fields.

"Jonathan!" wailed Bill. "Answer me!" He thought Jonathan was lying hidden among the sorghum. He plunged down into its midst and ran across the orderly rows, looking up and down them. Nothing. No one.

They had husbanded the lower slopes; they had dug ditches across the fields to drain the wallows, the buffalo wallows where children disappeared.

It was crazy, but Jonathan had gone.

Dreamtime and Zeandale, Kansas

1883

*It seems that spring has come once more and farmers go forth to seed
their fields. Some oats are already sown. The rain has moistened the
earth, making a good outlook for rich harvests. Though nature seems to
smile upon the fields, yet some heavy hearts rest among us, grieving over
the departed soul of Sister Reynolds.*

> *. . . Though her body was broken*
> *Through her misery unspoken*
> *Though deformity changed her aspect*
> *Though earth's duties were hard,*
> *She complained not a word,*
> *For all these she could leave in the casket.*
>
> *She was gentle and kind*
> *Always bearing in mind*
> *That she had a work to perform*
> *And with meekness and love*
> *All things were performed in their turn . . .*
>
> *To those children so dear*
> *To their mother while here,*
> *We would say in their anguish and sorrow*
> *Be strong in the Lord*
> *Abide in his word*
> *Eternity is only tomorrow . . .*

—Lines written by "True Friendship" on the death of Etta
   Parkerson Reynolds, as published in the Manhattan *Nationalist*,
   March 18, 1889, as recorded by Ellen Payne Paullin in her
   edition of *Etta's Journal*

Inside the cyclone, Dorothy dreamed.

She dreamed she was still on the road westward, walking toward Wichita. Wilbur F. Jewell was with her. Wilbur was still thirteen. He was now as old as Dorothy. Wilbur was dressed like an Indian, with a colored headband with feathers and painted lines on his face. He had gone to the Territory and found the Indians and lived with them. Dorothy's heart swelled with happiness for him. Wilbur had come back from the Territory to find her and take her with him. The Territory would be full of Indians and buffalo and magic. Wilbur was tall and bony and gangling, and he looked so young to her now. Dorothy knew in her dream that she loved him, would have loved him if he had lived.

America walked with them, westward out of the East. Dorothy dreamed that they had stopped in a wayside camp. There were wagons and tents. There were women in gingham dresses and children in smocks and narrow-eyed men in black hats. The men mumbled with metal bars in their mouths.

The adults were in harness. Great thongs of leather led out from the bits in their mouths, and their eyes were circled with rings of exhaustion and shielded by black leather blinders. They wore them even as they sat slumped on the ground, sprawled carelessly around small grubby fires. There was ash and blood on their hands, and they were burning coffee black in greasy tins. Beside the camps there were mounds of buffalo bones bleaching in the sun. Children ran up them barefoot. Under their feet, clattering hip bones had sockets like eyes. All around them, on either side of the road, there were stumps of trees, lined up like tombstones.

There was a constant sound of chopping. Dorothy saw, beyond the stumps, the blue-green tops of conifers. They waved back and forth and then fell out of sight with a distant crash. Wilbur and Dorothy went to look. The sound grew louder, multiplied many times.

There were Mechanical Woodsmen. They were a labor saving device, a sign of progress like telephones. They went on chopping and chopping, cutting out sections of living wood. The Mechanicals were steam-driven, jets of it coming out of funnels in their heads. Wreaths of acrid orange-brown smoke came out of their mouths. Their faces, their arms, their legs, were coated in thick black grease. Whirling gears and belts moved them and they dripped scalding water. They couldn't keep themselves from cutting down the trees.

One of them looked up at Dorothy and she saw he had living eyes. He wept boiling water. The eyes were Uncle Henry's. It's not my fault, he seemed to say, I can't help it. He looked embarrassed, ashamed, as he slammed an ax into the trunk of a cedar.

Dorothy knew then that she was frightened of men, almost all men except for Wilbur. She wondered how she would ever learn to love men or live with them.

A whistle blew, a long mournful sound like all the loneliness that drove the men and the machines. The Mechanicals hissed and chuffed and came to a halt, ready to move on.

"All aboard!" someone cried.

The people of the camp groaned and stood up. The leather harnesses creaked and stretched. The adults were hauling their houses behind them. They were all moving West, to escape the past, escape the East. Why didn't they ever look behind them? Did they never wonder why they were so weary and mean? Dorothy knew and despised them. They were all pulling the East with them.

They carried guns. They shot things. They shot anything that moved. They shot a black man running toward freedom. There were flocks of deer, bounding away, white tails like the waves of the sea. Rifles crackled and the deer fell, their legs suddenly breaking under them like twigs. There were clouds of birds in the sky, darkening the sun. The men raised their rifles like thunder, and there was a rainfall of blood, blood and feathers, and pelting corpses of pigeons. People slipped on blood. Without thinking, without even knowing, the men raised their rifles and fired.

Lift the rifle. Crack. Lower the rifle. Lift the rifle. Crack.

One of them turned to Dorothy, coated in grease, grinning.

"We're civilizing the country," he said.

Dorothy knew that by the time they got to the Territory, it would be gone, always advancing away from them like a rainbow.

They all walked on, toward Wichita.

As the settlers drew near Wichita, there was a great lowing sound and a cloud of dust ahead of them. A herd of Bad Women was being driven toward the river.

"Yee ha!" the cowboys on horseback shouted and herded the

women down the banks so they could wash. The women were brown with dust and they skidded down into the water, their dirty stolen dresses billowing out on the surface of the river.

The settlers walked through a shantytown, between lean-to shelters with lace curtains and open doors with women standing in them. The Bad Women were not pretty; they were fat and sour or skinny and mean. Dorothy looked at the settlers but their eyes were fixed ahead of them and they seemed not to see.

They seemed not to see the women running races naked through the streets like horses. Men lined the course, wearing bowler hats and drinking straight from the bottle and laying down bets. The women ran with breasts swinging. Their smiles were fixed; their eyes were dim. Alongside the course, two Bad Women in all their finery got into a fight, tearing feathers and hair. Men gathered around the fight to laugh at it and to cheer them on. The women screeched in pain.

At the bridge, the gates to Wichita, the shantytown was left behind. There were bankers there to meet the settlers. The bankers were the guardians of the cowtown, with vests and rotund stomachs and extravagant whiskers. The bankers took away each man's gun. There was nothing to shoot in Wichita but people and that would be bad for business. The bankers took away the horsemen's blinders and put on blindman's glasses instead. The glasses were tinted green. They made the gray grass and the gray sky and the gray soil look alive. And the bankers sang!

Fine property, with water nearby, in balmy gentle climate!

The travelers sang too, swinging their arms out in front of them like blind people. The pilgrims stumbled through the gates, singing "Land of Goshen."

Wichita had streets of unpaved mud, churned up by wagons and human feet. There were wooden boardwalks and vast puddles and ramshackle tents, and cheap wooden buildings with lies painted on them. FINEST DRY GOODS, said one shack, sweltering in a puddle. FIRST NATIONAL BANK, said a sign over a tent.

Fights began to break out as people tried to camp. Women sat down in the mud and wept. Along the boardwalks, there were freak shows. One-armed men. Women with beards. Tattooed couples, all green and red and pink and lavender. There was a black man with no arms and legs, opening a box of matches with his teeth to light a cigarette. It was a show. In her vision, Dorothy knew that he had cut off his arms and legs himself, to make a living.

There were brass bands in front of the restaurants and emporia. The music they played was loud and squawking, harsh and blaring. They were in competition with each other. They had to make you hear them at the expense of the others. A man in woman's clothing lifted up his dress to step around a puddle. Dorothy peered at his face. He was Jesse James. His face was made of black lines, like an engraving. The look he gave Dorothy stilled her heart with fear.

Behind the shacks and false-front palaces, there were mounds of stinking hides, laid out, with scraps of meat still clinging to them. There were deer's heads, and bears' paws, all in mounds. There were slaughterhouses, full of cattle lowing, smelling blood, knowing they were going to die, voiding their bowels and bladders, so the stink and the flies rose up.

I want, thought Dorothy, to go home.

She didn't want to see any more, because she knew this was a truth. Would her father be here? How could she find out? Wilbur said there might be a list in the County Offices.

The County Offices were two stories high and were made out of brick, with stone arches over the windows. There was a gaslight outside them on the corner and signs by the door saying PROBATE and LAW OFFICE. There was a telephone. Dorothy could hear it ringing and ringing, with no one to answer it.

Inside, the County Offices looked like a bank. Ruined, desperate men lined up in front of tellers, all in peaked caps. Everyone was shouting. A policeman bustled a howling man out of the place. Telegraph messages squeaked like a flock of birds.

Dorothy was in despair, waiting in line. In her dream, she knew no one would be able to help her. They wouldn't even be able to hear her over the din. Wilbur took her arm and led her into another room. Great doors opened, and beyond them, the County Offices looked like a church.

There were Gothic pillars and fragmented, colored-glass windows and beautiful distant singing that was forever out of reach, like a colored scarf being blown away by the wind.

And all around them, the people worshiped, on their knees. Worshiped what was good, able to worship what was good by deliberately using it to cover up the bad. They worshiped the things they had destroyed.

Our Father, who art in Heaven

And Dorothy was afraid and knelt down and prayed.

They worshiped the buffalo. They had his head and horns on the wall, and his hide on the floor.

They worshiped the Indian, his blankets around their shoulders, a row of drums in a glass case. They worshiped their heritage. A heritage is something that was never yours, and which has been destroyed.

They worshiped a child in a manger. The Kings and Wise Men, the shepherds, the cattlemen and thieves had all gathered around the crib. They worshiped the mother of the Child, but only because she was a virgin. All other women were bad.

As Dorothy watched, the Wise Men and the Kings, the shepherds and the cowboys and the mayor of the cowtown lifted up the Child, who was plump and innocent and happy. "Dear little thing," they said. "Isn't he dear?" He smiled at them without guile. And they smiled back, knowing.

Knowing they had a cross. And Dorothy cried out, but all the people around her wore the Green Glasses and couldn't hear, because they were praying. They bound the Child tightly in swaddling clothes so that he could not move. They pulled tighter and tighter on the linen.

They drove a nail through his swaddled feet. The Child screamed and wailed and howled. The men looked around in embarrassment.

"I told you what would happen if you did that again," they said in warning, shaking their heads.

Then they placed a nail on his forehead, and they raised a hammer. No, said Dorothy, no, but the words came out like glue, viscous and silent. And the hammer struck home, piercing the skull, pinioning the babe to the cross, and the cross was raised, and his murderers knelt to worship him.

The Child hung, like a scarecrow, and the wood of the cross bent gently in the wind like a tree. There was a gentle, sighing sound, and the Child stared like the buffalo.

His mind had been ruined. He could only speak now in the language of words. And he looked to Dorothy and cried aloud, "I'm alive!"

I know, said Dorothy in silence, but she seemed to be the only one who heard.

"I think I'm alive, aren't I? Am I alive?"

One of the Wise Men turned and sat next to Dorothy.

"I was alive," said the Child, perplexed.

"Hello, Dorothy," said the Wise Man and hugged her. For a moment Dorothy thought she had found her father. She felt his broad male shoulders and his trimmed whiskers and her heart rose up into her mouth out of fear and desire, which for her were confounded.

Then the Wise Man pulled back and Dorothy saw that he wore a straw boater and had his jacket off, and that metal bands held up the shirtsleeves that were too long for his arms. He had a moustache and merry eyes. He was the Substitute.

Frank, whispered Dorothy, for she loved him too.

"What have you learned, Dorothy?" he asked her.

Dorothy thought a moment and said, "I learned to be disappointed and not to hope too much. I learned how to be beaten and how to beat others. I learned that I am worthless and the world is worthless, and that love is a lie and if it's not a lie, then it's wasted."

"They learned you wrong," he said.

Love is real? Where? How, how do we find it, Frank?

"You don't have to go the way they want you to go," he said. He pointed backward, behind her. And she smiled, and Frank kissed her chastely on the forehead, as a mother might.

Dorothy rose up full of joy in her dream, and she turned, and she walked the wrong way. She skipped out of the bank. It had fallen on hard times. The president had absconded with all the funds and the windows were boarded up. The city was a ghost town. Something about the extension railroad and quarantine lines. The wind whispered in the hollow eyes of its windows, and grass sprouted up between the planks of the boardwalks. Mrs. Langrishe clutched a nosegay over her nostrils. It was to kill the reek of death that rose up from her own body. She stumbled, blind.

The settlers had moved on, hoping to find the perfect pasture, the land that would make them rich. Dorothy saw the great trail they had left behind them, discarded pianos, broken clocks in the mud.

She laughed at them. Wheeee! she said, and spun on her heel. What did they think they would find, but more dust, more work, more dry wells and bankers and mortgages? There was no magical land in the West. They would all have to find another kind of Territory to explore.

One dream was over. Another began.

*　　*　　*

The train was hauled backward into St. Louis, with sgnilaeuqs and sgniffuhc. Dorothy stepped off it, wearing her white theater dress. It blazed in sunlight.

There was the wooden platform, the brick concourse, the stone frontage, just as Dorothy had forgotten they looked. She began to hear music. Somewhere there were calliopes playing, as at a fairground. The station was full of little people with funny faces she could not quite see, passing out pennants, tiny flags. It was a Day of Independence. Dorothy walked down the steps of the station and saw that everything was different.

St. Louis was a park, full of trees and great open areas. There was prairie grass and prairie wildflowers among them. Great gusts of laughter seemed to be blown across the fields, and Dorothy heard her best lace-up boots swishing through the long grass, with a cripple's uneven gait.

Ahead of her there were swings and a sandbox. There were rho-dodendrons and other ornamental plants. A flood of children suddenly broke out from under them, shrieking with glee. Surprise! they called. Surprise! Dorothy knew them, from long ago. They danced around her in a circle. Come and play! they said. Oh, Dotty, come and play! They were her friends, they liked her. She knew their faces from long ago. A little red-haired girl covered with freckles who had a high, round forehead. Her quiet little brother in black shorts. Andy and Violet: she remembered their names. Dorothy took their hands and ran with them, and she stood on the swings and pumped back and forth. In her dream, Dorothy felt her hair rise and fall, along with her stomach. She felt the wind on her face. Below, the children turned somersaults on the grass and didn't mind the stains on their clothing.

In the dream Dorothy knew that this was a place where children had been set free. She looked and saw that some of them were not children at all. They were a different kind of adult. They looked like Etta Parkerson. They were tiny and small and giggling, with funny whiskers and conical hats, and they played fiddles or sat with the children who were almost as big as they were, on their laps. They both started fires with magnifying glasses and hopped in sack races. The children and the adults were the same kind of creature.

Bison grazed on the grass and a wildcat lazed in a tree, flicking his tail. In the shade there were wigwams, with white smoke curling from the tops. Indian women sat on the ground sorting dried maize in baskets. The children and the Indians played together on the swings.

All around the park, there were rows of white houses with green shutters. Carts glided past them, pulled by huge gray horses with clopping hooves. The horses wore no blinders and the long white hair around their unshod hooves was flung from side to side by their dancing feet. Over the tops of the houses, there rose great domes of earth. Smoke curled out of them, and Indian ponies grazed on them. The bushes and trees seemed to hiss and whisper in the wind and the flowers made sounds like piano wires snapping.

A dog began to bark. His voice was echoing from far away. Dorothy swung back and forth, over ground that rocked like a pendulum. Then she saw him running toward her, as she always knew he would one day. She always knew he would come back.

"Toto!" she called. "Here, boy! Toto!"

She saw him charging through the long grass, partridge rearing up into the air around him. Dorothy launched herself from the swing and seemed to fly through the air. She landed in the grass and he burst through it and was all over her, whining and barking and licking her face, and she laughed and hugged him, remembered the feel of his tiny back and its wiry hair. He spun in a circle and his bark broke with joy. He picked up his red ball and dropped it at her feet. She had forgotten his red ball. It was covered with spit that smelled of him. Dorothy picked it up delicately, with two fingers only, and threw it for him. He sprang after it, rolled over the ground snarling, and caught it. Then, with a rambunctious toss of the head, he started to trot away, head and ball held high.

Dorothy followed him. She remembered the way now. She walked between the two huge chestnut trees and crossed the muddy street. She went to the front door, with the lion's-head knocker. Dorothy remembered that there was a latchkey dangling on a piece of string inside the slot for letters. She reached inside for it with fat, clumsy fingers. She had to stand on tiptoe to open the door.

She smelled their hallway. There was the wooden table with the vase of dried flowers and the umbrella rack. There were the beat-up old shoes of the woman who cleaned and lived downstairs. There was the stairway.

Dorothy climbed, past the old framed engravings of the Jews in the wilderness, the parting of the Red Sea, the breaking of the tablets. Coats were hung on hooks, red and green and blue, brightly colored, and she recognized them as if they had been people. Dorothy heard, from behind a closed door, the sound of a piano being played. The door creaked as she pushed it open.

"Mama," she whispered.

There she was, there she was, in a dress like a candy cane, red stripes, playing the piano, her back toward Dorothy, her hair in ringlets. There was her papa, sitting in his armchair, smoking his pipe, a brown-skinned man with black hair and black eyes and a moustache. I'm not Gael at all, Dorothy remembered. My name is Gutierrez. I am Dorothy Gutierrez.

Her mother saw and stopped playing. She turned and dazzled Dorothy with her smile. She was so young and pretty and she reached out to hold her. Dorothy ran.

"Dorothy. Where has my little girl been?"

Dorothy began to cry and fell into her mother's arms and was held. "Oh, Mama," she said. "I had a terrible dream! Daddy was gone and you were dead, and I had to go away, and I never saw you ever again!"

Dorothy buried her head against her mother's bosom, her mother's dress, her mother's smell of soap and perfume she could not afford, and Dorothy wept. Her mother rocked her and sang to her gently. The song was an old one, one that Dorothy had not heard since St. Louis. She let herself be rocked and comforted.

When Dorothy had stopped crying, her mother patted her back, and moved her gently away from her and looked into her eyes. Dorothy's mother was crying too.

"Everything dies, Dorothy," she said. "Everything gets taken away in the end."

Dorothy looked at the room. There was the rocking cradle in which her little brother slept. Toto peered into it, whimpering, his front paws resting on its edge. There was the divan with its lace covers. There was the black dresser with the cups with the gold edges and the dancing china pony on the piano, and the Nativity in the window, the china figures, the china manger. It was snowing outside.

Dorothy knew all of those things as if they had never gone, as if all she had to do was come here on a visit and find them there, solid, to be used. She looked at her father's face.

"*Muy linda*," he said, and smiled at her. It was Spanish, but Dorothy understood. He smiled at her. Her father's smile was not to be trusted. He was so young, young and handsome and not to be held by anything, even love. Everything about him was true, true to the point of cruelty.

"This is just a memory," her father said. "Here and then gone. But you have to remember, to have a heart, to have a brain. You have to remember in order to be brave. That's how you grow up."

"But all you've got," said her mother, who was pretty and quite tough, "is now."

Time left you in another world where everything was different, even you. Memory held it together. So where was home?

Her mother's face crumpled with a tolerant, forbearing smile, and she leaned forward and kissed Dorothy on the forehead and said, "Look around you, Dorothy."

And Dorothy looked and saw she was lashed to a fence post in Kansas. It was as if she had made a stupid mistake. She had been in a field in Kansas all along, and it was full of wildflowers. They were tiny, red and white and blue, scattered by the wind. And there was the sky, blue, streaked with pale white.

The world was haunted. It needed to be haunted. The Land of Was was cradled in the arms of Now like a child. Was made Now tender. Death made life precious. The wildflowers were shriveling and they shook in the dry wind. Dorothy looked down and saw the theater dress, brown and stained, still hugged to her breast.

Dorothy heaved her legs out of the mud. Thick and glossy, mud coated Aunty Em's pioneer green. Dorothy unwound the wire from around herself and stood up and looked around her, feeling the dust caked on her face, and she grinned. The world was always beautiful. With a light heart she turned and began to walk, to anywhere.

Through those same fields, Bill Davison tramped up and down. The police were there with dogs now and the sky was orange. It was going to rain. Sunlight peeked under the shelf of clouds. The bald hill was green and red.

You can't just disappear, Bill told himself. The dogs will find him somewhere. He felt humbled by the world, by Jonathan himself. This was what Jonathan wanted, Bill told the fiery light on the hillside. He wanted to stay here. He wanted to disappear. He wanted to find Oz.

Do you believe in miracles?

The rain came, cold, in huge drops that splattered over Bill's bare arms, his striped shirt. The scent of running footsteps would be washed away from the fields. Bill looked up and saw the sunlight broken by rain. He saw rainbows, a corridor of them all along the valley, parallel to the hills, lined up over the straight, flat Kansas road. On his right he saw the sun, and all the sky there had flared orange. This is the rainbow too, he thought, this is what it looks like when you stand in a rainbow. For someone else.

"Oh, Jesus," he murmured, in astonishment, in wonder. He started to pray and found he didn't need to. Kansas prayed for him.

It moved inside his eyes. The hills seemed to rear back, pull away, and swell in size. His own eyes seemed to swell, like balloons. The fields seemed to rear up, their even, man-made rows distorted. The whole land rose up like a wave, and he could see it, bearing them all along with it, the police cars like surfboards, the people balanced precariously, space and time moving as one, a never-ending wave that never broke. The hillsides gaped their mouths and furrowed their brows. The hillsides had a face.

Something huge in the land, like a shark, like a whale, moved past him. Sparing him? A living land that was also a person. After a lifetime of prayer, Bill Davison had finally had a vision. Of God?

And Dynamite Dot lay in the snow, beating her angel wings, the snow cupped in her fingers as thick as air. She was flying and singing and dying at the same time, and she was looking up at the winter stars in a sky that was clearing, but snow still fell, fell past her face as if she were moving through the midst of stars. The stars spoke to her.

"Dah do la ti sang," they said. "Ming ming ming."

They had voices like bells. They were not stars or snow, Old Dynamite realized. They were people.

And Ira Mildvan read a newspaper ringed around with handwritten words:

M'dearest Ox [it began]

You came to see me this morning. You were waiting by the Coke machine. You were 20 years old in blue jeans and you had thick hair, and wire-rim spectacles. You were the Ira who was going to become a lawyer to help Cesar Chavez and the lettuce pickers. Nowadays that sounds like the name of a band. I don't know if this will help, but we both changed. We both went neutral on each other. Whatever happened really wasn't your fault. I always made you do everything. I made you do too much.

It's dawn here. The air is beautiful and clear and I want to get out in it, so I'll try to write this quickly. I'm going to stay in Manhattan. It's small and quiet and friendly, and better than that, it's haunted for me. All this search for history was a search for home.

The old movie house here is called the Wareham and it's a theater supper club now with a semi-pro production of *Dinner at Eight*. I could die on stage in a dinner jacket. If things got too bad, I could just walk into the River Kaw, where the Kansa Indians used to cross.

I found Dorothy. Or at least, I know where she went to school. Today, Bill and I are going to look for her. Even if we do find her, nothing magical is going to happen, except that finally, the circle will be complete. Bill and I will stand where she stood, and I'll be able to stop humming those songs and flapping my arms for that part I will never play.

I keep seeing ghosts, Ira. In a dance. What would God see and hear, Ira, except a ghost dance, a chorus of people all at once, whole countries, outside time and place, all together, and alive?

Maybe you could come and visit me here.

Love, JONATHAN

In 1916 a book was published in a secure and settled Kansas, called *Sunflowers: A Book of Kansas Poems*.

Bill Davison had a copy, and he often read it. The poets of Kansas did not write about banks or clapboard cities. They did not write about Wyatt Earp or cattle or railways or dry-goods stores. They wrote about freedom and John Brown and marching truth. They wrote about Arcadia and knew their ancient Greek. They wrote about African cities of the future ruled by black people. They wrote about Shri Khrishna.

On his return from Kansas, Bill Davison reread the book and came with a start upon a poet who signed herself E. A. Branscomb.

For Aunty Em, the Kansas wind was like the brush of a child's eyelash on her cheek. The teeth of the river gnawed the banks, hungry for land. She had visions of Indians rising from the dust, poppies springing from their spectral feet.

In one poem, an old woman paces the hollow, thumping floorboards of her house late at night, unable to sleep. Then she hears the laughter of a child. She opens the door and sees only darkness and calls out "Dodo?"

Outside her door is a town. An electric light shines on her porch. Somewhere in the night she hears the creak of wagon wheels, the protest of an ox under a yoke. Creeping out of the darkness toward her and into the electric light come the tired faces of those long gone, men and women in plain dress, standing amid the new, not surprised, not confused or outraged. Simply standing.

Rose Lawn Farm, near Syracuse, New York

Summer 1861

It's always best to begin at the beginning.

—THE GOOD WITCH

There were chickens at Rose Lawn and china soldiers. The hens were brown and white with feathers cleaner than sheets. They were alive. The soldiers were tiny and perfect, and for Frank they were alive as well.

Frank liked the soldiers' pink cheeks, their tiny perfect eyes and the feel of their china faces under his fingers, smooth but slightly rough at the same time. The soldiers were French because their arms moved loosely under their uniforms. Their arms were held by threads. Frank lay one of them down very carefully next to him on the stone steps. Things got lost. Things got broken.

Was that snow glinting on the grass? Was it water? Did grass cry? Eagles flew. Frank looked up. It was as though he could leap up into the sky. Clouds sighed overhead, across the face of the sun.

Frank was running away. Frank was always running away to secret places and Rose Lawn was full of them. Frank was running away now. But he knew he had been found, sitting on two stone steps between cedars.

He heard the crunch of his mother's boots behind him on the gravel walk. He did not look up. His mother began to speak. The words fell, as individual as stars.

"Where's Nanny?" she asked.

Frank shrugged. He heard the rustle of cloth as his mother knelt down beside him. He could smell soap and scent. Frank rubbed his eyes.

"I don't like her," Frank said. Nanny smelled of sweat and washed his face with her own spit daubed on a handkerchief. Frank looked at his mother's green dress with what seemed to him like thick green ropes embedded in the fabric. He wondered vaguely if they were for hanging things on. Or hanging up the dress? Hanging up his mother, from the walls?

"Nanny doesn't always understand," said his mother.

That was not Frank's problem. He felt his mother stroking his hair. He looked up at her face. The eyes were full on his.

"She doesn't remember what it is like to be a child," his mother explained.

"Why not?" Frank asked. It seemed to him to be a simple enough thing to do. Overhead, the clouds had faces, and they smiled.

"Because it was such a long time ago," said his mother. She whispered, in case the trees were listening.

Frank looked at the clipped hedges and the white fences, the water snaking its way from the fountain's mouth. He looked at the china soldiers and his wooden duck with the wheels on the stone steps. The steps glinted in the sun as if blinking. The hens, feathers billowing in the slight breeze, looked like clouds with legs. They kept kissing the ground.

"I'll remember," promised Frank.

Reality Check

I am a fantasy writer who fell in love with realism. Because I am a fantasy writer, I am particularly aware that every work of fiction, however realistic, is a fantasy. It happens in a world that is an alternative to this one.

There is a town called Manhattan, Kansas, that is very like the one in this novel. It was settled by people called Purcell and Higinbotham and Pillsbury. There was a Professor Mudge, an Etta Parkerson and her Mr. Reynolds. There even was a Dr. Lyman. To my knowledge, however, he was not related to Lyman Frank Baum, nor did Baum visit the town, though he was in Kansas in the 1880s.

To my knowledge, no Chinese people lived in Manhattan in the 1870s. There was, however, a Mr. Win Tsue who lived in Deadwood, South Dakota, and who invited local women to meet his wife on New Year's Day.

There was a Blue Earth village on the Manhattan side of the two great rivers. At one time, it consisted of 128 lodges, each sixty feet long. The marks in the ground were visible for many years afterward, still remembered by people writing in the 1920s.

There is a Zeandale; there is a Pillsbury's Crossing. The Aiken family still lives in the area. There were indeed two Sunflower Schools, one of which has disappeared, leaving only a clearing in a small hump of woodland where a lane meets the main road. That lane does lead to a smooth, ziggurat-shaped hill.

There is a farm rather like the one my Dorothy lived on, except that the people who lived there, the St. Johns, the Eakins, have been moved over by about a mile to make room for the Branscomb Estate. My Zeandale is a much bigger place.

The real one did have buffalo wallows which are remembered as having swallowed one child whole. If memory serves, the last buffalo in Zeandale was seen at Pillsbury's Crossing, by a member of the Aiken family, in 1882.

There were many other sources in reality of this fantasy.

Mr. and Mrs. Aiken spoke to me and showed me where the first Sunflower School had been. They told me the story of the buffalo wallow and another story of lilacs planted on the hills to commemorate another child who had died.

The interior of Mrs. Baker's farmhouse is rather like that of Mrs. Marjorie Sand's, who in two interviews told me much about Riley County and life in the old days. It was Mrs. Sand who managed to produce for me one of the last available copies of *Pioneers of the Blue Stem Prairie,* an exhaustive and invaluable work tracing the family history of all the original settlers of a huge area of Kansas.

I am indebted to Charlotte Shawver of the Registry Office in Manhattan and to Nancy Gorman and Dala Suther, who provided enthusiastic help during my brief visit there.

I could not have written the book in such detail without the days of personal help given to me by Cheryl Collins and Jeanne Mithen of the Riley County Historical Museum. They found and allowed me to photocopy unpublished memoirs, census records, historical books, photographs and plat books. These memoirs provided the basis for those of Aunty Em. In particular, the memoir of Anna Blasing was a source of much of the material. Aunty Em's description of the burning of Lawrence in 1856 was based on that of Sara T. L. Robinson in her book of 1856, *Kansas: Its Interior and Exterior Life.*

The Manhattan Public Library is to be thanked for preserving their store of local newspapers from the nineteenth century. Wilbur F. Jewell got his name from them—he was a thirteen-year-old boy who committed suicide. The description of the celebration of the Congregationalist church came from those microfilms, as did the text of Aunty

Em's poem. It was in fact recited at the banquet. The Kansas State Historical Society in Topeka also keeps a very large store of such material, from which information about Professor Mudge was derived.

Descriptions of life in Wichita in Dorothy's dream and elsewhere are derived in part from *Wichita: The Early Years, 1865–80* by H. Craig Miner (University of Nebraska Press).

Acknowledgments on page 370 give credits for those sources quoted in the chapter heads.

Thanks are also due to the Lancaster, California, Public Library. Special attention is reserved for the person who stole the microfilm of the Lancaster local newspaper for the year 1927. It was the only publicly available copy of the microfilm, and the newspapers from which it was made have disintegrated.

The chapters on the childhood of Frances Gumm and the life of her mother, Ethel Milne, owe a great debt to *Young Judy* by David Dahl and Barry Kehoe.

I must acknowledge a great debt, too, to *The Making of the Wizard of Oz* by Aljean Harmetz. It is extremely difficult to retrieve the amount of in-depth detail that this author managed to find.

The real film was made in a slightly different way to mine. For example, Judy Garland's makeup would have been done by a man. Millie Haugaard did not exist. At first I called her Millie Shroeder; I then found that by coincidence Millie Shroeder was the name of Bert Lahr's wife.

I couldn't find out where MGM staff parked their cars, so I have Millie take the bus. There were many things I could not find out about MGM during my short stays in Los Angeles. Most of what is available is old publicity material. A lot of the MGM archives were used as landfill under the freeway system. In one hundred years' time we will know more about Manhattan, Kansas, in the 1870s (the high-school newspaper is preserved) than we will about the working lives of MGM staff. But we will still have the films.

There was a Corndale, Ontario, Canada, under another name. There was a very similar house to Jonathan's, long ago, in Was.

The chapter set in Manhattan High School owes an enormous debt to an unpublished manuscript entitled "A Teacher Learns" by Major John Hawkins. He is in part a model for the character of Baum as portrayed in this chapter, and the particular incidents described in it are drawn from his experiences as a teacher. Dorothy's singing death is also inspired by a Hawkins family story. Thanks also to John Clute for reinforcing the idea of Jonathan's disappearance. Johanna Firbank has been a continual inspiration in long discussions on such subjects as childhood conditioning and the nature of literature.

My greatest debt is to L. Frank Baum and *The Wonderful Wizard of Oz*.

Books make authors, not the other way around. Books come out of their own accord, authors just write them. Books can be written without authors. They can come, like epic poetry, out of many different mouths.

Oz was first visited upon a kindly man who wanted to set children free from fear. Oz grew out of *Alice in Wonderland,* and out of Kansas and the people who settled there, and Baum's own life.

It also kept on growing. It grew out of improved Technicolor cameras and out of the MGM studio system, which meant the first footage directed by Richard Thorpe could be thrown out. It grew out of Herman Mankiewicz and Ogden Nash and Noel Langley; Florence Ryerson and Edgar Allan Woolf, and Ben Hecht's secretary, John Lee Mahin. Can a script with this many writers be said to have an author? Oz grew out of Arlen and Harburg, who wrote the songs. It grew out of the singers, who knew how to sing them. It kept on growing, because of television; it kept on gaining meaning with each repeat. Oz came swimming to us out of history, because we needed it, because it needed to be. A book, a film, a television ritual, a thousand icons scattered through advertising, journalism, political cartoons, music, poetry. Had Oz been blocked, it would have taken another form in the world. It could have come as a cyclone.

That doesn't make it true.

I fell in love with realism because it deflates the myths, the unexamined ideas of fantasy. It confronts them with forgotten facts. It uses past truth—history.

I love fantasy because it reminds us how far short our lives fall from their full potential. Fantasy reminds us how wonderful the world is. In fantasy, we can imagine a better life, a better future. In fantasy, we can free ourselves from history and outworn realism.

Oz is, after all, only a place with flowers and birds and rivers and hills. Everything is alive there, as it is here if we care to see it. To-morrow, we could all decide to live in a place not much different from Oz. We don't. We continue to make the world an ugly, even murderous place, for reasons we do not understand.

Those reasons lie in both fantasy and history. Where we are gripped by history—our own personal history, our country's history. Where we are deluded by fantasy—our own fantasy, our country's fantasy. It is necessary to distinguish between history and fantasy wherever possible.

And then use them against each other.

Acknowledgments

Grateful acknowledgment is made to the following for permission to reprint previously published material:

CPP/Belwin, Inc.: Excerpt from "If I Only Had a Brain" by E. Y. Harburg and H. Arlen. Copyright 1938, 1939 (renewed 1966, 1967) by Metro-Goldwyn-Mayer Inc. Rights assigned to EMI Catalogue Partnership. All rights controlled and administered by EMI Feist Catalog. International copyright secured. Made in USA. All rights reserved. Used by permission.

Centennial Committee of the City of Lancaster: Excerpt from Lancaster Celebrates a Century: A Pictorial History of Lancaster, California, 1983. Reprinted by permission of the City of Lancaster.

Doubleday: Excerpt from Adolf Hitler by John Toland. Copyright © 1973 by John Toland. Reprinted by permission of Doubleday, a division of Bantam Doubleday Dell Publishing Group, Inc.

Elinor Anderson Elliott: Excerpt from The Metamorphosis of the Family Farm in the Republican Valley of Kansas 1860–1960, M.A. thesis, Kansas State University. Reprinted by permission.

Harcourt Brace Jovanovich, Inc. and Faber and Faber Ltd.: Excerpt from "Little Gidding" in Four Quartets by T. S. Eliot. Copyright 1943 by T. S. Eliot and renewed 1971 by Esme Valerie Eliot. Rights in Canada administered by Faber and Faber Ltd. Reprinted by permission of Harcourt Brace Jovanovich, Inc. and Faber and Faber Ltd.

Sheila Johnston: Excerpt from the *Independent,* February 4, 1988, London. Reprinted by permission.

Alfred A. Knopf, Inc.: Excerpt from *The Making of the Wizard of Oz* by Aljean Harmetz. Copyright © 1977 by Aljean Harmetz. Reprinted by permission of Alfred A. Knopf, Inc.

Alfred A. Knopf, Inc. and *Peters Fraser & Dunlop:* Excerpt from *The Parade's Gone By . . .* by Kevin Brownlow. Copyright © 1968 by Kevin Brownlow. Reprinted by permission of Alfred A. Knopf, Inc. and Peters Fraser & Dunlop.

The New York Review of Books: Excerpt from an essay "The Oz Books" by Gore Vidal. Copyright © 1977 by Nyrev, Inc. Reprinted by permission of The New York Review of Books.

Pantheon Books: Excerpt from *Wisconsin Death Trip* by Michael Lesy. Copyright © 1973 by Michael Lesy. Reprinted by permission of Pantheon Books, a division of Random House, Inc.

University of Oklahoma Press: Excerpt from *The Kansas Indians: A History of the Wind People 1673–1873* by William E. Unrau. Copyright © 1971 by the University of Oklahoma Press. Reprinted by permission of the University of Oklahoma Press.

Ellen Payne Paullin (ed): Excerpt from *Etta's Journal,* Manhattan, KS, 1981 (as published in the Manhattan *Nationalist,* March 18). Reprinted by permission.

A NOTE ON THE TYPE

The text of this book has been set in Goudy Old Style, one of
the more than 100 type faces designed by Frederic William
Goudy (1865–1947). Although Goudy began his career as a
bookkeeper, he was so inspired by the appearance of several
newly published books from the Kelmscott Press that he
devoted the remainder of his life to typography in an attempt
to bring a better understanding of the movement led by
William Morris to the printers of the United States.

Produced in 1914, Goudy Old Style reflects the absorption of
a generation of designers with things "ancient." Its smooth,
even color combined with its generous curves and ample cut
marks it as one of Goudy's finest achievements.

FOR THE BEST IN PAPERBACKS, LOOK FOR THE

In every corner of the world, on every subject under the sun, Penguin represents quality and variety—the very best in publishing today.

For complete information about books available from Penguin—including Penguin Classics, Penguin Compass, and Puffins—and how to order them, write to us at the appropriate address below. Please note that for copyright reasons the selection of books varies from country to country.

In the United States: Please write to *Penguin Group (USA), P.O. Box 12289 Dept. B, Newark, New Jersey 07101-5289* or call 1-800-788-6262.

In the United Kingdom: Please write to *Dept. EP, Penguin Books Ltd, Bath Road, Harmondsworth, West Drayton, Middlesex UB7 0DA.*

In Canada: Please write to *Penguin Books Canada Ltd, 10 Alcorn Avenue, Suite 300, Toronto, Ontario M4V 3B2.*

In Australia: Please write to *Penguin Books Australia Ltd, P.O. Box 257, Ringwood, Victoria 3134.*

In New Zealand: Please write to *Penguin Books (NZ) Ltd, Private Bag 102902, North Shore Mail Centre, Auckland 10.*

In India: Please write to *Penguin Books India Pvt Ltd, 11 Panchsheel Shopping Centre, Panchsheel Park, New Delhi 110 017.*

In the Netherlands: Please write to *Penguin Books Netherlands bv, Postbus 3507, NL-1001 AH Amsterdam.*

In Germany: Please write to *Penguin Books Deutschland GmbH, Metzlerstrasse 26, 60594 Frankfurt am Main.*

In Spain: Please write to *Penguin Books S. A., Bravo Murillo 19, 1° B, 28015 Madrid.*

In Italy: Please write to *Penguin Italia s.r.l., Via Benedetto Croce 2, 20094 Corsico, Milano.*

In France: Please write to *Penguin France, Le Carré Wilson, 62 rue Benjamin Baillaud, 31500 Toulouse.*

In Japan: Please write to *Penguin Books Japan Ltd, Kaneko Building, 2-3-25 Koraku, Bunkyo-Ku, Tokyo 112.*

In South Africa: Please write to *Penguin Books South Africa (Pty) Ltd, Private Bag X14, Parkview, 2122 Johannesburg.*